NO LONGER PROPERTY OF
SEATTLE PUBLIC LIBRARY

D0344666

ROAR BACK

ROAR BACK

John Farrow

This first world edition published 2020
in Great Britain and the USA by
SEVERN HOUSE PUBLISHERS LTD of
Eardley House, 4 Uxbridge Street, London W8 7SY.
Trade paperback edition first published
in Great Britain and the USA 2020 by
SEVERN HOUSE PUBLISHERS LTD.

Copyright © 2020 by John Farrow Mysteries Inc.

All rights reserved including the right of
reproduction in whole or in part in any form.
The right of John Farrow Mysteries Inc. to
be identified as the author of this work has
been asserted in accordance with the
Copyright, Designs & Patents Act 1988.

British Library Cataloguing in Publication Data
A CIP catalogue record for this title is available from the British Library.

ISBN-13: 978-0-7278-8937-9 (cased)
ISBN-13: 978-1-78029-681-4 (trade paper)
ISBN-13: 978-1-4483-0385-4 (e-book)

This is a work of fiction. Names, characters, places and incidents
are either the product of the author's imagination or are used fictitiously.
Except where actual historical events and characters are being described
for the storyline of this novel, all situations in this publication are
fictitious and any resemblance to actual persons, living or dead,
business establishments, events or locales is purely coincidental.

All Severn House titles are printed on acid-free paper.

Severn House Publishers support the Forest Stewardship Council™ [FSC™],
the leading international forest certification organisation.
All our titles that are printed on FSC certified paper carry the FSC logo.

Typeset by Palimpsest Book Production Ltd.,
Falkirk, Stirlingshire, Scotland.
Printed and bound in Great Britain by
TJ International, Padstow, Cornwall.

Not an *X*, yet they marked the spot.

Lift the gate's rusty latch. Enter the small backyard. Avoid exterior stairs to the first and second floors. Instead, step through an unlocked door that led underground.

When he decided to count the experience as being a superior's psychological ruse, he rallied. He would not succumb to panic. Nor bolt. He was being tested; he'd breeze through the challenge. He stiffened his spine. Prepared himself to endure. It took a while – three-and-a-half minutes, although it felt longer – before he realized that he was not alone.

He detected a breath in the room, not his own, and spoke into the darkness. 'You're here.'

'You, too. Here,' Captain Armand Touton replied, his voice a disembodied entity.

In locating the voice, the visitor discerned that the other man was seated. Slightly behind and to the right of him. Thinking of his inquisitor in a chair triggered an inexplicable creeping anxiety. For the first time in the black cavern, the man grew fearful.

Captain Touton took this first contact to extremes. He had labeled the concept a cockamamie idea, and the coal bin underscored his contempt for the project. He only went along with the notion after his countervailing arguments were dismissed. If he did not participate, somebody else would. A naive dimple-cheeks in charge might transform mere failure into catastrophe. Better if he ran the show.

Pax, his boss, the mystical romantic, agreed and insisted they push ahead. Forces of evil were aligning for a fight. He wanted a head start and a decent chance of coping, even if the plan was harebrained.

Obliged to listen to BS of that nature, Touton's response was a protracted sigh, which got his feelings across, if not his point. He had survived his own fight against evil, a conflagration known as World War Two. He didn't believe the battle anticipated by Pax would be more than a skirmish by comparison. Pax was a civilian, a bureaucrat, brilliant in his own way, a courtroom wizard, but what did he know of war? Of evil?

An ardent reformer, Pacifique 'Pax' Plante – commemorated as the Eliot Ness of the Montreal Police Service from the forties into the fifties, taking a page from Chicago of the thirties – stood a

1958

He persevered, cautiously, down a brief flight of stairs.

With each step, the darkness intensified.

At the base of the stairwell he lifted a latch, crossed the threshold, and let the heavy door swing shut behind him.

The latch clicked into place.

Total darkness.

He had landed in an unused coal cellar. The switch to oil in the 1950s left coal bins vacant, their walls and floors impregnated with decades of black dust. He kept his breathing shallow. He did not carry a flashlight; the glow would be extinguished if he did. The man had not anticipated stumbling into a vacant tomb.

No lighter. No matches.

Little air.

He tasted dust on his tongue.

In the utter blackness of the cellar, the man waited.

For someone. Something.

A sound. A light. A distraction. An appearance.

A specter, even. A ghoul.

He had arrived yet possessed no further directive.

He checked: his own hand, inches from his eyes, was invisible.

He was invisible, even to himself.

One hand gripped the other, assurance that he existed.

He felt taken in.

He had followed the instructions to the letter: proceed to the district in Montreal known as Park Extension – commonly referred to as Park Ex, as though the community's best days were done. Locate the laneway betwixt rue de l'Épée on the east, Bloomfield Street on the west. Avenue d'Anvers and rue Jarry crossed north and south. Search for a high wood fence, faded green. One impossible to see over without standing on a rock. A pair of yellow slash marks, each the width and length of a thumb, knee-high on the gate, confirmed the location.

The twin dashes were tilted off the vertical. Close to parallel.

head below the mayor yet head-and-shoulders above the chief of police. The chief would not be informed of their gambit. Only a trusted few would be privy. Their operation had to be that strict. Pax insisted, and Touton did, too. Even the mayor, a valued confidant, was kept outside their inner circle, although Touton pointed out that too few were involved to form a circle.

'Fine,' Pax deadpanned. 'We'll be a straight line.'

The other person who helped form their straight line was the sacrificial lamb, the one ready and willing to be gutted and hung on a rack. The one willing to be bled dry. The one standing in the dark in a coal room. Full of ambition and, in this environment, as blind as a bat.

A fine young man, according to various accounts.

In time, all mayors decamped. Police chiefs, too. Some in disgrace. Men like Plante might die young. A slaughtered lamb, though, could be eternal. Even if its life proved short.

With luck, the lamb might escape bleeding out on a platter. One way to spare him that fate was to shock his senses first. Touton would meet the guy, assess his character, plumb his will, determine his chances of survival. Maybe coax him into changing his mind.

He'd been forewarned. The new man was a mule. Pax maintained, 'He won't be swayed by you, Armand. Imagine that.'

But Pax knew he'd try. Perhaps he was counting on Touton to do exactly that.

The meeting was set up between the police captain and the neophyte. Touton chose both the site and the terms of engagement. The young man's name had not been revealed to him; not yet. He might be advised of it, eventually, but by then it would likely be an invention. He hoped the man wouldn't be reduced to a code word, like 'Apricot' or 'Lynx'. If a man was going to die on him, he'd prefer to inscribe a proper moniker on his gravestone. In his head, he took to calling him *the guy*, although he couldn't bury him under that name either, and tried not to think of him as an innocent lamb being prepped for the slaughter.

His code name better not be 'Lamb' or 'Easter'.

In a moment of honesty, Touton admitted that he wanted to meet *the guy*. Somebody willing to sacrifice his life without a specific cause might be worth looking at square-on. He'd make his own evaluation then. How much of the man was composed of courage and conviction? How much hellbent on self-destruction? What balance had he struck between those two prevalent and competing forces?

How long would it take for the man to be torn apart? Before his psyche – a shrink's good word – was shattered?

He'd talk to him first, in the dark, both men distilled to their marrow as disembodied voices, before switching on the overhead and glaring into his eyes.

'Is there no light?' the invisible recruit inquired.

'You want to live in darkness. That's the idea, no?'

'In a way. I guess so. Yeah.'

'Make up your mind.'

'It's made up.'

'I heard that, too.'

'You want to know why.'

'I don't. Why should I?' Touton baited him.

'Really?' the recruit asked, then inquired again, 'There's no light?'

'Later, maybe. When you're ready. If you're ready.'

'I'm ready. Sir.'

'You are when I say so. Not until.'

No response.

He sounded well-spoken. That could be a problem.

'Do you have good teeth?' Touton asked him.

'Excuse me?'

'Are you deaf?'

'I'm not. I have good teeth.'

'A liability. What loser, Apricot, what upraised screwball has good teeth?'

'You think somebody will check my teeth?'

'First impressions, Apricot. You need to rely on them.'

'My teeth?'

'First impressions.'

'That's true. Why *Apricot*? Why call me that?'

'Think about good teeth. What impression do they give? Like you wore braces. A rich boy's teeth.'

'What do you want me to do? Pull them out?'

He didn't mind the sarcasm. He played along. 'Slowly. Prolong the agony. You should know what pain is, how much you can endure. Or eat candy. Your choice.' Plying a tooth out wasn't the worst idea he'd heard, even in jest. At any rate, he was enjoying yanking the young man's chain.

'How serious are you?' the recruit wanted to know.

'Everything we say is serious. Eat candy. Take on more than one bad habit, Lynx. I read your weight, your height. That tells me you're fit. As if you're in training. As if you go to a gym, do sit-ups every morning. If so, quit. Get fat. You're ex-military, I heard.'

'Commando. Black Watch.'

'I didn't ask. Don't reveal yourself. Action?'

'The damn war ended first. Korea, I mean. Peacekeeping duty after that. No firefights. Risky at times. Bad people. Buddies got killed in front of me. That's not why, in case you're wondering. I don't want the job to make up for a lack of action.'

'I don't want to know why, Lynx. Do you want to know why I don't want to know why?'

'Sure. Tell me.'

'Because you don't know why yourself.'

'I think I do.'

'That's the problem. You only *think* you do. You've written it up in your head. You *think* you've got it figured out. You want to go deep underground, be a snitch inside the mob. Only, you won't have nothing to do as a snitch for years and more years, because you're going deep, so deep you'll bury yourself in muck. Only when you can overturn the whole fucking applecart will you come up for air with the good stuff stored in your head. Names and numbers. Methods, bank accounts. Then the whole world comes crashing down around you, Lynx, because of you, Apricot, because you lived inside for years, let's say for decades. And you want to tell me now why you want to do that in the years to come? I'm telling you, Easter Mutton, you don't know why. Whatever you think the reason is, that's not it.'

'Really.'

'Don't be arrogant with me, kid. I'm not in the mood.'

'Don't call me "kid". Sir. If you don't mind.'

'Easter Mutton is better? I mind. Find a wall. Rub your hand against it.'

'What?'

'Tone deaf, huh?'

'I'm not deaf. I'll do it.'

They both heard his hand being wiped along a wall.

'Now rub the floor with your other hand.'

This time he didn't object, he just did it.

'Now your face.'

'What?'

'Deaf? Rub your face.'

'Against the floor?'

'With your hands.'

'Blacken it, you mean?'

'Blacken it. Be thorough. After you've done it once, do it again. Coal dust on your hands, from the floor, the walls, then onto your face. Every part of your face. Over and over again. Cover your nose. Your cheeks. Forehead. Your jaw. When I turn on the light to look at you, I don't want to see you. I don't want to ever recognize you. Blacken up. Do it. You think I'm not corrupt, but anyone can be corrupted. You do not want to be recognized. No one can know you. You're invisible. Blacken up.'

Touton could hear him, scraping the walls, the floor, blackening his features.

'What's the point of turning on the light?' the man asked. 'You won't recognize me if we stay in the dark.'

'The time may come when you want me to recognize you, Lynx. Or I want to. I can do that by looking into your eyes and remembering them forever. Won't notice you on the street, passing by. I don't stare into people's eyes as I stroll by. Do you? But if you ever want to be known, ask me to look into your eyes and remember the blackened face. Or, if I need to identify your corpse, I can peel back your eyelids and know it's you. If I designate a surrogate – someday I might be dead – that man won't know your eyes, but he'll know a story I told him, and this is one story you won't forget in your lifetime.'

'That's true,' the man said.

'Are you ready?' Touton asked him. 'For the light?'

'Sure,' the man said.

'Really? Are you ready for your new life? Because your old one is over. Who you knew, what you knew, who you are – finished. If I turn on this light, you're a new person, undercover. To go this deep, there is no *you* anymore. You're done with your old self.

That world has vanished. You don't have family. You don't have friends. You're alone and forgotten. That's for all time or until you come out, and if you do this the right way you're not coming out until you're an older guy who even you won't recognize. So, no, I don't want to know why because you don't know why. There is no why anymore. There is only your new shitty self. You're a punk now, a bag of shit on the make sniffing fresh manure. Don't talk to me about why. Why isn't good enough. Why will get you killed. There is only who you are and who you are has nothing to do with you. That guy's dead and gone. Quit this bullshit right now or face the facts, Sonny Boy, Lemon Pop, Apricot, Lynx, whatever your code name is, because you may not be able to come out on your own ever again. It'll be complicated.'

Touton gave his speech and waited for a reaction.

He didn't get one.

Finally, the recruit said, 'Now what?'

'I turn on the light.'

'Turn it on.'

The man blinked under the sudden brightness of the bare overhead bulb. Slowly, he grew accustomed to the light and returned Touton's stare, although, given the light's angle, he could scarcely see Touton's eyes, while his own were exposed.

The two stared at one another. One memorized the other's eyes. The other accepted that he was being observed down to his core.

The blackness absorbed light before it reached a wall. As though they floated in mid-air.

Touton said, 'You'll find a bucket in the corner behind you. Towel, cloth, soap, water. Clean up. Dry up. Then be on your way. I'm leaving now.'

'How do we keep in touch?'

'Don't you get it yet? You're out of touch now. You're on your own.'

'But someday.'

'Someday is your problem.'

Touton stopped at the door. He turned. First, he said, 'You're an idiot.' Then he said, 'Good luck.' He turned once more and departed.

The man cleaned up. Without a mirror, he was thorough. The water was warm. He was liberal with the soap. Any spots he missed he could attend to later. He left the way he'd come and walked down the lane. He had no idea that Captain Armand Touton was keeping an eye on him and followed his progress through binoculars. When he disappeared out of sight, Touton knew it would be a while before he vanished from his mind.

Back downtown, Touton dispatched a technician to collect the neophyte's fingerprints from the coal dust. A set on file might come in handy someday, in making a positive ID on a corpse, perhaps. That way, a record-keeper wouldn't be obliged to take his word for it based on the color of the man's irises.

PART ONE
1978

PART ONE

ONE

A detective opens his eyes.

Before dawn, an island city awakes. A phalanx of delivery vans lumber across aging bridges; others wheeze and rumble through tunnels. Ships navigate canals, avoiding the river's more turbulent currents. In the dark by the water's edge, a young woman sheds her clothing. She slides into the stream where it's rapid, impervious to the cold. Drifts away. Her head bobs on the surface. Following a turn onto her back and a final glance at the stars and waning gibbous moon, she exhales a bubble of air. Goes under.

Her body will be recovered downstream, if not in days, then in several weeks' time. No one has spotted the sorrow of a young person's surrender to life's travail.

The city neglects other lives regal in their essence. A man who dwells in quiet servitude to his hovel is kingly there as the sun pokes up. He shaves. The scratch of a razor across his whiskers invigorates: no one to admonish or correct him, no one to direct him, no one to say boo. Outside, chased by light, mice and rats retreat from the alley – literal and metaphorical rodents, both – and across the street, boxcars shunt and slam in the railway yard. Citizens rise early to spare themselves being blasted from their sleep.

Nearby, men in their outdoor slumber pull their clothing tighter. Adjust cardboard walls and roofs in a ditch. On the roadways, cabbies ease off their gas pedals. The only lull in the day diminishes their natural aggression. Bars closed their doors at three a.m.; by four, the busted and the broke, the brawlers, the beaten and the bored, the euphoric, the lonely, the rowdy, the half-asleep and the half-dead, the happy revelers and the blissfully inebriated have been delivered to their homes. Now it's both too late and too early to drive anybody anywhere – a few prowl for that one fluke ride to the airport – and with nothing to do, drivers congregate in all-nighters over coffee. Not caring for the habits of breakfast, a few indulge in a slice of sky-high cheesecake with a glutinous strawberry glaze.

Cops arrive, too, nearing their shift's end. Take a seat. Spread their limbs. Wrap their fingers around a mug. They're too depleted to worry a glance at the worn hookers and pimps, the muggers and beggars. All are equally subdued. No one looks up as smatterings of crooks stumble into this café or that diner. After their overnight skirmishes, cops, thieves and stragglers blend together. Morning a truce. First light a line of demarcation, a demilitarized zone, between hunters and prey.

Elsewhere, a pack of burglars who have enjoyed a decent night converges in an empty parking lot to divvy loot and swill beer.

In his diminutive dwelling, gray light outside, Émile Cinq-Mars stirs. His first day on the job with a new rank: *Sergeant-Detective*. The thought is in his head the moment his eyes blink open. He's not expecting whistles and cheers. Nor even a salute. The opposite, more likely. Casual ribbing. An upraised middle finger behind his back. Yet he's keen to jumpstart this new chapter of his professional life and feels bolstered by subliminal adrenalin.

Sergeant-Detective Émile Cinq-Mars. The sound of it feels right.

He, too, scrapes whiskers from his jaw, the blade of his razor in need of replacement.

Late in the month of May, the year is 1978.

Émile Cinq-Mars had been enjoying a tumultuous career as a young police officer. After tugging the robes on life as a priest, he had found himself wanting with respect to that calling – the calling itself insufficient. He'd then considered veterinary medicine. If he was not to minister among people, he'd do so among animals, pull a modern-day St Francis act. He'd forged his way toward that goal by following a course in what has become a defunct section, with a name that delights his peers whenever it's mentioned: Animal Husbandry. A common refrain inquires, *'Who was the bride if you were the husband, Cinq-Mars? A goat? A sow? Were you rampant in a hen house?'* The ribbing pounds down upon him whenever he fails to keep his past concealed, especially inside the police department, which is where he eventually landed.

In a sense, he combined the first two inclinations. He'd not be a priest yet remain a moral persuader in his community. Not a veterinarian, yet he'd keep animals of the two-legged sort in check.

Weaned to plough fields, bale hay and raise horses, the country lad became a big city cop. Any straw poll predicted a staid life. He was tall and strong. Muscle was a useful component for a beat cop. He did not exhibit any particular flair for the service, and his country roots marked him as susceptible to the degenerates and slick deceivers in the big bad metropolis. That he held to his religious background, at a time when any man in his right mind was fleeing the Church for the secular world, indicated that he'd be eclipsed by his skeptical peers as time scooted by.

A surprise, then, when things turned out differently.

He was mentored early on by the captain of the Night Patrol, one Armand Touton, a folk hero among the general population as a reformer and crusader. Together they made a key contribution to the defeat of the FLQ, the *front de libération du Québec*, a cynical, quasi-militant group that murdered a cabinet minister and kidnapped a British trade commissioner to advance their interests in a Quebec independent from Canada. That success bolstered his in-house profile. His immediate boss was allied with the key reformers in the city. The mayor, Jean Drapeau, and the crime-busting prosecutor, Pacifique 'Pax' Plante, also found the newbie worthy of inclusion in their cabal. Touton brought him onto the elite Night Patrol and elevated Émile Cinq-Mars to the rank of detective. That quick promotion caused him to be despised among cohorts, and not only by those benefitting in a material way from criminal gangs across the cityscape of Montreal. A cop who aligned with the reformers was advised to be prepared: to fit himself out with his coffin of choice.

Cinq-Mars served on Touton's Night Patrol until that man retired and the Patrol was disbanded by the bureaucrats. Mayor Jean Drapeau was gone by then, and now Pax Plante was dead. The new brass did not want reformers with muscle in positions of authority. Older politicians who opposed them were defeated or in retreat. He was cast out to a suburb, a form of exile. He remained under wraps while rarely investigating anything more odious than minor felonies. To that end, he did his job.

Still, he managed to solve a few murder cases while officially investigating none.

Colleagues alleged that news of his impending promotion pointed to his old cronies. Others brayed that the rank of Sergeant-Detective was granted to keep him in line, to burden him with minutiae out in the boonies and out of everyone's hair. The brass – half corrupt, the other half largely weary of the battle for oxygen – were now free to sic second-rate partners on him while enjoying a chuckle at his expense over their evening cocktails.

The detective heard the chatter. He knew the chorus. Which took no great feat of detection. Officers meant for him to listen in and get the message. He was not wanted.

A toasted bagel with cream cheese and thin slices of lox suited his mood for the morning. Strong coffee was preceded by an extra tall glass – a celebratory aspect – of orange juice.

Morning light edged onto his street. The sunniest of days in the offing.

The jangle of the telephone gave Émile Cinq-Mars a start. A loner, few people rang him. No one at this hour.

'*Bonjour?*' More a question than a greeting. His inflection implied that the unknown caller must have misdialed.

'Sergeant-Detective.' There, for the first time. From a superior's mouth to his ear. His rank spoken aloud, suddenly official.

'Captain Delacroix,' Cinq-Mars answered in French. 'Good morning.'

'For you, maybe.' While he and his boss remained a long way from being bosom pals, they had progressed a fair distance. He surmised that the captain's respect and confidence had finally been earned. Captain Delacroix would never say so, yet Cinq-Mars harbored the suspicion that the captain had initiated the recommendation for promotion. If true, he was free to dismiss the cynicism of others who figured a fix had been on, or under, the table.

'What's up, Cap?'

'Saving you a trip in,' Delacroix announced. The streets being empty at this early hour, the *trip in* took six or seven minutes by car. Cinq-Mars could walk a shorter route in twenty.

'Sure. Why?' Had he been transferred? He'd been addressed by his rank; surely he hadn't been demoted already.

'The nightshift gave me a buzz, Cinq-Mars. I'm at home. They pulled down a case too complicated for their feeble minds.'

A lie. More likely, catching a case near the end of their shift meant overtime for that crew. The night captain was being protective of his budget, so asked the dayshift to take it.

'OK,' Cinq-Mars said, expecting more.

'Burglary. How complicated can that be? Anyhow, it's real close to you.' He read out the address on rue de l'Épée. The man was right. Two blocks away. Closer than that as the crow flies. 'Go straight there. Take it on.'

'Done. Anything on my new partner? He's supposed to be assigned today.'

'If he shows up, I'll send him over.'

'Any idea who?'

'Downtown's choice. Whoever they want to pass off as landfill. I expect riffraff.'

'That's how I arrived,' Cinq-Mars mentioned. He immediately regretted giving Delacroix that obvious an opening.

'Need I say more?'

'No, sir. I'll check out the robbery.'

'Plural,' Captain Delacroix corrected him.

'Excuse me?'

'Not one robbery. There's like a dozen or more.'

At the very least, his first case as a Sergeant-Detective held out a modicum of interest.

TWO

As if they were darkened ships off-loading contraband at sea, detectives Émile Cinq-Mars and Henri Casgrain transferred cases now and then. The lack of overlap on shift changes made it difficult to grab a case when ready for bed – often the situation for Casgrain – or hungry for a meal at a long dayshift's end – a typical circumstance for Cinq-Mars. Crooks rarely timed their operations to suit their pursuers.

Casgrain was a bald-headed man with a full brush mustache and an elongated visage. His cheeks were concave. He matched Cinq-Mars in height – north of six feet – except that a severe slope

to his shoulders and a stooped posture left the impression that he
was shorter. Cinq-Mars wondered if he'd fractured a vertebra or
sustained a neck injury, but the stoop was congenital. While the
posture made him appear dopey, Cinq-Mars knew his colleague
to be both wickedly smart and convivial. As importantly, he was
a man of character. He coached hockey teams in winter, baseball
in summer. In contrast to their dad's impairment, his three boys
were enthusiastic athletes. Cinq-Mars was inclined to trust cops
who were community guys and family-oriented that way, and he
trusted Casgrain.

Lately, the attitude struck him as ironic, as he himself was not
community-oriented, had no progeny, and was bereft of feminine
companionship.

Cinq-Mars never shook hands with cops on the job, it wasn't
done, but Detective Henri Casgrain was the exception. Their handshake conveyed mutual respect. Both men messed with the bad
guys yet stayed clean. As well, neither admired the day-to-day
drudgery contributed by their peers, even when diligent. They
preferred to stab routine with inspiration.

'Another rung up the ladder, Émile. Hope your feet are on the
ground.'

'My head sleeps on one cloud. I put my feet up on another.'

'I bet. Congratulations, bud.'

Casgrain was one man he could expect to be sincere.

'Thanks, Henri. You're next.'

'In a pig's eye. Anyway, happy where I am.'

'What do we have here?'

'I was hoping to keep this one. Boss says no. Time and money,
Émile, the two things we're lacking on the midnight shift. Why
is our budget constantly imploding?'

'Somebody has sticky fingers, maybe.'

'Hate to think.'

'A break-in? More than one, I was told.'

'We can walk through the janitor's apartment. I want you to
see this from the back lane.'

They faced a building five stories high, tall for the area. No
route existed to get to the rear that did not require walking to
either end of the block, as no gap existed between apartment
buildings, duplexes and triplexes lining the street. They were stuck

in the middle. Casgrain had more or less claimed the janitor's basement quarters for his operations and guided Cinq-Mars through to the rear. The late arrival took an interest in what he observed, in what was out of whack. Back outside again, he moved onto the lane to gain a broader vantage.

Casgrain tested him. 'What do you see?'

Exterior back stairs connected each floor. They served as fire escapes and gave access to the lane. Children played there, and folks washed their cars or changed the oil on their sedans. Men leaned over carburetors, contemplating the universe. Smaller buildings sported gardens and kiddies' sandboxes, and often a few vines for making dreadful wine in the fall. Stairs that served the upper floors of duplexes were wooden and straight: kids loved sliding down the bannisters. Steel stairs spiraled between floors of the apartment buildings. On each metal-grate balcony, wooden storage huts, notorious as firetraps, cluttered the panorama.

'From a distance, not much,' Cinq-Mars concluded. 'Except . . .'

'You noticed.'

'Hard to see in this light. Circles of glass, cut out from the windows in each door.'

'Mode of entry. Seventeen times.'

'Seventeen! Whoa. Somebody was busy.'

'The storage sheds? Eleven broken into. The locks snipped.'

The newly-minted Sergeant-Detective crossed his arms over his chest and grunted. In the grand scheme of things, this was not a major heist – these were impoverished people – but the ambition behind the caper impressed him. A good one to catch first thing. 'What else you got?'

'A truckload of crazies. They're all yours, Émile. I'm jumping off here.'

Easy to interpret his going-away smile as a warning.

He was learning what Casgrain meant by 'crazies.' As if the circus pitched a tent. He tried not to deploy obvious mnemonics, but as he went along, he needed to keep the many victims straight. Serge the Spitter, who sent gobs over the back railing like artillery fire. Florence the Hen, who literally kept her eggs in a basket and offered Cinq-Mars a pair. 'Hard-boiled.' She added, 'Are you hard-boiled, Mr Policeman?' Chloë the Carrot Stick. Skinny as a sapling and equally shy. She wasn't a redhead, but her dress was orange. Youssef the Bombardier. Shirt off, big-bellied and wearing shorts, he'd caterwaul to anyone on the lane in a voice capable of drowning out the Blitz. He'd awakened the block to the robberies that morning. Constantly bellowing, he had nothing meaningful to impart.

Many had been robbed. In each instance, the thief removed a circle of glass from the back-door window, put it to one side to not be tromped upon, and reached through the hole to twist open a pathetic lock. On first impression, the busy crook went no further than the kitchens of each apartment. Pressed for time, he had little interest in waking the residents.

Looking down from the back balcony where Serge the Spitter was launching air-to-ground missiles, and from where the Bombardier lamented the collapse of civilization to a gathering of the curious, Cinq-Mars noticed a man with his hands on his hips gazing skyward. The gent was overdressed. He wore a long topcoat despite spring yielding to summer. His fedora, tilted back, ill-suited the times. After the cultural upheaval of the sixties, men stopped wearing hats, with the exception of hippies and *artistes* who discovered various unique forms of hat-wear. In Montreal, the fedora had become an endangered species.

One rested upon the head of the man now staring up at him.

A uniform stepped out from an apartment. 'Man, do I have a looney tune for you.'

Cinq-Mars felt the need to break from this clutter of humans. Either that or he was reacting to being addressed as '*man*' by a uniform. Time and place for familiarity. This was neither. 'Later. I need to check something out.'

He'd grow into his rank. For the moment, he did not need to explain himself to a uniform. He headed down, getting into a rhythm. Upon his descent, he felt a bit dizzy. The whole way down, the man on the ground never took his eyes off him. He was older than Cinq-Mars, in his late fifties, with an expansive smile and watery eyes. He kept his hands on his hips as though in a perpetual state of inquisitiveness. Or befuddlement. He introduced himself as Geoffrion, and added, 'Not related.'

Oh. Him. That guy.

Cinq-Mars knew of him: nothing complimentary, but nothing

drastic. His full name was Detective Norville Geoffrion. His surname was famous in Quebec thanks to the local hockey legend, Bernard 'Boom-Boom' Geoffrion, now retired as a player. The detective was infamous for adding a rider when he was introduced – 'Not related' – to the point where colleagues might remark, 'Don't ask me. Go ask Not Related.'

An irony persisted, given that the two Geoffrions probably *were* related. The original family name, Joffrion, went back to the founding of Montreal, many decades before the *Mayflower*. A different nickname had been applied to him, a cruel disparagement of Boom-Boom. Behind his back, cops referred to him as Poof-Poof.

Cinq-Mars presumed the moniker had no merit. Nor did he care. What names were dismissive of him behind his back – 'Damn Priest', the least offensive – were water off a duck's back. The same held true for any cop. What he drew from the general scuttlebutt regarding Norville Geoffrion was that he was not the crystal to give a chandelier its sparkle. No one knew how he made detective grade. Rumor held that he flunked out as a beat cop and some dope upstairs decided that he was best hidden from public view as a bumbling detective. Cruelties, Cinq-Mars assumed, borne from the usual run-of-the-mill grist mixed in with an occasional grain of truth.

Either way, his partner now, and junior in rank.

'What tale here?' Geoffrion asked.

'Seventeen kitchens robbed. Along with eleven storage sheds.'

'Kitchens? That's rich. What were they after? Knives and forks?'

'Purses. Not merely the contents, the entire purse. Six in all. A bunch of toasters.'

'Toasters!'

'Quite a haul, huh? Toasters, coffee-makers and radios. In every case, only kitchens. We're sorting out what's missing from the sheds. Assorted junk. A few tools.'

'A busy man,' Geoffrion deduced, which is what Cinq-Mars initially assumed.

'Nope,' he made known.

Geoffrion's hands finally came off his hips.

'Seventeen windows carefully cut out,' Cinq-Mars explained. 'Eleven locks clipped on the sheds. A boatload of small appliances and a few purses taken. A couple of wallets. Nobody did it on their own.' Both men gazed up at the rear of the apartment block. 'A coordinated gang. If I'm not mistaken, it was intended to be an exercise in precision, speed and cooperation among a high number of participants.'

'An exercise?' Geoffrion repeated. Cinq-Mars didn't mind that he sounded skeptical.

'Think about it. Park Ex is the juvenile delinquency capital of Canada. That's statistically true. Also statistically true, couples here are the poorest of any neighborhood in the country. I heard it on the radio. Now, I can imagine delinquents getting together to rob a bunch of apartments, but their precision is hard to get my head around. And why choose such a poor neighborhood? Are they local themselves? Could be. But I'm saying, this was a dry run. These boys won't be satisfied with toasters and purses going forward. The enterprise was too clever and too quick. A practice run, Norville. What they're practicing for, I have no clue. They pulled it off like clockwork, and what comes next, whatever that is, will require clockwork, and, apparently, practice.'

'Practice,' Geoffrion repeated. He seemed to be admiring the building. Then he said, 'I heard you were smart.'

'Anything you hear inside the department, take it with a grain of salt,' Cinq-Mars advised.

Whatever had been said about him should be deposited on the junk pile. He meant to suggest that he was willing to do the same with the tables turned.

The uniform who had wanted to speak to him about a 'looney tune' hadn't relinquished the thought; he'd come down the stairs and was walking over.

'What's up?' Cinq-Mars asked.

'This woman, sad case, hard to make sense of her. Man, if what she says is true . . .' The cop was in his early twenties. Little experience. Walking up to the investigating detective like this and interrupting his conversation with another superior indicated as much. Still, Cinq-Mars admired his persistence if not his choice of appellation.

First, he corrected him. 'My rank is Sergeant-Detective.' Then he encouraged him. 'Go on.'

'I think she was raped.'

'Why do you think that?'

'Because she says so. I think. Kinda hard to tell with her.'

That changed everything.

THREE

That mad cop, who had him blacken his face in a coal cellar, had been right. Where once he'd been certain, he no longer understood why he lived this life.

Or if he could survive it.

He'd been the intended victim of an execution.

Instead, the attacker was killed.

He might have considered bugging out, except a circuit hard-wired in his brain canceled the idea.

He had time-in. He had sacrificed. Now he needed the payoff.

Not a surprise he was targeted given the company he kept. Mafia on one side, Hells Angels on the flip. Russians in the middle. Yet no one had a beef with him. The attack sailed in from elsewhere. That told him the gangs had grown complacent; the soil was shifting underfoot.

Time to bury-in.

His death might have gone unnoticed, a mere blip marked down as a personal grievance. That he survived was bound to light up the airwaves.

An assassination attempt by an unknown player imploded the Vegas odds on him surviving another week. The house shut down that bet. No takers on his life expectancy.

The irony of survival: now more folks wanted him dead.

He assumed he was already deader than a Christmas turkey with its head chopped off. His own skin-and-bones the stuffing. Staying alive meant playing dead. Put hope aside. Squash it. Hope could be lethal. Hope could kill a dead man and bring him back to life. And that – *that* – could be fatal.

He was a corpse unsteady on his feet. Breathing, but lacking a pulse.

Go with that. Call it a last resort. Just don't call it hope.

FOUR

'We go up? See her?' Geoffrion prompted him. His new Sergeant-Detective, the guy with the gargantuan honker, had drifted off. The question brought him back to earth.

'I'll go on my own,' Cinq-Mars determined. 'Norville, locate the janitor. Ask if he saw or heard anything – not only last night, but recently. Then work your way through the tenants. Anything suspicious over the last few weeks? Make sure to interrogate the men who strut around in their undershirts. Or no shirts. If they're showing off how fat they are in public, they might've been out on their balconies when something of interest happened.'

'Got it.'

'And the son,' Cinq-Mars added.

'What son?'

'The janitor's. A teenager. Talk to him. When I got here, he was still in bed.'

'Teenagers. They can sleep through earthquakes.'

'Cops are crawling through the building and his own apartment – he's not interested? Can't rouse himself to crank open an eyelid? People were robbed, Norville. They're raising a stink. We have squad cars with flashing lights, guns on our belts. It's a big deal on the block. Bored teenagers are curious. When we show up, they do, too. Why is he the exception?'

'OK. The janitor, the son, the fat guys. I'm on it.' He did not seem perturbed to be taking orders from a young man whom a day earlier possessed the same rank as him.

'Nord, when you're not busy indoors, be outside at the rear. We'll find each other that way.'

Nord slipped off his tongue. He didn't want to call him *Not Related*: clearly derogatory. And he certainly wasn't going to call him *Poof-Poof*. Still, *Norville* felt too formal. He could address him by his rank, *Detective*, and forget about it. *Nord* felt better. A diminutive of his full name which meant North

City, or North of the City. So, *Nord*. North, in French. Familiar,
friendly, respectful as nicknames go, one that might work
between them.

So far, no objection.

Before he shared a word with the woman on the top floor, Cinq-
Mars enumerated a few rising suspicions. This was not in character
nor part of his professional process. His choice to be a policeman
stemmed from a natural inclination to side with victims, not perpet-
rators. He found his reaction, then, perplexing.

Concerns cropped up as he climbed the spiral stairs. He spotted
something previously missed. Outside a number of kitchen doors,
roughly at the height of mid-shin, a pair of vertical chalk marks
were etched on the red bricks. Each about three inches long.
Having noticed them, he returned back to ground level to start
over. This time he noted which apartments were marked and
which were not. A connection: only apartments scored with chalk
marks were left untouched by the robbery. Any that suffered a
break-in remained clear. Possibly, a cop did it, after the fact,
although it was not procedure. More likely, the property had been
cased in advance. The thieves had scored the dwellings they wanted
to avoid by scratching twin chalk marks.

A quick examination showed why.

Each of the marked apartments had either a deadbolt or other
serious locks on the backdoor. The apartments could not be entered
by creating a hole in the glass then tripping a latch inside. For
these apartments, a thief required a key or a modified battering
ram. Robbing multiple dwellings at night presented a difficulty:
how to quickly differentiate between doors with deadbolts and
those without. Chalk marks, etched ahead of time during daylight,
made the task easy.

Upstairs, Cinq-Mars took note that the premises occupied by
the woman issuing the rape charge had been marked by chalk.
Her place had been designated to be left alone. Sure enough, a
proper deadbolt protected the premises, nor had the glass in her
door been compromised. Her apartment, unlike most, also possessed
a screen door secured by a hook-and-eye latch. A frail secondary
defense, yet it provided an extra line of security. Before knocking,
Cinq-Mars considered that her claim of being violated required

close scrutiny – or viewed as a crime not connected to the rampant break-and-entries.

He rapped his knuckles against the doorframe.

No one showed. He pounded his fist three times upon the frame, then politely, twice, on the side window.

A woman emerged. Tentative, distrustful of him from a distance. He showed his badge. She stepped briskly to cross the room, unlocking the inner and outer doors to admit him.

'So many police. The neighborhood is overrun, like fleas on a blanket. Who knew we hired so many? Our taxes! The entire police department must be out today.'

Cinq-Mars relinquished the urge to correct her. A few squad cars did not constitute a significant police presence.

'I understand you've suffered an assault,' he said. He let go her reference to cops as fleas.

'Diabolical,' she said, and invited him inside.

Moira Ellibee dwelled in the apartment alone. She spoke softly and dabbed an occasional tear while seated in a kitchen chair, her brow furrowed into tight knots. Cinq-Mars sat facing her. He discerned that a daintiness, a kind of overt vulnerability, encompassed the woman in a protective cloak. He suppressed an urge to declare himself her protector – he knew better, but also because he harbored a suspicion. As the conversation continued, he had to build defenses to thwart her. Not that she was hostile. The contrary, she was so inviting, and so vulnerable, and so fragile in demeanor that he could easily lose his professional distance and act to shelter and comfort her. Every intuitive signal brayed against that response.

Of average height, the woman was thin. Late forties, early fifties. Mousy hair of medium length with gentle curls. She kept one knee crossed over the other. She repeatedly burrowed in the pockets of her flimsy house gown as if seeking a recalcitrant Kleenex, finding none. 'Thanking my lucky stars,' she said, in a voice that sounded grateful before Cinq-Mars could process what she meant. 'He wanted me to only use my mouth.'

He paused to deflect his momentary shock. 'Can you describe him, ma'am?'

'How can I? He wore a ski mask. What do you call those? Don't tell me. I think I know.'

'A balaclava?'

'Don't tell me, I said! Oh, you're wicked!'

Difficult to assess this woman's bearing. 'Was he tall, ma'am? Short? Stout? Skinny?'

'Muscular. The stomach muscles on that fellow. I closed my eyes for the rest.'

'A harrowing experience.' She didn't appear to be in critical distress, her upset under control.

'Are you Catholic?' she inquired.

'Sorry?' Not a welcome question. He was Roman Catholic, and practicing, although of late he hadn't given his faith much attention. That had been bothering him, as if his career was stripping away his internal fortitude one speck at a time. He wasn't calling it a crisis of faith, yet he could see where he might wake up one morning and discover that his spiritual life – vital to his sense of self – was slipping away to become a distant memory.

'It's important to know.'

'Why's that, ma'am?'

'Because of what I need to tell you,' she intimated.

'I'm Catholic, yes.' That he once intended to be a priest he kept to himself.

'Do you attend mass?'

'When I can.' Not strictly true. Lately, he'd been skipping. 'Why do you ask?'

She leaned closer. He noticed the veins in her temples, a translucency to her skin.

'It's all right,' she whispered. 'I cannot be harmed. His . . .' She stopped to hunt for the right word. 'His *goop* was never released. Do you know why?'

He couldn't believe the conversation. Her tone seemed off-kilter. Or off the planet. 'I don't. Why was that?'

'I'm protected. By the Virgin. Mary keeps me safe.'

She leaned closer still. The entwined fingers of both her hands hovered above his knees. Her head slumped below his own. She spoke so quietly that he had to lean closer to her. Their foreheads nearly touched.

'She appeared to me, the Virgin,' she whispered. 'When I was young. She gave to me, as you can see, the body of a sixteen-year-old. Mine forever. My body doesn't age, Detective. It's important to me that you're a Catholic man, a believer, or you won't understand. Protestants think I'm crazy. But I can tell. You're a Catholic man. You know how to believe.'

He straightened in his hardback chair. She was clearly nuts, but that did not mean she had not been violated.

'Did he enter by the kitchen door, ma'am? Or the front? Or through a window?'

She sat back herself. She appeared frustrated with explanations. 'How am I supposed to know? He *appeared*. Just like that. In my bedroom.'

'Did he leave by the kitchen door, then, or the front stairwell?'

'I didn't show him out, my detective. I was too stunned. Only when the police arrived outside did I dare leave my bedroom. You understand. He might have been waiting for me beyond the door.'

He thought to ask how she knew the police had arrived if she was in her bedroom. Hers did not look out to the street. He let his challenge pass, then stood, largely to re-establish his position as an investigating detective and to escape the role she imposed upon him as her confidant.

'This occurred, then, in the middle of the night? Are you aware of the robberies in the building, Ms Ellibee? Do you think your attacker was also here to rob you?'

'I checked. Looked everywhere. I'm not missing anything. As I said, I'm protected.'

'By the Virgin. Yes. Ma'am, do you require medical attention? We can take you to the hospital.'

'They never believe me, the doctors.'

'Never? You could talk to a nurse—'

'They're worse.'

'Have you been raped before?' Finding where her sense of reality began and vanished was proving difficult. Perhaps impossible.

'Raped? I wasn't raped, my detective. I was visited by a specter, a phantom, a ghost. They don't have the power to rape me. They're not *physical*, Detective. They don't have bodies. They have no goop. Although his muscles, as I said, they felt *very* real, and I was *violated* – I think I can put it that way – on the spiritual realm. It's difficult to tell the difference when it feels that real. I guess there's no big difference. Anyway, I told you, I'm protected. By the Virgin. I suppose where the phantom lives, in his world, you can call it rape and not be wrong. I will let you say it, if you wish, as long as you understand that ghosts or phantoms cannot hurt me. Did you think they could? Really? They cannot. I'm protected that way.'

Cinq-Mars took a breath. The help she required was not of a sort he could provide.

She went on: 'I told that wonderful policeman about my visitor, my detective. He seemed to like my story. He seemed a nice young man. I didn't tell him I was raped, of course. I have no *interest* in being raped. I don't want *that* going around the block. I only had to open my mouth for someone who was not there. You understand, my detective. Being Catholic.'

Cinq-Mars held in abeyance the notion that the specter with the muscular build and ripped stomach might well have matched her impression of the uniform who interviewed her. One image may have blurred with another. One body imagined from another. He'd have to tell Detective Casgrain, who had mentioned an apartment building of crazies, that he didn't know the half. Casgrain may not have wanted to give up the case to Cinq-Mars, but Cinq-Mars was now more than willing to hand it back.

'Thank you, ma'am, for your cooperation,' he said.

'I fibbed,' she told him. The corners of her lips turned up.

'How so?' Really? She'd been having him on?

Moira Ellibee pressed her thumb and forefinger together to express an infinitesimal space. 'A teensy white lie.'

'I see.'

'The Virgin Mary didn't permanently give me the body of a sixteen-year old.'

'To tell you the truth, I didn't think so.'

'Thank you. Sometimes people don't believe me. I cheated a little.'

'Ma'am—'

'I'm fourteen. Physically. Below the neck. That's my age. Fourteen-and-a-half. That's when she visited me. The Virgin. I was fourteen. My body hasn't changed since. It's permanent.'

'That's . . . wonderful. Thank you, Ms Ellibee. We'll be in touch.'

'Call me Moira.'

Cinq-Mars declined to do so.

'Is that nice young policeman coming back?'

'I can't be sure, ma'am.'

'Will you be coming back?'

Cinq-Mars shuffled out the door, somewhat awkwardly.

FIVE

I n a wife-beater undershirt, Serge the Spitter hacked up a spitball. Sent it flying off the balcony.

'I hope you looked down first,' Cinq-Mars commented.

'Look out below. Or buy an umbrella.'

'Only on a rainy day. Nobody takes it up with you?'

'Never mind. Find my wallet yet?'

'The thieves neglected to mail it back.'

'If they do, you'll take your cut. Help yourself like a mangy mutt on a bone.'

'Maybe I will. Thanks for the idea.'

'Oh sure. It don't matter anyhow. I'm smarter than these dumb-bells here.'

'How's that?'

'Insurance. I bought it. I keep up my premiums.'

'A poor man with insurance. That's suspicious to a cop.'

'Use a toilet. Don't hand me your shit on a plate.'

'Don't give me a shower on the way down. Or when I'm on the ground.'

The man spat over the side before answering. 'If you get hit, wasn't me.'

'Then I won't get hit.' One of those times when he had to have the parting word.

Down below, he found Detective Geoffrion in conversation with three tenants and a pair of uniforms. His partner split from the group to provide an update.

'Definitely talk to the kid. His name is Mikhail. Goes by Mick. He's Russian. Speaks French and English. We should bring him in, maybe? He resisted talking to me. Trouble is, he's not all there. The father's protecting him. I thought I'd leave him alone for now.'

'What do you mean, not all there?'

'Either a screw loose or he's missing a link upstairs.'

'I see.' He didn't, nor did he know what the difference could be. 'Anything from the dad?'

'Same as the other tenants. Nothing, not even with twenty-twenty hindsight.'

'Nord, the doors were marked in chalk. Two quick vertical lines. Apartments marked that way were spared.'

'No lines, they were robbed? Somebody cased the building.'

'Make sure none of ours did it for some reason. If not, mention the lines as you go around. Might twig a memory.'

'One odd thing, boss,' Geoffrion intimated. Cinq-Mars waited to hear it. The detective wet his lips, concentrating on the mathematics of his response. 'Twenty-eight apartments above ground level. Seventeen broken into. Eleven were not. Except, the storage sheds for those eleven got hit. One way or the other, everybody got hit except for anyone who lives in the basement. They were left alone. Of course, down below, they don't own sheds.'

Cinq-Mars appeared to fade away again and did not initially respond.

Geoffrion prompted him. 'Sir?'

He returned. 'Remarkable. Nobody hit twice, nobody spared.'

'One apartment we can't say for sure. But yeah, that's what it looks like.'

'What's different about one apartment?'

'Broken into, for sure. The tenant's been gone a few days, neighbors tell me. We don't know what's been taken, if anything.'

'Which apartment?'

'Top floor. Middle unit. I have to check which one exactly.'

'That's OK.' He was looking up to the fifth, where Serge the Spitter and Youssef the Bombardier surveyed the scene below. 'The neighbors can tell me.'

They did.

Cinq-Mars entered the apartment where the occupant was absent – a convenience of it being broken into and no longer locked – and shut the door behind him. He appreciated the opportunity. To be on the premises when the last person to spend time inside was the crook satisfied an interest. He felt closer to the perpetrator, as though an impression of him lingered. In other apartments, the tenants held sway. Their agitation obliterated any residual trace of the crook. Cinq-Mars did not mean to add a spooky sense to his investigative process, only that he'd learned to be quiet and contemplative at the scene of a crime. He functioned more effectively when the scene wasn't contaminated by the busyness of officers and forensic analysts, or a victim's shattered nerves. Stillness served him better than any fuss.

Daylight had been long-standing, yet he could close his eyes and feel the kitchen as had the thief in the dead of night. The faint buzz of an appliance, the mixture of scents of a life lived there. The slumber of the place. Opening his eyes, he walked through the other rooms by going down the hall and starting over in the living room at the front, a bedroom alongside it, then working his way back. The bed looked slept in. Perhaps not lately. Next to a Westinghouse TV, a few tubes lay at rest, most likely changed recently. These old units were starting to disappear; if the tenant continued to have trouble, it would not be long for the scrap heap.

Not many books. A selection of magazines on various topics, tidily arranged. Everything from dream vacation rentals to *GQ*. Tool catalogs jostled for position alongside car magazines, baseball and hockey magazines, *Time* and *National Geographic*.

The dining room extended the living room and offered a separate exit to the hallway. Across the hall was the bathroom. Tidy, brightened by a skylight shaft. In the rear, a second bedroom lay opposite the kitchen, an interior design typical of the neighborhood. Cinq-Mars went in. The blinds were drawn. He was wondering if the tenant was a businessman who traveled frequently. He'd left a straight row of black shoes under a shelving unit – more shoes than most men bothered to own, with little variation in style – and he opened the closet to see if he possessed as many suits to match. That appeared to be the case. Before he could count them Cinq-Mars noticed more footwear. He pushed the suits aside to the right and left, and discovered that feet, without socks, remained standing in a pair of slippers. He stepped back, startled, looked up. A man stood there, impaled through the neck with what looked like a machete, the blade entering the wall behind him deeply enough to pin him upright.

The neighbors had reported the tenant absent for days. A quick check revealed that this body remained somewhat supple. *Rigor mortis* had not had a significant head start. The victim was dead less than four hours in his estimation, more likely three. Possibly as few as two.

This changed everything once again.

Cinq-Mars stepped out to the balcony. Not wanting to create a scene with an avid public observing him, he signaled below for Detective Geoffrion to come up. Already he was thinking that this was his first case as a Sergeant-Detective, yet he would have to turn over the most intriguing aspect to homicide. Or turn over the whole kit-and-caboodle to homicide. The multitude of burglaries might keep him in the game, but that remained to be negotiated.

Returning to the apartment, he did another appraisal, different now that the crime was infinitely more serious. Perhaps that's why he noticed something obvious he'd neglected previously. On the dining room table, next to a buffet where dishes were stored, stood a toaster. Had it come from another apartment? Or did this one belong in the kitchen? Odd that it had made it only this far when so many had been stolen throughout the complex.

'Yeah, what's up?' Geoffrion asked. An inexplicable smile on his face.

'Back bedroom closet,' Cinq-Mars said.

He waited. Perused the premises again. A broken elastic band on a hall table near the entrance held his attention. Long, the band; the sort mailmen used to bundle letters. That struck him as peculiar as mail was delivered only to the boxes in the entrance-level foyer. The fact that it was lying around, broken, on a surface in an apartment where nothing else was out of place or untidy, was filed away.

He heard the bedroom closet door open.

Geoffrion exclaimed, 'Holy shit!'

Cinq-Mars returned to the bedroom to join him. 'Odd juxtaposition of words, don't you think?'

Geoffrion couldn't fathom what the hell he was talking about.

'Nord, use this guy's telephone. If you don't have gloves, use Kleenex. I don't want this on the airwaves. Keep it quiet around the building. No one should suspect a thing until the morgue shows up. Meantime, buzz homicide.'

'Yeah,' Geoffrion concurred. Then repeated, 'Holy shit,' as though he wanted that edict confirmed.

Émile Cinq-Mars continued to dwell upon the apartment's peacefulness. Nothing in the air signaled what had occurred, or how or why. The man's end was horrific and violent, yet his bedroom appeared undisturbed. His suits had been pushed back across to cover him up. Dust marks in the kitchen indicated that a radio, probably, had been removed, and a toaster relocated, but under the circumstances that didn't add up to a hill of beans. All he had to go on was the toaster in the dining room. Out of place. He'd want it checked for prints. Perhaps the eerie sense he was experiencing had been presaged by the woman whose ghost attacker, a fantasy attacker more likely, had simply appeared, then was gone. Unlike her, the dead man possessed no mystical protection, no Virgin Mary, to thwart an assault.

Departing, Cinq-Mars noticed the absence of chalk marks by the doorjamb, indicative that the apartment had been designated to be robbed. No further marking foreshadowed a murder. Down a door, the purported rape victim had had her door marked: no forced entry assigned. The marks, or their lack, surely indicated what was meant to transpire. He'd love to speak to whoever had etched them onto the bricks.

SIX

Willy, to those who knew him.

Coalface, to those who did not.

Out of the blue, somebody considered him important enough to kill.

That raised his profile. People who thought they knew him took another look.

Willy maintained a secret office that came with a sink and toilet. Years ago, he'd added a shower. Stowed a hot-plate in a drawer. Tins of beans and soup lay at the bottom of a filing cabinet. A half-size fridge that kept his beer cold was useful now to chill food.

The sofa opened into a bed. He kept a sleeping-bag in a closet.

Almost no one entered but him. Nothing for the cleaning lady to see. Office tenants on his floor nosy enough to inquire were informed that he kept the books for select clients off-site. That explained his lengthy absences. He wasn't Willy in the building. Not Coalface, either. He was Mr d'Alessandro.

He kept his communication equipment in a safe there. Never in his apartment.

Time to haul it out. Make contact.

On an ordinary telephone he could ring the head man in the Mafia; the boss would take his call. He could advise him to not take the news of his death to heart. Shed no tears. The trouble with that, the boss might be disappointed. Especially if he'd ordered the hit. Better to report his remarkable escape to a friend. Somebody a few rungs down. Let the news spread outward and upward. Allow his miraculous Lazarus revival to take on a mythological bearing by the time word reached the top man's ears.

He called up Teddy The Bear.

'What're you saying to me that makes sense?' Teddy asked.

'Skin of my teeth.'

'Who the dead guy if not you?'

'Nobody I know. Your world. You tell me. I only keep the books.'

'Yeah, but—' A big part of this was not adding up.

'I know, Teds, I know. Point is, he had no business in my bedroom.'

'You whacked him?'

'Hard to believe.'

'You whacked him? You?'

'Get used to the idea.'

'Willy. I don't believe this. You whacked him?'

'Teds. Come on. Who had a choice? It was him or me. I preferred it was him.'

'Holy goddamn shit, Willy. Where you now?'

'Holed up.'

'Where?'

'Can't say, Teds.'

'Willy, it's me.'

'I know who I'm talking to. Think a minute.'

'I'm thinking.'

'Teds! I don't know who ordered the hit.'

That gave Piergiorgio 'Teddy The Bear' Giordano pause. He took time to consider. 'OK. You're right. Lie low.'

'I'm lying low. Teds, I got this feeling. Somebody wants me out of the way. Me? That's strange-colored shit flowing downstream.'

'Like what?'

'Like what. Like we'll find out soon, like what. Tell the boss. I can't poke my nose outside until I know what's in the air.'

'I tell the boss that?'

'Please.'

They broke off their talk.

He had another call to make.

He got a machine. He gave his number and said, 'Field report.'

He waited for the next automated voice. He'd been in on a killing, and now the time had come to start a war. To finish this. To do what had to be done and get out. If he was a marked man, his usefulness had arrived at its natural conclusion. One more gambit to make everything worthwhile. Tear the house down. He had a vested interest. He'd put in the time. He recorded his field report and added, 'I need help.'

He hung up. Time to make up the bed.

He'd been on an adrenalin jag.

Dead men sleep, don't they?

SEVEN

Homicide detectives were designated *la crème de la crème*. The toughest, the smartest, the best-dressed. Émile Cinq-Mars found many to be sharp and rarely disputed their acumen. Toughness was difficult to gauge, but he agreed that they wore expensive ties. Yet, lately, a few members of this elite band were coming across as smug dickheads. As if the burden of being *la crème* churned their contingent into stinky cheese.

Case in point: the pair that showed up to the crime scene. He'd had run-ins with them. Back when Cinq-Mars thrived under the wing of Captain Armand Touton of the Night Patrol; when he was an untouchable. Other cops resented that. Now that he was a suburban outcast, these two in particular were eager to sully his existence.

'Cinq-Mars, how long does it take to find a stiff in a closet? Were you out sunning yourself? Humping an air mattress?'

'You guys are called in *after* a body's discovered. *After* a corpse is leaking maggots. The rest of us, we *investigate* the crime first. We *open* the closet door to see what's inside.'

He was talking to Alfred Morin, a gold shield detective who, as of today, held less rank than him. Which made not a nick of difference. Morin was in homicide, so for him, everybody else could go fish or enjoy a colossal fart. His red hair indicated Irish descent, his ancestors among the thousands absorbed into the Québécois people during the hard times of potato famine and cholera in an earlier century. Irish kids who survived epidemics when their parents did not were generously adopted into rural French homes. Through time, the physical features of the French and the Irish blended, and on occasion, generations on, redheads returned.

Cinq-Mars had met Morin ten years earlier. He had not liked him then; less so now. Joining homicide, the man had not only graduated as an A-1 jerk, he'd proudly stuck his diploma on the wall. Had Morin been first on the scene, Cinq-Mars believed, the cadaver would never have been detected until the stench ripened.

'Are you interested in what I put together?'

'How many days off my life will it cost me?' Morin asked.

'Start over at point zero, then.'

'I don't need your permission, Cinq-Mars. Oh, excuse me, I meant to say: Sergeant-fucking-Detective Cinq-Mars. It's time to run along. Look into bicycle theft. Somebody's probably shop-lifting socks. That should keep you busy.'

'What about the toasters?' Cinq-Mars asked him.

'What toasters?'

'You'll find out, Detective.'

Let him hunt them down. He wasn't going to warn him off Moira Ellibee, either. Let him work through the whole crew. With any luck, Morin might be spat upon by Serge the Spitter or have his eardrums pierced by Youssef the Bombardier.

'Show me the stiff,' Morin directed him. 'Then get back to speedbump patrol. Make sure those old ladies slow down, hey. Don't let them whack you with their canes.'

Morin did not have rank, but he had jurisdiction. He was working it to the limit. If Cinq-Mars pulled rank, some other clodhopper up the scale would arrive to verbally pepper-spray him. Not worth the trouble. He did as he was told: showed him the dead guy and departed.

Geoffrion had fared no better. He'd dealt with the senior detective of the pair who'd hosed him down for not wearing gloves. He pleaded that he'd been checking on stolen radios and coffeemakers; nobody had shown up dead when he first went through the building. Sergeant-Detective Jerôme LaFôret let him know that if he contaminated his murder case, he'd bust him down to clerical. A curious pathology. Cinq-Mars found it aggravating that both homicide detectives were inclined to piss on the shoes of every cop in the vicinity. Prone to anxiety, Geoffrion responded to them as they wished: he became unglued.

'How did I contaminate? I didn't touch nothing!' he whinged.

'Nord, don't worry about it.'

'My hands were in my pockets. Most of the time. You saw me.'

'You might've touched a few clothes in the closet.'

'Oh shit!'

'And the phone.'

'I'm dead.'

'Nord. Nobody's dusting a jacket for prints. You were careful with the phone.'

'Right. Right. Why is he busting my balls?'

'Good question. Focus on that. What's his problem?'

'I don't know.'

'The point is, his problem is *his* problem. Not yours.'

'He could make it mine. Seems like he wants to.'

Cinq-Mars gathered why some people called his new partner *Poof-Poof*.

'I got your back, buddy. Relax.'

The look on Geoffrion's face. As though no one had uttered a similar kindness to him in his lifetime. The glow – as if voted Most Popular in a high school yearbook.

'Talk to a neighbor, Nord. Find out the victim's name. Then we'll beat it out of here.'

'OK,' Geoffrion agreed, his spirit returning. 'Hey. You're assuming something.'

Good that he noticed. 'The victim, the tenant: probably the same person.'

'We can't be sure.'

'His shoes. His suit. Perfect fit. They match other clothes in the closet. Find out his name. We'll go from there.'

'Where do we go? Not our case. Homicide will have a bird.'

'Nord, think. The dead man had his toaster moved to a different room. Perhaps against his will. That's outrageous. Where's his radio? His wallet? Will we abandon him in his time of need, just because somebody speared him through the throat?'

'Ah. Right. Gotcha.'

Geoffrion had arrived on the scene in a squad car, Cinq-Mars in his personal vehicle, a Volkswagen Beetle. When ready, they traveled back to the station separately. Cinq-Mars said he'd find the new man a desk and introduce him around. He also wanted to check reports from other *postes*. If similar robberies had occurred around town, it would be useful to know that. If not, he'd be on the lookout for the next escalation in the new gang's progress. He now nursed an alternative theory, of course, that the robberies were an elaborate ploy to mask a murder. Had murder been the intention of the gambit all along? He had to consider the premise, although it made limited sense. Due to the robberies, the body was located sooner than otherwise, which undercut the theory.

Yet, somehow, did burglary facilitate murder?

Did a killer believe that a murder obscured by the heist degraded an investigation?

None of it made sense. More likely, the robberies and the murder, and for that matter the mystical rape, were unrelated. A scenario that shoved him back to investigating the rampant theft of toasters. Quite a thrill.

Strange, though, the killing. The victim, dressed in the middle of the night with his feet in his slippers, without socks, wearing a suit but no tie, slaughtered with a long, sturdy knife – machete-like – offering no resistance. No upraised protective palm, for it displayed no wound. The victim may not have seen the blade coming, despite being propped against the closet wall. Had he been hiding there, only to suddenly be revealed when the killer shoved aside the suits as Cinq-Mars had done? Perhaps someone had also noticed the slippers first, out of place given the rack of shoes nearby. Or had the man been threatened into standing in the closet, believing that that would be the end of it, that his attacker would leave, only to have the blood supply to his brain abruptly severed.

The power of the blow was impressive. Through the throat, then deeply enough into the wallboard that the blade held the victim upright. Not a short jab with a knife, but a mighty thrust, perhaps two-handed with the full weight of the attacker behind it. The victim waiting passively to be struck. But how did that make sense?

The knife wreaked destruction more typical of a spear.

What of blood from the wound? Rather, its lack? Why wasn't it all over his spiffy suit? Why had no blood splashed onto the suits nearest the victim?

Getting into possible scenarios, Cinq-Mars regretted losing out on the investigation. He wouldn't be watching speedbumps as Morin had intimated. Bicycle theft never rose above the level of cops in uniform who jotted a few notes, submitted a brief report, then forgot about it. Yet a truth was included in the mean-spirited jibes, for he had no other case as interesting to occupy his time.

Or so he believed. At the station, he was handed a message from his old boss, now retired, asking to see him, *pronto*. Cinq-Mars called first.

'On the double, kid.' Always, he was *kid* to the old man.

'Ah, you do know that I work days now. I can come over after dinner. Or *for* dinner if you want to fire up the barbecue.'

'Your ass,' retired Captain Armand Touton demanded, 'my doorstep, *right the fuck now*.'

'Anybody wants to know my whereabouts,' Cinq-Mars whispered to Nord Geoffrion as he was going out the door, 'tell him I got a lead on a bunch of toasters.'

'Do you?' his new partner inquired. 'Already?'

Overall, the new guy did not seem to lack intelligence as his reputation foretold. Then again, there were moments . . .

'I'll be back, Nord. Can't say when. Make yourself look busy.

Check for similar thefts around town. Also, write up an obit on the corpse. Who is he? I want to know. Thanks.'

Hopefully, the man knew how to do that, both make himself busy and handle fundamental research. Good to find out.

EIGHT

Packed to travel.

Retired Captain Armand Touton's Ford Country Squire was hitched to a seventeen-foot house trailer. A canoe strapped to the car's rooftop. Tires appeared done-in and the hood bowed upward. Four fishing rods leaned against the trailer.

'Holidays?' Émile Cinq-Mars queried. 'Or do you camp out in your driveway now?'

'Blow it out your rear, punk. I'm heading up north for the summer.'

Touton carried a pair of suitcases from his house, the veins of his muscled forearms prominent. Thirty pounds each, he flicked them through a trailer door as if they were empty.

'I hope you don't expect me to paddle that canoe.'

'Give me a nickel's worth of credit, kid,' his former boss stated. If someday Touton was a hundred and Cinq-Mars sixty-five, he'd still call him *kid*.

'Always do.' He gave the man all the respect in the world, although they were not compatible on every matter. Touton was never shy about collapsing a suspect's defenses with a single blow to the gut or crunching a criminal's throat in his grip. Cinq-Mars preferred guile, and the law, to reduce a tough guy to tears. Both men harbored the keenest sense of right and wrong. When the heat was on, both believed in good and evil, something generally frowned upon in the modern age.

'I had you drive out here,' Touton maintained, 'because this is serious.'

Out here had been an hour's ride for Cinq-Mars. Touton had ditched life in the big city for the burbs, living off the north side of the Island of Montreal. He had chosen a modest bungalow, and added the house trailer, canoe and a private camp in the woods by a sprawling lake as retirement perks. Cinq-Mars was glad for him. Away from the job, the man was content with his fishing rods and solitude whenever his adult children were not a trial.

'Well, I'm here.'

'Inside, Émile.'

Cinq-Mars took a step toward the bungalow, then noticed Touton heave himself into the trailer.

Weird, sitting in a house trailer on a driveway in suburbia. Cinq-Mars bunched his limbs on the bench behind the small fold-down table opposite his former boss. Two large men in cramped quarters. 'What's going on?' he asked.

'Let me tell you about Coalface,' Touton began.

'This guy's been embedded in the Mafia for over twenty years?' Cinq-Mars was incredulous. 'What does he do for them?'

'Who knows? Robs banks? Kills people? I imagine he keeps the books or sweeps floors.'

'He hasn't come up for air?'

'Not to my knowledge,' Touton said. 'Don't ask about his headspace. I have no clue.'

'How much has he given us?'

'I won't say. Nothing can be revealed. Not ever. That could be his death knell.'

'You're telling me about him right now – that could be his death knell.'

'No details. If we have no details to keep track of, we don't need to keep track of them.'

'Armand, what's he giving you today that you brought me out here?'

Touton was distracted by a small wooden box nestled on a side shelf. He brought it onto the table, opened the lid. Fishing flies, beautifully knotted with colorful feathers and fake wings, concealed the lethal hooks. 'How I spent my winter,' Touton revealed.

Given the man's tenure in violent circumstances, as a soldier, a prisoner of war, a cop, a reformer in a corrupt department, this artistic side was unexpected. Cinq-Mars marveled at the intricacy and detailing of the delicate *objets d'arts*. They were functional, meant to catch fish, yet admirable on their own. 'Beautiful, Armand. Amazing.'

Touton took time to admire them himself, before gently placing them back in the box. Cinq-Mars was left with the impression that he'd be reluctant to put the wet flies into service, that he might begrudge a fish gobbling one into its mouth.

'If I was a fish, I'd bite,' Cinq-Mars said.

'If you were a fish, I'd throw you back.'

'Coalface,' Cinq-Mars reminded him, to get them back on track.

'My flies are like our guy,' Touton noted.

'How's that?' He was not normally a man who resorted to metaphor.

'Like I said, I made him mark up his face with coal. Coal is not his disguise. His whole life is his disguise. The Mafia will never know that inside his life lies a giant, very sharp hook.'

'Does he make contact often?'

'Extremely rare. We knew it wouldn't be about this heist or that homicide. His purpose is to rip the heart out of the apparatus when the time comes. When he can. Tell you the truth, Émile, I forget about him for years at a stretch.'

'You and me, not so long ago, we struck a blow.'

'A glancing one. Now we see the effect.'

'Meaning?' Cinq-Mars asked.

Touton gave the back of his weathered neck a scratch. 'Émile, you know as well as me, taking out the bad guys stops nothing. Trade away or retire players, the game stays the same.'

'There's always a new team, yeah.'

'New and different. You're new, but you're different from me. Inside the Mafia, it's the same difference. A new guard, respectful to the senior bunch, but waiting their turn. They'll be different, like you're different from me. I was muscle. You're a smart guy. The Mafia always had muscle, now they're acquiring brains, too. Their new boys are bright. That's bad enough, but it's gone beyond that.'

'Coalface says so?'

'Not just him. The old generation remains in place, doing it the old-fashioned way. But on their last legs.'

The postures of the two men were stooped in the cramped quarters. Cinq-Mars entwined his fingers together; Touton's massive paws remained face-down on the table. Other men in a similar moment might deflect their eye contact. Such was the long-standing resolve between these two that neither noticed the intensity of the other's gaze. 'Goes beyond, how?'

'What you mentioned, Émile, our most recent action, before I handed in my badge. We messed up the Mafia. Like always, we had to cut a deal. Scaled it back to a compromise. They were testing satellite gangs, then, to beef up their muscle. A lot of their own punks have been lost to attrition: jail, death. They need to recover. Next move, the Mafia's wise guys are inviting the Hells Angels in. You know this. For the first time, they'll partner across the board with non-Italians. Very significant. The Hells will provide their muscle. They'll have guys to break legs and crack skulls. Things get heavy, these animals are into chainsaws. Bombs, too. Meantime, the Maf gives the Hells expertise, political contacts, teaches them about organization that's local, national, international. Update me. How's that working so far?'

'Going well. The Italians are recouping their losses.'

'You're behind the times, Émile. It's not working out as expected.'

The opinion surprised the young detective. 'Why say that?'

'Turns out, the Hells aren't dumb punks with shit for brains, eager to kill for a tattoo on their arm. They're smart, too. They've picked up on how to organize from the masters of crime. You don't have an uneasy alliance between the Hells and the Mafia anymore, now you're stuck with a vicious gang that has structure. Local chapters are brutal, as we know. Chainsaws – no joke. Sets us up with a violent biker gang that has sophisticated leadership. Their guys are learning to implement, Émile. They have a vision for the future. International contacts. A business plan banks approve of. If they went public, I'd buy stock. Anybody who doesn't think this is a recipe for disaster will be hit with a hammer. Since nobody at City Hall gives a rat's ass, that surprise is coming harder and sooner than anybody knows.'

Cinq-Mars concurred that trouble lay ahead. 'You think they're good students, the Hells?'

'Their top guys are effing wizards. They've divided into cells. One cell doesn't know what the next one is doing. Taking one down doesn't help us. Let me tell you how different your life will be. The Mafia got by on organized muscle and intimidation. Enough to control a few unions and make life hard on the bosses. Tell me you can guess what's changed.'

Cinq-Mars shook his head.

'They still control unions, but they'll be the bosses, too. You want to have an Olympics? We had an Olympics. We saw what happened. Mafia contractors hire Mafia unions, who fund Mafia-controlled politicians to keep excessive money flowing. The new guard, they're learning to manage from the inside out. Be inside the police, worm their way inside the judiciary. Be inside business, not only unions. And finally, work inside political elites. We used to talk about their influence. Soon we'll talk about their *authority*. While all this is progressing, consider that the Hells are learning how to operate at the feet of the masters. Only, they're more cruel. More vicious. They're willing to sit in place for now, keep learning, but not forever. Remember, the Hells are way less civilized, less willing to keep the order. The Mafia figured out that they could thrive on order. The Hells think – not proven yet – that they can thrive in chaos. They don't give a damn if innocents get rubbed out along the way, or if the social order is wrecked. They figure they're better off if society's a mess.'

'All this from your guy?' Cinq-Mars inquired. Ominous news.

'He's not my guy. Never think so. I don't know who he is. I've seen him, though I'm not sure I could pick him out in a crowd. I almost forgot about him, until he gave me a call one day. Years ago. Now – first time ever – he wrote a report. I got wind of the highlights from a third party.'

'A third party.'

'Can't say. Won't say. Don't ask.'

'And this report, it's required reading?'

'Phoned in.'

Levels of intrigue he was unaccustomed to and did not appreciate. 'What's the long-range objective for the bikers, Armand? Take over the world?'

'You joke. Go joke.'

'I'm not.'

'This is no joke, Émile.'

'I'm not joking.'

'They're too smart to take over the world. They're looking for unlimited funds – nothing new there – plus they want to be invulnerable. They're setting themselves up to be impenetrable. What will you do then, when the bad guys can't be touched, when they operate with impunity? When they kill, maim, extort, control – and fill banks with money. Banks they control or, at least, influence.'

A dark vision. 'Except, we've got some guy inside.'

'Inside the Mafia, yeah. The Hells, no. Not the same thing. Although he might be connected to both. Don't get sarcastic with me, punk. I'll punch you out.'

Cinq-Mars skipped denying his sarcasm and took a moment to process everything else. 'As the kids say, Armand, this is heavy. Does your guy, who's not your guy, want to pass along a word of advice? Anything specific we can do?'

'That's where it gets tricky. This is where you come in and you won't like it, Émile.'

'Why's that?'

'We need someone who talks nice. I've decided. That's you.'

'Now who's being sarcastic?'

'Me? No. Not me.'

'Talk to who?'

'You won't like that either.'

He was given a perplexing task. Émile Cinq-Mars repeated it, to make sure he had it straight.

'This guy embedded in the Mafia emerges from his lair and says go talk to a priest—'

'A pastor. Or minister. Whatever Protestants call priests.'

'I'm to talk to this Protestant priest to make sure a certain con stays in prison.'

'I can't do it myself. I'm a cop no more. Besides, I'm going fishing. Has to be you. You're the new me, right? Even if you don't have the real juice.'

'I just got promoted. To Sergeant-Detective.'

'Whoop-de-doo, Émile. Congratulations.'

'Whoop-de-doo?'

'You have no power. Probably, thanks to your connection with me, you never will.'

'That's true. You're my kiss of death in the department until you're long forgotten. Thanks a lot. So where do I find this Protestant priest?'

'Your turf.'

'Meaning what?'

'Park Ex. Don't you live there?'

'Really? OK. So, I have to convince a pastor to *not* help a bad guy get out of jail. That's all?'

Touton rocked his head from side to side, as though to modify the assignment. 'Émile, our guy's been undercover for twenty-plus years. The shit that's gone down over all that time. He must've done some dark dope himself. What does he want when finally he communicates? This. More than anything, he wants to stop a nobody punk from being released. After the murders, the broken legs, the abductions, the drugs, the prostitution rings, the protection rackets, the bank heists – let's not forget the fucking bank heists; it's like crooks make monthly withdrawals, with pistols instead of withdrawal slips. Why can't they use a fucking pen and paper like the rest of us? After all that, *this* is what he considers essential?'

'Strange,' Cinq-Mars concurred.

'A minor-league punk denied early release. A guy who's out in two years anyway, what's the big deal? I don't know, but Coalface is counting on us. Either he's lost his mind, or this is more important than we're allowed to know. Don't let this priest, this whatever, this Protestant, help a young hood get out of jail. Do not permit the pastor to be a Good Fucking Samaritan. Apparently, he makes it a habit. Talks birds out of the trees. We can't let him convince a civilian panel to let a con go free. Go in there, talk to the sweet-talker. Convince the Protestant penguin to back off.'

'And say what?'

'That's up to you! I can't help you on this. Absolutely critical that you come through.'

'Can I research the convict, at least?'

'Run his sheet. Talk to his loved ones. Look at his baby pictures. Just make sure he does his full stretch.'

A bizarre, borderline ludicrous assignment. Yet no other option presented itself, and he didn't see the harm. If a mole, secretly embedded in the Mafia, believed that a convict had to stay behind bars, why argue? 'OK,' he said.

'Now get out,' Touton told him. 'Let me go fishing.'

His way, perhaps, of saying thanks.

NINE

Congested streets. Impassable intersections. Every manner of truck and more damned trucks. A chorus of blaring horns. The sun in his eyes and he'd forgotten his shades. Cinq-Mars was impeded further by a multitude of stop signs and seemed destined to hit every red light. He finally pulled over at a phone booth set back from a corner. Extra honks for that move as he bore through a pedestrian tide. He hung his badge on his lapel pocket on the off-chance a zealous uniform – were there any left? – wanted to ticket him. A lucky day: half the phonebook was intact; the section that survived chronic vandalism suited his purposes. Letters M through Z included a list of United Church congregations. He noted the address of the one he'd been directed to visit.

The phone being handy he called his new partner.

Geoffrion was summoned, he could hear his slow shuffle, then, 'Hey, boss, what's up?'

Boss. The appellation would take some getting used to.

Geoffrion reported that he was hitting it off with his new *quartier* captain. Delacroix had brought him into his office for coffee, toast and jam, then shown him the ropes. Surprising – and suspicious – news. Out of character for Delacroix. More than had been done for him. The contrary, he'd been given a hard time. Of course, he had arrived savagely hungover, flubbing his chance to make a good first impression.

Cinq-Mars had yet to be invited into the captain's office for toast and jam.

He asked his new partner to check the rap sheet on Johnny Bondar. Currently incarcerated. Touton had scribbled a note that his first name could be on the books as Jan, a Ukrainian take on John. 'I'll check back in twenty minutes.'

When he did call again, from a different booth, he was pleasantly surprised that his new partner had successfully pulled up the man's sheet. Reports of his incompetence were overblown. 'He's in jail under Johnny. Not even John. He's Johnny.'

'What's he done?'

'Car theft. Priors for assault. Hired one time to bust up a polling booth. Another time he trashed a mom-and-pop store. Short-changed, maybe.'

An unremarkable record that demonstrated he was not strictly independent, that he freelanced for others. He was connected.

'The car thefts,' Cinq-Mars wanted to know. 'Joy-riding or business?'

'In it for the bucks. Nabbed the last time in a chop-shop. Caught rubbing out VINs. Sixth arrest for a car heist, third conviction. He got forty-two months.'

Major time for minor crime, in the overall scheme of things. Hard to figure why anyone would be riled up about his release.

'Thanks, Nord.'

His new partner proved to be thorough. 'Parole hearing this Thursday.'

Confirmation to act quickly. 'The robberies today, anything similar elsewhere?'

'Getting to it next. Like I said, the boss took up my time.'

'Is he concerned about me at all?'

'Not my take. Seems a little pissed that we lost the case to homicide. He made a joke. Said we should've ditched the stiff in a sewer to keep the robbery our own.' Cinq-Mars wasn't sure he'd heard his boss joke before. Maybe he had to be eating toast and jam. 'He grunted when I mentioned you weren't in. Is he used to your jitterbug?'

He could argue that his excursion was no song-and-dance, although he might then need to explain what he was up to in detail.

'Catch you later, Nord.'

'I'll see what I find that's similar, burglary-wise. It's been a unique morning.'

Unique captured the essence of his day. He was now on his way to urge a minister *not* to help a prisoner win favor with a parole board. Likely, the minister would ask him why. Not a

question he was prepared to answer, nor had he devised a decent
lie to cover his tail.

Cinq-Mars drove his VW Bug into Park Ex. The church, which
he'd passed a thousand times without really noticing, was on
Bloomfield Street. Easy to miss. Remarkable only for being small.
It blended with its surroundings to the brink of being invisible.

Parking was tight; he got lucky, found a spot around the corner
on Avenue Ogilvy. Not unaccustomed to visiting parish priests,
both personally and professionally, he counted on them living next
door to their church. Walking closer, he recalled that the same did
not necessarily hold true for Protestants. The minister might live
in an adjacent manse, or miles away. The minister might rent,
going out of his way to be just plain folks. A wife and kids to
boot. Sure enough, no home was attached to the wee church. The
detective's expectations sank. Now he had to hold out hope for an
office on the premises.

Cinq-Mars located a side-door. Locked. *Protestants*! He rang
the bell.

He showed his badge and identified himself to the woman
who answered – the church secretary, he assumed, but you never
knew with Protestants, she could be the minister's wife. The
pleasant, freckle-faced woman greeted him warmly. He told her
that he was there to speak to Reverend Alex Montour. 'Certainly!
Come on up.' He followed her up a short stairwell, around
a corner, down a hallway, and into an office. When she sat
behind the only desk in the small vestry and relaxed her forearms
upon the surface, he suddenly realized the depth of his error.
Growing up with priests, he had never encountered this. He'd
heard about it, but this was a cultural chasm far removed from his
Quebec–Catholic roots.

'*You're* Reverend Montour,' he said, to make sure.

'I am.' Noticing his plight, she grasped that the concept was
new to him. 'We exist now. Women clergy.'

'Not in my church you don't.' He laughed at his own misjudg-
ment. 'I can't see it happening either. Not in this century. Or
the next.'

'Sad but true. I won't get up on my high horse, Sergeant-
Detective. Catholic women have taken orders as nuns for centuries.
Protestant ladies? They make tea.'

Her remark struck him as generous.

'Your name – Alex – threw me off,' he admitted. 'It should've occurred to me that Alex can be a woman's name.'

'It's thrown people off before. Short for Alexandra, in my case.' She lowered her voice, as though to convey a subterfuge. 'When I was invited here, most parishioners expected a man to walk through the door.' She was beaming with the pleasure of her tale. 'Please, Sergeant-Detective, have a seat. I take it this is not a personal visit.'

Thinking on the fly, his strategy evolved quickly. He had no lie to promote, and given that he couldn't be convincing, he opted for a version of the truth.

'I'm here with a request that's come through to me from others. Ah . . . I'm sorry for my ignorance, how do I address you? In my church an ordained woman might be Mother Superior, or Sister. That doesn't apply, I know.'

She smiled. 'Some say Reverend, some prefer Pastor, if they feel a title is necessary. If it doesn't offend your sensibilities too much, I'm content with Alex.'

Cinq-Mars rocked his head slightly. 'I'm old-school. Maybe if you call me Émile. I'm not used to Sergeant-Detective. I've had the rank for less than a day.'

'Congratulations! Let's go back and forth, Émile. Find whatever's comfortable.'

'I'll try. I have a request I really don't comprehend. I'm only the messenger, charged with persuading you to do something you may not want to do.'

'How odd.'

'Exactly. What I can tell you is that the charge to me comes from a superior I trust very much. I am to argue strenuously should you disagree with the proposal. I'm supposed to be convincing. The consequences of failure, I'm told, are dire.'

She clenched her lips. Then said, 'You argue well. I'm almost ready to agree with you, although I haven't the foggiest idea what you want.'

'My fogginess may exceed yours. Reverend Montour, I understand that you're preparing to appear before a parole board on behalf of Johnny Bondar this week. Is that correct?'

'On Thursday. Yes.'

'My task is to beseech you not to go. Please, stay home.'

Cinq-Mars thought he could hear a pin drop in the ensuing silence. As the moment expanded and grew prolonged, he heard a clock ticking more loudly than any falling pin might hit a floor. A muffled burr came in from the adjoining room – he suspected a small refrigerator as the culprit. From busy Bloomfield Street – one-way, well-traveled – came a cacophony amplified by the silence in the vestry. Children's ecstatic squeals, tires on the pavement, a bus lurching to a stop. Behind the foreground racket the thrum of a city. No pin could drop here and be heard, yet the silence felt all-encompassing, on the verge of deafening.

Reverend Alex Montour finally spoke. 'You want to keep Johnny in prison. Why?'

Damn that question. 'It's believed, by men of integrity, who possess critical knowledge that I don't, that his release will have serious negative consequences.'

'Such as?'

'In this case, I'm ignorant of the matter. Only that his release could precipitate an unfortunate, perhaps tragic, result.'

'For whom? The police?'

'Perhaps the police. Perhaps the public. Perhaps for Mr Bondar himself.'

'That latter point I dispute.'

'On what basis? We don't know—'

'On the basis that remaining in prison will probably kill him. I've visited Johnny in jail, Sergeant-Detective.' He was back to being Sergeant-Detective now, he noticed. 'Have you been inside St Vincent de Paul?' He had, in fact, visited that penitentiary. His memories of the place would only lend weight to her side of the discussion. 'Not to put too fine a theological point on it, but that institution is hell on earth.'

'It's unpleasant,' Cinq-Mars agreed.

'Unpleasant?' She took a moment to corral her thoughts. 'The first time I went in there, I returned home and was physically ill. To be graphic, I regurgitated my lunch. The second time nearly sent me into a free-fall depression. It's filthy and vile. Men are not merely incarcerated there, Sergeant-Detective, they are slowly reduced to rubble. Men who were once violent and terrifying at least had some life to them. Now? Bags of bones. Their brains reduced to pus. A few haven't sat upright in years. If I cannot get

Johnny out of there – no doubt he's an imperfect person; heaven knows, I have no clue what constitutes a "model prisoner" – but if I cannot get Johnny out of there, I will find it impossible to sleep at night. I won't be able to minister to my so-called flock. Johnny is eligible for parole. He can be home Friday. I will do everything in my power to see that parole is granted.'

If only he had arrived with a lie to support his side. Too late to foster one now.

'All I can do,' Cinq-Mars remarked, 'is try to find further information to help change your mind. In the meantime, I'm urging you to reconsider.'

'No, I'm sorry—'

'I have never known such a request to be delivered with this degree of urgency and alarm, Alex.' He added her name to see if it helped. It didn't. 'Johnny Bondar represents a significant danger, perhaps to himself, more likely to others. I say more likely, because who would take an interest otherwise within the police department? Consider, please, that his release may be a grave danger to others.'

'He steals cars. Is an officer worried about his Cadillac?'

The sarcasm was not appreciated. Cinq-Mars accepted that he deserved it, given that he had no alternative line of reasoning to present.

'I'll see what the dog digs up,' he grumbled, and rose.

'Thank you for coming in, Sergeant-Detective.' She offered a forced smile.

'Perhaps we'll talk again soon, if I have more information.'

'I cannot imagine that you will change my mind,' she warned, rising also.

Cinq-Mars's problem was that he could not imagine it, either.

TEN

The quick hop from the church to the *poste* crossed from an impoverished neighborhood into the lap of affluence. A fence partitioned the adjacent communities, which helped declare the disparity as jarring. An immigrant ghetto next door to the *nouveau riche*. Inner-city congestion slapped alongside suburban entitlement. Back alleys vanished, backyard lawns appeared. This time, driving through, Cinq-Mars paid little heed to his surroundings.

He felt vexed. In failing to persuade the minister to relinquish her crusade, he had let his friend Armand Touton down. Compounding that regret, he could not reach the old man, who'd gone fishing. He considered an impromptu appearance before the parole board himself, where he'd either beg or polish up a lie. One choice was pathetic, the other illegal. Grumbling to himself, he parked his Volkswagen Bug in his *poste*'s backlot, entered the yellow brick building, and sat at his desk. He didn't notice his new partner approaching until the last second.

Geoffrion hovered, perplexed.

'Nord?' Cinq-Mars inquired.

'I'm in shit.'

'What's wrong?'

'I was getting along with Captain Delacroix, thought so, then *wham-o*.'

Ah. Sometimes the captain came across as schizophrenic. '*Wham-o* how?'

'Beats me.'

'You were having your toast and jam, then what?' He expected the sarcasm to slip by unnoticed, and it did.

'That was over an hour ago,' Geoffrion pointed out. 'I was looking into robberies – can't find any similar to ours. I went out for a break, and when I came back, he marched right up to me and told me to eff off.'

'He told you . . . Nothing else?'

'Yeah, something else. In front of everybody. He told me to screw my grandmother.'

Even for Delacroix, that was beyond the norm.

'I'll talk to him,' Cinq-Mars said.

'What did I do?' Geoffrion bellyached. He was quick, as Cinq-Mars noted earlier, to turn on himself.

'What's bugging him, Nord? That's the question to ask.'

Delacroix could be illogical and prickly; this occasion appeared to be more than that.

*   *   *

'Hey, boss.' He slumped down in one of the two visitors' chairs in the captain's office.

'Welcome back to the Montreal Police Service, Sergeant-Detective. I presume you've been on leave of absence without pay?'

Cinq-Mars declined to engage, and asked, 'Cap, what do you have against my new partner's grandmother?'

They stared at one another while Delacroix's adrenalin burned off. The captain shuffled papers from one side of his desk to the other without examining them.

'Maybe that was out of line,' he admitted.

'His first day on the job. Plus, you softened him up with toast and jam. One minute, he thinks he's landed in breakfast heaven, the next, he's stepping off the roof.'

'What roof?'

'Any roof. Maybe one that's not too high.'

'He's suicidal?'

'Fragile. I was exaggerating, boss.'

'He's *fragile*? Fuck that noise. I'd prefer him to be suicidal.'

'I'm still exaggerating.'

'How am I supposed to know?'

From the get-go, Delacroix had always felt maligned by his officers. A stickler for the rules in an era when rules were being crushed, a teetotaler in a Quebec culture of drinkers, a puritan in a time of license and exuberance, he felt disconnected from the world around him. He tried to remedy his righteous inclinations by being aggressively gruff and profane among subordinates – he felt more like a captain when he behaved that way – although he never carried it off in a convincing fashion. Had he stopped to think, he might have noticed that he was closer in outlook to the spiritual bent of his Sergeant-Detective than he realized, but Delacroix never arrived close to that conclusion. Cinq-Mars poured whiskey down his gullet. He was single and smart. Delacroix never imbibed and resented the younger man's freedom and brain power. His rampant insecurities commonly manipulated his better angels.

'Maybe not fragile, either. Let's say he doubts himself. Lacks confidence. We can leave grandma out of it.'

'I don't know his grandmother.'

'That might be the point.'

Cinq-Mars was figuring this out. Delacroix had taken Geoffrion's reputation at face value, something he was prone to do with anyone. He'd figured that Geoffrion could be a true subordinate. Not more clever than him, not braver or more successful, and that allowed him to extend the warm hand of friendship. Since then, something had undermined that initiative.

'Sticking up for your new partner, Cinq-Mars, that's so sweet. What've you been doing all day besides handing over our case to homicide?'

'Sorry. The dead guy got in the way.'

'He's sorrier than you, I bet.'

'Right now, he couldn't care less. Has anything come in on that case? Are you privy? Has the victim been ID'd?'

'I better be privy. Homicide should respect our turf.'

After a previous partner to Cinq-Mars had been shot – then taken early retirement – downtown consolidated the homicide unit. The brass upheld that the two events were not connected, a line not widely believed. Segregating the homicide squad had the unintended effect of granting detectives in the elite group a keener sense of privilege and superiority. No longer sharing office space with riff-raff detectives, they quit thinking of them as peers. The treatment Cinq-Mars received earlier in the day still rankled because it enforced that culture.

Delacroix pressed a magic button. Immediately, his secretary lounged in the doorway. Fern was perpetually caught in mid-pose, jutting a rather substantial hip. Cinq-Mars liked her. She was interested in important things and cordial. And yet, based only on a supposition, he didn't want to know what she did during her off-hours. Fifty and heavyset, that jutting hip signaled an adventuresome spirit. A wild-side personality. She departed, off to fulfill the captain's request for information on the morning's events.

'What happened,' Cinq-Mars pressed him, 'with Geoffrion?'

'First day at his new desk, he's sneaking around.' The adrenalin burn was returning. 'I was coming back from a piss, happened to glance out to the parking lot. Who's there but our new guy. I get it. He smokes in private. But that wasn't it.'

'What was he doing?'

'Drinking.'

'Drinking?'

'He met a guy. Not a cop. A young guy, rough around the edges, that type, who gets out of his car and passes a flask to Poof-Poof. They share a couple of pops. First day at his new desk, Cinq-Mars. Boozing it up in the parking lot. A secret meeting with a mister nobody.'

'You didn't ask who it was?'

'I told him to bugger his grandmother instead. Why not?'

'Yeah, that was helpful. I'll ask him.'

'He'll lie. They all do, these pricks. You know the type. These boozers.'

'Unless he's not a prick.'

'Spare me the bullshit tale! I saw him with my own two eyes.'

Fern struck a hip against the doorjamb again and recited news off a fax. 'No identity on the dead man, Captain. Homicide found nothing on his person, no wallet, nothing in the apartment to identify him. Neighbors said he goes by Willy. No last name. Weird, huh? Homicide is waiting on fingerprints. That'll take longer than forever, and like always give us nothing.'

Fingerprints held great promise for the future; for now, a process in its infancy.

The secretary left the room, her heels clicking on the linoleum floor.

Cinq-Mars and Delacroix absorbed the news.

'The corpse was a ghost before it became a corpse,' Delacroix mused.

'No surprise on the wallet,' Cinq-Mars pointed out. 'Stolen in the robbery.'

'Nothing else lying around? No phone bill? What name is on the apartment lease? I hope the boys in homicide know their asses from their elbows on a Tuesday.'

'Doubt it. Thanks, Cap. I'll get back to you on Geoffrion.'

'Don't bother.'

Geoffrion ventured over as soon as Cinq-Mars reclaimed his desk.

'Nord, the Cap gets nervy about stuff going on behind his back. I can't blame him, but he overreacts. Also, he really hates drunks. Pathological with him. I have a whiskey now and then, or a beer. I'm not a drunk, not by a longshot. According to the Cap, I should sleep in the drunk tank if I even *think* about having a nip. You?

You were drinking with a stranger in the parking lot. On the job. He no longer wants to see your face unless it's immersed in a toilet bowl – or you have a damn good explanation. Which I doubt, by the way.'

'I have an explanation. Why do you doubt it?'

'Sharing a bottle in the middle of the day? Looks bad, Nord.'

'The guy? In the lot? Son-in-law. He dropped by to celebrate. Him, on the birth of his second child yesterday. Me, on being a grandad for the second time. My first granddaughter.'

He was beaming now. Cinq-Mars stood to shake his hand. He then announced the news to the dozen or so cops and half-dozen civilians in the room. His timing impeccable, as Delacroix happened to emerge from his office. 'Everybody! Our new man, Nord Geoffrion – he's not related, by the way – became a granddad last night for the second time.'

The man was swiftly engulfed with well-wishers. Cinq-Mars was stepping aside to let it happen when a thought clicked. He recorded the moment by tapping two fingers against his right temple, then crossed the room and intercepted Delacroix. They retreated to his office.

'The guy in the car lot?' Delacroix asked, sheepish now. 'His son?'

'In-law. We misinterpreted this one, Cap. But it gave me a jolt. Look, I need to go back to the crime scene. I'll wait a day, not to push it. I need you to provide cover, in case homicide finds out I'm playing in their sandbox. Thanks to you, I had an idea.'

'Thanks to me?' Words he'd not heard before.

'Mistaken identity. You missed on Nord's son-in-law. I whiffed on the scene this morning. I accepted what my eyes showed me, what my ears told me, yet totally missed the obvious. Also, you called the corpse a ghost. Maybe you weren't the first to do that.'

'Can you try, Cinq-Mars, to make sense?'

'Too complicated, Cap. I need to go back there. Bear with me. Give me cover?'

Captain Delacroix shrugged, sighed, and thought about it. 'If it comes up, you lost your keys. If that doesn't wash, I'll say it was your senses. Nobody will have trouble believing that.'

Was the man trying to tell a joke again? Hard to say. If so, it was for the first time within earshot of his newly minted Sergeant-Detective.

Cinq-Mars thanked him. Captain Delacroix had no clue what for.

ELEVEN

A city may slumber as the sun goes down. Or awaken. A pulse, a drumbeat, a music in the air quickens Montreal to come alive at night, spirited by the dark. If cold, bleak winters are to be endured, summer warmth and a festive heart is enjoyed deep into the wee hours of night.

Bars are packed.

At two a.m., folks continue to line up for smoked meat.

At three, taxis are like spawning fish.

Nights for Dominic 'The Dime' Letourneau were reserved for pleasure. Drudgery and work were daytime affairs.

'I believe in God the Almighty,' he pronounced once, preaching to an ambulance driver treating a pal for a gunshot wound that was both accidental and self-inflicted, 'and the Father, the Holy Ghost, and all that horseshit, but I believe also in those other buggers. The monkeys, gorillas and chimps. There's a ladder. You're at the bottom or the top, you're climbing up or falling down. Where you are is where you fight to be. I'm on my way up, me. To the top. If I slip, shoot me blind before I sink too far. Unless I shoot myself in the head, first, like this sap.'

'I thought he was your friend.'

'Until he pulled the trigger.'

He went out late at night. Early evenings, he put his feet up and watched TV and ate pizza or burgers, and that evening nibbled the ear of a girl lured from one of his gang's bars. Home was a high-rise apartment on the border of Westmount where rich English guys lived. Those even richer lived way up on the mountainside, high above his building's penthouse. He'd get there someday. Find the highest ground. For now, he lived right under the penthouse but above the slime dirt. He gazed across the lights of the city in one direction and up the mountain in the other, knowing that this town would be his one day. He'd own it. Money flowed like the river that encircled the island city, forever to the sea. Drug money was more lucrative every year. Whore money, and he included the strip clubs in that, was steady, his specialty. Gambling money. Protection money. Union money. Construction money. Money for political or business favors. In whatever direction he looked from his eyrie he saw the funnel of cash; so far, money from girls was channeled his way and more would flow his way from different sources. Bound to. Right now, he could buy the girl whose ear he was nibbling a pony if she wanted one. He could buy her a Kentucky thoroughbred and find out if it could run. He wouldn't do that, although he might let her think so, because he was more careful with his cash than anyone knew. What he waved around was only for show because he had to keep up appearances. He had expenses, though, and knew how to take care of business. Cops, judges and bankers came at a cost. Women were not an expense in his life, unlike with most guys. He didn't marry them, he didn't spoil any with jewels, and he never stepped out of his league. Why bother when he could get what he wanted with nothing more than a promise? Later, he'd enjoy the look of disappointment on the girl's face when he moved on after a few days.

This one cooed as he nibbled her earlobe. Cute, yet less tantalizing, less strange, than his usual inclination. Maybe if she was willing to be part of a three-pack, he could enjoy her more that way. For now, he was fixated on her ear and how she cooed as he whispered for her to turn on the TV.

'Thought it was busted.'

'Damn thing got fixed. Better be fixed. Fucker repairman left a whopper bill.'

'Whadyawannawatch?'

'Should be a ballgame on,' he said.

The young woman, scarcely eighteen – street legal, not that he cared, in from the countryside and fresh to the city – wiggled her bum as she crossed the room and turned on the set. Perhaps she saw the flash as the entire apartment ignited. She saw nothing after that. Heard nothing. Knew nothing. High above the city streets below, windows blew out, sending shards of glass flying through the air and landing half a block away. Furniture disintegrated. The pair in the room had no moment to be aware of their fate. They were instantly obliterated, the bomb in the TV that powerful. Walls were reduced to powder. After the fire department came and long after crowds gathered in the streets below to watch the blaze on high, and after the bomb squad came and went, and cops tramped through the soaking, charred ruins, portions of the man would be identified by his dental records and because he lived at that address. The second person in the room – forensics determined she was female – was never identified.

A Jane Doe from the countryside. Never reported missing.

In all likelihood, what bones survived would be procured by a lab and studied in a training program, used in a subsequent project, then incinerated. The ashes were not collected. She'd not be buried or commemorated, unlike Letourneau, who was lined up to have a grand funeral, thick with bikers and molls, rough hoodlums and genteel mobsters sufficiently sophisticated to probe their teeth with toothpicks, and the usual band of observant cops.

Reports on the bombing described the male victim as being known to police; another way to say that nobody cared who he was or why he died. 'A settling of accounts,' the operative phrase. The blast was public and dramatic, newsworthy that way, but another mobster who'd crossed the wrong person was a mere tidbit on the ladder of criminal life in Montreal. Nobody realized that his death marked a significant alteration to the criminal landscape of the city. Not a change anyone judged as being for the better, other than by whomever effected the kill.

TWELVE

The building where a murder and a rash of burglaries took place did not offer an elevator to the top floor. Sergeant-Detective Émile Cinq-Mars stopped taking the stairs two at a time after the third level to accommodate his sluggish companion. Geoffrion was catching his breath in awkward intakes and exhales by the time they knocked on Moira Ellibee's door.

'Remember,' Cinq-Mars reminded him, 'this could get bizarre. Hang back. Play along.'

'Won't budge unless she pulls a weapon.'

Geoffrion had no clue what he was in for.

The mingling of scents impressed Cinq-Mars on the way up. Mexican tortilla, Japanese tempura, Italian spaghetti, Ukrainian cabbage rolls, matzah balls from Poland. The day before, he hadn't noticed the culinary mishmash on the rear exterior stairs. The cumulative fragrance in the front stairwell was both intoxicating and disorienting.

He rapped on the door again.

'We may both need protection, Nord. Only not as you imagine.'

Moira Ellibee flung the door open without checking who might be there.

'Oh! I was expecting Jehovah's Witnesses. They're on the street. They like to drop by. Nice ladies. A little too . . . *dour*. But nice. We have tea and biscuits and discuss the end of the world. Who won't survive. They say I'm doomed. I think it's them.'

'Do you discuss the Virgin Mary?'

Her eyes slid from Cinq-Mars to the stranger next to him, then returned. 'Once,' she replied, 'I did.' She tucked a forearm across her waist and planted her free elbow onto the opposing fist. 'The oldest lady declared that she did not come to my home to entertain me. "That being the case," I said, "you may leave."' Ms Ellibee snapped her fingers. 'Boy, did that change her tune. They never want to exit. Usually I start the vacuum to get them going.'

She wore a yellow-green frock. She was slim, her movements lithe. Moira Ellibee marshaled the men into her living room and commanded they sit.

'Drinks? I don't, myself, but I have beer in the fridge. Gifts from others. They shouldn't go to waste.'

Either she was lying, and secretly drank, or she had suitors. Cinq-Mars could imagine the latter, as she seemed to put up no defenses. He might have interviewed her on his own, but given that their talk was likely to be tricky, he felt safer with Nord Geoffrion along.

'Ms Ellibee—'

'Moira,' she corrected him. 'Ground rules! Amuse me. Call me Moira or giddy-up and go.'

Cinq-Mars consented to her rules of engagement. 'Moira,' he

said to appease her. 'On the night of the robberies and the murder next door, you were visited by an apparition.'

Geoffrion glanced his way.

For a moment, it appeared as though the woman might deny her previous claim. Then she said, 'A good word. Apparition. Fair. There's a difference between ghosts and spirits. I was visited by a *spirit*. But apparition. Yes. That word is fair.'

Geoffrion asked, 'You mean like a ghost of Christmas past? But wasn't he a spirit, too?'

She scowled. Cinq-Mars censored any further comment from him with a stern glare. 'Nord, Ms Ellibee endured a sexual predator. She warrants our sympathy.'

'Of course. Sorry.'

She held her head higher, her shoulders more square, as though to purposefully indicate that she now felt elevated in the world.

'Apparition, then,' Cinq-Mars encouraged her. 'Let's agree on that word. I wonder if you can describe him in more detail. I know it was dark. You mentioned his stomach muscles. Is there anything else you recall?'

'Stomach muscles on a ghost,' Geoffrion murmured, unable to hold the comment in. He noticed that if looks could kill, he'd be a dead man, Cinq-Mars the shooter.

Moira Ellibee paid him no mind. 'Dark. Confusing. He had a smooth face. When I was imploring him to stop, I touched his face. Smooth.'

Cinq-Mars slowly looked over to Geoffrion as if daring him to say peep. She'd forgotten about her attacker's balaclava.

Learning, his partner remained mute.

'Excellent. His height?'

'A little taller than me. Hard to tell.'

'Then five-eight to five-ten, approximately, would you say?'

'Sounds good.'

'His clothing?'

'The light from the back lane into my bedroom is not very bright, my detective. He was an apparition. They tend to be dullish, although some are capable of changing their appearance, even the color of their outfits.'

'Was he wearing what might be called an outfit? Or regular clothes, a man-in-the-street kind of look? To fool you that way.'

'More like that.'

'Was he wearing a jacket?'

'A reddish shirt, I think. Maybe bright red, but in the dark . . . And his trousers.'

'Yes?' Not one to take notes, Cinq-Mars signaled Geoffrion to do so. His intention having to do with encouraging Moira to continue rather than as an aid to memory.

'Pleats. A fine sharp crease. As if they were dry-cleaned. It's not like a man to have a crease in his trousers unless someone else put it there. Like a dry-cleaner, or a wife.'

Cinq-Mars began to work a suspicion. 'Ms Ellibee, do you think there's any chance – and you would know—'

'Moira,' she reminded him.

'Moira, apparitions can have such extraordinary abilities to project themselves, to seem real. People perceive them to be real. Don't you agree?'

'Of course. Absolutely.'

'Then, is it not possible that you might have mistaken a real person for being an apparition? I mean, wouldn't that be an easy mistake?'

Her puzzlement proved temporary. 'I thought of that. If the spirit was real, he'd have goop. He would . . . you know . . . you know . . .'

Cinq-Mars shot a glance at Geoffrion as though warning him not to breathe.

'That confirms it, don't you think? No goop. A spirit. Not a man. Tell me . . . on a different subject. Did you know the man who was murdered next door?'

'Willy! Yes! That's so *terrible*, I can't even say.'

'How would you describe him? What was he like? We don't have a photograph, Moira. I saw him briefly, but he was dead. I'd like to have a good description of him.'

'Oh, Willy was a quiet man. Almost like he didn't have a voice. He could say hello sometimes. Once he asked me if Tuesday was garbage day. For him, that was like reciting the entire Old Testament. He listened to news on the radio. I heard it through the wall. No music. He never played music.'

'How heavy was he?'

'Thin. Not heavy. Soft, I think. But trim.'

Cinq-Mars created a pretense of searching deeply for his next question. 'How did he wear his hair? Long, like the fashion these days? Short? Neat? Scruffy?'

'Oh, scruffy all right. He seemed to always have day-old whiskers, and of course those long sideburns. His hair was medium. On the long side of medium.'

'Excellent. I want to thank you, Moira. You've been a great help.'

'You're welcome. The beers? They're cold. If not now, you could come back. Anytime. Even the one you keep shutting up . . .' Moira looked at Norville Geoffrion for the first time. 'Even you,' she said, 'can come back. Maybe on a hot day?'

Cinq-Mars interrupted her move on his partner. 'Thank you for your generosity, Moira. We may do that.' He stood. Geoffrion stood with him, and a moment later they were safely on the landing outside her closed door.

'You're kidding me, Émile. She wasn't describing Willy.'

'I think she was.'

'If that's true, Willy wasn't the dead guy in the closet.'

'Take a bow. You were right to warn about that.'

'Who was it then?'

'Smooth-shaven. Slick hair. Taut stomach. Who does that sound like?'

'The dead guy. But not the guy who had sex with her.'

'Why not?'

'He wasn't wearing a red shirt. He had on a jacket.'

'What does that tell you?' Cinq-Mars asked him.

'Nothing makes sense, that's what it tells me.'

'The dead guy was wearing Willy's clothes. Except his socks. The killer never put socks on the corpse.'

'The killer . . . what?'

'The killer. He dressed the dead guy. Put Willy's clothes on him.'

'Why?'

'To make us think that he was Willy.'

'OK. Same question. Why?'

'Because maybe *he* was Willy.'

Nord Geoffrion blew out a gust of air. 'He kills the guy having sex with his neighbor? Then tries to make us think the dead guy was him?'

'Close. No cigar. The killer arrives. With, or separate from, the gang of thieves. That part remains to be figured out. The killer enters the wrong apartment, looking for Willy.'

'Her apartment. Since he's there anyway, he has sex.'

'In her mind. Remember, Nord, no *goop*. That tells me the man was either a spirit, like she says, or there was no man. Or, a man who didn't stay for sex.'

'She just likes to say so.'

'Or think so. Captain Delacroix mistook your son-in-law for a bad guy because that's how he was inclined to interpret what he saw. Mistaken identity. Before we think too badly of him, bear in mind that I assumed the dead guy was the same person who lived in the apartment. You were smarter.'

'Thanks. I guess.'

'Another case of mistaken identity. Moira comes across a man in her bedroom. Maybe she really thinks he's an apparition, or she thinks she has a new secret lover. Either way, mistaken identity. The killer, if that's him, went into the wrong apartment. Easy to do in the dark from the rear of this building. He comes across the wrong person. A woman. Not a man. No chance of mistaken identity there. He leaves. He enters the correct apartment, and because he's an assassin on a mission, he hides in the bedroom closet. When he didn't find Willy, he waited for him to come home. What he didn't know was that Willy – for now, a huge assumption – was onto him. Maybe he heard him enter his apartment so hid under the bed, or something similar. Maybe he knew he was coming. Maybe he saw him go into Moira's place. That way, the killer is taken by surprise, totally, when Willy whips open the door and slams that huge butcher's knife through his larynx.'

'You know,' Geoffrion pointed out, 'we're not supposed to be investigating this case. You might be solving it, but how will you pitch this to homicide?'

Cinq-Mars shook his head. 'Worry about the case, not them. Willy has a dead guy in his closet. He removes the killer's bloody clothes, stuffs them in a bag he'll take away. Then dresses him in one of his own suits. It's obvious it'll be a decent fit. He even puts a pair of slippers on him. Socks are too much trouble. That's why the dead guy has hardly any blood on his clothes, despite being stabbed in the neck. I bet when we read the autopsy report, we find out that he had blood on his body. That'll confirm the theory.

Blood on his body, not much on his clothes, yet he's wearing clothes. How does that happen unless his clothes were removed while he was still dripping from the neck, and a new outfit – a new suit – was put on him? As though he was a mannequin. Next, Willy goes through his apartment removing any trace of his own identity – bills, photographs, his wallet, etcetera. It's easy for him, he knows where to look. Then he takes a hike. Why? Because he wants this death to be a case of mistaken identity. He wants to *be* alive but to be considered dead.'

'The killer's dead,' Nord said. 'Long live the killer.'

Cinq-Mars looked at him.

'Sorry. A little humor on the job.'

'That's all right,' Cinq-Mars told him. 'I don't mind.'

'We solved one murder today, maybe, now we have a new one. What's next?'

'We haven't solved a thing. As for what's next, we take your advice.'

'Mine?'

'Back when this was our case, you said I should talk to the landlord's son. Let's do that.'

'Should we mention that it's not our case?'

'I wouldn't. Not to anyone.'

'Gotcha.'

Cinq-Mars believed he did.

THIRTEEN

Cinq-Mars had pegged the janitor's son as indolent, which didn't jive with the young man in the back lane repeatedly chinning himself to a maple's stout limb. Slick with sweat, the boy proudly showed off his prowess. Cinq-Mars waited for him to drop to the ground.

'You're in shape,' he remarked. The boy wore a loose-fitting basketball shirt with the team logo of the Boston Celtics. He was lean and muscled.

'I know you?' the boy asked.

'I was in your place yesterday. You were in bed.'

'Sleeping it off.'

Another boy snickered.

'Leave us,' Cinq-Mars directed the second youth.

When the lad didn't budge, he showed his badge. The boy moved along then, but not far. Cinq-Mars circled around to put the second teen at his back, so that the two friends could not easily check in with each other.

'What's up?' the janitor's son asked. Cinq-Mars assessed that he was neither keen on cooperation nor looking to bolt.

'I'd like to ask what you know about the robberies.'

'What I know? Nothing.' The boy wiped sweat from his eyes with the hem of his shirt.

'You go by Mick?'

'Mick, yeah.'

Cinq-Mars formally introduced himself and his partner. 'The murder last night must have surprised you.'

'What do you mean?'

'You weren't expecting it.'

'Why would I? Who expects that?'

Cinq-Mars glanced at Norville Geoffrion. He had thought him indolent, and Geoffrion had doubted his intelligence. Had they both been wrong? Geoffrion indicated that he couldn't explain it, either.

'What were you on?' Cinq-Mars asked the boy. An educated guess.

The boy returned only a quizzical expression.

'To be so sleepy?'

'A couple of beers maybe.'

'That's not what I asked you.'

'I thought it was.'

'Think about it.'

The boy did. He scratched the side of his neck. Smiled a notch. He said, 'I'm not going to stand here and tell a policeman I was taking drugs or anything dumb like that.'

'Why not?'

'Maybe you heard? Drugs are against the law.'

'A man was murdered. I'm not interested in drugs.'

The boy seemed legitimately confused.

Cinq-Mars tried to put him at ease. 'Being doped up explains why you didn't get out of bed yesterday morning. It tells me you were doped up overnight. Puts you in the clear, no? Doped up, you were not carefully and precisely breaking into apartments. Gives you an alibi.'

'I need an alibi?'

'You need to tell me where you were and what you were doing last night.'

The boy thought about it some more.

'I might've been high, yeah. Hanging out in the park. Bunch of us. Looking at the stars. A lot of stars up there, holy cow, once you look.'

'Name the pharmaceutical for me, Mick. Helps with your credibility.'

Mick tried to look over at his pal, but Cinq-Mars was too tall and too close to him. He said, cautiously, '*If* I was taking a drug it was LSD.'

'How was it?'

'What do you mean?'

'Your trip. How was it?'

'*If* I dropped acid, it was good. Mostly. When the cops were in my apartment, maybe I was still sleeping it off. *If* I took a pill. I wasn't totally convinced you guys were real going through my place.'

'Hmm,' Cinq-Mars said. He allowed his doubt to show. He nodded toward his partner. 'Detective Geoffrion thought you were stupid.'

'Geoffrion?' Mick asked. He looked excited.

'Not related,' Nord told him.

'He's not related,' Cinq-Mars confirmed. 'It makes me wonder.'

The boy waited for whatever came next. When the detective remained mute, he asked, 'Wonder what?'

'If you're related.'

'To Geoffrion?'

'To anyone connected to this case. What can you tell us about the dead guy?'

'We're not *related*.'

'What can you tell us about Willy?'

Mick looked up to the apartment where the murder took place, as though the victim's ghost might be gazing down from the balcony. His compulsive shrug felt elaborate, indicating that he meant to convey a lot. He said, 'Not much.'

'Not much.'

'I hardly ever talked to him. Why would I? He was a real quiet guy. Spooky, that way. The most we talked was this one time I fixed his leaky tap.'

'What did you talk about?'

'Girls, mostly. He wanted to know what they're like these days.'

'These days. Like he hasn't seen any for a while?'

'More like he's remembering some olden time. That maybe never was.'

'What did you tell him?'

'You know.'

'I don't, actually.'

'Girls are girls.'

'Hmm,' Cinq-Mars noted. He was beginning to circle around Mick, and the boy followed him with his eyes by turning his torso. 'What's his last name?'

The teen gave the query serious thought. 'I don't know.'

'I can get it from your dad, I imagine.'

'Maybe. I guess.'

'He must pay his rent every month.'

'In cash, yeah.'

'I see.' He made a mental note to check the man's phone records, his hydro bill. The thought instigated a worry. 'Mick, is the hydro included in the rent here?'

'Yeah, it is.'

'Heat?'

'Everything. Yeah.'

Not a confirmation, but if a man was looking to live anonymously, off the public grid, he'd look for a place like this. And pay cash.

'What about the chalk marks?' A technique he'd been developing. Ask questions straight out of left field.

'Chalk marks?' He seemed honestly confused.

'The ones next to the apartments that were spared. The sheds got busted into instead. You didn't mark up those apartments?'

'I don't know what you're talking about.'

'Did you see anybody marking doors with yellow chalk?'

'No.'

'Anybody hanging around lately who looked suspicious?'

'Everybody looks suspicious.'

'Try not to be a smart-ass, OK? You've been good until now. Don't start.'

'OK. No. I haven't seen anybody look more suspicious than usual. Why ask me?'

'Because half a squad of cops went through your apartment. You could barely open an eyelid. Makes it look as though you knew what was going on. That you didn't need to ask.'

Cinq-Mars gave him marks for coming across as honest. He took a point off for willfulness. Cinq-Mars treated their exchange as a contest; the boy had no reason to do so.

'Anyone come around trying to recruit kids like you?'

'Kids like me?'

'Kids in general.'

He shrugged. 'The usual. If that's what you mean.'

'What's the usual?'

'Pedophiles. Pushers. The usual.'

The world kids lived in these days. A big word for him to use, though. *Pedophiles.* Rather than a street slur. Cinq-Mars was struck by that. Possibly, the response was prepared in advance, in case somebody asked. But he might be overthinking it.

'Nobody else?'

'Nope.'

'Would you tell me if there was someone else or something new?'

'Like what?'

'A gang. Or an individual recruiting thieves.'

'I guess I'd tell you. Why not?'

'Will you tell me if it happens in the future? Give me a heads up?'

'I guess so. Sure. Why not?'

'How many chin-ups can you do?'

The boy looked across at the maple. 'Thirty. The bark cuts into my hands or I'd do more.'

'Then I won't challenge you. I could blame the bark, but you're doing too many for me.'

'You have more weight to pull up. That matters.'

Modest of him to say so. Generous, also.

Cinq-Mars asked, 'How many dogs in this building?'

'Dogs? None. Not allowed.'

'Who made that rule?'

'The landlord, I guess. The owner.'

'There's other dogs around. Across the lane. Down the lane. Why do you think none were barking last night? You'd think they would, a bunch of thieves around.'

'A *bunch* of thieves? Not one or two?'

'A killer, too. Why wouldn't they bark?'

'They'd bark. But they always bark. Who'd notice?'

'Good point.' He had him there. Cinq-Mars pulled out a card and passed it to Mick. Although it did not signify his rank, the number was good. 'Call, if anything comes up.'

'What can come up?'

'Somebody tries to sell you a toaster real cheap. Or who knows what? Call.'

Sergeant-Detective Cinq-Mars walked away, heading down the lane to take the long way back to the street. Detective Geoffrion fell into step alongside him. Then Cinq-Mars stopped, turned, and went back to the boy. He walked right up to him, nudged the boy's pal aside once again, and leaned over to whisper in Mick's ear.

'You must know Moira Ellibee? Do you fix her taps, too? Do you stay away from her, Mick? Do you? You know what I mean.'

Taken aback, Mick nodded, to indicate he understood.

'You stay away?'

He nodded again.

'Other boys? Do they know her?'

Finally, Mick spoke up. 'Men come and go. Older guys. My age? Never seen that.'

'That's helpful. See, that wasn't so hard. Thanks.'

He joined Geoffrion and they continued their stroll down the lane. His partner wanted to know what he'd said to the boy, and Cinq-Mars told him.

'Why ask him that?'

'I'm trying to get a handle on how mad she really is.'

'How mad is she?'

'My hunch, she's halfway sane. But she has her things.'

'Don't we all.'

'Speak for yourself.'

'You got your things, too. What I heard.'

'Like what?'

'Crazy religious, like what.'

Cinq-Mars walked on in silence for a time. Geoffrion feared he'd offended him. He didn't say anything more, suspecting he'd make the matter worse. He was wishing he'd minded his tongue. They turned the corner and exited onto the street. De l'Épée. In English, *the street of the sword.*

'Crazy can be religious,' Cinq-Mars noted. 'I've seen that. Religious can be crazy. Seen that, too. They're not mutually exclusive. But just like crazy is not automatically religious, religious is not automatically crazy, in my opinion.'

'I'll keep it in mind,' Geoffrion said, not with any conviction.

'Try to,' Cinq-Mars suggested. 'I'd appreciate it.'

He was keeping to himself that he hadn't felt religious lately, and not particularly crazy either. That was bothering him. In the same way that the case was bothering him. Something was off; the world as it should be was out-of-sync. As though the planet wobbled more than usual. Privately, he summed up: *something's wrong and I have no clue what.*

The case, he thought, emitted an odor; one difficult to define, hard to locate.

Late in the afternoon, at the *poste*, after failing to find a record of the tenant known as Willy or evidence of his last name, despite a call to Mick's father and another to the building's landlord, Cinq-Mars took a call from Armand Touton. His former boss succumbed to an illustrious rage.

'Calm down, Armand,' he told him.

'Who're you telling to calm down? Who?'

'You, if that's a serious question.'

'You're not telling me to calm down!'

'As a matter of fact, I am. What's going on?'

'He's out already, you numbskull!'

He wanted to ask who was out, and out of what, but the likely answer froze any response. The best he could do was say, 'It's not Thursday.'

'His hearing got bumped up. That minister sweet-talked the parole board—'

'She's a she, by the way. The minister. A woman. I presume you didn't know.'

Touton spoke slowly, to more evenly and powerfully vent his rage. 'Is that something,' he asked, 'I should care about deep inside my crotch?'

'Sorry. He's out? Bondar was released?'

'Thanks to you. You did nothing to stop it.'

'Armand, I know you don't look twice when it comes to protocol. For you, the rule of law means next to nothing.'

'Correct. There's right. There's wrong. That's it. What more do you want?'

'You've handed me that line before. I get it. Trouble is, the rest of us live and work within the law. There are rules, procedures. The minister wasn't budging off her position. No matter what I did or said, I had no hope of changing her mind. She wanted Bondar out. Period.'

'Then do something about it now, Émile.'

'What do you mean, "do"? I can't put him back in prison.'

'Who said? You won't know until you try. Why is it so important that he stays in jail?'

'I don't know. That's the trouble. Maybe if you told me—'

'I don't know either! But you can find out. Tail him, Émile. One step over the line, arrest his skinny ass. A guy like that, a parole violation can't be hard.'

Even Johnny Bondar had civil rights, but, yeah, it would probably not be a challenge to nail him on a misdemeanor. Out on parole, depending on the terms, he might not be allowed to consort with known felons. That might be difficult to avoid. If push came to shove, Cinq-Mars could make it unavoidable. Not kosher, but he could live with it.

'Armand, how do you know about this? I thought you were incommunicado. Gone fishing. Out in the wilderness with the moose, the wolves, and blackflies.'

'A village is close by. I was picking up an order for worms. They got a phone box. I put in a call, like I'm doing with you right now, wise guy. Lucky you didn't come out with me. I would've throttled you on the spot.'

No doubt. 'I'll put a tail on him. You go fishing.'

'I'm too upset for that.'

'Give me the number where you buy your worms. Where I can leave a message.'

'Don't, unless it's good news. Anything else, fix it first.'

He could remind the older man that he'd retired, that he was in no position to give commands. Figuring his blood pressure was already high enough, Cinq-Mars laid off. He wrote down the phone number, returned the receiver to its cradle. Then noticed Geoffrion waiting for him. 'Punch in much overtime lately?' he asked.

'Me? I don't pull extra duty.' A cross he'd learned to bear, judging by his tone.

'Saddle up, Nord. You're working late. Find out where Johnny Bondar lives. Find out where he's hanging out after his release—'

'He's out?'

'Free as a bird. Find him. Tail him. Call me at home if anything comes up. Leave a message if I'm not there. Arrest him if he spits on a sidewalk. Got it?'

'Are you exaggerating, boss?'

Cinq-Mars glared back at him. Geoffrion, perhaps, required very specific instructions.

'Use your best judgment,' he told him. 'But before you do, call me.'

'Will do, boss.'

Boss. Like *Sergeant-Detective*, he might not get used to that.

He wasn't going to tail Johnny Bondar himself. Not tonight. He wanted to patrol the neighborhood of Park Ex. See what packs of boys were hanging out. Maybe see if anyone anywhere wanted to sell him a toaster.

FOURTEEN

Detective Norville Geoffrion had a choice. Stay put or take a risk. He was staking out the Bondar family home on Bloomfield Street in Park Extension. A party in full swing. Beer flowed, guests continued to arrive. He should stay in his car, and if he had to take a leak, find a stout maple. Instead, he made a toilet run to the deli a half-block down on Jarry Street. Then picked up a sandwich, coke and chips. And Jujubes. Candy went well with all-nighters.

He gambled that Bondar wouldn't leave the party in his absence. He was right. Nord walked away and when he returned the festivities had moved onto the front balcony of the upper duplex. The flat swelled with well-wishers. Older folk arrived, some with kids; even hoodlums had families. A woman wearing a clerical collar showed up. Religion, too. Tough guys arrived, on foot, in hot-rods. Girls sashayed down the sidewalk in their high heels, the world their oyster as they joined the throng. Nord spotted the young man, once through his living room window, once on the balcony. Matched him to his mugshot.

He wrote everything up in exacting detail, omitting his deli run. Then chowed down in peace.

With his radio on, he didn't feel lonely. Happy for the assignment. Early days, but he fell into reflections on his new partner. A lofty rank for his age; still, he came across as a stand-up guy. Standoffish, and damn smart, but a couple of times he'd spoken kindly to him. Rare in his life.

Geoffrion polished off his ham-and-cheese, half a bag of chips, and was digging into the Jujubes – he'd bought three packs – when the party abruptly went quiet. The music switched off. People on the balcony were squeezing back inside. The cacophony of voices ceased, as if everybody wanted to hear one person speak. The minutes ticked by with no sign, then the music went loud again with a thumping bass, the thrum of conversation picked up steam. Out of the front door came two men he recognized. He needed a moment to place them. They clambered into their sedan, and Geoffrion lowered himself down below the top of his steering column as they passed by. No doubt: the two homicide detectives from the other day. He wrote down their names – Sergeant-Detective Jerôme LaFôret and Detective Alfred Morin. He noted the time of their departure from Johnny Bondar's house on his pad.

Their appearance spurred consequences. Three minutes later, Johnny Bondar was on the move.

* * *

His target slid onto the vinyl passenger seat of a red Plymouth convertible. Norville Geoffrion again eased down behind his steering wheel as the car passed by. He waited, wrote a note, then casually pulled out from the curb. At the corner, the convertible gunned it as the light turned amber, zipping across the intersection.

Geoffrion respected the red light as the convertible bombed up Bloomfield. Two cars turned off Jarry and traveled behind it, more slowly, single file. He took a gamble then. He ignored the red and did a quick left onto Jarry. Went right on Querbes, ignoring a red light there as well. He sped down that four-lane boulevard at impressive speed. Half-a-dozen blocks later, at busy Jean Talon, he slowed to let the green change to red and waited to see if he'd guessed correctly.

He gambled that, with only a few exits from Park Ex available, the odds were in his favor. He came out on top. The convertible went past him on Jean Talon. The boys were probably headed for the downtown lights of the big city. On a wider, faster street now – southbound on Park Avenue – Geoffrion could keep the car in view, travel fast, without drawing undue attention.

They sped down the immigrant corridor and over the hump of the lower mountain into the Student Ghetto. Geoffrion got on his radio. He told the dispatcher to telephone Cinq-Mars at home. 'Tell him, Johnny Bondar is headed downtown. Got that? Over.'

He'd abandoned a party in his honor. Something was up.

In the Ghetto, the Plymouth diverted from its downtown trajectory, making a left onto narrow Milton Street, one designed in horse-and-buggy days. The detective followed and was dead behind the car at the first red light. They carried on straight then made a right down Ste Famille. Geoffrion took the turn and pulled in next to a hydrant to let the boys gain separation. Good thing, as they parked halfway down the block. Geoffrion disembarked and crossed the street. He dug out a couple of Jujubes to plop into his mouth as he sauntered along, then entered an apartment building where he kept an eye on the street from the lobby.

The boys did not remain at their address for long.

Johnny Bondar came out with a rifle carrying-case – the detective would bet his eyeteeth it wasn't empty. The ex-con put it down on the floor of the backseat. The two boys were off again, and the cop hustled back to his car.

This time, he identified himself then hollered into his two-way: 'Call Cinq-Mars! Bondar's got a rifle! Headed downtown on Sherbrooke Street from Ste Famille. Red convertible. Over!'

'License plate?' the pleasant lady's voice at the other end inquired.

'It's a red Plymouth convertible! What the hell do you want from me? It's probably the only one downtown right now! I want every car responding.'

Two minutes later he was back on the radio.

'Suspect entered the Bar El Paso with a rifle. I'm going in. Over.'

'Wait for backup, Poof-Poof. Acknowledge.'

He didn't know who was giving the orders now. A man's voice, not the pleasant lady dispatcher's. Who had called him that? A voice he gladly defied.

'The gang's all here. Out.'

Call him that? Poof-Poof? Over the radio? *Over the fucking radio*! His fury seized him by his diaphragm and that adrenalin drove him into the club.

Patrol cars gathered behind him. More lights were flashing in the distance, coming to his aid. Cops were organizing outside. *The hell with every last one of them. I'll Poof-Poof them.*

The detective went in, pistol in hand. He ran into eight guys in Stetsons. Cowboys? 'What is this,' he taunted them out loud, 'the wild fucking west?' They'd take it up with him but noticed the pistol, then the first shot from Bondar's rifle was fired. Sudden screaming. A stampede. Geoffrion found cover, looked around. He didn't have a shot in the melee. Then he did. In the light of the stage from where the band had fled stood the silhouette of a man with a rifle. Norville Geoffrion didn't take time to identify himself or the gunman. He aimed. Who was the fucker calling him Poof-Poof over the radio for every cop to hear? Who was that? He fired.

Sergeant-Detective Émile Cinq-Mars drove onto Sherbrooke Street under the sudden gaze of high-rise hotels, apartment and office towers, into the flashing lights of squad cars and ambulances.

Cops did not admit his Volkswagen Bug inside their perimeter. On foot, he penetrated more easily. That he had no business on-site was no one's concern, he had rank, and in the chaos of the night's events he wandered with impunity. Just off the sidewalk, wedged into a corner of a first-floor balcony, a young man with a rifle in his lap lay dead. A bullet wound in his forehead, two more in his chest. One in his left kneecap. A mess. Cinq-Mars took a long look before a medic covered the corpse with a sheet.

Moving around, he spotted the homicide cops from the other day, LaFôret and Morin, and skirted behind a supervisor's car to avoid them. Geoffrion was nowhere in sight. He showed his badge and asked a uniform if detectives were inside. The cop explained that the gunfight started there, then came back to the street. Cinq-Mars entered the El Paso. Overheads had turned the space bright. Cops were conducting multiple interviews with traumatized witnesses. He went deeper and came upon a white sheet over another victim. He showed his badge, gestured with his chin.

'Ours,' the uniform told him.

'Name?'

'Like the hockey star. Geoffrion.'

Cinq-Mars stood stunned. He didn't speak. He didn't want to speak, then he said, 'Let me see him.'

'Sir?'

'Pull the sheet back. He's my partner.'

Confirmation. Norville Geoffrion was dead. A single bullet to the left temple. Cinq-Mars bent at the waist. He felt ill. He could have taken the assignment himself but had not done so. He'd sent this man to his death. He could not blame himself for doing his job, but in the moment, regret soaked through him.

He straightened up.

'The dead kid outside. Do you have a name?' The uniform was young, possibly a rookie.

'I could ask.'

'Ask.' They were being gentle with one another because one man had lost his partner.

Cinq-Mars looked around, then approached the stage. Another body on the floor, covered. 'Who's that?' he asked.

'Don't know,' a different uniform told him. 'The detectives have a name. They think he's the guy the other guy came to kill.'

'They say why?'

'Over a girl, what I heard. She's in back. Two lovers. One gets out of jail. The guy who's been doing her in the meantime gets whacked.'

Cinq-Mars went back to the front of the bar. The uniform who'd gone outside returned.

'Johnny Bondar,' the cop said.

'Yeah,' Cinq-Mars said. The man he had failed to keep in jail had killed his partner and was dead himself. He was doubly to blame. Living with himself was not going to be easy.

'I told the detectives outside that our guy's partner was here.'

'Mmm,' Cinq-Mars said. 'Who'd you tell?'

'Me.' Sergeant-Detective LaFôret stepped up behind him. 'Real sorry about Poof-Poof.'

'Geoffrion. That was his name.'

'Sure. Any idea what he was doing here?'

Earlier, Geoffrion radioed the station to ask dispatch to contact him. He could not now deny their involvement in a case, although he hated admitting anything to LaFôret.

'The shooter was released from prison today. We had a tip. Not this. Nobody expected this. Norville tailed him.'

'Who tipped you? A tip about what?'

Cinq-Mars shrugged. He was exercising the limits of his cooperation with this second-rate detective. 'No clue. Geoffrion took the tip. The info died with him. Bondar kill him?'

'Ballistics will confirm. Look, we don't get along. That won't change. But this. I don't want this for nobody. Real sorry.'

'Yeah. Thanks.'

'You should go home, Cinq-Mars.'

He didn't know why he should, but he had no fight in him. 'Sure. I will. Say, Nord called the station about a red convertible. I didn't see it outside.'

'Not accounted for. The only extra car is Geoffrion's unit.'

'Bondar wasn't driving. He was a passenger, one message said.'

'We know. We'll track down the car. Go home.'

At first, he thought LaFôret was being kind sending him home. Now he felt differently.

Cinq-Mars went outside. He looked up at the sky. City lights obliterated any starlight. The moon was not in view. On his way back to his Bug he noticed yellow tape around an unmarked squad car and presumed the unit to be Geoffrion's. He ducked under the tape.

The driver's side door was open. Inside, a sandwich wrapper.

The remains of a coke. A bag of chips, half-eaten. Crumbs. Two unopened packs of Jujubes. An investigator's pad. Kneeling in the doorframe, Cinq-Mars glanced inside the small book. A couple of names popped up. He pocketed the pad. Damn the consequences. His partner had been killed, he was entitled to take measures. Anyway, he could hand it back in the morning.

Or not.

Émile Cinq-Mars drove to the lookout on Mount Royal, which surveyed the eastern half of the city from a high promontory. The moon above him at half-mast. He put a hand across his brow. Time had passed since any prayer he murmured contained conviction or import, yet he fell into a sorrow that eclipsed his previous inattention. He said words for the soul of Detective Norville Geoffrion, who wanted the world to know he was not related to a famous man. The poor fellow would not enjoy his latest grandchild, and that broke Émile's heart. His prayer surprised him when it transformed into a resolve to get to the bottom of the case they'd worked on together. He implored himself to be stronger and smarter; intuition told him he'd need to be. He'd be calling Touton to say that Bondar was dead, no longer their problem, and recite the sorrowful news that a detective had fallen in the line of duty.

Life went on. He needed sleep. He'd wake in the morning. Start over. A cop was killed by Johnny Bondar. Then Bondar was killed by cops. Who was the other dead guy in the bar? Why was Bondar so important that Cinq-Mars had been instructed to keep him in prison?

As well, why on earth did LaFôret's and Morin's names appear in Geoffrion's case pad? Why were those two at Johnny Bondar's shortly before he left on a rampage? Why were they even out at night? He could have blurted his queries to the relevant individuals had it not been for instinct: he might be better served if he had answers *before* asking difficult questions.

He came down from the mountain, flush with a gentle grief for a man he hardly knew. He drove home, and with sluggish labor prepared for bed.

Cinq-Mars yearned for a girlfriend, at times more powerfully than at other times. His anger was misplaced as he grumbled to his ceiling and to the walls, 'I'm not supposed to live like this, OK? Like a fucking monk. I *quit* the priesthood, remember?'

He rarely swore. His rage got away from him, even if the vitriol felt necessary. Living like a monk wasn't the thing. He knew that. He was living like a prisoner, like the guys he put away. Not a life. Half-asleep, half-dreaming, he felt the world roaring, roaring, all around him. Why did he have to think about gangs and racketeers when what he wanted was to keep good citizens safe from harm inflicted by thieves and pickpockets, by muggers and scammers. The big picture didn't interest him. He wanted to focus on petty criminals. That was his bailiwick. His forte. His purpose in life. Protect the little guy from the bad guy. Keep the peace. A necessary component in the social order. A worthy occupation. Why was he obligated to contemplate convoluted plots and organized carnage? Him, of all people, in his little cell. Monk-like. Convict-like. He'd rather contemplate the universe. Gravity. The Big Bang. S-Matrix theory – what some were calling string theory. Energy and light. Fresh notions were being devised every day. Like quantum chromodynamics. Hard to keep up when he had to worry about the mob. He didn't sign on for the tumultuous commotion of vast criminal enterprises, yet the tumult kept seeking him out. His previous partner had been shot and wounded and his current partner shot and killed. He wanted to rage against his own inclinations, show a little mercy for his own life, yet also roar back against those whose criminal enterprises constantly interfered with his desire and the desire of so many for a simple loving life. They made it so difficult, these killers, if not impossible. They hijacked peace, the mobsters did, and he wanted them to stop that. It wasn't supposed to be up to him. He preferred countering small fry. Yet once again, he was coming up against the really bad guys. He could feel it coming on. He'd have to roar back against them again.

Something was in the air. $E=MC^2$.

As though the night itself roared in his ears.

PART TWO
THE LAMB

FIFTEEN

He studied fear. Learned how to be afraid. No one expected him to be brave; even so, fear required strategies.

He went by the tag name Willy. He thought it would suit him, but the name never fit right. It didn't help him become the guy he imagined. He held out hope that the boys would give him a nickname as they did one another. No such luck. Which indicated that he was useful enough to keep around, but still not one of them.

He studied fear.

First thing to know: everybody dies. Get used to the idea. Pack it away. Grow accustomed to a reality where you're already dead. When a bullet slams through the back of your brain, it's done. Nothing to worry about then. The trick is not to worry when you see it coming. Such as when your ears pick up the click of a gun cocked behind your cranium.

Way easier said than done.

Then don't say it.

Step forward with the notion that it's over. No bones to protect. No life to save. No breath to take that hasn't already expired. *Ashes to ashes.* As the fear rushes in, work it, knead it, *dust to dust*, massage it through your limbs. Diffuse it. Make fear your next of kin. Use it like a hit of adrenalin. All time is borrowed. All payments are past due. There's nothing to lose that hasn't been lost already.

He gave up his life decades ago to take up a separate existence.

What was gone was not worth mourning.

Yet he remained on the shelf, long past his expiry date.

He'd learned to live with the irony that thinking himself dead kept him alive.

Teddy cruised by to pick him up. Lucien was sitting in the front. That was usually Willy's seat, but this time he sat in back. No great inconvenience, although a degree of caution was warranted. Lucien Grenier was known as Le Gris. For a living, he killed people.

He never really got along with Lucien.

'Heading out,' Le Gris said. He wore an overcoat when on a kill to keep his pistol or sawed-off concealed. Wearing it today. 'Bumped into Teddy. I ask him, "Teddy, my main man, where you going?" Turns out, he's going to the same place I am. I ask him, "Why two cars?"'

'You don't need a car,' Willy pointed out. 'You're practically next door.'

'Next door? What you talking—? Oh. You don't know. It's moved, the meeting. You don't keep up? On account of the bomb, the Dime blown out of his shoes. The boss wants better security. A meeting like this, somebody might get an idea. Who, we don't know.'

'Where we going?' Willy inquired. He feared a change in venue. He'd been targeted. The change of venue could be related. Or not. Nothing he hadn't experienced before. Or not. The key was to stay calm. Show nothing, as if you trust your fellow man to the bitter edge of time.

'Joe's place. Meeting's still there, in a way.'

'In a way?'

'His country place now. For the security.'

Security. Not necessarily his own. *Change the subject.* 'How you doing, Teds?'

He and The Bear were the best of buds. Obese, The Bear's name was in deference to his size. Over the years he was considered a Teddy Bear more than a grizzly. His nickname evolved to comply with his personality. His real name was Piergiorgio Giordano. These days only his banker and his doctor called him that. Even his accountant called him Teddy. His bookie. His physical therapist. She smiled when she did so; it gave her a kick. *Teddy Bear.*

Teds apparently was doing fine. He had no complaints.

'Going to the country, huh?'

'All that fresh air, I dunno.'

'Don't know fresh. I prefer pollution. Fumes.'

'Don't worry about it,' Teds said.

He stayed worried. 'Why not, right? Fresh air. It's not poison.'

Like they say, a good day to die. He had to wonder why him, why now. He wasn't going to bring it up. He wasn't going to betray himself by suggesting that somebody might have a legitimate reason to off him, or that he was asking only because he was curious about which thing it was that he did wrong. A guy should never ask that. Basic. In no circumstance does wanting to know why you were going to be whacked help you not be whacked. It only helped the guy doing the job. The one thing worse was to plead for your life. The one thing worse than that was to cry. The one thing worse than that was to piss your pants. The one thing worse than that was to lose control of your bowels. The key was not to get started on a downhill run. Don't ask why you had to die. Just die. You were dead already.

He'd been through one assassination attempt lately. Maybe he'd survive another.

This time, he knew who wanted him dead.

He'd called Teddy, who'd passed on the message. The boss wanted him in.

They talked baseball, him and the other two in the car. The Expos.

In the West Island, Teddy turned off the expressway onto Boulevard St Jean. Willy commented, 'You call this the country?'

They were in the suburbs. Malls, single-family dwellings, car dealerships and restaurants.

Teddy said, 'You know Massimo.'

'Sure. Met him a bunch of times. Massimo The Coat.'

'We're picking him up.'

He wanted to ask, *How many Italian mobsters does it take to whack a guy?* He didn't. Still, four in the car. Three killers. One victim. Why?

Teddy went up the walkway to Massimo's door. The two men who remained in the car talked about the Expos. Specifically, the pitching. Massimo answered the door while he was on the phone at the same time. A long cord and he brought the phone onto his stoop. Then he went back inside. Teddy waited. Then Massimo came back to the door and invited Teddy in, as if he'd forgotten him the first time. Teddy went in. This whole thing was strange. Then Teddy came out and called to Lucien. He'd had his nickname since forever, not only Le Gris, but also, in English, The Gray. He looked like a corpse. Gaunt and narrow – and gray – as if perpetually taking chemo. Not necessarily his skin tone, more like a general demeanor, as though he slept in a coffin at night yet lacked the vampire's allure. He possessed none of the gumption, none of the sex appeal. He just happened to look three-quarters dead on a good day. Le Gris. As if he'd been labeled a boring corpse. He came alive talking about the Expos, he had opinions, but otherwise a dull talker. He spoke as if behind a curtain and never pointed his mouth to the person he addressed.

Teddy asked him inside.

Le Gris went to the door. Teddy followed him inside, leaving Willy alone in the car. A funny way to be assassinated, sitting by himself in the backseat of a car in the goddamn suburbs. Undignified. He could flee but didn't. That would be worse than his bowels running loose. He stayed put. Stayed calm. Waited for the bomb in the trunk to blow his ass off.

The first rule of survival: understand you won't. You can't.

Teddy came out of the house with Massimo. The garage door opened. Le Gris climbed into the driver's seat of Massimo's car. A Pontiac. A muscle car. Massimo got into the front seat of Teddy's car where Le Gris had sat on the ride over. Squeezed behind the wheel, Teddy announced, 'Change of plan.'

He wanted to ask, *What? I'm not whacked today?* Instead, he asked, 'What change?'

'They want The Gray in town,' Teddy explained. 'Massi in the meeting instead. So it's us. We're going to the country without him.'

'Le Gris is pissed,' Massimo said. 'He was looking forward. Like a little kid, excited. He wanted to be in the country at the big house.'

'Oh yeah?'

'Yeah. He wanted to visit the barn, pat the horses' butts. Or what they call them? Flanks. Trip a pig, see if he could. Strange guy. Don't you think so?'

Willy knew better than to express an opinion. An opinion could get you killed on a good day. No telling what it might do for you on a bad day.

In the backseat, Willy knew for sure that he was going to die.

This was an old ploy. The Gray was a killer who left the city with a man destined to be a corpse. He would now go back to the city and make certain that he could account for his whereabouts. If he'd been seen in a car with the future corpse, he could prove he was elsewhere at the eventual time of death. The new guy in the car – Massimo Sanna, The Coat – wasn't seen with him when he left downtown, and out in the suburbs nobody saw anybody. Massimo was not a guy people thought about as killing people in his spare time.

Willy knew better. Massi killed people. Not casually. Only when the situation warranted.

They traversed a bridge off the island. Drove west from Montreal into the countryside. Turned onto a back road. Then onto an unmarked trail. Peaceful there. Like a cemetery.

'You been out here before?' he asked his old friend. Teddy was driving slowly and cautiously, as if looking for a sign.

'A few times.'

That many? he wanted to ask, except that he was being calm and polite today, and he might lose it if he asked *How many guys you whacked out here? More than, I dunno, seven?* He wanted to know, *Why here?* But he knew why. This was a lonely old road. Well treed. Out of sight. They would walk into the woods where nobody ever walked without a no-good reason. The only no-good reason for a walk in the woods was to shoot somebody.

They stopped off at the side of the road and Massimo climbed out first. Teddy stalled getting out long enough to say, 'Be cool, Wills.'

Willy got out and asked, 'Why here?'

'You fucking idiot,' Massimo said.

'Why am I a fucking idiot?'

'Because we dug the hole here, you fucking idiot.'

'That much I figured.'

Held low at his hip, Massimo was pointing a pistol at his chest. A Glock. Willy was thinking that he might have sold him that gun. He should've asked more for it. If only he'd known. His heart was pounding in his chest right where the gun was pointing.

'Walk,' Massimo said.

'Maybe I'll ask you to drag me. Shoot me here. Drag me there.' He never understood why any man cooperated with his assassin.

His chance to do things differently. He felt his bowels loosening. *Damn.*

Massimo lowered the aim of the pistol. 'I'll shoot your nuts off first. One at a time if my aim is that good. I think it is. Then I drag you. Screaming and wailing away. Next, blow off your kneecaps. I hear that hurts. Then I stick one in your armpit. Then bury you alive. Do it slow. Sing you a lullaby before saying bye-bye, nighty-night.'

Willy didn't know why they called him The Coat. All he had on was a jacket.

'I'll walk,' Willy said.

'Thought so. Hey, so you know. This ain't personal. I don't know the reason.'

'There is none. Remember that for yourself. Whatever it is it ain't worth shit to me.'

They walked on through the woods. Teddy in the lead. Massimo behind. Willy in the middle. His legs felt like Jell-O that hadn't set right. His toes were marshmallows. He didn't let on. He thought about it but had no hope of jumping them. He could try. Either way, he'd end up in the ground.

'You're not pissing your pants,' Massimo said. 'I'll let people know.'

'Sure. But I wouldn't mind one. A piss. Can we stop here?'

That seemed a reasonable request, and they stopped. It took a while. Willy's stream gave Teddy the same idea and then Massimo unzipped also. Then they zipped up one by one and walked on.

They went over a knoll through leaves that fell a year ago, surviving the winter, and at the bottom of the slope the gravesite had been dug. The rains would pour down the slope onto his final resting place. Muddy. Could be worse, he thought. He said it out loud. 'Could be worse.'

He wasn't that calm. His belly was twisted, his heart hammering in his chest. A heart attack might come first. His blood in his veins felt like sludge. His skin was lifting off the surface of the earth. If he gave in a tiny bit, he would bluster and moan, cry out and beg. If he let himself go just a speck. He held onto himself instead.

Right to the end.

He stood over the grave and two quick shots blasted through the woods and across the sky. He heard the shots. Two of them.

Rapid. Urgent. Like air punching through tin. That wasn't his body falling into the grave. Massimo 'The Coat' Sanna – *his* body fell. Not into, but alongside, the grave.

Teddy holstered his gun.

This was harder, to recover from a near death. Worse than dying, maybe. He went to a knee. Tried to control his breathing. He was at risk of hyperventilating, and while that was not a story, it was an embarrassment on one level.

Eventually, he pulled it together. He stood up. Teddy watched. Big grin.

He tried to breathe more calmly. 'What happened? Christ!'

'You saw.'

'Always him? Or is this a change of heart? I hope not. Because then we're both in shit.'

'Always him. Never you. We had to get Massimo out here without he suspects. Made him think it was you. Couldn't tell you ahead of time in case you start playacting. Tip him off if you did. Wanted you to be yourself. You got balls, I'll say that. You got stones. Willy stones.'

'Jesus, Teddy.'

'Yeah, you could've been shot with that "shoot me here, drag me there" horseshit.'

'Now what?'

'Roll him in the hole. We bury him.'

'He might've whacked me, you bastard, you take too long.'

'Could've. Would've. Life's a risky business. It's all about timing.'

'We're having this out, you and me.'

'Don't bother. I'm bigger than you.'

'I'm smarter than you.'

'Just remember, I'm bigger than you. Roll him in, smart boy.'

He was on the same side of the grave as the dead man. The bullet holes had gone through Massimo's forehead and below his throat. He started rolling the body and Teddy turned to take off his jacket and that's when Willy made his move. Fast and slick. Then back to the body and another big heave and it fell into the hole and the dead man's limbs lay akimbo.

Teddy gazed at the dead man, at Massi The Coat.

Willy asked if they shouldn't step down into the grave and

straighten him out. Put him on his back. Cross his hands over his chest. 'It'll be more dignified.'

'We're not here for his fucking dignity.'

'You're right. This way he can see where he's going.'

He had landed face down.

Teddy grunted and commenced shoveling him in. 'Two shovels,' he mentioned. 'They don't dig by themselves.'

Willy pitched in with the shoveling. One man on one side, one on the other. They got Massimo covered, with another five feet of backfill to go. Graves weren't usually dug this deep by killers. He knew why this time was different.

'Hot,' he said. He went over to where Teddy had dropped his jacket on a rock and removed his own due to his exertion. When he returned, he aimed Massimo's pistol at the back of Teddy's head. He had confiscated the gun when Teddy took his jacket off. He'd stuck it under his belt and the flap of his own jacket. Something The Coat would do, only he wasn't Massimo The Coat. He did it anyway. He aimed. He hesitated. He fired. He didn't say anything. He knew why the grave had been dug so deep. He blew off the back of Teddy's head and then he shot him once in the spine for good measure. That was not necessary. He just did it.

He wouldn't have to roll the big man into the grave. Teddy The Bear fell in on his own. He didn't land in a dignified position, either. But he wasn't here for Teddy's dignity. He had to finish shoveling him into the ground, though.

The work was strenuous for just one man. Whoever had planned this had planned on two diggers for part of the time. Willy dug and contemplated what came next. Twice, he'd been set up to vanish. Twice, he'd escaped. This time, no doubting who the killers were. The mob. His own people. His own crew.

Willy was now, officially, on the run.

Too late to change sides. The other side would never trust him. They might pump him for information, then he was a dead man. They might call a meeting to decide that he was better off dead.

He might not disagree.

The backfill took over an hour. He was worn out when he was done, and hungry. Adrenalin kept him upright. He walked out of the woods to the car. He felt as though he was on the verge of suffering whiplash, like he'd need to put his neck in a brace. But he could still think. He picked out a tall birch. One of rare size along that road. He tore two strips off the bark. That old signal, once used for him by a cop. Reused recently. Not an *X*, which was too overt. Twin strips to mark the spot. If he had to, he could find this tree again. He could show people the bodies if he had a reason for that.

He'd use the car to get away, then ditch it. The number one objective was to get away.

He executed a three-point turn before he changed his mind.

Wait.

A different thought.

He should get the hell away from the gravesite. First, he had to figure this out. This new thought might be his only option. Trouble was, he'd need what Teddy The Bear called his Willy stones. Still. A plan.

Anyhow, wasn't he dead already?

What the hell did he have to lose?

SIXTEEN

Sergeant-Detective Émile Cinq-Mars checked the map drawn for him on the back of an old envelope by an adolescent at the General Store. Outside, in large block letters a sign advertised: BEER WORMS FUDGE ICE. Inside, he explained that he only wanted directions. The hesitant twelve-year-old brought in from the storage room instilled no confidence, but it turned out he knew his stuff. Each landmark into the backwoods appeared exactly as indicated: a mossy rock outcropping, a clump of five skinny birches, and now – Armand Touton's silver trailer shining through the trees.

A rutted, sharp descent. Tall, stiff grasses between the tire tracks brushed his oil pan. Harder nudges indicated rocks and uneven ground. Touton's station wagon and trailer had handled the pitch somehow; the Bug struggled. He parked in the weeds on an upslope and lugged himself out to be welcomed by a thirsty array of mosquitoes.

No point thrashing and dancing, attracting another contingent.

He walked past the trailer down a near-vertical descent where Touton slept in a lounge chair on the rickety wood wharf.

Cinq-Mars reached the water's edge before being noticed by Touton, who looked groggy as he roused himself. He'd already learned the bad news, which Cinq-Mars knew because the pimply kid at the General Store said so while diagramming directions. The message had been picked up when Touton dropped by for a pound of coffee. He'd sworn out loud, startling many.

The younger detective sat down on the dock and neither man spoke a cheerful word.

Cops hated hearing that one of their own had been shot dead. They inhabited their mutual gloom. The air they breathed deflated inside them.

In the sunlight, the mosquitoes left them alone and Cinq-Mars took in his surroundings. Touton's property had evaded development due to the steep descent to the lake. The jut suitable for his trailer would not support a house; regulations demanded a further setback from the water. He occupied one end of a finger-shaped pond and had the surrounding woods to himself. The opposite end, with flatter topography, supported cottages, the nearest a mile away. On the dock, the shining lake before him, the forest rising like a concert hall around him, Touton was buttressed from the world. Cinq-Mars experienced the sensation that the retired captain dismissed his old life here, that it merely trolled along behind him as a sparkling lure below the surface.

Cinq-Mars blinked into the sunlight. 'Fish biting?'

'We'll eat.'

Like an aging relative, their silence took up residence between them.

Cinq-Mars watched clouds drift. Then said, 'Any of your guys get killed over the years?' Opening up that can of worms.

'Luck of the draw,' Touton determined.

Cinq-Mars took that to be a no.

'You can't blame yourself.'

He was thinking, *I assigned him.*

'You know this story,' Touton continued. 'Let me tell it a different way this time. End of the war, almost. The Germans in retreat. We were force-marched out of our POW camp in Poland. Scrounged our own food along the way. Anybody who fell by the wayside took a bullet in the head. Time came, it was over for me. I had dysentery, I was weak, I was done. Last day alive. We heard tanks coming up over a hill. I noticed how they sounded different.'

'Not gas engines,' Cinq-Mars remarked. He had heard the story before and waited for what was new. 'Most German tanks ran on gas. These were diesels.'

'I told my buddies, my fellow prisoners—'

Cinq-Mars finished his thought. 'American tanks.'

'The Germans surrendered without a shot. An American lieutenant poked his head out of a turret and asked if any German mistreated us. I always told you, guys pointed to the officer who shot us if we lagged behind. The American took out his pistol, climbed down, and shot the German in the head. Instant justice.'

Cinq-Mars gave him time, then asked, 'What's different?'

Touton inhaled deeply. An exhale rattled out of him. 'No bunch of guys pointed to the German. The lieutenant climbed down. He didn't ask the question. He was looking at us like we were nothing more than rags on sticks. I spoke up. "See this guy?" Pointed to the German. "He's been killing us off, one by one." That Nazi bastard would have shot me before nightfall, when my legs and my will gave out. I knew it. The German knew it, too. The lieutenant took out his pistol. I looked at him. He handed it to me. I never told you that part. I changed it before. I'm the one who fired the shot. Point-blank. Through his left eye. I let the German blink. Then killed him.'

Was it the lakeside retreat? The killing of a policeman? His sleepiness after waking from slumber? The older man was coming clean in his old age. Some memories failed to stay submerged forever.

'Today they call that a war crime. We called it what it was. War. Just that. War.'

'Why is it on your mind, Cap?' He was impressed by the scene. The old warrior, half-falling through the webbing on his lounge chair which had seen too much sunlight, half-buried in bad memories, speaking to the forest and to the lake. And to a friend.

'Those were my guys getting shot coming out of Poland. None had to die. We tried to keep them going. Winter. Without boots. Without clothing. Amazing what a man can endure. To a point. Those were my guys being shot. Day after day after day.'

Cinq-Mars gave him that ground, that memory. Touton had lost men, too.

'War, Émile,' his old boss said. 'I feel one coming on.'

He didn't argue. Nor did he tell him that he felt it, too.

'Tell me,' Touton asked, 'did Geoffrion have a family?'

A cluster of perch were filleted and fired up in lemon juice and butter. A rock cairn had been cobbled together on the shore that contained coals and perfectly supported a cast-iron pan. The older fellow diced the cooked fish, adding shallots and tartar sauce, salt and pepper, and inserted them into hot dog buns, buttered and toasted over the open flame on the end of a fork. They ate on the dock, and the simplicity of the meal did nothing to deflect from the feast. Cinq-Mars removed his shoes and socks, rolled up his pant legs and dipped his feet in the lake. Minnows nibbled his toes. He had two more fish dogs.

Touton called them fishwiches.

They quaffed beer before they got down to business.

'Hear anything I should've heard by now?' Touton asked.

Cinq-Mars let his toes dry in the sun. 'A love triangle, homicide says. The man in the club Johnny Bondar came to kill was sleeping with his girlfriend.'

'Makes sense. Except, you're not buying it.'

'Dominic Letourneau. The Dime.'

'His ass landed on Atwater Street, I heard. One big glob of fat. Or in pieces?'

'Dental had to confirm it was his ass.'

The two men couldn't help themselves. It made no sense, but they chuckled. Clinked beer bottles as though to toast The Dime's inglorious demise.

'Here's something,' Cinq-Mars explained. 'The guy killed by Johnny Bondar was Nic Jobin. Yeah, bedding his girlfriend. That part they got right.'

'What's a nice lady supposed to do when her man's in jail?'

'Do better for herself, why not? Nic Jobin was The Dime's right-hand man. Together, they were in charge of the entertainment at several dozen strip clubs. Ran a fleet of hookers. Escort services, call girls, you name it. Is it an accident the two top pimps in the city are knocked off the same week? I'm not big on coincidence, but I am inclined to consider that somebody didn't want their deaths to look related. The Dime is blasted out of a high-rise. Jobin goes down in a love triangle shootout. Different methods, but with the timing, I'm skeptical.'

'The bombing,' Touton noted, 'has the feel of a war coming on. A bomb does more than kill. It sends a message. I don't mean to the dead guy – he's not listening anymore.' He swatted a mosquito gunning for his neck. 'Word of caution, Émile. Two ring pimps were whacked. Does somebody want the business? Could be. Could also be that Nic Jobin blew The Dime's ass out the window. Number Two wanted to be Number One. Then he's iced by Bondar. A love triangle, or payback for offing The Dime? Was Bondar a jealous lover or a hired gun? Hard to say.' Touton slapped another pest, on his jaw this time. He examined the tiny carcass before flicking it into the lake. 'None of this involves you, by the way.'

'It involved my partner. That involves me.' Cinq-Mars is not cross and they're not arguing. 'Something else. Nord Geoffrion kept a surveillance record. Who do you think visited Johnny Bondar at his party *before* he shot up the bar?'

'My ears are barn doors.'

'Morin and LaFôret. Know them? Homicide.'

Touton sat with his mouth agape a moment. 'Never liked them. Never thought they're dirty, just highly unlikeable.'

'They could've had a legit excuse to disrupt the house party. Lay down the law, that sort of thing.'

'You didn't ask?'

'I won't. I picked up Nord's book. Just took it. I don't want them knowing what I know until I find out more.'

Touton grimaced. 'This is how a police department comes apart at the seams, Émile. Trust and respect fly out the window.'

'Sue me.'

'Just saying. For now, I'll let that sleeping dog lie in your bed. Not in mine.'

They both gazed at the lake shimmering in the sunlight, sinking into private contemplations. Eventually, Touton asked to hear about the great toaster caper in detail. A ritual that Cinq-Mars knew well. Re-examine a scene endlessly, until a nugget of interest crops up. Like panning for gold.

He stopped talking when Touton asked him to hold on.

Suddenly, Touton shot up like a Jack-in-the-box, from seated to standing in a flash, and demanded, 'What? What did you say?'

'There's a spitter—'

'Before that! Before that!'

'What? I don't know. I told you about the chalk marks.'

'Tell me again!'

'Parallel marks, in yellow chalk, denoted apartments with deadbolts. All left alone.'

Calm again, Touton said, 'Those were my marks.'

'Ah, sorry? Explain.'

'I forgot. The day I met Coalface. I put two parallel marks on the gate. With yellow paint. A single line would be hard to find, like looking for a needle in a stack of needles. Doesn't every gate have a scratch on it? A single slash might not stand out. An X? Too obvious. Too overt. Stands out too much. Other people might notice, ask questions. Or remove it. I did twin lines to mark the gate Coalface went through to find me.'

'Twenty years ago. More.'

'I told Coalface, when the time came, he had to find his own way to make contact.'

'He could pick up a phone.'

'We don't know that. We know nothing about his situation. We've had tips in past years. A recent report. But in the moment, he might have to reach out any way he can.'

'Sounds out there to me.'

'Don't start believing in coincidence now, Cinq-Mars. Where's the building located?'

He told him.

'Yeah,' Touton pointed out, repeating what Cinq-Mars said, 'on de l'Épée between Jarry and d'Anvers. Same block where I met Coalface. One street over. Not even. In the lane *between* the streets. Add that to your coincidence pile.'

'Either way,' Cinq-Mars concluded, 'he's been underwater long enough. Time to pull him up for air, maybe?'

'We don't know where he is. Or even who he is.'

'You've seen him once.'

'Once. The Ice Age has come and gone since then. Look. He relayed a message. *Keep Bondar in prison.* We failed. Well, you did. Same day we spring him, Bondar's a stiff and he took Jobin with him. Coincidence? Or planned that way? Imagine. Somebody wants Jobin taken out but is worried about repercussions. How to do it? One way, release Bondar. Whisper in his ear about his girlfriend. Let him know where to pick up a rifle. Tell him there's something in it for him, more than getting his girl back.'

'Who did the whispering?'

'I know what you're thinking. We don't know that.'

'Only a thought,' Cinq-Mars said. 'Look, we have two state funerals coming up. The Dime's tomorrow, then Jobin's. I'll run the photographs of the grieving mourners by you. See if you can pick out Coalface.'

'I only saw his eyes close up. His whole face at a distance. Years ago.'

'Give it a shot.'

'Don't get your hopes up. More likely, if he's trying to alert us, he will.'

The two scaled the embankment. Touton lugged up the ice chest with the last of his morning catch. He noticed that his young visitor seemed in no hurry to depart.

'Émile, you came out here to commiserate over Geoffrion. Only natural. You came to discuss your case. We did that. You came out here to lick your wounds. I get that, too. But I know you. You're goddamn efficient. You don't know how to waste your time.'

'I have no clue what you're on about.'

'You want something from me, punk. I'm not like you. I don't have the power to pull stuff out of thin air and know what another person's thinking. Tell me what you want. I'll probably say no. If that's the worst thing that happens to you today, it's not so bad.'

Cinq-Mars smiled to himself. 'You just proved that you know what another person is thinking.' He kicked a stone around with his right shoe.

Touton waited, then admonished him. 'Enough soccer.'

'I don't know if a war is starting but *something* is going on. Armand, I'll be assigned a new partner. That's what happens when yours is killed.'

'Don't beat yourself up.'

Cinq-Mars looked forlorn and a little lost. 'If there's a war,

I'll need help. There's a guy working nights. Henri Casgrain. Know him?'

Touton had heard the name.

'Pull strings. Make him my next partner. He may not want to work days. He may not want to work with me. I don't care. I need someone I can trust.'

'I'm retired.'

'Bullshit.'

Armand Touton smiled to himself. 'OK. Promise me something, Émile. If you do, a good chance you'll get the new partner you want.'

'Promise what?' In the past, he never liked these trades.

'Visit Detective Geoffrion's daughter. He was divorced, you said? Visit his daughter. Go see the new baby, his grandchild.'

He didn't like this trade, either. 'OK. Fine. Why?'

'It'll do you good. Not negotiable. Do it, you'll get the partner you want. Anybody but me.'

He had witnessed this sentimental side to Touton before. Always, it surprised him. They shook on it, and Cinq-Mars was free to head back to town.

SEVENTEEN

Willy stopped the car, a brief hesitation before turning up the long drive. The farm lay on the edge of a broad plateau adjacent to wooded hills: house, barn and a large utility garage perched on a man-made nub. The view to the distant horizon quite peaceful.

Twice, men failed to harm him. The three who'd tried were dead. The luck that granted him such good fortune derived from believing that his time had already expired.

He did not think of his own death as imminent, rather, he saw it in the rear-view mirror. He just wasn't official yet. He'd either be alive when the sun went down, or underground. No more Mr In-Between.

He didn't want that to be his nickname, the years that he walked upright chiseled on a grave marker. If he'd even be given a grave marker. If he was even admitted to a cemetery. He might not be granted that dignity.

The man who called himself Willy, known in one quarter as Coalface, although he was unaware of the moniker, drove up to the farmhouse. *The valley of the shadow of*. . . The meeting among mobsters had either been called off or had been a ruse. The only vehicle on the property looked too tame to be a gangster's preferred mode of transportation.

The boss saw him drive in and donned a protective vest. He cinched the webbing fasteners as Willy stopped the car and climbed out. No weapon was visible in the hands of either man in the bare barnyard. Willy raised both his to indicate that he had arrived peacefully. Slowly, he lowered one hand and with a thumb and forefinger extracted Massimo's pistol from a jacket pocket and tossed it on the ground. He raised that hand back up again. He lowered his other hand and extracted Teddy's pistol from a hip pocket and tossed it on the ground. He hoped that would appease the boss because he didn't have a third weapon to show him. The boss came over and at the last second pulled out a pistol from the holster at the base of his spine, and with his other hand reached across diagonally and clutched Willy by the shoulder. He forced him to pivot and face the car. Willy obediently placed both hands on the roof line and spread his legs.

As if he was under arrest.

The boss frisked him.

That was undignified. But appropriate.

The boss turned him around again.

'Teddy?' Ciampini inquired softly. 'Massi?'

'They were coming here after? You were expecting them?'

'After what?' He spoke softly, a whisper. Willy resisted the urge to lean in to hear better.

'You know, Mr Ciampini.'

'They weren't coming here. Don't fuck with me, Willy. Where are they?'

'Not my decision. Heaven or hell. Maybe one in each?'

'Jesus, Willy. Did you hide the bones, at least?'

'No worries. I did unto others as they would do unto me.'

'You're religious now?'

'By now I should be.'

'You come here with your new religion. Figure to do me next?'

'I hold no grievance against you, Mr Ciampini. I had no grievance against them. Maybe they didn't feel the same way. You should hold no grievance over me.'

'You say.'

'The only thing between me and you is my loyalty. That's all. That's what I think.'

'Maybe you think too much.'

'I thought we could talk about it, Mr Ciampini. I mean, if you want me dead, I'm dead, right? What can I do? Maybe we can talk first. I got nothing to hide. What we have here is a bona fide, no-doubt-about-it, humongous misunderstanding.'

'Is that what we have?' Ciampini sparked. 'Think so?'

'Speaking for myself, I don't understand it, that's for sure.'

Ciampini stared him down, looking for a flicker of doubt, or of fear. 'You got some balls.'

'My Willy stones, Teddy called them.'

'Did he, yeah? Teddy was your buddy, no?'

'A good friend of mine, yeah. I killed him anyway. On account of he was going to kill me first. Wait. No. Second. He was going to kill me second.'

'He was not supposed to tell you that.'

'He didn't. He stuck to the plan. I figured it out is all.'

'Always the smart one, Willy-boy,' Ciampini said. 'Why we kept you around so long.'

'I'm still smart. You can still keep me around.'

Ciampini gave him a hard, long look again. Willy did not relent.

'It's always the smart guys who wanna fuck with you.'

'I'm not that smart.'

Ciampini kept staring at him, boring holes in his head.

'Walk away ten strides,' the boss ordered.

Willy did so, and the mob boss took advantage of the distance between them to pick up the two pistols dropped on the ground. He emptied out their shells and sniffed the barrels. Both weapons had been fired recently. He tossed the guns into the front seat of the car and dropped the bullets into a front pocket of his trousers. He slammed the car door shut.

'You can't come in the house. My youngest is here with her

youngest who's taking a nap. Some kids got it soft, you know? A nap! I didn't get those when I was a kid. You?'

'I don't recall. Maybe a few. Don't hold it against me.'

'What's he need a rest for, my grandkid, middle of the day? Does he work at a job?'

'How old is he?'

'Eight months.'

'He's got a lot to think about, I guess.'

'Like you.'

'Maybe not the same.'

'We'll go in the barn.'

He could die there. Or they could talk there. Not his decision.

'I don't know why he visits me,' Ciampini groused, 'if he naps all day.'

Ciampini kept a hard grip on Willy's right biceps as they strode to the barn. The farm had not seen rain. Their boots kicked up dust. Ciampini's pistol was pointed at the ground. Willy took solace in that. Maybe he had a chance to be resurrected. Or not.

His boss showed him his three horses. They were big horses. The two men went into an empty stall at the far end of the barn and Willy was told to kneel down. He did so. He knelt down on the straw. It seemed very clean. He was told to take his belt off and he did so. Ciampini used it to lash his arms together above the elbows behind his back. He could easily squiggle free if left alone for five seconds, but not with Ciampini watching. Those five seconds would cost him his life.

He adjusted his weight on his knees.

Ciampini sat down on a low stool, the kind that might be used for milking a cow if they had cows. Willy could be shot through the back of the head at any moment, what the papers liked to call gangland-style. He'd never see it coming unless the boss wanted him to see it coming.

He didn't mind. He was already dead. This was only about climbing back out of his grave into the light of day if that was possible. His heart was thumping. He could feel his pulse beating in his neck and head no matter how calm he looked.

He had his back to Ciampini yet was staring into the eyes of death.

'Talk,' Ciampini directed. And forewarned, 'Don't waste my time, make sure.'

EIGHTEEN

The parking spot Sergeant-Detective Émile Cinq-Mars had snagged previously was free again, around the corner from the United Church. He crossed the street just as kids on bicycles raced past him, hooting away. To be that free, that delighted with the world.

He rang the bell on the vestry door.

A diminutive, olive-skinned gentleman answered. Gripping a mop in one hand, he nodded with great vigor, as though he had news of essential importance. Cinq-Mars introduced himself in French. The fellow kept nodding. He tried in English. When the minister came down the stairs, she explained that the janitor was stone deaf.

'He reads lips, but only if you speak Portuguese. We communicate in gestures. Apart from that difficulty, we're glad he gives us a few hours. We couldn't manage without him.'

That gave Cinq-Mars an idea. 'Does he do apartments?'

'Maybe, but how do I ask?'

She went to sit behind her vestry desk. Cinq-Mars took the chair facing her. To his left, the window was dull opaque glass shaded by a maple. Precious light filtered through. Cinq-Mars stared out anyway, feeling glum. A mood the minister shared.

'Are you here to berate me?' she asked. 'Johnny's death is my fault.'

He had not come to scold. Too late for that. He did feel a need to augment her thinking. 'The police officer Bondar killed was my partner.'

Reverend Montour believed that she deserved his rebuke. She summoned her reserves to both commiserate with him and apologize. 'I'm sorry for your loss, Sergeant-Detective. I can't express how sorry I am. Especially for my part in it. I'm ashamed.'

Cinq-Mars let her off the hook. 'I'm more to blame than you are. I failed to convince you, then sent my partner to follow Bondar. I sent him to his grave.'

He saw that she was about to assail his personal sense of guilt, or of self-pity, if it was that. He put a hand up to stymie the impulse.

'Colleagues remind me that I didn't pull the trigger. Blame belongs with the young man who fired the gun. I'll say the same to you, Reverend Montour. Let's admit that it's true. We didn't shoot anybody. We're not responsible.'

'I appreciate . . .' she searched for the right word, 'your generosity, Sergeant-Detective.'

'Émile,' he said. 'And I will call you Alex.'

'Forgiveness is a virtue,' she remarked. 'Thank you, Émile.'

'It's an ever-flowing stream. I'll let you in on this. For me to stay in the Church has not been easy. It means I must forgive the church for appalling wrong-doing, both down through the centuries and presently. I know the rhetoric: blame the people responsible, not the whole of the realm or the grand notion behind the realm. I try. Also, it hasn't been easy for the Church to keep me, either. In my way, I'm a heretic. Forgiveness all around, then, on both sides. I could talk the same way about the Police Department. Good works and wrong-doing walk hand in hand. As in any human enterprise, except that cops are sunk in the mire early.'

She was struck by the depth of his malaise. Various upsets drawn from different quarters flowed into the distress of losing a partner. Delivering the order that precipitated a death intensified his anguish. He might be dealing with it, but it was not a simple thing.

She asked about Norville Geoffrion and his family. He told her what he could. Good to talk. The story of the newborn grandchild cast both a pall and a restorative note. She caught a slight, sly smile on his face. 'What?'

'You're trying to quit,' he said.

She cocked her chin to question his meaning.

'No ashtrays. The scent of fresh smoke. You smoke out the window to hide it.'

'Guilty as charged, Detective.'

'Me too. That's how I know. This time around, I've extended my time off the weed. Not easily done. I'm quick to anger. Slow to kick off an unnecessary mood when one comes over me. With what's going on, I'll probably start again. You?'

'I haven't quit, as you've *detected*, Detective. I may have let a few people think I have.'

'A spouse?'

'My girlfriend. She's on my case.'

He wasn't sure how to take that. She noticed.

'Baby steps, Émile. First, let's get you accustomed to the idea of female clergy.'

They laughed.

'You're talking to someone who gave up on the priesthood partly because of celibacy. Look at me now.'

'What do I see?' she asked.

'I'm celibate anyway. I haven't had a girlfriend in a dog's age.' They laughed. 'Yet you do. How is that fair? I might as well be a monk. My apartment is no larger than a monk's cell. Look, I'm sorry. Not smoking. Maybe that brought this on.'

'It didn't. You know that. Good on you for quitting, Émile. Hold onto the victory. Be my inspiration.'

'If you offer me one now, Alex, I'll accept.'

They exchanged a long look.

'Nice try,' she said.

'Damn,' he said.

They broke off their staring contest.

The minister swept a touch of dust from her desk with her pinkie.

'I'm glad you came by,' she mentioned. 'Not only for this talk. There's something else, but first, why are you here, if not to condemn me to wherever Johnny Bondar's soul has traveled? You didn't come to bum a smoke, either.'

He grimaced. She was right. 'I have a few questions. Alex, my partner was following Johnny Bondar. To see what he might be up to. He was outside Bondar's apartment during his welcome home party.'

'He saw me there.'

He liked that she was straightforward with him. 'Norville recorded your arrival in his notebook, yes. At least, the arrival of a woman with a clerical collar. You helped spring Johnny Bondar. Perfectly natural to go to the party. Did anything occur that I should know?'

'Occur?'

'Did he say where he was going when he left? Did he threaten anyone? What was his mood like? Was he drinking heavily?'

She spoke with evident care. 'I spent remarkably little time with Johnny. That made sense, with all the young people around him. His parents had invited me over. I talked to his mom. She was crying half the time. Crying because he was home and crying because he was always in trouble. Since birth, she said. We discussed how he might start over from scratch, which is how Johnny put it when I visited him in prison. Such a tough guy, but when I visited he cried. That sorrow felt real. Once out, he was surrounded by his rough crowd again. They bucked him up, I guess. Perhaps because you spoke to me, I worried.'

'Did you notice two men arrive during the party? The music went quiet when they did.'

'Your partner kept detailed notes.'

'He did.'

'Everybody noticed them. I can't say I liked the cut of their jib. Somebody said they were hoodlums. Somebody else said policemen. The whole apartment went silent. It made more sense they were police.' The way the fingers on her left hand wrestled with those on her right indicated an itch for a smoke. 'Johnny was out on the back balcony. The two men walked past me to go there. Everybody turned to look. The music was switched off, like you say. I think people were hoping to eavesdrop on the conversation. My impression.'

'They spoke to Bondar?'

'Out of earshot. They came back soon afterwards. Really, it was shocking how everyone stayed so quiet. I didn't understand it. They left. The music came back on. Way too loud, of course. Everything returned the way it was. A few minutes later, maybe five, ten, Johnny races back through the apartment and leaves. His mother's in tears. The party fizzled out after that. Sorry, Émile, that I can't be of help.'

Cinq-Mars shook off her apology. 'You can never tell what helps. There was something you wanted to bring up?'

The minister looked to the side, as though she'd rather not broach the matter. 'Another tragedy in the making, I suspect. A young woman, twenty years old. She doesn't live nearby; her parents do. She's gone missing. Right out of the blue. The parents filed a missing person's report, but they don't think her disappearance is being taken seriously. She's twenty, after all, not ten. Her folks are going round the bend. I have little hope given how I let you down, but could you look into it? You're the only policeman I know. I want to help the parents.'

Cinq-Mars wrote down the particulars, which were scant.

He had one more box to check off. 'Will you be going to the funeral, Alex? Bondar's?'

'Going? I'll be conducting the service. In church and at the gravesite.'

Not expecting that, he realized that he should have. 'I'm not asking you to compromise any professional or ecclesiastical oath—'

'Then why do I feel you will?'

He smiled. She was right again.

'If, in the course of the day, you hear anything that might aid our understanding of what happened, leading to Bondar's death and the deaths of his victims, even if you don't think it significant, I'm all ears. Really, I'm hoping you'll share whatever gossip falls your way.'

The minister wore the coy smile this time. 'Protestants don't do confession well. We confess our lives as sinners – a generalized admission of wrong-doing. We accept God's forgiveness as if it's our due. The specifics? We keep those narratives to ourselves. On the other hand, we're quite excellent at gossip! Other people's sins and foibles fascinate us no end. I'll let you know if anything arises, Émile. Does this make me your secret snitch?'

In a way, it did. She was teasing, but Cinq-Mars left it at that.

'I'll see about your missing girl,' he said. A gentle reminder that this was not only friendly but also tit-for-tat.

Leaving, the cop bumped into the janitor sweeping up day-old confetti from the sidewalk. He tried to ask if he'd be interested in cleaning up his apartment from time to time but failed to make the request comprehensible to the deaf Portuguese man. The janitor kept nodding happily, as if to confirm a shared agreement, despite not comprehending a word and being totally flummoxed by the detective's crazed gestures.

A passing pedestrian, though, walked on, feeling entertained.

NINETEEN

On his knees on straw. A pistol to his head. 'Your daughter's inside,' Willy said.

'My youngest. You know where my eldest is.'

'For shooting a cop, yeah. Light sentence, though, right? You worked that one.'

'Maybe I did.'

'Your grandkid's in the house.'

'Wasting. My. Time. Willy.'

'No, no, not wasting, not wasting. Wondering, is all.' Willy was reminding him that he had family in the house, including the mother of a baby boy who might not be accustomed to a man being murdered in the barn by her dad. He took the boss's silence to indicate that he might have tweaked that nerve. Willy remained on his knees, his back to the man, head exposed to an angry bullet.

'Wondering something myself, Willy. Do I stick a slug in your right ear or your left? Any preference?'

'If you want it that way, sure, the job's done. Still, can't a man ask himself how come? Out of his natural curiosity? I'm asking, how did this happen overnight? I go from doing my job to finding out I'm worm-food to you. Why so different so fast in your eyes?'

'Talk, I told you. I said nothing about asking questions.'

'You're right. Sorry about that, boss.'

'I can shoot you through the head, Willy. One and done. Or I can shoot you slowly.'

'Slowly? You mean—'

'Work my way up. By the time I do, you're begging for the end. Tell me you know what I mean.'

'I got an inkling, yeah.'

'A what?'

'I know what you mean, boss. No questions. Whew. I know what you mean.'

'You better.'

'You don't want to do it on your farm, though, right? With your grandkid around. You'll wake him. I hope you think so, anyway.'

Willy rocked on his knees a moment, to both reconfigure his posture, his arms pinioned behind him with his own belt, and to parlay his time to properly finagle his redemption.

He kept talking. 'So fucking fast, the way things go down, hey? The Dime blows up. A bomb in his TV. I mean, who can watch the news anymore, catch a ballgame, without first you flinch? Like you gotta shut your eyes when you turn the knob. It's a reflex. Not necessarily you. Me, I mean. Anybody. We flinch.'

'You're telling me what I already know. You think I got time on my hands?'

'Course not. Putting this together is all. The Dime blows up. Then Nic gets whacked.'

'Unrelated.'

'Some say, yeah. Supposed to look that way anyhow.'

'Meaning?' For once, Ciampini conveyed genuine interest in what Willy was saying.

'Suspicious, no? But you get it. The punk, released from the can. A little early somehow. Something strange there. Same night, he takes out Nic Jobin.'

'Nic was screwing his girl. His decision. Old news.'

'Right. Still, here's a guy who's never done nothing except jumpstart a few cars. Suddenly, he's driving around with a thirty-aught-six? I mean, I'm the guy who supplies the weapons around here. I should be the one who's upset. Somebody cut in on my action? Not that I'm unhappy to be high and dry on this one. I mean, the kid, just out of the slammer, no clue where to find a gun, not only finds a rifle but picks a fight with cops who are waiting for him – *waiting for him* – outside the bar. Jobin gets whacked. His killer, too. Convenient, no? If somebody wanted a convenient kill, that plan worked out fine.'

'Interesting. Still leaves you with a hitman in your closet.'

'That bothers you why? I don't see it. OK, either you were trying to kill me, and I might never find out why, or somebody else was out to get me. After today, I'm thinking it was you. You sent Teddy. You sent out Le Gris to confuse the issue. You sent Massi The Coat to finish the job. Pretty obvious you want to do me in. But the first time, I had to ask if that was you or somebody else. Because if it was somebody else then I see the pattern.'

The boss's voice was low and a little weary, as though he wanted to get on with shooting him. 'What pattern?'

'Nic Jobin. Killed by the Bondar kid. We think it's a boy-and-girl thing, right? Jealousy. But what if Bondar was sent there? Sent. His job: kill Jobin. Make it look like a love triangle thing. Same with me. Kill me, but make it look like an outside gang was killing one of yours. That way, you think I'm doing something with an outside gang that's worth finishing the job for them.'

'We're aware, Willy,' Ciampini said.

'Aware of what?'

'You're the mole.'

An undercover cop who'd infiltrated the mob might be called a lot of names by a crime boss, but Willy didn't think 'mole' would be one of them. They were confusing him with somebody else.

'What mole?'

'We have a mole.'

Not somebody reporting back to the police. Somebody reporting to another gang, maybe?

'You think it's me?'

'Odd stuff is happening with you, Willy. Killing that hitman like you did. Made us think we don't know you. The Willy we know would've had a hard time taking out a spider with a broom. The Willy we know tracks our shipments, hocks our guns, keeps our books. Knows too much, maybe. Who's he been hanging with lately? He have enemies? Who's he been talking to? What's he doing our enemies want to smack him dead? He's not hardcore. *Our* Willy's the kind of guy you have a cappuccino with, gives OK advice from time to time. Keeps things rolling. He don't act tough or talk tough, too smart for that. If he acted tough, we'd laugh. The Willy we know, he don't slam a sickle through a man's skull and pin his head to the wall.'

'Butcher's knife. A long one, I admit. Not a sickle. Through the throat.'

'A machete, a sickle, a cleaver. Head. Throat. Do I care? I give the order to dig your grave and you put two of my best guys in it. Who did that? Not *my* Willy. I'm not saying you didn't have cause, you had cause. Teddy woulda offed you. The plan. But where did you find the stones for it and how did you off *him*? Confess, Willy-boy. Come clean. I'll let you go out with dignity if you confess to me. That's all I care about when you talk. Your confession. I'll give you a quick one, for old time's sake. Nothing prolonged. Because I care.'

You'll chop my legs off then my arms. You won't sharpen the axe, neither.

'One favor, boss. The fucker who let all that suspicion fall down on my head? Now's the time – let suspicion fall down on *his* head. Let it *rain* right down. I'm nobody's mole. That's airtight. I'll take it to the grave and you can, too. Give me a slow death, crack my balls in a vise. I'll scream, I won't like it, I'll beg for your good mercy, but that don't change the honest truth. If you had a mole, you still have a mole. Only he's deeper and better hid after I'm dead and presumed to be the rat when I'm not. I won't plead for my life, boss. No point. Don't want to waste your time. But whether you off me or not, promise me you'll keep looking for your mole. Because I'm not the guy.'

'Why we listened to your good advice sometimes. You had good talk in you.'

'Want to know how I see it? The Dime gets blown up. I heard people whisper, *maybe it was Nic Jobin*. The Dime's been tasting the candy for years. Spends his days doing the girls instead of running them. So Nic maybe had a good thought to take over. Nic was good pals with Massimo. Massi's old man has a TV store. That's where The Dime sent his set for repairs. Boom. Like that. So we think, was it Nic? With help from Massi?'

'I heard those stories,' Ciampini said.

'Nic gets whacked. Why? Love triangle. OK. Call it that.'

'You don't?'

'Somebody tries to do me, I see it coming, turn it around. Why me? Somebody thinks I'm useful to you. But *you* think, what's up with Willy? Stuff is happening with Willy. You order me dead. While you're at it, you order Massi put down. For the TV set, maybe. But now we're killing each other. Forgive me, boss, for speaking plain, but now's the time – what you don't see, we're getting picked off one by one. Like we're in a war, except nobody's calling it a war. We got excuses for everybody. But what if that's the plan? What if this *is* a war? Doesn't look like it, so you don't declare one. You don't retaliate. You don't call New York for reinforcements. But maybe somebody wants you to keep New York out of this.'

Willy fell silent. Still on his knees. His arms strapped behind him, his boss with a pistol. He was desperate, but he had to give his speech time to sink in. He was feeling more alive than dead now. Shaking inside. Suddenly, he wanted to live. He tried to suppress it, but he couldn't deny the feeling. Now that he might live, he was suddenly afraid of death. He was wanting to live and didn't welcome the emotion. Wanting to live did him no good. This is what hope did to a man, it messed him up.

'Who're you putting behind this big plan?'

His boss's tone of voice indicated that he was not convinced.

'Who's been learning at your feet, boss? Last couple of years? You needed more muscle. You went out, you hired more muscle. But this muscle has brains.'

Rather than answer, he let the notion float in the air. He wanted the boss to figure it out for himself. He was more likely to be convinced that way.

'The Hells?' Ciampini asked him. The question sought confirmation, yet his skeptical tone was gone once he said it aloud himself.

'I know, boss. We think they're thugs on bikes. Ugly hair. Tattoos. The whole bit. But they been learning. You hire them to be your muscle and you got what you want. But *they* see *you* as weak when you hire them to do the dirty work. They fear you less. They hang around. Do what you want. Get close. The whole time they watch. They learn. When they put a plan into action, guess what? Nobody thinks it's them because nobody thinks they have the smarts for a plan. So, yeah, if you want my opinion, it's the Hells. I'll tell you one thing, I'd sure like a chance to find out.'

He didn't appreciate the ensuing silence.

'Something else needs saying,' Willy added.

'What's that?'

He was hoping for that question.

'You know who's who in the Hells. You trust the guys you brought in. The leadership. But in your life, men tried to take you out. You put them down. But if men try, from inside the Hells, to take out their top guys, you will see a new regime. Then who do you know inside the Hells? Then who do you trust, if the ones you trust are dead?'

Not hard to sound convincing when he was telling the truth from the ground up. He knew more of what was in the air and on the ground than any kingpin. For its part, the mob had a grievance against him but not the one they imagined. He'd said his piece. He'd shown he had value. Willy adjusted his weight on his knees, took a deeper breath. Perhaps his last. He didn't know. He waited.

PART THREE
THE SLAUGHTER

TWENTY

Promises made were meant to morph into promises fulfilled. Émile Cinq-Mars visited Detective Norville Geoffrion's daughter. Not wanting the pendulum of obligation to swing over his head for long, he embarked in the shank of the evening.

High above the city, overlooking downtown, 'The Vic' – The Royal Victoria Hospital – was a congested conglomeration of ornate structures on a slope of Mount Royal. Nine Scottish baronial pavilions with a multitude of romantic turrets probed the skyline, yet a century of service had taken a toll on the physical plant. Gloom dulled window glass and settled like dust through the complex grid of corridors. Cinq-Mars had visited the Women's Pavilion before, which was fortunate, as it was not easy to find, tucked away in the rear of the labyrinthine muddle of dark gray buildings. He wound his Beetle up the hillside and parked in an upper lot that offered expansive views to the east.

Over two days, the young woman had given birth and lost her father to violence. How that confluence of joy and grief had affected her he could not imagine.

'Dad mentioned you,' the new mom revealed. Her name was Gina, which rolled off the tongue as Gina Geoffrion. Her married name, however, was Gina Malinger, which sounded fine out loud, but read off the nameplate over her bed called her character into question. English names often flummoxed Cinq-Mars. His tongue failed to glide around them easily and he'd muff the proper accent. 'He was looking forward to working with you. He hated being a cop, so that's saying something.'

She wept, briefly. And apologized – needlessly – for doing so. Cinq-Mars worked to keep himself stitched together. 'Sorry for your loss, Gina. Your dad was delighted to welcome your little one into the world.'

'You should have seen his eyes! He lit up like a candle for wee Marguerite!'

He kept the opinion to himself, but he was pleased whenever

a French–English couple chose a French name for their child. For one thing, he could pronounce it properly, whereas he'd butcher 'Margaret', and never repeat it the same way twice.

The infant slept peacefully in her father's arms.

'I think she misses her granddad already,' Gina said.

A fallacy Cinq-Mars was willing to accommodate.

Nord's death cast a pall. Focus naturally shifted to the newborn. Coming away from the visit, Cinq-Mars carried the impression that his former partner – under-appreciated, mocked, divorced, diminished by the nickname Poof-Poof – would be granted short shrift in death.

The funeral – delayed for a few days to give Gina time to recuperate – would command the attention of departments across the continent. Officers killed in the line of duty received royal send-offs. Nord would have that, at least.

Cinq-Mars felt saddened, and something Gina had shared under-scored his low spirits. She remarked that her father never wanted to be a policeman, that he signed up only because the force offered steady employment. He persevered for the sake of his family. The job was demanding; to carry on solely for the income made the hassles tougher to endure. Whatever Touton was hoping Cinq-Mars would gain from a visit to his partner's family never clicked in. He came away from the hospital even more deeply mired in the doldrums and needed to kick his mood. The detective took a walk up the mountainside on trails leading from the parking lot to help himself snap out of it.

He'd been promoted. He should not be acting as though he'd been booted to the curb.

Dark out now. Standing on a trail in the forest. The thrum of the city rose up to him. A vast array of house lights to the eastern horizon flickered like stars; a galaxy sequestered for the night. Amid travail and pleasure, yearning and hardship, among a multi-tude of children, somebody had to keep folks safe. Cinq-Mars came to a determination. Time to get back on the stick. Nord had not wanted to be a cop, or a detective when the promotion came his way. Cinq-Mars was sorry to hear that, but they were not built of the same material. He regretted the man's death, his part in it, and hated the ease with which Nord would soon be forgotten. Still, he'd dwell on him no more.

Out with the old. In with the new. Tough as that was. Call it life.

A walk in the woods was not good enough. Time to crack an internal whip. Don't mope another second. Or grieve. Time to do what he expected of himself.

Hands in his pockets, Cinq-Mars quick-marched back out of the woods.

In the lobby of the Women's Pavilion, he made a couple of calls to solicit a phone number, then dialed the detective he wanted to have assigned to him. Touton had come through. Detective Henri Casgrain had been notified of his transfer and granted the night off. He started in the morning on his new shift.

'Good,' Cinq-Mars affirmed.

'For you, maybe,' Casgrain said. 'I'm not doing the Watusi.'

'Let's meet up. We'll have a drink. Talk about it.'

'Beer in the fridge. Come on over.'

'I don't want to impose on your family,' Cinq-Mars demurred.

'I'm babysitting. Impose.'

Casgrain lived on the vast, flat, dense urban table east of the mountain. Into that vale of flickering lights known as the Plateau, Cinq-Mars sped off to meet him.

The man who called himself Willy also took stock of his troubles, ruminating on a different set of choices. He'd not been a violent man, although he was familiar with the milieu. He'd bartered guns to killers. Observed malcontents being pummeled. Chosen the gravesite for a family man delinquent on his payments. Lately, he'd survived an assassin's trap and terminated the man's life with a carving knife thrust through his windpipe. He'd had help. Only one person knew that. Foiling the assault was critical, but he remained a marked man, his name inscribed on a gang's roadkill list.

Suspicious of him, 'friends' decided that if he was courting nasty enemies, he must have something serious to hide. The next step in gang logic he anticipated and understood: if he could not be trusted and kept his own secrets, he was better off dead.

Willy welcomed a secret irony. Something he could share with no one. Having survived, he now wanted to live. At last.

A challenge.

So far that day, he had foiled one execution and talked his way out of another.

Still, best to remain on his toes.

Willy returned and stood near to his apartment, behind a pathetic excuse for an ash tree. He wanted to observe the building, confirm that no one lingered in wait for him, that no one was watching before he made his move.

The coast seemed clear. He hunched his shoulders, pulled up the collar on his jacket. Not much of a disguise. He strolled down the opposite side of the street from his building and crossed at the last minute. Not much of a ploy. Inside the front door he listened for trouble. People were indoors, televisions turned on. He headed up. He pressed an ear to his own door on the top floor. Not much of a precaution. He inserted his key and entered.

He was in.

He locked the door behind him.

Strange, to be home, where he was no longer welcome.

He couldn't stay.

Would pack a few clothes and essentials.

Cops had no reason to return here. No one would notice if anything was missing. No one would know that he'd come back to confiscate extra clothes and a few pairs of shoes.

He turned on a light.

His suits remained in place. Where he'd slaughtered his assassin, his beloved shoes were lined up in rows. People never understood his wardrobe. Why wear identical suits and similar shoes? Back in time, he had once helped himself to the proceeds of a gang heist, a hijacked truck. Six copies of the same suit, same size. After that, his preference was to maintain an appearance as bland as dust, while enjoying the feel of fresh duds. His secret: to look like a man who owned only one suit, except that the suit he wore each day hadn't been worn in a week, appearances to the contrary. His way to indulge in a luxury that went unnoticed.

His way to pass through the world unnoticed.

Suddenly, a rapping. He switched off the light.

Realized his mistake too late. He had confirmed that someone was inside the apartment.

He moved toward the kitchen door that emptied onto the back balcony.

The rapping persisted. Furtive. As though someone wanted the sound to be heard only by the one inside.

He peeked. Saw a form.

Took a longer look.

He knew who it was.

'Willy,' she was whispering at the door. Not loud but urgent. 'Willy!'

Sooner or later, she'd draw attention to herself.

He went to the door. It wasn't locked. She had only assumed it was. Opened it a crack.

'Let me in.'

'Moira, not a good time.'

'I know that. Let me in.'

He did. She closed the door quietly behind her, then turned to be very close to him. He took a step back. She took another step forward. Clutched a sleeve of his jacket.

'Moira.'

'Jesus, Willy, it's all right. I didn't tell them a thing. I was very discreet. Rest assured.'

'Tell who what? What is there to tell?'

'I didn't say I knew you. That we know each other. That you put your hands on me. That I put my hands on you.'

'That's good, Moira. Thanks.'

'I didn't tell them about the cameras. Let them find that out themselves.'

He was quiet a moment.

'Moira? What cameras?'

'You know what cameras. Oh, Willy, you killed a man. Jesus! That was bad. I guess you had to. Is that why you had the cameras? For protection? What now? Are you on the run? You are, aren't you? You're on the run. Oh, Willy, I won't betray you. You can put your hands on me.'

'Not the time, Moira.'

'Let me put my hands on you. You'll feel better.'

'Moira, what do you know about the cameras?'

'I didn't tell! That's what's important. Nothing else. Let me put my hands on you.'

He let her. He felt paralyzed. He couldn't get into a loud fight with her or chase her out. She put her hands on him and unzipped him and he let her do that and he didn't stop her when she went down on her knees. As if he were a long distance away, he remembered that this could be pleasant.

The moment came. Passed. She stood. She put her arms around him.

She whispered in his ear. 'Put your hands on me, Willy.'

'Moira, it's not the time.'

She spoke harshly to him under her breath. 'Put your hands on me! Or I'll tell the police. I'll tell everybody about the cameras. People will know who you are, Willy! You're a killer. Everybody knows that now. Put your hands.'

He put his hands on her. He didn't know what else to do. This was a mistake, coming back here. He should have waited, or never returned and purchased new clothes. He touched her intimately. She was moaning in his arms, standing up, and then it was over. Moira was always sudden that way.

'Don't be a stranger,' she said. Vaguely, a warning. She kissed him on the lips, a peck, really, then left the way she arrived, as a wraith in the night, a wisp.

He washed up. The man referred to by a few as Coalface finished packing a bag and stole away from his home. *This time*, he was thinking, *for good*. Moira was only half-right when she inferred that he was on the run. He was also on the hunt. Half a block down on Jarry Street he hailed a cab to drive him to his car.

He murmured to the driver, 'I might need to kill that woman.'

The driver laughed, assumed he was joking. Willy lightly chuckled along with him, not really knowing how serious he might be. Summer was coming on. He knew that much. He feared a bloodbath, generally.

When Cinq-Mars was formally introduced to Henri Casgrain's two youngest, they shook hands. Buoyant, happy kids, six and eleven. His sixteen-year old was hanging out with friends after being relieved of the babysitting chore when his father's schedule changed. Henri's wife, whom Cinq-Mars had yet to meet, was attending choir practice.

'One night of the week totally her own. That ends soon, for the summer. Usually, I sleep days. Evenings, my turn to look after the kids, then work at midnight. I do my coaching in the evenings, too. We think we can adjust to the new regime. Émile— By the way, do I still call you "Émile", or do I call you "boss"?'

'Your Royal Highness will do.'

'Your Royal Ass it is. What you have to accept, because it's non-negotiable: my family gets my time at night. Used to be, overtime ate into my days, into my sleep. Fine. No big deal. Overtime with you? That takes away from family hours. Won't happen. Take it or leave it.'

'Anything else I need to take or leave?'

'That's it, that's all.'

'Then we have a deal. Put in for extra hours, I'll boot your rump.'

Casgrain was content to secure their arrangement, although he remained skeptical. 'Once the clock strikes five, your Royal Ass, my golden carriage arrives. Doesn't matter whose shit hits what fan at what velocity.'

'I prefer working solo anyway. *Especially* when shit hits a fan.'

'Heard that about you. You're a pain. Beer?'

'Why I'm here.'

The kids glued a plastic battleship together as the men took their bottles onto the back porch. The night was cool, comfortable. Quiet voices. Neighboring families were cleaning up barbecues or taking their ease with a nightcap. Casgrain's flat was the second floor of a duplex. The porch overlooked the lane's backyards. Patchwork flower gardens amid struggling grass. A few cement parking spots. An assortment of fences: planks, wire, latticework. Older boys sat on their bicycles and in the dark chatted over fences to the girls who'd been on their minds.

The detectives compared notes on the Park Ex robberies, on the crazies in the building, on the murder, on recent gangland slayings. Casgrain saw no interconnections. Cinq-Mars advised him to stick around, that he might. They talked briefly about Norville Geoffrion. Casgrain knew him from years ago and declined to say a negative word, which Cinq-Mars appreciated, although he detected the usual reticence to praise the man.

Casgrain cut to the chase. 'Why did you abduct me to be your partner, Émile?'

'Abduct?' Cinq-Mars repeated.

'What else can you call it? No one I know can make that happen.'

'Old connections, let's say.'

'That part I get. What I want to understand is: why?'

'We've never worked together, Henri. Only crossed paths. Yet I trust you. Right now, it's critical for me to be with someone I trust.'

'Why? What's special?'

'The apartment robberies. What you passed off to me.'

'Homicide took it over. The whole nine yards. They know you're working it?'

'Maybe I forget to mention that.'

'I bet.' Casgrain savored another swallow of beer. Swilled the liquid in his bottle around. 'Look. You have the horses to get me onto the dayshift. You probably have the horses to keep our necks free of the guillotine. I'm not going to sweat this. But *why*, Émile? What's the big deal about toasters? Why go at this?'

'My partner was shot and killed.'

'We know who did it. He's dead, too.'

'Yeah. And before Johnny Bondar shot up a nightclub and killed my partner, he was visited by two homicide detectives. Pretty good, don't you think? Visited by homicide *before* killing people. Why were they talking to a car thief anyway? I mean, those guys deserve a commendation. That's some kind of super police work, predicting the future like that.'

Casgrain let the news hang in the evening air, like clothes dripping on a backyard line. 'This isn't about shit hitting the fan in a windstorm. More like falling out of the sky, a cloudburst.'

'Why I want you around, Henri. Your way with words.'

'Finally,' Casgrain ventured. 'A good reason.'

They shared a quick grin. As hard as the days ahead might be, they sensed they'd have a good time.

'OK, tell me why Geoffrion was tailing Bondar.'

'I ordered him to. Yes, I feel guilty about that. Over it, to a degree.'

'Bondar wasn't out for a day. He steals cars. Not toasters. Why follow him?'

Cinq-Mars told him of his talks with Touton, his failure to convince the minister, Geoffrion's careful notes which made mention of detectives LaFôret and Morin. He concluded, 'Right out of jail, how did Bondar know where to find a rifle? Did our homicide dicks tell him?'

They dove into silence for a time.

'OK,' his new partner said, 'you're right to pull me in.'

'That's not all.'

'It's enough.'

'It's not all.' He then solicited an oath from the man and reminded him that he needed someone he could trust implicitly.

'What's going on, Émile?'

He related the story of the man Touton referred to as Coalface. He concluded by saying, 'We have to find him. Our job? To bring him in.'

Casgrain exhaled a breath he hadn't realized he was holding. 'Sounds like he's gone under. I don't expect him to come up for air, not after what he's put himself through. Try to imagine what he's done to stay inside. Arrest him on a charge, cut him an inch of slack for his sacrifice. Otherwise, let him be.'

'I don't care about the shape he's in. I want him in now. I want to know what he knows. Besides, he might be in danger. This might be a case of now or never.'

'Why think that way if you never hear from him?'

'Touton has a theory. The slash marks I told you about? They relate to Coalface. Touton thinks he's communicating. Besides, it was Coalface who told him to keep Bondar in jail. That seems like the right call today. That was straight-on communication. Except he used an intermediary. Not slash marks or smoke signals.'

'He can't always? That's his thought? Touton's?'

Cinq-Mars nodded and sipped. 'Has to go out of his way, maybe. Not always convenient if he's in a crowd of bad guys.' He finished his soldier and Casgrain returned to the kitchen and came back with two more.

They sat quietly and drank, deep in thought.

A balcony light came on across the lane. Casgrain patted down his salt-and-peppery mustache. He was the first to emerge from their stupor.

'What you said about the thefts being practice. Could be. Or, could be they provide cover for the murder. Exactly how, I don't know. Also, as I said before, there's another possibility.'

As much as anything, this was why Cinq-Mars wanted them to partner up. The man was thoughtful and smart. Smug of him, he knew, but he considered Henri Casgrain a peer.

'The robbery,' Casgrain continued, 'implicates the thieves in a murder whether they deserve to be or not. If they are being indoc-trinated into a gang, the murder bonds them to the gang. They're accessories to the bigger crime. Also, different tack, if murder was the motive for the robberies, then, officially, the robberies are out of our hands and in the hands of homicide. That's true in the normal course of events, failing His Royal Hind-ass Émile Cinq-Mars arriving on the scene. Keep in mind that that might've been the plan from the get-go, to keep everyday detectives away from the scene. Not you, specifically. I caught the call, remember. But homicide gets to take it over. You indicated your disdain for LaFôret and Morin. Maybe some people appreciate what they offer. Not for the right reasons.'

'I don't know them. Can't say. Their attitude leaves a bad taste.'

'Reason enough to work our own case. We neglect to mention it to them, of course.'

Cinq-Mars had had expectations, yet was more impressed than anticipated. 'You've given me stuff to think about, Henri. Were the robberies an initiation into serious crime? Was the murder a way to strike fear into the hearts of young recruits? Was a plot in place to select who investigates?'

'Your lead. You said, maybe it was practice. Let's say that's part of it. If a group of young recruits was *practicing* a heist, then two questions shake out from that. One, what are they practicing for?'

'That I get. What's the second?'

'Who's to say they pulled off their practice run without a flaw? Put the murder and that so-called rape on a side burner for a minute. What if we go over the scene again, scrape the toaster robberies with a fine-tooth comb, look for amateur mistakes? If they were only practicing, it follows that they made errors, no? Maybe a bunch.'

Cinq-Mars got it. They clinked glasses.

'Tomorrow,' he said.

'Oh God,' Henri Casgrain lamented. 'I can't believe I'm working days now.'

'You'll survive,' Cinq-Mars assured him.

'Maybe not with your track record.'

TWENTY-ONE

M ick, the janitor's son, sent out word to his buddies. After midnight. The back lane. Bring who you know, if they're big, tough, if they want some action. Fourteen said they'd be there. A few copped out, but the core group was augmented by strangers who got wind of the rumble. Fifteen young men and older adolescent boys waited in the lane. There to defend their turf, protect a friend, catch an adrenalin rush.

Ukrainians, Russians, Poles and two Latvian brothers up against Italian youths and a few French pals. The scenario they expected.

A half-hour after midnight, the opposing force congregated at the lane's north end. Mick's friends noticed they were outnumbered when they'd expected the advantage. A few worried. Too late to cop out now. They stood their ground as the other side sauntered toward them. Getting closer, the arrivals made noise. Rattled lumber against fences. Made hooting sounds, as if they were owls. Not that one of these city boys had ever heard or seen an owl. In unison, they sounded frightening.

Lights were being turned on in the duplexes and apartments.

People peered outside.

Neighbors were alerted.

The lane boys howled back to embolden themselves, but really, they wanted everyone who lived nearby to wake up, to help, to call for help, do something to keep the battle brief. They could engage, but they could not sustain the brawl for long.

'Form a U-shape,' Mick instructed his line of defenders. A general to his troops. 'Surround them that way. Keep them in the middle.'

They formed a U.

One way to combat superior numbers.

A few more than twenty were coming at them.

Too many. Bad odds.

Insults were hurled in both directions regarding nationality and sexuality.

The sides roared together. First contact was erratic. The attackers had numerical advantage, except they were partially encircled. The sounds of combat grew raucous, the thudding, the taunts, the grunts. Alarmed cries were emitted by women on their balconies. Men shouted warnings. They dressed and came down their back-stairs to stop this. High above the fray, the man Émile Cinq-Mars had designated as the Bombardier, a megaphone voice, bellowed profane encouragement.

'Piss in their eyes, the motherfuckers!'

Also on high, Serge the Spitter readied himself should visiting punks attempt to mount the building's spiral staircase. He looked nervous, though, a man ready to run.

'Shit in their ears!' the Bombardier instructed.

Mick did well with his first opponent. His punches landed. The other guy's were deflected. They could scarcely see each other in the dark, but Mick's fist connected with the other boy's chin and a sharp elbow between the eyes convinced his attacker he'd not chosen his opponent well. He sprang to a different fight, making it a two-on-one. Mick leapt ahead to make a three-on-one more fair. He prospered in that punch-up until accosted from behind. In trouble then. Clasped by a much heavier boy, he could not fend against punches to his belly from a second assailant.

Overpowered from behind. Controlled. Panicky as he went to the pavement. Pinned.

Mick kicked and squirmed under a ton of weight. To no avail. He shouted out.

Help arrived, an adult in the dark. Other adults were evening up the side. The marauding boys started to back away as the men pulled them off and a jeremiad of police sirens wailed through the night. Cops were close and coming fast. On the ground with an elephant on top of him, Mick held on for rescue and strained with all his might, heaving under his transgressor and wanting to cry out but not wanting to come undone. What blows he had absorbed scarcely affected him in the chaos – then the other boy was gone. On the run. More of a fast waddle in his case. Cop cars were coming up the lane from one end, blue-and-red cherries flashing and sirens echoing off the tenements. The marauders raced and hobbled away on foot toward the opposite end to escape.

His own father helped Mick to his feet. He tugged him toward their basement apartment. Mick was thoroughly bloodied. Once they were both safely inside, his dad had nothing to say. Neither rebuke nor criticism. The janitor washed blood from his son's face.

They sat at the kitchen table and had a beer. The janitor had never had a beer with his son before. Mick dabbed his nose with a towel, and the scrape across his cheek where he'd landed on asphalt.

'God and Jesus,' the father said eventually.

'Yeah,' his son said.

'You knew it was coming?'

'Not so many guys. Was supposed to be a fair fight.'

'What you fight about?'

'Nothing,' the boy said.

'Nothing? That's worth it, fight for nothing?'

'Nothing much, Dad.'

'What so important? Why so mad?'

A knock on the back door.

Uniformed officers wanted to talk to the boy.

'He defend himself,' the father pointed out. 'He has a right. Who those boys?'

'That's a question we want to ask your son. Can you call him out here, please?'

'Mick!' the janitor shouted over his shoulder, not realizing the boy was only arm's length away. 'Come talk.' To the officer, he asked, 'You no arrest?'

'If we catch the guys who ran, maybe. We want to know what happened first.'

Outside, at the scene of the battle, Mick told his story to a pair of uniformed officers. He kept his version brief. The cops went along with the premise that boys will be boys. There'd been no knives, dusters, rocks, no hammers or screwdrivers. Fists and a few pieces of lumber, but no bats. Little more than an inept wrestling match as far as they could tell. Injuries would heal. The kid with a broken nose was driven to the hospital in a squad car, otherwise the lads were sent home to tend to their cuts and bruises.

*   *   *

Sergeant-Detective Émile Cinq-Mars was awakened from sleep. The night watch commander knew he'd been called to a certain address previously, so sent him again. The commander was short-handed. His best detective had been stripped from him and put on the dayshift. As retribution, he phoned Cinq-Mars after one o'clock in the morning.

Cinq-Mars could call Henri Casgrain to pitch in. They were supposed to work in pairs, but he'd been disruptive enough to his new partner's routine, so didn't bother him. The uniforms filled him in on an altercation where the robberies had occurred. Another night in Park Ex, they summed up, now that it was summer.

Cinq-Mars agreed they had the season right; otherwise, very little made sense. How did local boys know that outsiders were coming? Occasionally, fights were booked, but usually on neutral turf, not on one side's home ground. Late at night in a lane was not something he'd heard before. What set it off? There had to be a spark beyond boys being boys. More importantly, what was the connection, if any, between recent criminal activity and this brawl?

The one to talk to, he was told, was the janitor's kid.

'Why him?' Cinq-Mars asked a uniform.

'I wouldn't call him a ringleader.'

'Sounds like you want to call him something.'

'He seems to know more about it. Some kids had no clue why they were fighting.'

That also made no sense. 'Names? Addresses?'

'A few from this side got away. Everybody on the other side ran off. Those we spoke to, yeah, names and addresses. I'll find the sheet for you.'

Cinq-Mars waited in the lane and gazed up at the apartment building where toasters had been stolen and a man knifed through the throat. Followed up by a roughhouse midnight brawl. He noticed something interesting and filed it away. Then he accepted the sheet from the returning officer and folded it to fit his jacket's inner pocket.

The boy and his dad had gone to bed. His bedroom being in the rear of the apartment, Mick answered the knock on the back door.

'You look beat up,' Cinq-Mars said.

'Sucker-punched.'

The boy was wearing the basketball jersey and sweatpants he slept in. 'Mind getting dressed? I'd like to talk to you outside.'

'No prob. Give me a minute.'

He did. In less time than that, Mick came outside.

TWENTY-TWO

'You see my dilemma,' Cinq-Mars told the young man. 'How this looks.'

The youth didn't. Cinq-Mars expected that.

They sat on the bottom steps of the spiral staircase that ascended to the apartments, the eighteen-year-old two steps higher than the policeman.

'How does it look?' Mick asked.

He had recited a credible story. At Jarry Park, which lay beyond the tracks on the east side of Park Ex, a baseball game let out. Fans dispersed, heading for buses, their cars, or the walk home. Mick was there but had not attended the game. He hung with a few guys, chatting up girls who hailed from the neighborhood further east, on the other side of the large park. The girls were Italian, the boys a mix of Russians and Poles. They were getting along, flirting, when four Italian guys, who knew the girls, drew them toward their home district. Mick's group objected. They were seven strong. A fight seemed imminent and the two sides discussed how it could go down. Three among Mick's crew could sit it out, to keep the battle fair. The Italians, probably for good reason, didn't go for that. 'They didn't trust us. Probably smart. I mean, our guys sitting out wouldn't watch us get beat up, right? The Italians wanted more guys.'

'More guys,' Cinq-Mars repeated.

'I told them we weren't waiting around to find out if they had any friends. A lot of talk.'

'Seven on four,' Cinq-Mars acknowledged. 'A nice advantage.'

'They said they'd come to our lane later. Midnight. How did they know our lane? A girl told them, turns out. I guess we mentioned it to her. What could we do? We agreed to fight. I added a few bodies. Not enough it turned out. Like they say, the rest is history. No big deal.'

'You see my dilemma,' Cinq-Mars repeated. 'This doesn't look good for you.'

Mick didn't get it. The detective explained his point.

'A gang broke into these apartments, and you have demonstrated to me that you can pull together a gang of young men on short notice. The uniform on duty told me that you organized your side into a U-shape or a V-shape to defend yourselves. Neighbors reported that, also. So, you can pull a gang together, Mick, then direct the gang to defend itself. We didn't only have burglaries here. We had a murder. You haven't implicated yourself in that, but let's face it, you've climbed up the ladder to being a suspect.'

'A suspect?' The boy took that in. The suggestion hadn't occurred to him. 'Seriously?'

'Seriously,' Cinq-Mars assured him. 'Anything you want to say? I appreciate a man who wants to be a man and come clean.'

'I got nothing to come clean about. I came clean already about the fight.'

'The robberies?'

'Nothing to do with me.'

'Can you prove where you were? Who you were with?'

'I told you. I was dropping acid. Guys won't want to say they were dropping with me.'

'They'd rather see you in jail. Good friends, huh?'

The boy shrugged. 'If I had to, I guess I could prove it.'

'That's probably true,' Cinq-Mars concurred. 'You could've been nowhere near the building when the robberies went down. Let me show you something. Follow me.'

The detective lumbered up and crossed the yard to the edge of the lane. Mick came along. Earlier, Cinq-Mars had spied an effect of moonlight. In the narrow range of sky afforded by the laneway, the moon itself was not visible.

'Turn around.'

They faced the building.

'What do you see?'

'What do you think? An apartment building. Where I live.'

'Go on. What else?'

The boy took a longer look, then didn't want to say.

'Tell me,' Cinq-Mars encouraged him.

Still no reply.

'Can you or can you not see the chalk marks?'

'Those? Yeah.'

'Kind of glow in the dark, don't they? I noticed that before. When it's dark, they pick up the lights in the lane, or from the moon. They glow.'

'Yeah,' he said. 'I see that.'

'Then you see my dilemma.'

'What' – he wanted to throw in an expletive but didn't – 'dilemma?'

'You can call a gang together. You can instruct a gang on a combat formation and they do what you say. You could very easily have marked these apartments – you have easy access. After that, you could have dropped acid while everything else was going down. Stayed clear. High and dry. Not necessarily innocent. That's my dilemma.'

The boy crossed his arms. 'Wasn't me,' he said.

'We'll see, Mick. I hope if anything comes up that can help me, you'll let me know. That's the only way I'll be able to help you, whether you're innocent or not. For now, go on back to bed. That's where I'm going. Goodnight, Mick.'

The boy didn't say goodnight, or anything else. Cinq-Mars remained standing where he was, and observed the boy return to his basement apartment. The door was opened by his father and shut behind him. Cinq-Mars headed back down the lane where he'd parked his Volkswagen.

'Copper!' roared a voice from on high. As though God, or an illustrious devil, wanted a word.

Cinq-Mars hadn't gone far. He turned and looked up, spotting the Bombardier on his balcony. Moira Ellibee was fastened to his side. 'Lady wants to talk to you.'

The lady had an effective method of gaining his attention.

Cinq-Mars took a breath, calculated the possible pros and cons of this solicitation, and chose not to resist. He returned and climbed the exterior stairs.

The Bombardier had departed by the time Cinq-Mars reached the top floor. He was to be alone with Moira, who insisted he enter her apartment. An angel on one shoulder counseled, '*Run!*' The angel on the opposite side: '*You're armed. Go in.*' He wasn't certain who was the good angel, who the bad. Either way, he went inside.

He was immediately glad to have done so.

'Willy was here,' Moira told him. 'He came for clothes, I think. Belongings. He was here.'

'Here?' Cinq-Mars remained skeptical at first. 'In this apartment.'

'Don't be silly. In his own apartment. He doesn't keep his clothes in mine.'

'How do you know he was here?'

'I saw him. I talked to him. He seems good. A little agitated. I calmed him down. Don't ask me how.'

'Where was he going?'

'Didn't say. He wouldn't, would he? Mum's the word with our Willy.'

'So he came by for his clothes.'

'What he could carry away, yes. I don't think he took a lot. I guess he's a man on the run now. Travels light.'

'What did you talk about? You said you spoke?'

'I wanted to know if he was planning to take his cameras with him. He seemed upset by the question. I don't think he remembered that I know about the cameras. I helped install them. I played a small part, anyway. It bothers me that he didn't remember that.'

'Moira,' Cinq-Mars said, 'what cameras?'

'The ones,' she said, 'in the roof.'

He remained mute a moment. Then asked, '*In* the roof. Not on?'

'In,' Moira Ellibee confirmed.

TWENTY-THREE

A fresh country morning. Summer firmly in the air at last. The Mafioso don, Giuseppe 'Joe' Ciampini, drove into town in the burgundy rear seat of his Chrysler New Yorker. His car of choice. He disdained the gangster cliché of the Cadillac.

'Announce who you are, why?' Two men, his driver and bodyguard, had come out to fetch him in a separate vehicle, a Caddy, that would remain on his property until their return. The two sat in the front seats of the boss's vehicle, Ciampini in back. He never traveled without a chauffeur, and lately the bodyguard made sense. Way of the world now. Nobody knew how to keep the peace. He had a guy blown out of his apartment onto the street in pieces, and nobody could find all the pieces. Punks today. They had no clue. To swat a fly you fire a bazooka? Who wants to bring the attention? When Ciampini slipped into the plush rear seat of his car his bodyguard handed him the morning newspaper and no one said a word until he was willing to speak up. That would take about ten minutes while he caught up on the news.

The drive steered them down a pleasant country road. They slowed for a tractor pulling a hay wagon. 'Don't honk,' Ciampini instructed, without bothering to look up, his first words of the day. A man could easily be lulled into thinking that out here everything was right with the world. Out here, a man might listen to the birds sing and follow along behind a hay wagon without giving a toot.

When the farmer came upon a spot to move over, he did, and the New Yorker pulled out and around the wagon.

Still reading, Ciampini spoke. 'How're you guys?'

'Good, boss. Good. You?'

The driver drove. The bodyguard did the talking, if there was any talking to do. Always the case when he came along.

'The Expos got beat again,' Ciampini lamented.

'The pitching.'

'They need another arm.'

'No argument, boss. None.'

He went quiet again with his nose in the paper. Once he had double-checked the financial pages and scanned the stock listings, he folded the paper neatly to a quarter its size and tucked it down on the seat beside him. By this time they were merging onto the expressway to draw them into Montreal.

The bodyguard figured he'd raise the subject uppermost on his mind. 'Boss, I know you said last night not to worry about it or nothing like that, so I'm not worrying myself, but I still never heard from Teddy. You? No answer when I call.'

'Don't worry about it. Nothing I could say on the phone.'

'He's all right then? Our Teddy? Good. That's good.'

'Not that good. Worms in his eyes by now.'

The bodyguard turned part way around in his seat. Not easily. He was a big man who found it hard to maneuver his form. His jaw went slack. The driver, a large but less substantial man, also looked back. He returned his eyes to the road except to glance over at the bodyguard. This seemed like a crisis.

'Our Teddy,' the bodyguard said. 'That's a sin.'

'It hurts me,' Ciampini admitted.

'Massimo did this?'

'Worms slide through his eyes, too.'

Another jolt. 'With Massimo they're supposed to be, the worms. Who then?'

'Don't ask.'

'Jesus's mother and Joseph's dad. Poor Teddy.'

'Yeah. Poor Teddy. I guess he got slow in his old age. A lesson to everybody.'

The two men in front took that as a warning directed at them. They glanced at each other but had nothing more they dared say. They had questions they didn't want to ask. They were hoping to hear the answers anyway.

'Who can tell me what Willy does for us on a daily basis? You guys know?'

The bodyguard volunteered a reply. He twisted his torso around again. 'He's like the guy in the middle. Isn't that right?'

'How you figure?' Ciampini put to him. As if he was testing the man's knowledge.

'Like, for example, if a gun is gonna change hands, right, there's a buyer and a seller. The buyer could be dirty, a cop, the seller could be dirty too, an enemy. One way or the other it could be a trap. The consequences, they're worse if we're talking about drugs and money. Or the women we move in bulk. You never know. With Willy, see, you know. He does the buying or the selling. Depends on the situation. He negotiates the fee. Either way, we know he's not dirty, right? None of us gets nailed, because he's representing us. Somebody gets nailed – well, look at that, it's only Willy. He goes down, it's him, not one of us. Better that way for everybody that he's in the middle.'

'Maybe not for Willy.'

'Maybe not for him, no, but it's only Willy.'

'We stay clean because Willy is exposed. He stays clean because he's good at it. That's what you say,' Ciampini summed up.

'That's right. Isn't that right?'

'Seems that way.' The boss propped an elbow on the window frame and with his elevated hand rubbed his chin. He had another question for them. 'OK, if that's true, then why do we want him dead?'

No one was quick with a reply.

They drove on in silence. Mile by mile, more traffic clustered along the route.

Eventually, Ciampini remarked, 'Do you remember what Massi did wrong in his life?'

Everybody knew. The men in front assumed the question to be rhetorical and remained mute. They merely nodded.

Ciampini answered his own query. 'His old man owned the TV store. The Dime took his television there. We put two and two together. We did. We figure it's Massimo living out in the suburbs pulling the plug on the organization. He's the one. It's him. But what do we know for sure, really? Nothing. We'll never know now. Worms are squirming down his throat, so he won't say nothing to us.'

Something in the old man's tone. The boys in front didn't like this. As though they were suffering his unprovoked rebuke. They both felt that way. They were aware of an assumption, one they didn't want to admit to or provoke further.

'We let Massi think he's going to do Willy, right?' Ciampini continued. 'Before he gets to do it, Teddy will do him. That takes care of Massimo. Willy helps with the body, the digging. Then Teddy takes care of Willy. Tic tac toe. That's the plan. Anything wrong with that plan?'

'Don't know, boss,' the bodyguard admitted. The plan struck him as being foolproof. Pretty damn brilliant. Pretty sweet. Except that the guy who was supposed to walk away didn't walk away. Maybe nobody did.

'Willy's smart,' Ciampini said. 'Nobody thought about that. That's what went wrong with the plan. Willy's smart. Goodbye, Teddy.'

'Willy? Willy did Teddy? Willy? That fucker. Boss, we'll find him. For sure, we get him.'

'No. You won't. You'll let him be or be next. You follow?'

'We'll let him be. Whatever you say, boss. Can I ask why, but?'

'You can ask,' Ciampini said. He didn't answer the question. 'Why'd we decide to take out Willy? Ever wonder? Because a man we don't know about – we hear he's a killer from LA, some Russian circus bear – comes into town and what's his purpose? To take out our Willy. Why? That's the question. Except that Willy takes out the guy from LA. How? That's the next best question. Is something up with Willy we don't know nothing about? Is he spoiled? Has he gone to rot? Must be the case. Our enemies must be working him if they want him iced. Otherwise, he's got nothing to do with them, right? Plus, it's in our heads like electric shock: *he* kills the killer? Our Willy? How come our Willy can do that? Our Willy can't do that. He's not capable. What is he, a tough guy now? What do we know about him anyway? We start to think it's like it is with Massimo. They both must go. Now, who was real busy promoting that point of view, I'm asking? I'm asking you. Who made the case? It wasn't you guys, I remember that. Who was it among us so sure Willy and Massimo had to go to the worms, the both?'

Neither man wanted to say. Answering a question like that could land a person in treacherous territory. Better if Ciampini answered his own question once again.

He did. 'Pasquale. You remember?'

Willy had provoked the thought. It had swirled around Ciampini's head. Willy said to let suspicion rain down on the man who wanted suspicion to rain down on him. Willy made a good case, saving his own life that way, for now, altering the course of action.

'Yeah, boss,' the bodyguard admitted. 'I remember that.'

'Me too,' the driver said, speaking for the first time.

'Pasquale,' Ciampini repeated. 'He was so sure, eh? Massi had to go because his old man's shop did the TV repair. But what does that prove? Tell me this, when was the exact day when Massimo got so stupid? He used his old man's store to plant a bomb in a TV? That's way too dumb even for Massimo. Since when is he so brilliant to make a mistake like that? Nobody asked that question. Then Willy, he had to go because he was marked. Who knows the reason? We don't know what he's been up to. He knows too much and anyway, what do we really know about him? He works for us but he's not one of us. All that came up. Pasquale made the case. Le Gris, too, the both. Together, they made a good case.'

The men up front didn't join in. They didn't want to be part of a chorus if it was the wrong chorus to be part of.

'You two will keep your mouths shut,' Ciampini let them know. 'A leak, it came out of the mouth of both of you.'

'Mouth shut, boss. Sealed like a rock.'

As though the two of them had only the one pair of lips.

'You bet,' the driver said. 'You can count on us.'

'I have no doubt,' Ciampini said. 'About Pasquale, I'm looking into this. Le Gris, too. No more rash decisions around here. Too many guys are feeding their balls to the worms. We can't afford no more. Except maybe Pasquale. Maybe Le Gris. That's something I'll find out. I'm looking into that.'

'If you need help with anything, boss, ask me.'

'I don't ask. I tell.'

'Anything you want, boss.'

'That's all right. I got a man on it.'

'If you don't mind my saying, boss, I hope he's somebody you can trust. Trust him like you can trust one of us.'

'I'll find out. That's part of it. To find that out.'

The men up front didn't understand that last statement, but they declined to question him further. Too risky. Besides, they wanted quiet time to grieve. Massimo The Coat and Teddy The Bear, long-time colleagues, were gone. They'd almost been pals. A surprise and a sorrow, although they were unsure if their sadness was something they should own up to or not.

'Willy did Teddy,' Ciampini said. 'Leave him alone about that. For now. Time comes I change my mind, I'll let you know. Take your revenge then. Only if I say so. Only when I say.'

'OK, boss.'

That made sense. They drove on into the city. The streets opened before them, swallowing them into their usual urgency and the cacophony typical of morning's mayhem. As though a street wasn't a street in Montreal until some guy toted his massive belly over a jackhammer and jackhammered away.

The dust. The noise. The bedlam of morning.

TWENTY-FOUR

Coalface lied. He lied.

The man who called himself Willy was not going to tell the boss anything the boss might already know. Far too dangerous. Since he had no idea what the boss knew or didn't know, he kept the factual information he possessed to himself. Had he said anything the boss knew to be false, even if he didn't know that it was false himself, he'd be a dead man. Within the minute. As well, if he told only the truth but it turned out that the boss already knew what he had to say, he'd be seen as unnecessary. Therefore expendable. He had to spin a yarn that made sense, one that would hold together, one that would set himself loose to learn more. To do that he needed to extend the boundaries of what was known and perceived.

He needed to convince others that his life was necessary. That the space he occupied could benefit them. He had to concoct a lie, a tale, to ensure that his news was news to the boss, and that the boss would want to hear more of the story. The idea being that if he did plumb the depths of what was going on, then and only then could he return with what was true. Only then could he provide his boss with sufficient knowledge to sustain his existence as someone whose life was worth maintaining.

He needed to push his end game a little further. He needed more time.

He would not be looking into the actions of the Hells Angels. Far from it. That had been a resourceful, a knowledgeable, lie. He was ahead of the game on that one. He'd told the boss what was coming, because it made sense and was believable because it was true. Yet Willy knew enough to know that what was coming remained a long way off. The Hells were still putting two-and-two together. They'd not arrived at their D-Day landing just yet. They weren't ready to embark. Preparation stage only. Mum's the word. In the meantime, another challenge was afoot, one that had gone undetected. He knew very little about it. No one did. He'd take aim at this matter and not signal his trajectory until after the arrow of his life struck the mark.

He was still way undercover. That's what no one knew. Not those he spied on and gathered intelligence against. Not those for whom, supposedly, he was working. With pay, but without acknowledgment. This was the only way to go to the heart of the matter and blow it to smithereens.

His handlers, who from the outset were not permitted to handle him, agreed. He was going so deep that everyday contact was out of the question. Forge ahead on his own, under his own rules and with his own schedule and guidance. He alone would determine the results and when to reveal them. He helped with this and that along the way. His true masters reaped rewards. But only in secret. He kept his eyes on the greater prize personal to him: ripping the racketeers apart at the seams, not only in Montreal, but in the States as well.

After all this time, he wasn't quite there yet.

He knew it, too.

He might never be.

In this horserace, if he fell a nose short, it might as well be a furlong. He'd fail. He'd trail the field.

For the first time in his life, Willy was admitting that he required help. For the first time he was willing to seek it out, too. In his line of work, he knew that nothing – absolutely nothing – was more dangerous than trying to make and solidify an alliance. It's why he'd never done so, why he'd stayed under on his own. The time had come to alter his circumstances. Although he really had no clue how, he figured he'd find a way.

A start was the best that he could manage for now.

Something to begin the process, then he'd follow through.

TWENTY-FIVE

The worse for wear after his extended night, Sergeant-Detective Émile Cinq-Mars fell back on a copious intake of caffeine. He had clocked between five and six hours of sleep, not consecutively. His go-to breakfast when in a rush – bagel with cream cheese – was consumed with crocodile-like efficiency. Lately, quickie breakfasts were becoming routine, as being in a hurry had become a habit.

He lugged himself into work where he introduced Casgrain to the dayshift in the suburban *poste*. His new partner noticed the telltale dark rings under his eyes.

'Émile, did you have a nightcap after our nightcap?' As far as family man Detective Henri Casgrain was concerned, single men could dump their social lives in the waste bin.

'Am I under investigation? You work for Internal now?'

They were seated at side-by-side desks. Casgrain's abysmal posture was more pronounced when he slumped forward in a chair. With his bald pate, white mustache and cute bulbous nose he resembled a happily sedated garden gnome.

'Tired, Émile? Midnight oil?'

'I was called out. Notice, I let you enjoy your beauty sleep. You need it. You can thank me now or owe me a massive favor later.' Unable to prevent one coming on, Cinq-Mars emitted a broad yawn as though to underscore his sacrifice.

'What call?'

'Our murder scene. The toaster heist.' Cinq-Mars filled him in on the brawl and his talks with residents there. He brought up the cameras mentioned by Moira Ellibee.

'I saw no cameras,' Casgrain noted.

'Sounds nuts. And she's nuts. Still, she might be on to something. You wanted to check out the building anyway. We can look for cameras while we're at it. I sure as hell wasn't climbing up in the dark last night, but I have no qualms sending you up a ladder in daylight.'

Glancing up, Cinq-Mars swiveled in his chair as Captain Delacroix arrived for the day and rushed past his desk. 'Cap! Hang on. Meet the new man: Detective Henri Casgrain.'

Delacroix stopped, turned back, checked the new fellow out. Hunched over, with that mustache and those droopy eyes, the new guy in his mind resembled an under-the-bridge troll. The captain offered his hand. 'I think we've met,' he said.

'We have, sir,' Casgrain agreed. 'Back in time.' They shook.

'You're welcome here, Detective. Between you, me and the bedpost, I'm not happy with how you came through the door.'

'Me neither. Not my idea.'

'Good to hear. Don't want it to become somebody's habit. Are you listening, Cinq-Mars?'

'A one-time thing, Cap.'

'Better be. His previous partner,' Delacroix reminded Casgrain, 'lasted a day. May he rest in peace. You know about that. Did you know that his partner before Geoffrion was also shot? Took early retirement. You see where I'm going with this. I mean it when I say good luck.'

'Ah, thanks, Captain.'

'Requisition request,' Cinq-Mars cut in. 'Unusual one, boss. Emergency basis.'

'Good luck with that.' He was about to walk away and turned his back to do so.

'Two Polaroid cameras, Cap. Film to go with them.'

Delacroix stopped and faced him again. 'What for?'

'I can explain. I'd rather not. Trust me, money well spent.'

'Are nude women involved?'

'Course not.'

'Too bad.' This was meant as a joke. Captain Delacroix was a straighter arrow than any ascetic in a cave. His spine, some said, was a ramrod inserted up his rectum at birth. As usual, he laughed at his own joke, and as usual he laughed alone.

Cinq-Mars placated him on the attempt at humor. 'Good one, Cap.'

Delacroix declared, 'One camera only. Take it or leave it,' and carried on to his office.

Casgrain asked in his wake, 'Polaroids?'

Cinq-Mars ignored the question. 'Here's a list of the brawlers from last night. The ones who hung around long enough to show ID. Anything strike you?'

Casgrain gave the names a glance. 'Russian. Polish-sounding. Ukrainian. Others from that part of the world.'

'No English. No French. Zero Italians.'

'You're saying the pattern's no accident?'

'Gangs form for different reasons. Different criteria. Ethnic origin, often a factor.'

'The Polaroids?'

'I want pictures of the brawlers. I'm putting together a photo album. Come on. Camera shop's nearby.'

Cinq-Mars fostered the notion that the toaster thieves were on a test run or training mission. Casgrain augmented that idea, speculating that if the culprits were learning the ropes, it followed that they'd make mistakes. The theory was one Cinq-Mars was willing to test, and now with the tip about cameras, a return to the apartments took on fresh import.

Initially, outside Willy's apartment, they saw no sign of cameras. Casgrain, in wandering the full length of the hall beyond Moira Ellibee's door, detected a wire leading from an overhead light. It traced the seam where the ceiling met the wall, then dropped down in the corner and followed the rim of the baseboard after that. It could be the wire for the light fixture, but why would it not be inside the ceiling? Sure enough, the wire entered a hole drilled into Willy's apartment. Painted the same color as the ceiling when on the ceiling, and the color of the walls when on a wall. Subtle shades of beige.

'Let's find a chair,' Cinq-Mars suggested. 'I prefer not to announce myself to Moira. One of these two doors is either the Bombardier's or the Spitter's. Either guy can lend us a chair.'

Better, the Bombardier offered a stepladder, then graciously shut his door behind him. Casgrain noticed how the man had been acutely curious yet had backed off anyway.

'Émile, I see what you do. You glare. People slink away. Good technique.'

'My nose is slightly large, some say. It seems the right size to me. When I stare down my nose at folks, a few get nervous. They don't stare back because they're embarrassed that they want to. Their problem, not mine.'

'*Slightly large*, Émile, is not an understatement. It's an oxymoron.'

He loved being with a partner who could use a word like oxymoron, even if he used it improperly. He warned, 'Don't go there. Anything you say I've heard before.'

They were setting up the ladder beneath the lamp.

'Then you probably heard,' Casgrain teased, 'that people want to ski off it.'

'Grade Two when that one came up the first time. A toboggan run, back then. If you want to make fun, be original.'

'I accept the challenge.'

Casgrain went up the ladder. He peered over the lip of the shade.

'Guess what?' he asked.

'Camera?'

'Yup.'

They left the stepladder outside Willy's door, went downstairs and walked around the block to return via the lane. They could enter Willy's place through the unlocked rear door. In the apartment, they found where the wire from the front corridor entered behind a bookcase, then followed a baseboard to terminate in the dining room. It looked as innocuous as a discontinued wire to nowhere, once again painted the same color as the walls. Two more wires terminated nearby, arriving from the opposite direction.

Cinq-Mars studied the dust marks on the surface of the small mahogany cabinet. Where a toaster had been left behind.

'He had two screens. Took them both away when he beat it out of here.'

'He saw his attacker come up the back stairs. Maybe among thieves,' Casgrain noted.

'Or he came home and played back a film. If he'd been recording. That would warn him if somebody was already inside. Our guy creeps into the bedroom, jumps open the closet door and knifes him through the windpipe.'

'Or,' Casgrain postulated, 'if he watched him come up the back stairs he ducked under the bed. When the assassin hides in the closet to wait for him to come home, our guy slides out from under the bed and does the dirty.'

'Either way, he might strip,' Cinq-Mars chipped in. 'Pretend he's getting ready for bed.'

'The killer waits in the closet for his victim to undress and crawl into the sack.'

'Instead, our boy rips open the door and slams him with a butcher's knife. Naked, the blood that splatters him washes off in the shower.'

'He dries himself off. Gets dressed in fresh duds. Removes all trace of his existence and blood on his clothes by getting rid of those clothes. He cuts the wires from the cameras and takes out the screens.'

'Let's check for more cameras. Moira told me where to look.'

They couldn't accomplish the next task without acquiring an audience. The Bombardier thought he was helping by yelling down to the lane, 'Nothing to see here! Everybody! Disperse! Go about your business! Scram! Don't cha got nothing better to do with your lives today?' He himself did not and his barrage assured that the viewing audience would be large. After hauling the ladder out from the corridor, Detective Casgrain grudgingly climbed onto the roof. On his belly, he peered back over the ledge. At opposite corners above the narrow balcony, half-sized bricks, protected from the elements, replaced full-sized ones, permitting cavities behind them. Both contained cameras. Their wires went up, unnoticed, onto the roof, coming down above Willy's back door where they entered the apartment. From there, they ran back to the cabinet where at least two screens had been set up but were now gone.

'Do you think the robbery's on tape?' Casgrain wondered, back in the living room.

'Who's that lucky?'

'People say you are. Or were they being mean?'

Success on the job was dismissed as luck by many. 'Depends how sophisticated our man is,' he mused. 'Can't imagine he was interested in evidence, only in security. If there's a tape, why would he keep it?'

'Either way, the man was frightened. Or big-time paranoid.'

'Paranoid and sophisticated. Could be our guy. Could be Coalface.'

'No evidence to support that. Anyway, how do we find him now?'

Cinq-Mars mentioned the mob funerals, that Touton might be able to identify the missing man if he turned up there. 'A longshot. Touton only saw him from a distance.'

'You could show the residents photos of mourners we can't identify. Won't be that many. They could say if one of them is Willy or not.'

'Hey, you're not just another pretty face with a mustache.'

'Like you're not just another huge nose. Although that's debatable. Yours is unique. Hey, have you ever used it as a shovel?'

'Not since high school,' Cinq-Mars assured him. 'Back when it was first suggested.'

'I'll keep trying. Do we canvas the building again?'

'We do. Find out how these beginners butchered the robbery.'

'Don't kid me, Émile. You're not counting on that, either.'

'Henri, it's your idea. How can it fail?'

They confirmed that rookie thieves were prone to err. Nothing that might tip their own investigation – officially they had no jurisdiction to call it that. Glass in the doors had been repaired, and Casgrain discovered a canister that contained debris. Shards of glass, primarily, including sections cut out by toaster crooks. On one, a few dots of blood. Cinq-Mars discerned threads with a close examination. 'A cloth glove. A gardener's, something like that.'

'Put out an APB for a thief with a cut thumb and a few threads missing from his glove. We'll haul in ten thousand gardeners over the next week.'

'We could do that,' Cinq-Mars deadpanned. 'Or check the thumbs of the young guys on our list. In case.'

Fair enough. They both knew they might as well be looking through the lens of a telescope while searching for galaxies extinguished for millennia. Still, their work paid homage to the theory that mistakes can happen, especially with respect to junior thieves. When mistakes were interbred with related errors, misshapen progeny might form.

The theory was borne out in the apartment of the woman Cinq-Mars referred to as Florence the Hen. She kept eggs in a basket and baked pies. Her kitchen floor had been washed since the break-in, but she pointed out where a culprit's footprints remained visible on her balcony, and partially on the steel stairs going down. The thief had stepped through flour dust on her floor where she baked her pies for morning deliveries. He then tracked the imprint of his shoes behind him for a distance.

'Let's play Cinderella. Canvas the neighborhood, Émile. Check everyone's shoes.'

'We can do that. Or check the footprints made by the guys whose names are on our list. Do it while we're checking their thumbs.'

That seemed almost as viable as it was absurd.

They thought they were done when Cinq-Mars spotted Mick on the lane below them.

'Hang on a sec!' he called down to him.

'You there! Mick!' the Bombardier echoed at full throttle. 'Hang on a second!'

'It's OK,' Cinq-Mars said. 'I got this.'

The Bombardier shrugged. 'Helping the Man,' he said. 'I'm a good citizen.'

The boy and his dad waited for him to descend. Casgrain followed along behind. He had met the father on his first day and the two greeted each other.

'I need a photograph,' Cinq-Mars said to Mick. 'Mind?'

He gave the boy no chance to respond and snapped the Polaroid without bothering to look through the viewfinder. Then he, Mick and his dad watched the miracle of the photograph developing on a stair and in the shade. Everyone agreed that it was amazing, and the purpose of the snapshot was almost lost.

'What's this for?' the dad inquired eventually.

'Routine,' Cinq-Mars told him. 'Helps me keep track. Mick, I know who you are. In your case, I wanted to test the camera. Pretty amazing, don't you think?'

They gazed at the snap again as the details sharpened. Mick, and in the background, his dad, gradually came into sharp focus.

'What's the play?' Casgrain wanted to know when they were on their own again, walking back to their unit.

'Track down the names on our list. Interview them. Ask about the brawl, be cute about the robbery. And no, Henri, I'm not checking their footprints.'

'I'm not checking their thumbs either, unless I see blood or a bandage.'

'Agreed.' Cinq-Mars shook an open palm in the air. 'These boys were on hand for the fight last night. Let's come around to the toaster heist at an angle, see what that brings. Also, I want their Polaroids. I need to show them to someone who was at Johnny Bondar's party. I want to find out if any of our young brawlers were friends of his. If so, who, how many, and what do they know about him or about anything at all.'

Casgrain scanned the list again. 'Not everyone lives in Park Ex. No one's far away. We can get through this.'

'Want to be the photographer?'

'Sure. Be aware, I have an artistic side.'

'Oh God. Don't take twenty shots to get the perfect one.'

'Don't interfere with my craft. Why'd you want two cameras, anyway?'

'I didn't. I needed to give Delacroix something he could say no to. Pure hustle, that part.'

Casgrain whistled, impressed. 'Keeping an eye on you.'

'Keep your eyes peeled for a cut finger and a frayed cloth glove.'

'Not to mention flour on some guy's boots.'

They smiled together, knowing that such incidental clues could make a needle in a haystack look like a guided missile on a launchpad.

TWENTY-SIX

Afternoon visits to a strip club on Boulevard St Laurent were neither common nor unusual for Willy. His favorite spot was convenient to his home – now his former home – halfway between Park Ex and downtown. He preferred the relaxed insouciance of spending midday on a barstool to the gyrating frenzy of an evening in the place. For one thing, the dancers were often in a better mood.

More talkative by day. Case by case, more compliant.

Shy loners showed up in the afternoon. Never belligerent, generally less creepy. Like the strippers, he judged them on a case-by-case basis. He looked like one himself. Typically, they weren't drunks – alcohol was less expensive when waitresses kept their clothes on – and they weren't regulars. These were the once every month or two types, and the once a year or twice a decade on a whim types. They didn't want to wave bills in the air or stuff them in a girl's thong or clamor for a favorite's attention. They didn't pass around Cuban cigars. They desired only a glimpse of what life might be like if only life had been radically different.

He had another reason to arrive by daylight. The dancers and wait staff recognized that he was connected to the administration of their lives. What he did exactly was unclear. In the business in some way, and when he arrived in daylight it meant he was doing his job. Nothing remotely sad about that, even if he had a squirrel on, whereas arriving at night signified a transgression. As if he intended to take liberties on the sly. Once in a blue moon, he and a girl might decide to give each other a nudge on her afternoon break, then share a pot of tea or a joint. Or they might have long wandering conversations on the vagaries of life. None of that went down at night.

He went there both to do his job and to keep the company of friends, be they younger women or older hoods. Apart from customers, those who showed up during daylight hours included gangland heavies and their lightweight goons. Cronies all. He might have reason to chat to a few. From time to time, some niggling thing might need working out.

Bigger problems today. Such as who, if not the Mafia, sent a killer to his door, and why?

Other things, too. Such as what's to be done about it?

'Who stuck your face in a toilet after he forgot to flush?'

The day manager was an olden-days hood named Slew, from the easy time when the city was as corrupt as a politician both wired on smack and addicted to freakish sex. Back then, the city was overloaded with burlesque clubs and gambling dens. Brothels outnumbered churches in a city of churches. Cops being tough meant they troubled themselves to padlock a madam's broom closet while keeping the door to her boudoir open. That would show her. Those were the days, and that easy time was the envy of the younger crowd and gave old-timers, such as former hitman Slew O'Grady from the West End Irish, stories to tell while keeping one eye on the tiller and another on a john's dark gaze. In modern times, you had to know how to assess risk factor when you were no longer permitted to take a spooky guy outside and burn a testicle. He'd been warned *three times* not to touch the merchandise; in the old days he'd learn a lesson while he healed.

Now, to save that trouble, you had to intersect early. That required a good eye.

Slew had pulled hard time. He was closing in on seventy-five years of age. A killer in his day. His head didn't turn in that direction anymore, most folks believed. Willy knew better. He still carried around that old-world attitude and had proved in his time that he'd rather split ten years between the slammer and parole than spill the beans on a bud. His reward: the Hells allowed him to be a daytime manager amid an ever-flowing cascade of young beauties and loser inebriates. Or, at least, people thought so, and Slew was content to look the part. Willy knew better.

'What've you heard?' Willy inquired. He didn't bother to deny the crack about his face in a toilet, nor did he believe Slew was referring to his physical appearance. Slew had the aptitude to be metaphorical, while Willy possessed the wisdom to understand him when he spoke that way. That allowed the two of them to be confidants at the best of times, and at the worst of times they could look out for each other without arousing undue suspicion.

'Yo-yo-style. Up and down. You're out then back in. Ping-pong much? I only get the retread buzz down here on the sidewalk. What's happening up in the airwaves, man? First you're dead meat, then I hear you're an untouchable. You got an out-of-towner's braid in your hair. How does *that* make sense? Can I touch, see if you're still made of flesh? Not a stiff come back alive?'

'Pure wax, Slew. Taking time-off from Madame Tussauds.'

'Figures. The story I don't get? You offed a guy.'

'Trespassing in my closet. You can't do that.'

'Not allowed, huh? My house? I agree with you. He's dead. Your place? Maybe you call for help. Or run. You don't spike him.'

'I know. That part's confusing. But there's a limit. A killer in my closet pisses me off.'

'A limit. I guess. What'll it be, Willy? Beer or cheap champagne? Either way, it's on the house. In honor of your first official whack.'

'The usual, Slew. Thanks.'

Molson Ex.

Slew was sat beside him on a barstool. Now he went around behind the bar that was unattended and opened a fridge door. Uncapped a couple of cold ones. He stayed behind the bar. Spread his arms and hands wide, leaning forward against it.

'We're not square,' Slew reminded him.

'Did what I could.'

'Failed.'

'Hard case.'

Slew had warned him to keep a con named Johnny Bondar in prison. 'Who he wants to kill might be detrimental to my business.' Willy saw it as more complex than that. Johnny Bondar had been conscripted to kill a high-up Mafia manager in the name of jealousy and revenge. He was being conned. Who by? Slew didn't tell him that part, nor did he give him the scope of the enterprise. They exchanged metaphors to indicate that they understood the ramifications. War was never good for business when you did your business in the trenches.

'Did you take it up with Ciampini or not?' Slew had expected that he would, that Willy would cajole Ciampini to fix the situation before it became a situation. Instead, Willy wrote a report to Armand Touton.

'Put a different plan in motion,' Willy explained. 'A good one. Nobody knew they would move up the hearing, spring him early.'

That made sense to Slew. He'd heard that already. Reluctantly, he let his grievance drop. 'What brings you in?' Time for contemporary business. Given what was going on in their world, no way could this be a social call.

Across the street from the club stood a warehouse for carpets and tiles. A competitor in floorings had owned what was now the club's premises until it mysteriously burned. Resurrected as a nightclub open from noon, it maintained that industrial feel even as girls and women removed their clothing and writhed around a pole or on a stage floor. A thick wallet could order a private dance in public, or be private without the dancing. That was up to the sorry mark and his budget. Small backrooms existed that were difficult to access. People had to know you. Then a person, even one who was very well known, had to be guided through a series of locked doors, as in the slammer, tipping each doorman on the way in and out. Anybody who wanted out quickly after misbehaving or neglecting to pay in full – a rare occurrence but shit happens – was in trouble beyond his imagining. Begging was not a currency with value. In those rare cases, a man might live, but not without first ceding ownership to his life. Even enforcers considered the results tragic.

Hell's inferno had no fury like a stripper with a bruise.

Rules are rules, man. Like being offered options on a car. 'I can remove a thumb and three toes. Or an ear. Your choice.' There were backrooms notable for their sound insulation. 'Why are you complaining? Last guy it was an eye.' The begging that went on; if it did have currency, a man could be independently wealthy in no time. Some choices were tougher than others. 'You prefer, we can arrange a suicide. What'll it be?'

'I'm hunted,' Willy pointed out. 'Nobody knows why. Overall scheme, nobody cares except me, and I don't always.'

'Sorry to hear tell.'

'Life's a long drive, Slew. Map never showed the road was gravel.'

'Amen, buddy.'

'My situation is of no importance,' Willy calculated.

Slew concurred. 'It's the overall scheme.' He got it.

'That's why I'm here. You want to know what's up in the airwaves, but I want to know – more important, Ciampini wants to know – the sidewalk news. What's below the curb?'

The two men took their first slugs of beer for the day, then put their bottles down. Willy sat back, waited. Slew crossed his arms, stood straight.

'Anything in the wind that's recent? Developments?' Willy asked. 'Any thread unravel you can knit me a sweater?'

'Funny you put it that way, Willy,' Slew started in.

'Yeah? I'm not getting the joke.'

'Kind of your domain.'

His domain. Interesting. A connection? 'I don't want to brag or nothing, Slew, but what domain? I have a few.'

'Girls.'

He wouldn't call *girls* his domain. But he'd call it a connection, yes.

'What about them?'

'A slowdown, are you aware? A glitch. Has to do with Bondar being sprung.'

He wasn't aware, although the thought had occurred that trouble might brew. Dominic 'The Dime' Letourneau had been the principal supplier of young women from the hinterland of Quebec to the bars of Montreal. His activity concluded when his

TV incinerated his apartment with him in it. The next in line, Nic Jobin, was gunned down in a nightclub by a guy sprung from prison that same day who didn't appreciate being two-timed. Their deaths left the supply chain vacant at the top.

'Define glitch.'

'Never like The Dime or Nic Jobin were combing the boonies, right? They had their own supplier out on the road. The girls got funneled through that supplier to The Dime and Jobin. Then to the club managers.'

'Right. So talk to that supplier until the boss decides who's the new authority.'

'Exactly my thought. Other guys think the same way. The problem is, we don't know the road guy's identity. A hiccup. But we found it out from Jobin's secretary. A surprise. A pair of suppliers. Even better, right? Two connections, one in Sorel, one in Drummondville.'

'We'll talk to them. Keep the pipeline intact. Rebuild.'

'Too late.'

'It's never too late. Why say that?'

'Both dead.'

This, then, was a more serious disruption than anyone knew.

'That I did not know,' Willy said.

'Nobody's aware. Now you are. Tell Ciampini. Look, both guys went down a while back. One a couple of weeks ago. The other guy more like six weeks. Traffic accident, him. The other guy OD'd. Accidents? Flukes? Some say so. Some don't.'

'Who's talking?'

'It's in the airwaves.'

Willy thought about it. 'OK,' he said. 'Interesting in different ways. One guy's loss is another's guy's big opportunity, right? It's not like we can't rebuild the pipeline, have it flowing real quick.'

'You might expect that that's true.'

'It's not?'

'There's a glitch.'

'You told me that already,' Willy said. 'The two dead guys—'

'They're not the glitch. I haven't started on it yet. Building up to it.'

'Are we there yet?'

'Now we are. We get girls from the countryside and from the city. The locals, they show up with baggage.'

'Boyfriends. Parents. Other opportunities. Different priorities.'

'Like that. It goes on and on. A guy with a camera offers a mint and they're gone. Country girls . . .'

'Lonely. Unaware. Lost in the big city. More compliant. I get that. What's the glitch?'

'The Rabbit brings in the city girls. His role. You know that.'

Local thug. Notorious for brutality. He did grunt work for the Mafia and ran his own club. With the acquiescence of Ciampini he recruited city girls for all the other clubs.

'His supply's not dry,' Willy said. 'Can't be. Work with him until you're over the hump.'

'That's not it,' Slew said. He put his elbows down on the bar top and leaned closer to Willy to whisper. No one was remotely near them. 'Few months ago, The Rabbit comes in. Says he's got a corner. New supply. If we're ever short, count on him.'

'This is a side gambit? Ciampini's cut out?'

'Don't know. But he has an overstock. I'm guessing foreign. We didn't need them at the time and we're not opening new gates. But now, just like that, our supply line is snipped. Next girl who slips away with her deadbeat soulmate to run drugs from Panama, we have no quick replacement. Next one too sick to pose? The next OD? Next one who thinks she's free to marry? You get the picture.'

'You're saying The Rabbit's the only game right now.'

'With rigged machines. In the past, if he wanted too big a cut, we go heavy with The Dime. If The Dime plays favorites, sends the prettiest newbies to somebody with more taps, we go heavy with The Rabbit. Now? There's no competition. Supply line cut. Yet fresh supply is available. It's a move, Willy. I'm only telling you because you're a hunted man. You don't know why. I do. You know how the books were cooked with The Dime. How stuff got arranged. How a fix got done when a fix was required. You're the last man standing who understands how the deal goes down when the night comes up. Somebody thinks you need to be retired. Somebody tried to take you out, Willy. I'm giving you a clue why.'

Willy drank from his bottle, taking it all in. In coming here, he'd expected to learn something, not this much. 'Were you going to call?' he asked Slew. He also reverted to whispering.

'You have no phone, Willy. What should I do? Put out a missing person's bulletin? What does that do? I was waiting for you to come in is all. Bound to happen, one reason or another.'

'Yeah. I came in. Maybe I could use a little solace. There's that reason.'

'Up to you. You're a growing boy.'

'Better to keep my feet moving, you think?'

'Don't disagree.'

'That figures. Thanks, Slew.'

'For the beer, yeah. No problem. You got nothing else from me.'

'For the beer only. Thanks.'

'Hey, you're welcome.'

TWENTY-SEVEN

After lunch, Cinq-Mars chose to handle the driving and stopped at an address on Durocher Street, corner of Saint Roch. A narrow white brick walk-up with a semi-subterranean flat and a TV repair shop elevated above the pavement. An exterior staircase served the shop and an interior one continued to a third-floor flat. Homes for the working poor. Cinq-Mars seemed reluctant to be stopping there.

Henri Casgrain double-checked their service pad. 'Not on the list,' he pointed out.

'Different list,' Cinq-Mars murmured under his breath. 'I'll do this one on my own.'

'You don't need a photographer, or don't like my pictures?' Casgrain was hamming it up.

'No pictures,' Cinq-Mars said. He took a deeper breath. He might as well explain. 'This is a side adventure. A sorrowful one. I promised to look into this for . . . Well, for a friend.'

'A friend you're not sure is a friend.'

'Professional contact, let's say. A minister. Not government. Church. Protestant.'

'OK. We've got time. What's the sorrow part?' Casgrain had cottoned on to his partner's mood. He was clearly apprehensive.

They had done a good job of covering their list. At one stop, they were guided to a backyard by the mother of a brawler where they found four of the boys they were looking for. Two were brothers. That saved time. The boys put up no resistance to the camera and politely answered questions.

Cinq-Mars and Casgrain reviewed the fight in the lane with them and queried their whereabouts on the night of the break-ins. Each boy stood in as another's alibi, and in that sense their responses held up. Cinq-Mars had no mind to push. Not yet. No youth claimed to be home in bed, and they admitted to being together. Significant details. None confessed to being out on the town stealing toasters.

If these boys were forming the next ruthless gang, the city was not in urgent peril.

'A young woman's gone missing,' Cinq-Mars explained, answering Casgrain's question. 'Her clothes were found by the side of the river, down where the current is quick.'

'You think she was dumped? Not with her clothes onshore.'

'She's a floater. That part I don't doubt. Most likely, she did it on her own. A couple of possibilities. I'm told that swimmers go down there, especially in the spring when the water's frigid and the ice is breaking up or has recently melted. It's a new kick, to swim nude in ice water. The kids feel alive. A good swimmer can make it in and out if he – or she – doesn't succumb to hypothermia. The further out you go, the stronger the current, by a knot. Wander too far out and alone, people will call it suicide. We might never know for sure. In this case, did she get caught in the current? Did she plan to get caught? Or did she overestimate her strength? Did the cold get to her? Without a note, who can say?'

'No note. This house?'

'Her folks.'

'Jesus, Émile.'

'Like I said, I can do this one on my own.'

'Nope. Coming with.'

Although the men had plied coffee into their veins over lunch, they accepted the tea offered by the young woman's mother. Too polite to decline. The drowned girl – Debra – fit the mold Cinq-Mars anticipated. An adventurer. An interest in art; she had created a number of murals around town.

'What kind of murals?' Casgrain asked.

Cinq-Mars wished he hadn't.

'I choose to call them that,' the mother said. She pulled in her chin. A gesture of defiance. 'Some call them graffiti. I do not. Her walls are beautiful.'

Saying that evoked an emotional crunch. She gave it time to pass and the men waited. She was alone, her husband at work. Immigrants, they had been in their new country long enough to see their daughter integrate into a different culture. The mother's accent was distinctly British, specifically Liverpudlian, although she'd been born in Burma before being raised for most of her early life in Liverpool. Her husband in the merchant marine before settling in Canada. The daughter had bright and expressive, mischievous eyes, Cinq-Mars observed, according to the forest of photographs that lined the mantelpiece.

'Tell me where I can find the murals,' Cinq-Mars requested, and he copied a list of the streets where the illicit artwork might be viewed. He wanted to establish a sense of the girl. He also assured the mother that the search was continuing. Not that it was. The river was too massive, the current too swift, no one had a clue where to dredge. What he meant was that people lived, fished and worked on the river and alongside it; sooner or later the submerged corpse was likely to surface. In the sense that the police department was passively expecting a call someday, they were still looking for her.

While he could offer no comfort, a visit from a policeman seemed respectful in regard to her daughter. The mother dried her eyes and thanked them for their sympathy.

Outside, Cinq-Mars leaned up against the hood of their Ford, subdued.

'You helped, Émile,' Casgrain told him. 'You're good at this.'

'Not something I want to be good at.'

'It's the priest in you. Comes through.'

For a moment, it seemed that Cinq-Mars wasn't listening. He was following a girls' game of hopscotch kitty-corner from them.

Then he declared, 'The priest thing gets around. It was a long time ago.'

'Why didn't it happen?'

'Can you hack celibacy? Not me. The sad irony of it, Henri, is here I am, still without a lady in my life.'

'You thought wearing the uniform would get you a date?'

'I'm a country boy. I might have been that naive. First, I pursued becoming a veterinarian. Then didn't. When police work came along, I snapped it up.'

They both remained still, leaning on the car, immersed in the despondency of the moment.

'This girl,' Cinq-Mars mused. 'Debra. Creative. Artistic. An adventurer. A bit wild. I bet she preferred her work described as graffiti. Not as wall murals. Tough combination: creative like that and looking for action.'

'Why tough?'

He rocked his head from side to side a moment. 'Some kids who aren't hard enough for this world are still compelled to take it on. They won't hide. They won't run from risk. That's tough.' He took another deep inhale. 'We should get a move on.'

Casgrain patted down his mustache. He said, 'Celibacy didn't keep you from the priesthood, Émile.'

'Yes it did. I should know.' He tried to make light. 'If I knew it would be inflicted on me anyway, I might be a priest today.'

'Bullshit.'

'Excuse me?'

'Don't tell me you couldn't pass muster on celibacy. I don't know you, but I *know* you. Give you a challenge, you come through. Celibacy is the *excuse* you used to quit the priesthood. Something else drove you out.'

'Borderline heretic, I admit.'

'That's not it, either.'

These pronouncements, unprovoked, driven and forceful, caught Cinq-Mars off-guard.

'Why then, smartass? Why am I a cop, not a priest? Trust me, celibacy was a deal-breaker.'

Casgrain stood up as straight as he could with his warped posture. He looked at him briefly, then cast his gaze elsewhere. 'There's a reason you don't have a girlfriend, Émile. You didn't *choose* to be celibate, but you are. The priesthood still has a hold on you. I saw that inside. Upstairs, you weren't a cop, you were a priest.'

Cinq-Mars made a motion with his shoulders as though squirming through an invisible crowd. He went around to get in their car. In a way, his partner kept him on his feet by declining to follow suit. Casgrain leaned his elbows on the roofline of the car instead and kept talking.

'I'll tell you something for free, Émile. When you figure out why you left the priesthood, that's when you'll find a girlfriend. Not until. For now, you're out of luck, because you never owned up to why you're not a priest. That's why you're *still* a priest, and celibate.'

Cinq-Mars opened the driver's side door. 'It might be easier to go find a girlfriend than have this talk with you.'

'You tried it, Émile. How did that work out?'

'Will you knock it off?'

Henri laughed, freely, easily. He opened the passenger door finally. 'I'm curious. You were a young man in the sixties. What did you do during the crazy days?'

'I was a beat cop in the sixties. What do you think I did? I busted hippies.'

'I guess hippies weren't that much into cops.'

'I had a girlfriend, if that's what you're dying to find out. In fact, I busted my girlfriend back then.' The moment the words were out, Cinq-Mars regretted telling him that. A chapter he'd rather keep closed. Mentioning the episode rushed everything back to mind.

'You busted your girlfriend? You really are some kind of saint. An idiot, but a saint.'

'She wasn't my girlfriend when I busted her. She threw a rock at the Prime Minister during a demonstration. Remember the St Jean Baptiste Day riot? I chased her down. That's how we met. Later, we hit it off.'

'Then what happened?'

'We broke up. Politics did us in, maybe. Not meant to be.'

'A broken heart. I see that. That's all right. Better than not living. Since then? Do you still date the women you bust? Maybe that's your problem. Maybe you should date them first and *then* bust them. Keep them under arrest.'

'Funny. Haha. Nothing's worked out, that's all.'

'Instead, you live alone in a little monk's cell in Park Extension.

That's how you described it to me. You can't get a new life because you're stuck in your old one. Figure it out, Cinq-Mars.' They both clambered into the car. Cinq-Mars started the engine, hoping it would silence his partner. It didn't. 'Do your future girlfriend a favor, Émile.'

'Will you shut up? Thank you.'

'My advice? Don't bust the first woman you're attracted to. What did you do? Crack her head open then drag her away by the hair, caveman-style? Don't do that. Instead, go deep, figure out what your problem is. A man like you, smart, handsome, with only one major liability, being a cop – OK, two, your nose – the point is, you shouldn't have a hard time. You should be dating up a storm.'

'I see I'm going to regret having you as partner.' He turned the car off the curb, driving on.

'Yeah,' Casgrain said. 'Don't get comfortable with me around. Soon as we're done with this case, I want back on nights.' He said this kindly, a twinkle in his eye. Cinq-Mars gathered that he said everything with kindly intention.

'Soon as we're done here, I'm shipping you out,' Cinq-Mars confirmed, both in jest and somewhat seriously. Having a personal shrink on the job was not something he'd bargained on. Especially not someone who came across as half-assed good at it.

TWENTY-EIGHT

T he retired captain of the Night Patrol never referred to himself as a war hero, as his engagement in World War Two was limited to being wounded at Dieppe, then captured and force-marched through Europe to a POW camp in Poland. As war's end approached, Armand Touton was force-marched back to Germany before rescue by an American brigade. Not a hero, then, in the sense that he had saved no one and put no dent in an enemy's defenses. Yet his life in the military was decidedly heroic to many, an epic tale of fortitude and endurance.

No man is fearless, yet fear never governed his actions in a crisis, neither in combat nor in his years as a tough, street-smart cop. He was recklessly brave. The tabloids loved to splash his image across their front pages, once with a shotgun cracked open across a forearm, his coat bloodied from hand-to-hand combat that followed a gunfight. Usually, he wasn't covered in his own blood, except for telling scrapes across his knuckles. Many exceptionally violent men had endeavored to intimidate him. Those who lived, lived to regret it; presumably, those who died also regretted it. In his city and province, no officer of the law was held in such high esteem by the general population. Amidst the proud Québécois people, he was a folk hero, and wore his fame and executed his responsibilities with humility, valor and grace. Not always by the book. He exhibited a working-class, man-of-the-people, nails-tough elegance.

Now, in retirement, he rowed a boat.

Touton tilted the trolling motor out of the water; on a lovely sunny day, opting for the oars. He conned the shoreline toward the far end of the lake's tongue where the cabin-people lived. He never understood how anyone who lived on a lake did not fish. Many did, of course, but those who did not were happy to accept his excess of perch, frying them up for dinner. Today, he had plenty to go around. Despite his customary grumpy demeanor, the aging captain enjoyed the occasional interruption to his solitude. To their delight, he teased the children. He supposed that he was a peculiar fellow to them, a strange lonesome old guy from down the lake where nobody else lived.

In late afternoon, he motored back down the lake again, this time trading quiet for a bit of speed.

Home in his trailer, he checked his supplies. Bereft of worms. Short on coffee and fruit. Especially bananas. He thought about it, considered a nap first, then chose to head into the local village while he had the energy. A trip now left time for a nap before dinner, induced in part by the cocktail hour.

In town he turned into the dusty parking lot for the General Store, braked, slammed shut the driver's door of his Ford wagon and mounted the stairs. An old-timer who often lingered on the porch sat there. He lived two miles away and walked in supported by a cane. Together they shared a few pleasantries, talk of the weather and the fishing. Both critical aspects in life were fine, for a change. Inside, although no messages awaited him, he was informed by the bright yet laconic lad that 'Stuff came for you.'

'Stuff?'

'Like mail. Only it's not mail.'

He was led into the rear supply room. Three large canvas sacks were piled up, each with his name on a tag. They'd not been delivered by the Post Office, nor by any other agency.

'Some guy in a Pinto.'

The sacks had bulk and rattled when lifted. Not light, but not that heavy, either. He shook a sack violently to make sure it wouldn't explode. It didn't. Good thing. He untied the knot in the drawstring and peered inside. Quickly, he opened the other two bags. The contents the same in each.

The sacks contained a variety and multitude of used electric toasters.

'Help yourself,' he invited the lad who worked there. 'What you don't take home you can sell. It's stolen property, but who cares? I'm not a cop anymore. Knock yourself out.'

That said, he had a few things to think about. A message had been delivered and, retired or not, he had to figure out what it meant and how in the world this had come to pass.

TWENTY-NINE

Tracking down the last of the brawlers took time. The afternoon raced to a close as Émile Cinq-Mars backed into his usual parking spot when visiting the Reverend Alex Montour.

That the spot was perpetually available verged on the miraculous. Teasing himself, he wondered if her Protestant God or his Roman Catholic deity intervened.

Henri Casgrain was curious. 'Another drowned girl?'

'Don't stay for this one, Henri. Drive back to the *poste*. I'll walk home, then either get my car later or leave it. Safer in the lot than on these streets.'

'Is it?' Casgrain asked. The man patted down his mustache, a habit.

Cinq-Mars was confused. 'Safer? Sure. Probably.'

'I meant, is it another drowned girl?'

Cinq-Mars explained. 'This is the minister who's looking out for the girl's family.'

'Showing her my Polaroids?' Casgrain maintained a proprietary interest in the snaps.

'End of shift, Henri,' Cinq-Mars reiterated. 'Go home. No overtime. See your kids.'

'*My* pictures. *My* artwork. I'll go in with you. *Then* I'll go home.'

Casgrain meant to make fun of himself when he spoke of his photographs as artwork, although Cinq-Mars recognized the defense mechanism. He had diligently done a super job with the snapshots. He analyzed each one as it developed and critiqued the outcome, saying what could be better, what turned out well. Handing the task to him had been sheer serendipity, no big deal. He'd had no advance warning that the man would accept the task exactly as forewarned, as an art project. Cinq-Mars wanted and expected quick functional portraits; Casgrain desired memorable ones. He then made fun of himself before his boss did.

Cinq-Mars was amused, yet impressed, by his partner's steady hand and incisive eye. The man trained the camera's lens to capture personality and nuance. And character. Even when his subjects were unwilling to cooperate, or especially then, Casgrain succeeded. Cinq-Mars gleaned that the man's innate talent at detection stemmed from a genuine interest in what lurked beneath the human façade, which uncannily emerged from several portraits.

'Did I tell you? The minister's a woman.'

Casgrain had no response.

'That doesn't surprise you? Surprised me.'

'Émile, in what century were you born?'

'Don't give me that. Just because I don't say "cool" and "far out" doesn't make me Victorian.'

'Nobody says "far out" anymore. I'm supposed to be the old fogey, Émile. You're the young one. Try to keep that straight.'

They were climbing out of the car and locking up. Casgrain hitched his trousers. Cinq-Mars adjusted his holster where his pistol dug into his hip in the car seat.

'Henri, you coach these teams, baseball, hockey. Do they win or lose?'

'It's how you play the game, Émile.'

'You're saying they lose.'

'Some years.'

'Most years?'

'It's not about winning and losing.'

'That's old school. *Old*, old school. We young guys, we're into winning.'

'It's about building character.'

'Nope. Winning.'

'Having fun?'

'Nope. Winning.'

'Your generation sucks, the way you think.'

'And you're an old fogey. Saying "sucks" doesn't change that.'

'My kids taught me that one. What's the minister's name?'

'Alex. She sleeps with women.'

'What?'

'Are you shocked?'

'You are. That's why you mention it. Proves my point. You're from another century. How did you find that out?'

'She volunteered the information. Maybe to shock me. I'm not sure.'

'Alex what?'

'Montour. The Reverend Alex Montour.'

'Got it. She was at Bondar's party.'

'Helped get him out of jail. I tried keeping him in. From that, we're friends. Maybe.'

'And you don't want me here, why?'

'Not that. It's your kids. We have a deal. No overtime for you.'

'Well. Maybe a dribble.'

'A dribble, then.'

Cinq-Mars rang the doorbell.

'Hope she's still here,' he said.

She was. And showed them in.

The reverend had already received a call from the girl's mom and been filled in on the talk with the officers. 'Thank you, Émile.'

'I haven't helped yet.' Switching gears, he said, 'Alex, about Johnny Bondar's house party.'

The minister grimaced. 'Nothing new to report, Émile.'

Henri Casgrain's head came up. His partner was on a first-name basis with the minister. He smiled to himself and seemingly filed something away.

'The other night, we had a brawl in Park Ex. Detective Casgrain has taken Polaroids of a number of participants. I'd like to know if you recognize any young men, and specifically if you recall seeing them at the Bondar party. Will that be all right?'

She consented, and Casgrain stood and arranged the portraits on the desk facing her. He took care to keep each snapshot perfectly aligned with the others, as though presenting them at a formal gallery. The slowness with which he presented his pictures allowed Reverend Montour to undertake a careful study.

When all the snaps were down, Cinq-Mars asked, 'Recognize anyone?'

She identified a few of the boys by name.

'I'm pretty sure this young man was at the party. But I don't know him. These two were definitely there.' She indicated the brothers that the policemen had interviewed in a lane that morning. She waved a finger over a picture on the edge. 'And this one.'

Cinq-Mars double-checked. 'This boy was there?' He moved the picture closer to her.

'No, sorry. Not the boy. The man in the background.'

The one picture that Cinq-Mars had taken, not Casgrain. The snapshot of Mick and his dad. The minister was indicating that the dad, the janitor, had been at Bondar's party.

'The older man? Not the younger one?'

'That's right.'

Cinq-Mars inscribed notations on the back of the photos she identified while Casgrain gathered up the rest of his artwork.

'These are good pictures, by the way,' Reverend Montour said.

'Thanks,' Casgrain said.

'You took them, Detective? You missed your calling.'

'I find Polaroids to be, you know, somewhat limiting.'

'You did very well.'

'Thanks,' he said again. Almost wistful in his appreciation of her compliment.

Cinq-Mars thanked her upon departing. He wanted to kick up his heels on the street. A good end to their workday.

Casgrain spoke up. 'Interesting, Émile. You're formal with some people yet insist on informality with others. First-name basis with the minister. I'm learning about you.'

'You're putting me under a microscope again. Mind saving that for the bad guys?'

'You wanted me as a partner, Émile. What you get is what you get. Now, since you forced me to work overtime—'

Casgrain put up a hand to block the obvious protest coming back at him.

'Buy me an ice cream cone before we head in,' Casgrain said.

'Ah, what? *What*?'

'We'll review the case.'

They did exactly that, licking ice cream while mulling the investigation. The first real taste of summer while discussing the cameras, the young guys, the missing man known as Willy, Bondar's association with at least a few of the brawlers, the janitor's association with Bondar, the homicide detectives' appearance at the party, Bondar killing an associate of a man assassinated by a bomb in his television set. So much circled around so much else that it was a good thing they ordered double-scoops. Cinq-Mars enjoyed a conflicting combination, maple walnut over black cherry. Casgrain doubled up on pistachio over pistachio.

They drove back to the station together to retrieve both their personal cars.

'Gotta hurry!' Casgrain suddenly exclaimed. 'Ballgame tonight.'

'Hope you win.'

'Émile, it's how you play the game.'

'Henri, that's only true if you lose.'

THIRTY

Like sewer gas, the street excretes its true nature. Congested, tumbledown and grim. Cretins roam the streets at night amid the gentle homeless. Hoods park black vans in front of hydrants, defying cops to ticket them. They don't. Hookers slouch in doorways. Muggers lurk. The bars are merely rowdy; violence in a few nightclubs is controlled by a tap the owners turn on to suit their inclinations.

Street-fighters remain numerous down on rue Notre-Dame Ouest, around the corner from the check-cashing, money-loaning, money-laundering, leg-breaking agencies on Atwater Street. The West End Irish don't hang out there, but they visit. French heavyweight gangs keep their profile visible. Burgeoning bikers maintain a modest clubhouse with plans to expand. Mafia crews are still prominent but a tad uneasy as their numbers dwindle.

Rue Notre-Dame Ouest was perfectly located for The Rabbit's bar salon.

He called it Dino's, the name it had when he bought the place. He'd given the previous owner a choice between a low-ball offer or arson. He wouldn't guarantee that the premises would be empty when a fireball sealed off the front door, or that the rear exit wouldn't be stuck.

The Rabbit did not run the district, as many assumed. No one had the army to control that district. Too many competing forces, all lethal. The Rabbit ran his club, and he strong-armed a variety of businesses near and far, maintained a drug corner, and prospered on the avails of women. Call girls, hookers, strippers, underage runaways. Country girls who worked the city didn't know him; The Rabbit brokered local talent exclusively. He operated his enterprises with a serrated edge. Rumor held that when he scrunched his brow, pimps lost control of their bladders. In recent years, as the intimidating might of the local Mafia was being compromised by attrition, he was a fist, a gun, and commanded a crew for hire. No light between him and the Mafia, he claimed. Mafioso agreed. With reluctance, they consented to adding the Russian to their contingent of Italian henchmen.

He increased his influence by day, his ferocity by night.

The man's last name was Lappin. Close to *lapin*, French for rabbit. Hence his moniker. Despite the English nickname that derived from a French-sounding surname, the man's origins were Russian. Not that he was known to speak the language. He was comfortable in French and spoke a fractured English he'd learned from others who talked that way. As a child, he had not known the company of children or of women, only of sailors upon a sea.

Older, he moved through both his English and French lowlife connections as a man to be feared, a bearing perfected in prison.

He accepted being called 'The Rabbit', but never 'Rabbit'.

'There's a difference.' No one dared ask him to explain.

After midnight, the man a few referred to as Coalface and others knew only as Willy stepped into The Rabbit's dark warren. A quiet night. A few stragglers in the nightclub looked up. His arrival was bound to cause a stir. The boss would learn of his entry before Willy crossed the floor and planted his posterior on a barstool. Despite the dim murkiness, a somnambulant troposphere, some news traveled more speedily than light.

The bartender inquired if he was in his right mind. As he put it, 'In your head, Willy?'

'More or less, yeah.'

'Your funeral.'

'Hope you show up for it. Somebody better.'

'Not if it means my exit.'

'Won't come to that, maybe. A guy can hope.'

'Dream on. Beer?'

'Ex. Yeah.'

'On the house. Drink up. Might be your last.'

'That's been suggested lately. Still standing.'

The bartender put the bottle down.

'Thanks, Luc,' Willy said.

'No worries,' the bartender replied. 'Behind you.'

Speed of light. No time at all. The Rabbit sat down beside him. Put his forearms on the bar. His eyes were small. Somehow that emphasized the blaze of scar that cut through his left eyebrow. The scar tissue picked up what light was emitted by the overheads and shone.

'New thing for me, Willy,' he said in French. 'Bourbon. Got a kick.'

'I'll stay true to my Ex, thanks.' He spoke French, also. A proper courtesy to his host.

'Wasn't offering. Too good to waste on the likes of you, right? Luc,' he instructed the bartender, 'Eagle Rare.'

The bartender was already pouring. He set the glass down on the bar top.

'The likes of me,' Willy said.

'Don't go all sensitive. Heard you were in the fry-chair. Real sorry to hear. I got nothing against you myself. Hoping I didn't get the call to clock your time. So, one minute, your ass is wired, next thing, hallelujah baby, you're allowed to live again. You're like Christ. Roll back the rock after taking a nap for a few days. A born-again fuck without no religion.'

'Been a ride,' Willy agreed.

'Don't know how you turn that ship around. Somebody can do that? Find a way to live when there's no way out? A man who does that I don't trust no more.'

'Not asking you to, The Rabbit.'

'Then why the fuck're you here, Willy? Makes no sense to me, you here.'

'My job.'

The Rabbit shook his head. 'Don't like the sound of that.' He took a moment to savor his bourbon. Struck both palms on the bar as the spirit slipped down his gullet. 'Shit's good,' he said.

'*Salut*, The Rabbit,' Willy said.

'*Salut*, Willy-boy. You, back from the dead.'

The two clinked glasses.

Visible in the mirror aft of the bar, a young woman took to the stage with a blanket and an inflated exercise ball as large as a chair. The music came up. She began by sitting on the ball in her sequined thong and tassels and nonchalantly gazing into space. Sexier than gyrating, Willy thought, the way she stared into nowhere. A man might be provoked into being tender.

'Talk to me, Willy-boy. How come you still breathe when you ain't got the right?'

'Never mind that, OK? OK? I'm here for a good reason, The Rabbit.'

'What reason?'

'Finding stuff out.'

'For who? What stuff?'

'For who. Who do you think for who? For who.'

'Ciampini. What stuff?'

'I know what you're doing, The Rabbit. Want I should grease the fat end of the bat for you?'

Willy said this looking into the mirror behind the bar, where he could observe the woman staring into nothingness and simultaneously observe both himself and The Rabbit. His eyes met The Rabbit's gaze amid the bottles of vermouth and gin. Nobody ever challenged The Rabbit. Nobody. Ever. To threaten him in any way was suicide. The moment was worth commemorating with a protracted pause.

'A cat now you think you are?' The Rabbit queried. 'You got nine lives?'

Willy swiveled on his barstool and met The Rabbit's gaze directly. 'How about we take our drinks upstairs? Talk in private.'

Not that there was anyone around. Even the bartender had separated from them.

The Rabbit took his time responding while he considered the situation.

'Pat you down first,' he forewarned.

'Get a hard-on doing that, save it for the next guy. I'm not interested.' An old line. One he'd used before. One The Rabbit had heard before.

They headed for the private stairs going up. Once through the upper door, Willy submitted to a thorough pat down, arms spread wide, legs apart. Joking aside, he endured a sexual component beyond what he expected.

'You got your jollies off that,' Willy said.

'No jack-off's getting by me.'

They went into his office.

The room was dark, and The Rabbit turned on a desk lamp only, which left both their faces in shadow. The Rabbit took a pistol from the back of his belt and placed it on the desk.

'In case,' he said.

'Of what, you think?' Willy sat in the chair opposite him.

'The unexpected.'

Tantamount to a commitment of trust, although Willy knew The Rabbit didn't mean it that way. Inadvertently, he had revealed that he did not expect Willy to pull a fast one.

'Talk,' The Rabbit directed.

The telephone awakened Émile Cinq-Mars from sleep. A call had been received at his *poste*, a woman demanding to see him immediately.

'What's the caller's name?'

'Moira Ellibee.'

'I'll pass. If she calls again, I'll see her tomorrow. If she's in trouble or danger, send uniforms. Not a detective.'

'Roger that.'

Roger-keep-your-phone-calls-until-the-morning, Cinq-Mars silently mumbled as he returned the phone to its cradle. He rolled over and went back to sleep with remarkable ease. In itself, unusual.

Willy couldn't put his finger on what struck him as being odd, then it hit him. The Rabbit was behind a desk. A contradiction in perception. The Rabbit. Behind a desk. Had he gone to a bank and found Al Capone's ghost working as a teller, he'd be less surprised.

'You're like a regular businessman,' Willy said.

'I am regular businessman. You are pencil-pusher fuck, but everybody got to do his thing. When business is complicate, you give best advice like my ladies give good head. Ciampini, he figure out to keep you close by.'

'I hope I'm worth keeping close by.'

'Too much maybe your hands stay clean. Like schoolboy. Then you go kill somebody. Like that. People amaze by you. Now you talk to me, I don't know why. Amaze me, Willy. Tell me something out of this fucking world.'

'The Rabbit, I know what you're doing.'

The Rabbit clamped his hands together. 'What is this I do, fuck? What you think in your stupid head you know? Somebody told you something? A rumor, like that? You know what you can do with that, where to put.'

'Just saying.'

'You sound like some tough guy now, Willy. Try to shake me down. Two things wrong with that, do you know?'

'I can guess.'

'Go ahead. Let me see.'

'One, I'm not a tough guy.'

'You right. Number two?'

'You don't shake down so easy.'

The Rabbit slouched lower in his chair. He was impressed by Willy's confidence. He knew which side was up, yet he was still in the room, speaking as though he had conversations like these twice a day. He'd never had a conversation like this with Willy. Never before had he let him into his office. Some people, if they left his office alive, wished they hadn't, and he presumed Willy knew that. Yet he was still bravely seated in front of him and keeping his piss off the floor.

'I begin to understand in my head why Ciampini gave you free pass.'

'Temporary, I'm sure.'

'You know that, too?'

'I'm supposed to be the smart guy, remember?'

'Then talk to me, smart guy. What you want?'

'The Dime went down, blown up. Nic Jobin, gunned down. Accidents, people think. Or that's how things go when you live the life. Couple of country boys went down, too.'

'Country boys,' The Rabbit said in a flat tone, but he betrayed his concern with Willy's level of knowledge.

'One in Sorel. The other in Drummondville. Both ran girls for The Dime and Jobin. Suddenly, there's a dearth.'

'A what? A death, you mean?'

Funny, he hadn't noticed that since arriving in the office, they'd switched to English. If French was the language of love, English was the language of business, though The Rabbit's diction was a lot more fractured in English.

'Dearth. Means a shortage,' Willy explained.

'Short of what?'

'Women. Everything in life is supply and demand. You understand the demand. You have the supply. As I see it, you're taking over the stripper and prostitution rackets right across town. All yours. Maybe you'll give the big boss a taste, but from here on out, you're in control. Right, The Rabbit? Isn't that the facts of life? You're cutting Ciampini out of prostitution and he doesn't know it. He won't find out until it's too late. He doesn't see it happening even when it's happening. He'll probably think you're doing him a favor.'

The Rabbit's silence was heavy, penetrating. He had patted his visitor down, done the necessary examination even in the vicinity of his sexual organs, but he still had to worry that he'd missed a wire or some minute transmitter. He had to mind his tongue in this discourse. That worry inhibited any inclination to listen to the man gargling on his own blood, which was a large temptation. Fearless, rapacious, The Rabbit nevertheless was wary of danger. He understood that he was stepping in it – they both were – at that moment. Cops could be right outside. The Italian mob could be outside. Either way, he had to conduct himself accordingly.

'As weird for me as it is for you,' Willy assured him. 'Me, talking to you like this, like I got the right. I got the advantage, though. I know that.'

'What advantage, you prick, over me? *You*?'

'You don't know my game. You don't know my call. Am I a radio or not? I know you're not. You didn't know I was coming. Am I a radio, The Rabbit?'

'You tell me. I could strip you down and find out.'

'If I say a safe word, you'd be busted if I am. Can you take the chance? If you wanted to, you would've already, right?'

'What your business, Willy-boy? Tell me it.'

'Wanted to tell you a war story, The Rabbit. You might find it an education. For me, it's been like an inspiration, this story.'

'What war?'

'Real one. Number two. Out in the world.'

'I like war stories. Tell me yours.'

'Germany. Used to be the Kaiser in charge of all the German people. Wearing their lederhosen. Drinking good beer. But he had help. You need help to run a country. The Kaiser had people who worked for the government, what you call a bureaucracy.'

The Rabbit smiled. 'You think I don't know English big words.'

'Trying to make my story clear is all. This Adolf guy comes along. Lots of goose-stepping. The Fascists are in power now. The bureaucracy? Goes on like always. The Kaiser, the Fascists, makes no difference. Then the war goes bad for him, Adolf takes the poison pill, and the commies take over the eastern half of the country, the big money guys the west. Totally opposite regimes, but the guys who run things, the men and women who see that bills get paid and taxes collected, all that, once again, they stay the same. Same people. Doesn't matter if they're in the west or the east, they keep their old jobs. How is that possible? Because, The Rabbit, they know what they're doing. It doesn't matter if it's a commie or a Nazi or the Kaiser in charge, or a democracy, it's the bureaucracy that's necessary. Each new guy in power is smart enough to choose the people who know how to run the works, and the people who can do that are the same people who always run the works.'

He didn't explain why he was telling The Rabbit the story. He let him figure it out for himself, knowing that it should be obvious. Indeed, his gambit demanded that he play to the man's intelligence. His survival depended on it.

'That you? The bureau-crazy?' The Rabbit asked. Not really a question.

'That's me,' Willy said. Partly an answer, mostly a prayer.

'Lay it out, Willy,' The Rabbit told him.

He did so. The Rabbit knew better than to take on the Mafia, especially now that they were making nice with the Hells Angels and starting to rely on a mercenary arm instead of their own muscle. The Mafia had The Rabbit do their dirty work in recent years, but he wasn't enough. The Rabbit was getting the message. He was honing in on his own action, not taking on the Mafia but fooling them into releasing their hold on running the prostitution rackets at the wholesale level. Ciampini didn't even realize that the operation was being taken out of his hands, because he wasn't looking, and anyway he didn't know where to look.

'Unless you tell him,' The Rabbit said. 'Which is what you here for. So how you live until morning? A question I keep to ask myself in my head.'

'You figured it out in advance. You figured I'd know where to look, that I have the knowledge only a bureaucrat has, that I'd spot the play. You figured I'd shine a light on your face. Why not take me out, too? Who'd notice? Who'd care? Maybe nobody. Sad to say.'

'Interest to me that you agree, Willy.'

'Get an outsider to do the job. Nobody would figure it out.'

'Not agree, me. You think I'm that smart?'

'I know what you're saying, The Rabbit. And why you're saying it. But how much easier everything will be and how much more stable – that's a key word, the *stability* of the enterprise – how much more stable if you don't get rid of me. Replace me with me, The Rabbit.'

'You with you.'

'Makes everything work. Like clockwork. Not only better than before, for you, but it can work in a way that Ciampini won't figure it out in his lifetime. You take over the entire prostitution racket in the whole city, but it still *looks* like it's Mafia run. Once you have it, the Hells don't. That's important, because you know they want it. You know it's the first thing they're gunning for even when they really want the drug trade. You, maybe you want the drug trade, too. Maybe you're satisfied without it. Either way, first the women. I can do that for you. Make you seamless. Seamless is good, The Rabbit. You should definitely consider my proposal.'

The Rabbit appeared to be doing so. He located an elastic band on his desk and was pulling it and twisting it over one finger and then another. His thought processes, the turns and mis-directions and alternatives, seemed to be duplicated by the elastic. Then he scratched an eyebrow, the one without the scar.

'You take big chance coming here to me.'

'With you. With Ciampini. Big time. Big chance. Two most feared men in the city. You know why I'm taking my chances.'

'Dead meat otherwise.'

'That, too. Mostly because I'm right. We can do this. I can run what needs to be run the way I run it. Only difference, a different boss. Two, not one. A real one, and one like a figurehead. You've pulled this off so far, The Rabbit. After this, it's the day-to-day, the books, the problem-solving. What're you going to do when the next big convention hits town and you need to pull in girls from twenty different clubs for private shows, and another three dozen hookers to work the room, without disrupting your regular client base? That takes expertise. Planning. It takes me, The Rabbit.'

As he spoke, he realized that he'd been right to hold back a suspicion. The killer who'd come to his apartment might not have arrived with an intent to kill. He had shown up with an intent to abduct. They'd wanted him alive. The Rabbit had wanted him alive, without anyone knowing that he'd been taken. He was supposed to be missing, not dead. In a sense, Willy was offering him now what The Rabbit had wanted all along. Unfettered access to his knowledge and expertise.

'I see how you talked Ciampini into not blowing your stupid head off.'

'This is a harder talk. I think you see it. It's the boring stuff that I look after, so you don't have to.' He shifted his weight to the forward lip of his chair, as though to emulate leaning across the desk to whisper in The Rabbit's ear. He spoke more quietly, which caused The Rabbit to incline himself forward as well. 'Ciampini has to be placated. He has to see this move as a defense of his operations as a whole.'

'What you talking? How?'

'He's working more with the Hells. You know that. I'm telling you what I'm telling him. They're not planning to stay in place, be the poor cousins because they're French. This is *their* turf, when you think about it. Ciampini has to see your move as a way of thwarting the Hells, of keeping them in their place, because what will they come after first?'

'Drugs.'

'Second, then. But I'm telling you, I told you already, it'll be first.'

'The women.'

'The Hells don't have a move against you if you take over the sex trade, not if you have Mafia support. Their first big move gets sunk. I'm the only one who can convince Ciampini that you take the prostitution racket and the dancers for yourself, cut him a nice slice, that that diversifies the market. Makes it less attractive, less accessible for the Hells to penetrate his operation. They'll have to figure something else out. Buys him time. He'll see you as a loyal confederate, thanks to me. Sooner or later, you will need that. You don't want him calling in reinforcements from New York against you. Against the Hells? That's down the road. Meantime, we'll make an alliance and he won't even know that anything changed.'

The Rabbit worked his elastic band until it broke, then worked the single strand some more. Winding it around the fingers of his left hand, then his right. Then he spoke.

'I think about it, Willy. Finish your beer at the bar. Then walk out of here with nobody bust your legs, crack you off at the knees.'

'Can't tell you how much that's appreciated.'

The Rabbit tossed a notepad toward him, then a pen. 'Write down how I keep in touch.'

Willy made a motion to follow through on that, then stopped himself as though he had a new idea, one that was only occurring to him in the moment. He moved the pad back toward The Rabbit, leaving it blank.

'I'll call you, The Rabbit. I'm the one at risk.'

'Don't make me go look for you, Willy. Hear me clear?'

PART FOUR
ROARING

THIRTY-ONE

'Humor me,' Sergeant-Detective Émile Cinq-Mars requested. He put down his lox-on-a-bagel without taking a bite. Opposite him in the booth, Detective Henri Casgrain carved four crispy bacon slices into bite sizes. His plate included a Spanish omelet and home fries. The man had an appetite in the morning.

'About what?' Casgrain responded.

'A theory.'

'Lay it on me.'

They were seated in the Daisy Mae restaurant on busy rue Jean Talon in Park Extension. A relic of the fifties that two decades later was still hopping. Patrons could sit on stools at the soda-fountain bar or in red vinyl booths. A flip-chart satellite unit in which to insert quarters and select songs from the jukebox was placed at an end of each table next to salt-and-pepper shakers and dispensers for sugar and napkins. Cinq-Mars had already flipped through the songs to find spelling errors. No new ones, although his favorite, *Knockin' on Evan's Door*, remained.

'What if we're wrong about everything?' Cinq-Mars put to him. 'Right from the get-go?'

'Won't be the first time. What's your thinking?'

Cinq-Mars didn't seem sure.

'For argument's sake, Henri, let's say I'm wrong and you're right. The purpose for stealing toasters was *not* to train a crew, but to kill the guy named Willy. To do that, they'd need to take out Willy's defenses. Specifically, the cameras. Let's say they knew about them. They created a robbery. Toasters and purses, tools from the sheds. Here's the key: they removed the cameras from Willy's apartment, too. It wasn't Willy later on. It was the whole point of the robberies, to get rid of the screens and any recording equipment. The killer arrives when he's confident Willy's not there. Either he knows his movements, or he caused him to be elsewhere. The thieves go in. They take out the electronic apparatus. That

makes stealing toasters easier, obviously, but it's the whole point
of the toaster heist. Take away the evidence without anybody
thinking there was evidence to take away. It also allows a killer
to hide in the apartment waiting for Willy to come home.'

Casgrain's manners at table passed muster. Aside from the oddity
of meticulously cutting up his bacon – something Cinq-Mars could
live with – the man chewed quietly and possessed the air of a
gentleman. Cops weren't slovenly as a rule, but Cinq-Mars had
had to endure more than his share of piggish partners.

Casgrain mounted an objection. 'Willy comes home. First thing
he sees: the missing screens.'

Cinq-Mars snapped his fingers. 'Got it!' he announced.

'Oh yeah?' Drily. 'What took so long?'

The younger detective lit up. 'Henri! I got it. What was the
toaster doing in the dining room? That's bugged me. If I'm right,
they took the screens out later. After the guy in the closet is dead,
but the thieves probably think Willy is in there, not the assassin.
The killer's had time to do him in, they believe, then get out by
the front door. Or maybe they don't even know that somebody
was meant to die. Not their role. Their job is to take out the screens
but make it look as though it's part of the overall robbery, so
nobody notices. Along the way, they bring the toaster into the
dining room to be carried out with everything else. In the end,
they either forget it there, or it was one too many items to carry.
They leave it behind in the dining room.'

Casgrain wiped his mouth with a napkin before responding.
'Say that's true, Émile. I don't see that it puts us any further ahead.'

'The elastic band!' Cinq-Mars exclaimed, a lightning strike.
Although he scarcely moved, his inflection emulated a man jumping
out of his chair. 'Henri, you weren't there, you didn't see this, but
I saw an elastic band on a hall table near the front door.'

'What about it?'

'It was snapped and left lying around. Everything is as neat as
a pin in that apartment. How did that elastic get there? Why was
it just left?'

'You know?'

'Could be another line of defense. The tenant was obviously
obsessed with security. Our Willy leaves his apartment. On the
way out, the door ajar, he places the band around both parts of

the lock on the inside. When he returns, he opens the door slightly, flips the band off one side of its mooring. If he returns and the band has been broken, he knows that someone came in while he was gone. I mean, the man had cameras. Security was an issue.'

Casgrain was as fixated on his breakfast as on his partner's theory. When he spoke again, he pointed with his fork in one hand, knife in the other. 'Flawed theory,' he declared.

'Tell me.'

'They broke into the *rear* of Willy's apartment. No sign of forced entry in the front. No need to go in and out by the front.'

Cinq-Mars resorted to his lox-and-bagel, chewing on his food while masticating on the problem. 'For appearances?' he posited a few minutes later. Not enamored with that answer, he tried again. 'How about this? Killer comes in the front door, long before the thieves.'

'How?'

'Let's say he has a master key for the door locks—'

'Come on, Émile. You're stretching. No evidence for that.'

'Not stretching. I'll tell you why. Moira Ellibee was visited that night, maybe. Not quite as she remembers it, but visited. Her apartment was not broken into. Was her back door left open? Possibly, but what intruder would expect that? The killer has a master key. He goes into the wrong apartment – Moira's – from the front and encounters the nutcase lady. He gets the hell out of there before she fellates him. I mean, the man's busy. He then goes into the right apartment – Willy's. It's next door. Without knowing, he breaks the elastic band. Willy comes home. Immediately, he knows someone is either inside at that moment or has come and gone. He's had the elastic on his lock for a decade and finally it's broken. He picks it up. Drops it on the hall table. Looks around. In this scenario, his screens stay in place. Maybe he detects the man breathing in his closet. Strips off. Opens the closet door. Kills him in a half-second. *Wham!* He spears him. Then washes up. Dresses the dead man in his own clothes so that we will assume he's the dead guy. Clears out his stuff. Leaves the screens. He doesn't care. The thieves break in. All of this has been timed out because I bet they knew when Willy was supposed to come home. They pick up the kitchen toaster. Carry it into the dining room. Take away the screens and any recording apparatus. Either they forget the toaster or it's one item too many. Anyway, they got what they came for. They leave. They don't know the dead man in the closet is one of their own. Sure as hell not their job to go check. This is a well-oiled, professional machine. Nothing amateurish about it.'

Casgrain stopped eating. 'Interesting,' he said. 'Still flawed, though. The part about the master key wrecks it.'

'Not true,' Cinq-Mars defended.

'Of course not,' Casgrain said. Sarcastic now. 'Explain.'

'Who would possess a master key?'

'I'll play. Who?'

'A janitor. One of Russian extraction, for example. He fits the little we know of the gang's profile, if there is a gang, and he attended Johnny Bondar's get-out-of-jail party. He doesn't run with the best companions. Plus . . .'

'Plus what?' Casgrain bobbed his head. He had egg on his mustache. Cinq-Mars figured he'd discover it for himself soon enough.

'How could Willy have cameras without the janitor being aware?'

Casgrain was willing to concede that his new boss might be onto something. 'What's our next move?'

'We need to check on Moira,' Cinq-Mars said. 'She called the station last night. At my request, dispatch put her off. After that, we'll run a check on our janitor before we stick a knee in his back. Won't be a huge surprise if he has a history.'

Casgrain reverted to his meal; Cinq-Mars followed suit. In due course, the older man located the spill on his mustache and cleaned it up. Minutes later, he was waving his fork at his boss. 'Émile, just saying. Something to be said for you living like a monk in a cell.'

Cinq-Mars didn't wholly dispute the opinion. 'All I ask?' he pleaded. 'Let me out someday. Don't throw away the key.'

THIRTY-TWO

What Moira Ellibee said disturbed them.

She denied calling the police to ask Émile Cinq-Mars to drop by.

Skeptical, and intending to demonstrate the powers of a police department, Henri Casgrain dialed his *poste*. He requested the record of the overnight call from a woman identifying herself as Moira Ellibee, and to be informed of calls placed overnight using Moira's phone. He and Cinq-Mars waited in her kitchen while she fumed. Both gave her marks for expressing her indignation with gusto, and for once she sounded credible. The phone rang and Casgrain picked up. The call in question had been made from a payphone in the southeast quadrant of the city. As well, Moira had neither received nor initiated any call from her home the previous evening or overnight.

'Told you! Wasn't me!' Moira was exuberant. She bounced around the kitchen. Cinq-Mars thought she could have out-spit Serge the Spitter, she was so excited.

'I believe you now,' he conceded.

In entertaining their apologies, Moira alarmed Casgrain.

'I'm right. You're wrong. I might be bad, but you're so, so, so wrong, wrong, wrong.'

'Moira,' Cinq-Mars directed her, 'behave yourself.'

She contorted in sexual ferment, both hands behind her head, lifting her hair and swaying.

'Gonna make me, my detective?'

'Leave him alone, ma'am,' Casgrain butted in. 'I'm married, but Sergeant-Detective Cinq-Mars is like a priest. Not *officially*. More like a monk. Poor man has taken a vow of chastity. He's one of those chaste cops you've heard people talk about.'

Moira had not heard anything of the sort. Her hands fell limply to her sides and her mouth went slack. 'That true?'

Cinq-Mars saw the virtue in his partner's folly. He chose to play along. His shrug conveyed the impression that he'd be embarrassed to admit to his membership of a sect of chaste cops.

Bewildered, Moira collected herself and offered them tea.

Casgrain was in for a second surprise when his partner accepted. He'd have bet on him bolting. Instead, once the tea steeped and their cups were poured, Cinq-Mars took his out to the back balcony. Casgrain tagged along behind.

'Not Moira,' Cinq-Mars whispered. 'Then who?'

Casgrain posed a question. 'To what end? Why did someone try to lure you out at night?'

The cops mulled it over.

'A prank, you think?' Cinq-Mars suggested.

'An ambush has to be considered.'

He had a point. Someone had wanted Cinq-Mars outside at night. The outcome, had he responded, was both a crapshoot and a worry.

'Shot across the bow, Émile. Time to watch your step.'

'You too. Keep in mind, my last two partners took bullets.'

'Day and night, foremost in my head.'

He may have been kidding. Cinq-Mars took it as gallows humor. Truth in it.

Briefly absent, Moira rejoined them. She had slipped into something summery, a pale blue frock with a remarkably short hem.

'Henri, did you know this about Moira?' Cinq-Mars asked. Casgrain had had his sport with him; time to turn the tables. 'The Virgin Mary, Our Lady the Mother of God, gave Moira the body of a fourteen-year-old for life. Isn't that something?'

'Excuse me?' Convinced he'd misheard.

'You're Catholic, aren't you?' Moira asked. 'Must be. You're French.'

Casgrain stared back at her.

Cinq-Mars gave him a modicum of shelter. 'He's not practicing.'

She wasn't about to quit. 'Are you open-minded, Detective Casgrain?'

'Mind like a steel trap,' Cinq-Mars quipped.

'I wouldn't go that far.' Casgrain battled his way back into the repartee, changing his strategy. 'But yeah. It's pretty closed. Me and the Virgin, we don't see eye to eye that often.'

'Pity,' Moira concluded, an acknowledgment of defeat. She may have been enjoying a little fun herself. 'At least Sergeant-Detective Émile has an open mind.'

'He's a peach.'

They both expected Cinq-Mars to follow through, but he was gazing down at the lane. 'Hmm,' he said, without realizing he'd emitted the utterance.

'What's up?' Casgrain drew closer.

'Nobody's there.'

People were milling about down below, attentive to their chores and amusements. 'What do you mean?'

'Children. Adults. Girls. Notice, not a single teenage boy. Where've they gone?'

The janitor came out down below and dragged a child's empty wading pool from shade into sunlight. He looked up, as if checking for the sun's trajectory, and spotted the man who was observing him.

'Thanks for the tea,' Cinq-Mars remarked to Moira.

'Stay a while.' A directive. An ultimatum.

'Work,' he stated. 'Another day.'

Casgrain got in his digs. 'He'll be back in a flash with more trash, I'm sure.'

The remark caused Moira to titter. She'd never heard the silly line. Cinq-Mars returned an eyeroll, yet the delay prompted another question to arise. He noticed the chalk lines. Her home had been marked, unlike the apartment of the man the locals called Willy. According to his observations, her apartment had not been slated for a break-in. Her locks the issue.

'Moira, do you see these slash marks? The yellow lines on the brick?'

'Hoo-gee. I'm forgetful. I keep meaning to wash them off. I have no idea why they're here.'

'You've noticed them before.'

'I'm a very observant person, my detective. I saw the mark and washed it off. Only, it returned. The second time it became a pair of marks and I figured it might have a purpose. So I left it alone. Lately, I keep forgetting. I'll wash it off now.'

Casgrain wanted to confirm. 'You saw one mark. Washed it off. Then there were two?'

'Maybe it was ghosts!'

'As good an explanation as any,' Cinq-Mars noted.

The two detectives did not speak of the matter further, yet the curiosity of the marks resided with both men. First one. Then two. How come?

Not a great distance as the crow flies. A mile, a mile-and-a-half to Little Italy, east of Park Extension. On a street corner near the largest outdoor farmers' market in North America, two slow-moving trucks braked loudly. They jerked to a stop alongside the curb. Both drivers stepped down from their cabs and went to the rear of their rigs.

They shoved open the roll-up doors and unloaded trolleys of flower flats. The supply endless, a springtime magic. In Montreal, the third week in May signaled the beginning of the flower-planting season; anything earlier risked frost. A line of young men arrived to receive the trollies. They wheeled them toward the vendors' stalls, a vibrant parade of color. No one noticed the youths speaking English among themselves, and also Russian.

At their station house, Cinq-Mars and Casgrain ran into a visitor. Shooting the breeze with a young woman from the secretarial pool, Armand Touton was dishing out relationship advice.

'No matter what, never marry a *flic*.' The secretary was on hand specifically for English correspondence, so the two were speaking English when Touton inserted the French equivalent of *cop*.

She laughed. 'What about a fireman?'

'Now you're talking. They're smoking hot, eh?' He was half-seated on her desk. He pushed himself upright to leave her and badger Cinq-Mars instead, switching to French. 'This is what it means to work days? Show up any time you please?'

'It's a wonder we come in at all. Armand, meet my new partner, Henri Casgrain.'

The two shook. 'Why'd he want you?' The older man pulled a gruff tone. They were walking toward the detectives' desks.

'Did he?' Casgrain asked.

'Begged. I should know. I set it up. He got down on his knees.'

Cinq-Mars ignored the ribbing, confident that Henri would pick up on Touton's fun in a twinkling. Once he pulled up a chair, the other two followed suit.

'Give me good steak, or pork, or chicken, a barbecue and tongs, I'm a wizard.'

Touton had already lost the upper hand. 'Ah, excuse me?'

'Probably that's why,' Casgrain explained. 'My cooking.'

The old guy appreciated the response. He concluded that his former initiate kept good company on the force.

'We've met before,' Casgrain pointed out to him. 'I applied to be on the Night Patrol.'

Touton studied him a moment, remembering. 'I told you why I didn't take you on.'

'That hurt. Hard to roll with that punch.'

Touton looked over at Cinq-Mars. He smiled weakly, then sighed. 'He stoops over. I needed men with good posture.'

Cinq-Mars censored him with his look, then stated flatly, 'What an idiot.'

'I was a punk back then,' Touton concurred, and apologized to Casgrain. 'Sorry about that. I'm not so stupid now.'

The tone may have been in jest; Casgrain accepted the remarks anyway.

'I've looked through the mob's funeral photographs,' Touton announced. 'Ugly mugs.'

'Didn't know they came in,' Cinq-Mars admitted.

'Captain Delacroix showed them to me. Good man, Delacroix.'

'And?' Cinq-Mars asked.

'Familiar faces. How come these Mafia punks walk around with impunity?'

'Did in your day, too, Armand.'

'They limped, back then. Black eyes in their mugshots, more bruises. Anyhow, I saw nobody I can pick out as Coalface. Sorry, a dead end.'

'Thanks for trying,' Casgrain said.

'What are you doing here, Armand?' Cinq-Mars put to him. Impossible for the visit to be social. He'd wanted him to check the photographs but had not called to say they were in. That they arrived before he did was purely coincidental.

'I'm not welcome here no more?'

'Not especially. What's up?'

'I was returning stolen property, Émile. Except it got hijacked. Locals up north sold the stuff from under me.'

'Try to make a little sense, please?'

'The toasters, Émile. *Your* toasters were delivered to me. How do you like them apples? Can you believe it? I can't and I was there. Some kind of a message. One question is, what's the message? The other question – can you guess?'

He wasn't planning to test the new guy in their group, but Casgrain interrupted to supply an answer. 'Who from?'

'That's it. On the money. Who sent them?'

'And why to you?' Cinq-Mars tacked on the third essential query.

*   *   *

When the flower vendors sent their helpers to gather the brunt of the delivery, their people couldn't locate the trolleys of flowers. No petunias, geraniums, pansies, verbena. No nothing. A man walking by said that, yeah, he found it peculiar that young men unloaded flowers from a couple of trucks then loaded them back onto a bigger truck around the corner.

Italian vendors indulged in a collective conniption fit. Raucous; entertaining to many in the vicinity. Anybody would think Italy had lost a World Cup match. One among them was inspired to call the cops. He believed in both law enforcement and the Bible and incessantly prevailed upon Jesus to help, even as he demanded that the police get a move on. Another angry vendor telephoned the Mafia. They paid for protection, he pointed out. 'Where is protection we pay for when we need?'

The discussion in the police station was dominated by the strange reappearance of the toasters; the false alarm call overnight that Cinq-Mars had failed to respond to due to his general laziness, or so Touton decreed; and the weather. Initially, they spoke of the three topics in order, before they blended together. Touton threw in a few remarks on fishing. After that, Cinq-Mars felt his old boss's gaze as it burrowed into him, twisting inside.

'What?' he demanded.

Casgrain had gone silent. He noticed the intensity between the two men.

'Ask me why I'm here,' Touton stated.

'I asked. You didn't answer. Except about the toasters.'

'You didn't press. Was it for nothing I mentored you, taught you what I know?'

'Why are you here, Armand?'

Casgrain followed the exchange with increasing interest. Department lore often centered around these two men when they were both on the Night Patrol. He felt privileged to overhear their back and forth and noted how their mutual respect was also combative. They were not alike. But if they chipped away at each other long enough they might become alike.

'Your assassin. The dead guy in the closet,' Touton parried, 'has been identified.'

The detectives shared a glance. They hadn't heard.

'How do you know what I don't?' Cinq-Mars inquired.

'Connections, Émile. Told you a hundred times, forge connections. Is that cotton batting in your ears?'

'Answer me, Armand. How do you know what we don't?' Cinq-Mars repeated.

'The folks who identified him called me.'

'Why you? You're retired.'

'Something to do with not trusting police in general. Only certain officers in particular. I've given them your name for next time. Expect a call.'

'From who, Armand? Stop beating around—'

'CIA.' He leaned back, addressed Casgrain. 'Shut up about it, OK? You're not hearing this.'

Casgrain was waiting for Cinq-Mars to respond. When he didn't, when he sat there as though a pickpocket had pilfered his tongue, he spoke up for him. 'What the hell does the CIA have to do with stinky cheese?'

Cinq-Mars found his voice again. 'Answer him.' Not a demand. More like an entreaty.

'Your dead guy is a former – well, that's a matter of conjecture; he might not be a *former* anything – your dead guy is ex-KGB, or KGB. Somebody in your department put his mugshot on the wire looking for an identity. Police forces, God bless them, drew a blank. Either that or they didn't bother to pay attention. Like I said, God bless the buggers. The CIA, however, made a positive ID. They have no plans to tell a soul. Except, you know, me.'

'Why not?' Casgrain inquired, although he wanted to ask, *why you?*

Touton shrugged. 'A pearls-before-swine type thing. Not something you want to do, toss jewelry to pigs. Am I right, Émile?'

'Hold on. Are you calling cops pigs?' Casgrain interjected.

'Whoa. Easy. I'm one of the good guys, remember?' Both men smiled.

'What else?' Cinq-Mars inquired.

'Who says there's anything—'

'What else, Armand?'

Cinq-Mars waited.

Touton seemed to be waiting on something also.

Casgrain observed their contest of wills.

He had a thought. 'Do you want me to leave?' he inquired.

'Answer the man,' Cinq-Mars suggested.

'Do you trust him?' Touton asked.

'I requested him for a reason.'

Touton consented. 'This goes no further.'

The slightest of nods from Casgrain, virtually imperceptible, confirmed a shared oath of secrecy as if inscribed in blood.

Touton breathed in. 'Russian gang members, Ukrainians, others, East Germans, have been arriving. A few show up with purpose. To establish a criminal beachhead in the land of plenty.'

'Canada?' Cinq-Mars asked.

'The USA, you dope, but yes, Canada, too. They figured out how the Mafia in the US takes advantage of keeping a leg in a different country – Canada. How that is useful. There's already Russian criminal gangs in New York and Miami, although they're still scattered and small. For now. The move will be to coalesce. First here. Montreal is their exit strategy. Here they get out from under the FBI. They work first on their escape hatch. Since it's the KGB and maybe ex-KGB pitching in, it helps to keep the CIA out of the way, too. They would have succeeded, except one of their assassins showed up dead in a closet that belonged to an undercover cop. A cop, I'm advised, of questionable loyalties.'

'Can we nail down if Willy is Coalface or not?'

'We can,' Touton said.

'How?'

'Fingerprints,' he decreed. 'I've kept Coalface's prints on file. I had him rub his fingers in the coal bin I told you about. Sent in a unit after that.'

'Come on, we didn't use fingerprints back then.'

'Wrong. We didn't have a *system* for prints, that's true. Used to take years to find a match, but people have worked with prints for like a century. We expected it to become a big thing soon. I wasn't always an old fart, Émile. Was a time, I was cutting edge.'

Cinq-Mars laughed lightly. Touton was never more cutting edge than a sledgehammer.

The three men went distinctly quiet when Captain Delacroix emerged from his office and made a beeline for their assembly. He'd taken time with Touton while waiting for the detectives to show. The precinct captain didn't look comfortable that the legendary Armand Touton was now engaging with his officers. *Undermining his authority* was likely how he'd interpret the exchange. But another matter was on his mind.

'Gentlemen, a heist. Need you two on it.'

Two excluded the third person. Delacroix probably enjoyed making that distinction.

Touton stood immediately to get out of everyone's way.

'What kind of heist?' Casgrain inquired.

'Flowers. A bunch were stolen from the Jean Talon market.'

The four men fell silent.

The way he said it lacked both heft and urgency.

Finally, Touton remarked, 'Is this what you do now, Cinq-Mars? Chase down guys who steal tulips for their girlfriends?'

Cinq-Mars figured that was coming. 'The sad thing, Armand, most days they get away with it. Yesterday, my God, it was marigolds. The day before, daffodils. Still no arrests. We'll try to do better this time before the city falls apart.'

Delacroix wasn't certain why the men were so amused. He feared they were laughing at him. 'Get going,' he commanded.

'We're out the door, Cap,' Cinq-Mars assured him.

In the parking lot, Cinq-Mars gripped Touton's hand more firmly than usual. Then held onto it, as though commencing a machismo challenge.

'What?' Touton asked.

Cinq-Mars maintained his grip but turned his head to Casgrain. 'What's the janitor's name?'

The detective checked his notepad. 'Surname, Ananyev. First name, Bogdan. Sounds better backwards. Properly, his name is Bogdan Ananyev. Son is Mikhail Ananyev.'

'You got that?' Cinq-Mars asked his old mentor.

Touton looked over at Casgrain, who said, 'I'll write it down for you.' He did. He tore off a scrap of paper that he passed to the older man, who took it with his left hand.

Still firmly in the grip of Émile Cinq-Mars, Touton grumbled, 'What am I, your secretary now? I run background?'

'Use your contacts. Run his name past the CIA. Let me know if it raises a red flag. So to speak.'

They disengaged, and the two active detectives were on their way. For his part, although he would never say so, the retired man was pleased to have been given a chore, one that less than a few private citizens on earth could hope to undertake successfully.

He forgot to add that he'd be seeing them again shortly. In his dress blues. Touton had decided to attend the police funeral for Detective Norville Geoffrion the following day. He wasn't big on funerals, but given that representatives were arriving from across the continent to pay respect to one of the fallen – a detective from the department he'd served for so long – his request to march in the procession had been accepted.

Tomorrow he would look like a cop again. Today he'd act like one and get Cinq-Mars his information.

THIRTY-THREE

On rue St Denis, Le Gris drove north.

His passenger, Pasquale, a man of significant proportions, perspired at the temples in the noon-hour warmth.

'How about you step on it?'

Le Gris said nothing. The Cadillac's air-conditioning was on the fritz; he guessed that Pasquale desired the additional breeze that speed engendered.

Pokey traffic across four lanes. They hit each red light in sequence. Pasquale hemmed and hawed. He entwined his hands over the hump of his belly. He looked like a man who wanted to hawk a giant spitball and let it fly. At each red, Le Gris gunned the engine in neutral, as if to mollify the other man's need for speed.

Pasquale mumbled incoherently under his breath.

'You can't do no better,' Le Gris finally shot back.

'I'm better on foot than you driving.'

'That's a laugh. You can walk even?'

'Better in a golf cart than you in a car. Say that.'

'A bigger laugh. Ha! Swing a club. Hit yourself in the head.'

'Driving the cart, what I meant. Said nothing about golfing.'

'The hell is the goddamned rush? Big hurry to save flowers so they don't wilt? You care?'

'It's Tuesday,' Pasquale said. 'Keep that in your head.'

Le Gris was confused. 'So what it's Tuesday?'

'Don't piss me off on Tuesday.'

Le Gris knew that Pasquale meant to include any other day as well.

Leaving the Town of Mount Royal behind, traveling east through Park Ex, Detective Henri Casgrain was driving when Émile Cinq-Mars inexplicably slapped the bench seat between them repeatedly.

'A favor, Henri. Put on a heavy boot.'

'For stolen flowers? What's the deal?'

'I had a thought. Let's go.'

'Siren and flashing cherries, if you want.'

Cinq-Mars decided against that extreme.

'What's your thinking?' Casgrain pressed him. He sped up. Not always easy on congested rue Jean Talon. Little point to it, anyway, as red lights thwarted swift progress.

'Proximity. The boys on the lane were missing this morning. Now we have a heist of flowers relatively close by. That's about their speed. Toasters. Flowers. Light. Easy to pack.'

'Is this your legendary intuition, Émile? So-called. Your claim to fame?'

Cinq-Mars rejected the notion. 'No claim that I make.'

'I see no connection between flowers and toasters.'

Stalled again at a red light. Cinq-Mars appeared to be daydreaming before he spoke up. 'If you want to know, I think the mind works with and without language. It's that simple. Language is slow, it's cumbersome. The brain is capable of firing on all cylinders as long as it doesn't have to detail everything in words.'

'If you say so,' Casgrain noted. Traffic started up again, plodding on. A truck flashed a tail-light, looking to double-park.

'Say for example,' Cinq-Mars carried on, 'you drop a fork. In mid-air, you grab it before it hits the floor. That's a reaction. You don't think to yourself, "I should grab my fork before it hits the floor." You don't think, "Make sure I don't gouge myself on the tines." You don't *think* at all. You react and grab the handle. Perfectly. When the mind puts something together from various impressions, from observations, conscious and unconscious, and from hard information, sometimes the mind leaps to a conclusion. *Voilà!* The fork is in your hand again. That amazes you, even though you were hardly aware you dropped it.'

Casgrain darted into, then around, a knot of traffic. He irritated another driver who honked. Under his breath, the detective said, 'You don't say.'

'You just proved my theory. Driving without thinking. You didn't hit anybody.'

Cinq-Mars fell silent until they stopped again behind another delivery truck. He resumed his thread. 'Doesn't mean that your sudden thought is the right conclusion. It's only a thought. But if you ignore thoughts like that, and most people do, those ideas won't come around. Not early, not often. But if you give them the time of day, you'll be rewarded.'

'You sound as wacky as Moira Ellibee. Are you saying, if I think to give that truck driver a ticket for double-parking, I shouldn't think about it, just do it?'

'Exactly. Except, who has the time right now?'

To Henri Casgrain, his partner's remarks sounded like a description, or an explanation, of intuition. Cinq-Mars did have a reputation for oddball thinking that eventually came out as sound. He figured the younger man to be sensitive about his opinions as his point of view found no favor among peers. Armand Touton, notoriously the toughest of the hard-crusts and bravest of the valorous, had apparently been the exception that proved the rule.

Which might explain how they'd bonded.

'Faster,' Cinq-Mars whispered as the car started forward again.

Casgrain was glad to be behind the wheel. He drove a tad more quickly, whereas given the mood he was in, Cinq-Mars might have been hellbent down this busy street. Casgrain had the better chance of preserving both their skins. He paid attention to the traffic, no matter what his partner said.

The marketplace soon loomed.

'Why send us, you think?' Pasquale wondered aloud. 'Not my thing, pretty flowers. Pretty girls, that's different.'

'No idea,' Le Gris said, then promptly contradicted himself. 'Shortage of manpower, you know? Who're you going to send? Massimo's dead. Teddy's in the dirt.'

'Could've been you in the dirt. You started out riding with them.'

'Could've been. Not supposed to be, but who knows? I can't imagine in my head Willy could off me. Not him up against me.'

'Teddy would've said the same thing. Massi, too. Why'd our Willy do it?'

'So Teddy wouldn't off him first.'

'Not a bad reason when you think about it. So what's the deal? We do everything now? Like this here? Flowers?'

'Everything now, looks like.'

'We need more guys.'

'More guys. More bonus pay, too. But I don't complain. You don't hear that from me.'

'Neither me. No complaints. More bonus would be nice, since we do everything like this. Not like we're paid to go find somebody's missing flowers.'

'Not like.'

'Or beat the crap out of who the fuck stole them.'

'Neither that.'

'We just do it.'

'For justice. It's our job.'

'You got nothing you don't got justice.'

Arriving at the market, they got lucky when a shopper departed her parking space.

'Who do we talk to, you know?' Pasquale asked.

Le Gris shrugged. 'Who talks to us, we talk back.'

Pasquale shrugged also. 'Good enough sense for me.' He struggled out of the car, an everyday difficulty given his proportions and lack of physical dexterity.

Walking past a butcher's, Pasquale took the initiative to resolve their minor tiff. 'In my opinion,' he began.

'What you said to me,' Le Gris countered.

'What'd I say?'

'Tuesday, is what I heard.'

Pasquale figured out what that meant. 'I won't bother you no more, Le Gris.'

'Neither don't piss me off.'

He didn't.

Le Gris led the way in talking to the flower vendors. None

could provide a description. There'd been a truck, somebody said. Who saw this truck? Nobody saw a truck. Then how do you know about a truck? Other people said so. Where are they, these other people? They were just people. You know. Citizens. Shoppers. They bought stuff. They went home or wherever they go when they're not shopping.

'Let me try,' Pasquale said.

'Shit, yeah,' Le Gris said.

Pasquale addressed the contingent of vendors who were missing flats of flowers they had paid and signed for, then had stolen under their noses. 'Who the fuck do I shoot in the head to get a straight answer around here? Tell me which one of youse do I kneecap?'

A few vendors had wanted the Mafia on the scene to give them a piece of their mind. They paid for protection, why weren't they protected? Given Pasquale's reputation, the impetus for their grievance dissipated. They chose to calculate and absorb their losses.

'The next time flowers come in,' one merchant suggested, 'maybe guard the shipment?'

Some thought that that was a good idea. Worth considering.

'What do you think we do all day?' Pasquale asked them. 'Twiddle our fucking thumbs?'

'If we find out who did this, we'll let you know,' Le Gris spoke up. 'Get your flowers back if they don't wilt. Otherwise . . .'

His alternative hung in the air.

'Otherwise what?' a faint voice in the back of the group inquired. More curious than belligerent. Hard to tell who spoke.

'Otherwise fuck off with your problems. You think we don't got none of our own?'

'We pay for protection,' a bolder man whinged.

Pasquale glared at him. Then he said, 'You want to repeat that once more out loud for the people in the back to hear?'

The man chose not to do so.

Pasquale and Le Gris took their leave. They both noticed two cops arriving at the other end of the marketplace. They could tell they were cops despite the plainclothes. Their walk, their demeanor, that they parked illegally, and mainly because both of them had had run-ins with each man. Not big enough run-ins that they could identify either one by name, but big enough they'd not forget the face. Each man was about to mention it to the other. Neither man, preoccupied that way, saw a pair of gunmen directly in front of them. Standing still. Waiting. Letting them walk close to them. Le Gris and Pasquale looked up. They saw the two guys raise their arms. Guns out. Neither man heard the bullets that killed both of them instantaneously, dropping them to the pavement in spreading pools of blood while panicked, caterwauling shoppers raced off in a multitude of directions.

Cinq-Mars and Casgrain spotted the gunmen as they fired. They drew their weapons on the run and shouted their presence. 'Police! *Arrêtez!* Stop!'

One shooter turned. Saw them. Fired in their direction.

The detectives saw a bystander drop. She'd been hit. Both detectives instantly stopped in mid-stride, as if they'd pulled their hamstrings. Between the two pairs of men with guns, people leapt out of the way, but a woman was lying on her side between them in shock and dismay, blood visible on a shoulder. Hundreds of other people were behind the two policemen. Any shot aimed at the detectives that missed would probably hit another innocent.

The chance of missing everyone was close to nil.

No place for a gunfight. Not the right situation.

'Hold up,' Cinq-Mars said.

No need to give the order. Casgrain knew what to do and both men holstered their weapons. They pursued on foot, but cautiously and more slowly than their prey. Only when the gunmen lit out down a lane did Cinq-Mars sprint after them. Casgrain broke into a gallop, somewhat lumbering, favoring his left leg over his right, not ineffective, although he was less swift than his partner. One gunman broke out of the lane and onto the next street before Cinq-Mars had a clear shot, but he had to hit the deck as the second man reappeared and took aim. The shot missed; Cinq-Mars figured by as much as a city block. At least the only person behind him now was his partner and he was still on his feet and running. Or lumbering. Cinq-Mars was up again, the shooter out of sight, and when he made the turn onto the next block, he assumed that the vehicle using the street as a drag strip belonged to the killers. A getaway car, waiting where traffic was light and in one direction only. Too much of a blur to make out a dusty plate. A Pontiac or a Chevy, pale blue, with twin exhausts. Now out of sight. Gone.

Casgrain caught up but they were both out of breath and had to get back. Two men and an innocent woman shot before their eyes. Possibly two homicides to which they were eyewitnesses.

The woman was being cared for by passersby, including a physician. She was made of stern stuff, her dismay under control. An ambulance had been called. The police, too, the detectives were informed. Cinq-Mars and Casgrain worked their way through a circle of the curious around the two men dormant on the pavement. They knelt and checked. Both victims were dead. Their wounds and the blood spatter made their faces unrecognizable even to each other had they survived. Wallet identification told the policemen who they were. Well-known names among the criminal elite. Casgrain went back to their unit to radio it in. A mob hit had taken down two Mafioso killers in the Jean Talon market.

This was news.

Whatever the war was about, whenever it began and whoever was involved, some sort of roaring battle was heating up.

THIRTY-FOUR

People fled when the guns were fired, driven on a wind of panic, then congregated in the aftermath, wholly absorbed by the sight of two dead men on the pavement in broad daylight. They hovered on the edge of that excitement. Then many who were absent at the time of the shooting swarmed to the crime scene, summoned by the clarion call of sirens.

Uniforms jumped to the task of crowd control.

Homicide Sergeant-Detective Jerôme LaFôret and his partner Detective Alfred Morin arrived amid a phalanx of squad cars, lights flashing, sirens at full wail until they reached the market square. An abrupt silence followed the caterwaul.

'Jerk-offs,' Morin steamed, addressing Cinq-Mars and Casgrain. His words kept private. 'Get it through the lead in your heads. You investigate domestic disputes and the theft of penny candy. Anything else, call in the big boys.'

'That would be you,' Cinq-Mars noted. 'A big boy.'

'Think otherwise, jackass? Oh, sorry, Sergeant-Jackass-Detective? What are you doing here? Playing tourist?'

'Waiting to be interviewed. We're eyewitnesses.'

'Oh yeah? You were witnesses? How can you be an eyewitness when you're a cop? What did you *do*, Cinq-Mars, as a *witness*. Pee your pants?'

'We gave chase. Are you interested? The getaway car was a pale blue Plymouth or Chevy. Twin exhausts. Didn't catch the plate number.'

'Course not. That would be doing your job.'

'Shots were fired. At us. A woman was hit. Consequently, the ambulance.'

'She's not with the dead guys?' The question was posed by Sergeant-Detective LaFôret, who thought the input of two officers present at the time of the shooting ought to be taken seriously. Morin took note of his boss's displeasure with him.

'Innocent bystander,' Henri Casgrain informed him.

'They fired at you. Did you fire back?'

'We were in a crowd of hundreds,' Cinq-Mars told him. 'What would you do?'

'How about you let me ask the questions and you curtail the attitude?'

'Seriously?' Casgrain interjected to short-circuit his partner's rising pique. 'Attitude?'

LaFôret acknowledged that it went both ways. 'Let's chill, guys,' he suggested. 'Two hundred people around. We don't want them going talk-radio on us.'

'Fine,' Cinq-Mars consented. 'Just keep your dog on a leash.'

LaFôret forestalled any further reaction from Morin, holding up a hand. His junior officer backed off.

'What were you doing here?' the senior homicide detective inquired. Politely.

'We were called in. A significant quantity of flowers was stolen. Two truckloads. As we arrived, *pow-pow*. That quick.'

'Two shots?'

Casgrain and Cinq-Mars glanced at each other. They answered simultaneously. 'Four.' Cinq-Mars added, 'At first. Two from each gunman, most likely. They were in sync. A single shot as they ran off which hit the woman. Another one after that down the lane.'

'How far away were you?'

'Here to the street,' Cinq-Mars said. 'They saw us, fired once. Hit the woman instead. Then ran. Once they were away from the market we pursued. They shot at me. Sadly for you, they missed. The rest you know.'

'Since when do thieves steal flowers?'

'Look into it. My opinion anyway.'

'How's that?'

Cinq-Mars indicated a group of vendors to his left. 'Italian merchants. They're robbed. Who do they call? Us and . . .?' He let the homicide detectives fill in that blank. 'The Mafia sends a pair of thugs. Somebody was waiting for them. That part looks obvious to me. It might explain why the flowers were stolen.'

'That's a stretch. How would anybody know who'd be sent?'

'Could be it didn't matter.' Cinq-Mars kept another thought on the subject to himself.

LaFôret was satisfied. Given his run of good manners, Cinq-Mars informed him that he wanted to take statements from the vendors – strictly to do with the theft of flowers. Then be on his way.

All parties were content with that. Cinq-Mars and Casgrain investigated the flowers' heist, took names and numbers, and noted the vendors' opinions on the murders. 'Like they were waiting,' the consensus view. The most common question posed: 'Who shoots Mafia?'

Cinq-Mars considered the question valid. He wondered if homicide would agree. When he and Casgrain were done with their interviews, he said, 'Let's separate those two. Henri, take LaFôret. Talk about anything. Leave Morin to me.'

'What are you up to, Émile?'

'Investigating my case.'

'Flowers or toasters?'

The slightest of smiles barely informed his lips. 'Neither,' Cinq-Mars declared. His smile became more evident. 'Murder.'

'You're trouble.'

'You're a good man, Henri.'

They approached the homicide detectives. Both men played the moment by ear. Casgrain asked LaFôret if he was going to the funeral tomorrow and the detective almost replied, 'What funeral?'

before catching himself. He said, 'I guess so. Don't know if I got time off yet.' Which meant that he hadn't put in for it. Casgrain kept talking to him about it anyway. With his man, Cinq-Mars skipped the pleasantries. He beckoned to Morin with a jerk of his chin and the detective disentangled from a group of uniforms and came away.

'What's up?' Morin asked.

'Had a question. About the party. How was it?'

Morin's expression went blank, cold. 'What party?'

'You know, Johnny Bondar's. The night he was killed.'

The detective straightened perceptibly, turned defensive, although he tried to project the same disinterest as before. 'What are you talking about?'

'Johnny Bondar gets out of jail. He throws a party. You go to the party. I'm curious. How did you end up on his guest list?'

'You think I answer to you about something?'

'I'm asking out of my own curiosity. Friendly basis.'

'There ain't nothing friendly between me and you.'

'I gathered that, Morin.' He spoke under his breath, terse, tense. 'Why did you visit Johnny Bondar *in his house*, the night he was having a party, the night he was going to be killed, the night *my partner* was shot and killed by him? What reason did you have?'

'Screw off, Cinq-Mars.'

'I'm the senior officer. Answer the question.'

'Who said I was at some damned party?'

'Norville Geoffrion did. It's in his notes.'

'What notes? He had notes? If he did, the man was mistaken.'

Cinq-Mars clutched Morin's elbow as he was breaking away. 'You need to do better than that. It was a *party*. A lot of people were there. You weren't invisible. You need to come up with a better response than denial.'

Motionless, Morin gazed at his elbow until Cinq-Mars let it go. 'LaFôret and me, we were working, Cinq-Mars. What do you need to know more than that? Sweet fuck all.'

'Yeah,' Cinq-Mars said. He almost agreed. 'We'll see. Although when you said you weren't there, you were blowing smoke. I want to know why.'

Morin bolted from him. Casgrain was still yammering on to LaFôret, even though the man wasn't listening and had noticed his partner's fury. Casgrain broke away from him; he and Cinq-Mars trundled off to their squad car.

Away from them, Cinq-Mars said, 'Interesting.'

'What is?' Casgrain squeezed in behind the wheel.

'The whole road. Drive. I need to spin a few thoughts on a loom.'

'The way you talk, Émile. Women should like you more than they do.'

'Quit it.' Then he amended his edict, tried to diminish his testiness. 'Not now.'

THIRTY-FIVE

Willy planned his escape years before he felt the need. A safety hatch prepared for the day when he required a sudden leave of absence.

Mythologies were prevalent in the culture. Some based on reality, others on fantasy. One mob myth implied that if you ran, the mob would hunt you down to the ends of the earth and find you. That was only true, in Willy's observances through decades, when the person on the lam was a complete idiot. The movies put someone in a bus depot laying eyes on someone on the run. Phoning in the tip for a cheap bottle of gin. In reality, if someone with a brain wanted to hide from the mob, all he had to do was use his brain and hide from the mob. Proven often, although the wise guys didn't repeat those stories. They didn't want word getting out.

The Mafia was not the RCMP, the FBI, the CIA or Scotland Yard. Those guys had resources. Cameras everywhere and credit card receipts, phone and bank records. If they felt the need, they could post photographs on the moon. The mob had none of that. Slipping free from their grasp, in reality, was as easy as slipping free from their grasp. A man had only to be smart and careful. Calling up your best buddy to request a loan was decidedly stupid. Some guys did that. Calling your mother or your girlfriend to say you were all right and were going to change was strictly a dumbass move. Willy knew that if the day came when he had to run, he'd vanish into the woodwork where even the carpenter ants couldn't find him. He'd be smart enough not to advise the Post Office where to forward his mail or ask a utility company to reconnect the power under his regular name.

Hard to believe, but some guys did that. Flaming idiots. They deserved the dismembering they received.

Willy was both on the run and sticking around. He needed to meet with opposing forces, then be invisible between visits. Already that was working. He knew where mob guys hung out. He avoided those districts and the adjacent ones. The clothes he put on for a meeting were not the clothes he wore otherwise. He acquired hats. Not those that made him look suspicious, but hats that altered his appearance and suggested a cultural background not his own. In the past he'd resembled a nondescript gent in the evening, a proper businessman by day. His preference was for black suits, white shirts and polished shoes. All gone by the wayside. He wore plaid at night, cotton tees by day. Jeans and work boots. Shades in daylight and ball caps. When did enter a district for a meeting with tough guys, he might start out wearing a hardhat, as if he had work to do. Switch over in his car. Not into a cape like Superman, but back into the black suit people expected him to wear. Switch back again after he left. The car he drove on the last leg to the meeting would never be his own. He parked it legally where it was well hidden and departed when the coast was clear, sometimes on a bus. Mafia henchmen were not riding the bus. He took care of the car or cars later. He had ID for the rental nobody knew about. That ID declared his true identity, that also nobody knew about. Not even the cops knew him by his real name, and by now the men who originally hired him were retired or dead.

Of course, there were others who knew him, too. He kept them informed.

He was north of Montreal, eating lunch in a middle-class town that had grown out of itself and become a suburb to the city. The news came up on the black-and-white TV behind the counter. Faces of the victims were covered, although their bodies looked familiar. The reporter announced that they were 'known to police'. Pasquale was a big man with a distinctive build. He was huge and incredibly round at the waist, merely lumpy elsewhere. That had to be him on the ground. Five will get your ten, Le Gris slept alongside him. His body was not distinctive, but he was wearing the same clothes he had on the other day in a car with Willy.

Willy had not killed the two men, but he might as well have. He'd advised Ciampini that if anyone feared him for his knowledge, that individual would want him dead, because that individual was the mole inside the mob. More than just one, apparently. Willy would bet his bottom dollar that Ciampini had taken his own guys out.

Who else would dare?

Pasquale and The Gray, had they turned? Seen the writing on the wall? Thrown in with the Hells, or less likely, The Rabbit?

Or should they be counted among the innocent dead?

Everything was working, if not exactly as Willy planned it, then better: the way he wanted things to go.

THIRTY-SIX

They were headed west on rue Jean Talon, away from the farmers' market, when Cinq-Mars spotted two lanky male youths.

'Slow down a sec.'

Henri Casgrain did so. He spotted them, too.

'The one on the inside, that's Mick?'

Parked cars repeatedly interrupted their view.

Casgrain concentrated on the road.

Then Cinq-Mars lit up. 'It's him!'

A theft of flowers by a youthful gang had been followed by twin murders. Mick, once again, in the vicinity. Worth talking to him about the value he placed on coincidence.

Double-parking would create havoc. Casgrain pulled in alongside a hydrant. He was casual about it, not wanting to alert the boys to their presence. He and Cinq-Mars clambered out and paired up on the sidewalk, tracing the boys' steps, gaining on them with every stride. Mick's pal happened to turn. He nudged Mick with his elbow. Mick looked back, spied the policemen. He didn't hesitate. He lit out. He ran.

The second boy charged into traffic, dodging cars and sparring with drivers in their tangled congestion. Mick tore off straight down the sidewalk and both detectives raced after him. They were nearing the underpass into Park Extension which ducked under the railway tracks. Mick broke from the sidewalk and threw himself against the chain-link fence there, scaled it in a twinkling and hurled himself up and over, like a high-jumper. Casgrain broke off his pursuit, giving up. Cinq-Mars scaled the fence, more assiduously than the boy, cautious of his clothing. He didn't want to rip his suit. Mainly, he didn't want to be snared on the fence for a fortnight. Mick was putting distance between them. He'd deal with that later.

The fence separated railway property from city streets. When Cinq-Mars made it up the hill to the tracks he saw his prey hoofing it north. He followed. An early sprint got reduced to a fast run, tempered to a high-paced jog as they continued. A warm day. Beads of sweat broke across the detective's brow. He tried to moderate his breathing and to summon endurance rather than speed. This could be a lengthy chase.

He ran. He hated that cops wore Oxfords. He couldn't run in these damn shoes. He bet that Mick wore footwear suitable for fleeing cops. Cinq-Mars slipped on oily railway ties and tripped on stones. His attempts to be steady in his strides, to hold onto a rhythm that would carry him along, continuously failed. Damned shoes. Damned shoes.

Damned trousers, too. Tight at the knees. Not loose enough or cool enough for this activity. Damn his suit jacket. He considered peeling it off. But a jacket was worth half a paycheck.

They ran on. Despite his difficulties, Cinq-Mars didn't lose that much ground. Mick must be having his troubles, too, despite his youth, despite his desperation to escape him.

He could yell, 'Stop! Police!' Yet reminding him that he was the police might spur him on. He could try shooting him, a thought that made him laugh, lose his concentration and stumble.

He stayed on his feet. And ran.

Under the heat of the sun, he remembered chasing another youth in another time. Younger then, his first year on the job. A riot erupted during a holiday parade. A rock was hurled at the man running to be Prime Minister. Other rocks and bottles were tossed after that, but Cinq-Mars pursued with singular intent the person who instigated the barrage. Along the way he realized that the agitator was a young woman, and attractive. Only after he reached the point of exhaustion did he nab her, and only after hauling her into a crowded paddy wagon, overriding her lament that she was claustrophobic, did he manage to catch his breath. Only after that did he pursue her again when men and women broke out of the paddy wagon *en masse*, and only after that did he suspect that he'd fallen in love with the girl. That was hinted at, as a sly undercurrent, when he finally arrested the young woman in her home later that night and her mom phoned the police. Specifically, she called a friend of the family and the man who would one day become Cinq-Mars's boss. Armand Touton. That's how he met his girlfriend to be and his boss to be, both in the same overnight disaster.

In uniform back then, a rookie. He had handcuffed the girl of his dreams and later, without the cuffs, they became lovers, which was not proper police conduct. They adored each other, yet remained divided by politics and the culture of the times. Her revolutionary spirit didn't dovetail with his job. The country in ferment: the abduction of a diplomat, the murder of a politician, bombs in mailboxes, the army on the streets to maintain order, the arrest of hundreds, mostly the innocent. In the end, the zealots were shoved off to Cuba in a deal that released a hostage, with Cinq-Mars and his new boss, Touton, instrumental in bringing the rage to a conclusion.

She took him on over his Catholicism and his absurd Catholic guilt, even as they shared a bed. Stuff to work through. Now he found himself running after another teenager, his heart set to burst, the sweat in his eyes, and for the first time in a long time Émile Cinq-Mars felt like a policeman again. Not the joy of being a cop, although pride, and acceptance of what he did for a living, was involved; what he felt was the confluence of circumstances and personal journey and character to know that this is who he needed to be. He was not running this boy down to save his soul. He was running him down to cuff him, haul him in and interrogate him until his eyebrows scalded off, his skin blistered, metaphorically anyway, all from having his lies confronted by truth. If that saved his soul, fine. If not, fine. He was a cop, not a priest, and at that moment there was nowhere on Mother Earth he'd rather be than in pursuit.

He'd rather nab a culprit in the act than hear his confession later on.

Mick was the first to break stride completely, resort to a quick walk. None too soon for Cinq-Mars. He resorted to a walk as well. He'd collapse otherwise. Mick found the breath and energy for a quick jaunt, then a walk, then a run again, then a walk again. Cinq-Mars matched his pace, gaining no more than a few strides at best. Then surrendering the advantage back.

He knew where the boy lived. He could wait for him there. As he'd done with his future girlfriend years ago, having studied her ID when he first nabbed her. Although this one might not show.

Cinq-Mars had another problem with the chase, which was arriving from a distance. He was not certain of the direction, and direction had a bearing. A train from ahead gave him an advantage. Whatever side of the tracks Mick chose to run on, Cinq-Mars could do the same. If the train approached from behind, then as it was going by Cinq-Mars, Mick could cross to the opposite side and disappear over the railway fence.

The train declared itself. Coming from behind. Advantage Mick.

Way down by the Jarry Street underpass, Cinq-Mars noticed a figure emerge onto the railway grade and sit upon a rail. A suicide, his first thought. Then he made out the man's stooped posture. Henri Casgrain. He'd driven the long way around. Good job.

Train direction was not an issue if Casgrain stayed alert.

The freight that pulled out of the Jean Talon Station, while still slow, was picking up speed. Soon enough, the locomotive charged past Cinq-Mars. If he was careful in his execution, he could hop onto a brakeman's ladder on a freight car. He gathered up the last dregs of his stamina and ran hard – *damned shoes!* – and slipped and fought and clasped the handrail and ran alongside the boxcar for a half-dozen strides before swinging a foot onto the ladder's bottom step. He slipped slightly, panic splitting right through him, then held on, steadied himself, and prepared to jump off on a run.

He looked ahead. Casgrain had disappeared. He had crossed to the opposite side of the tracks where Mick had also gone. Cinq-Mars picked up his coordinates for the Jarry Street underpass, his approximate destination, but chose to jump before the train gained too much momentum. Leaping off the boxcar proved less elegant than getting on. He stumbled out of control, his knees jarred by the surface under him. He buckled, both at the knees and at the hips, then dove head over heels, a double somersault, his forehead sliced by stones on the first spin, his scalp on the second.

He came out of it on his feet again, bloody and wobbly and fit to be tied.

Hands on his knees, he noticed his right pant leg shredded. The train was click-clacking, click-clacking by, and when the caboose finally passed him, there stood Detective Henri Casgrain on the other side of the tracks, a goofy grin on his face. His right hand clutched the back collar of Mikhail Ananyev.

The boy's hands went down behind his back. Most likely into cuffs. Between the two of them, Cinq-Mars was the worst for wear, his cuts deeper and bloodier. Mick, though, was banged up. He and Casgrain had engaged in a roughhouse tussle.

'Police brutality,' the boy stated, as though Cinq-Mars should do something about it.

'No, kid,' he told him, his hands on his knees while he caught his breath and gave his head a chance to settle. 'Police brutality? That comes next.'

THIRTY-SEVEN

As they drove, the madness to their repartee contained its own method. Cinq-Mars and Casgrain never had had an opportunity to grill a prisoner together, yet both fell into sync with the other's foray.

'Plucking an eye out – can't do that anymore, Émile. Gone by the wayside.'

'The good old days, huh? Must be something we can do.'

'Burn the soles of his feet. Is that still permitted?'

'Trying to quit. Cigarettes, I mean. Not feet. I don't carry a lighter anymore. You?'

'No matches, either. Anyway, last time I did it the guy's feet stank. Not worth the trouble. All that screaming.'

In the rear seat of the squad car, Mick knew they were stringing him along. He sneered and scoffed in a show of contempt. More silly than threatening, the men did not expect him to fall for their hyperbole, yet he failed to grasp their play. Realistic threats might scare him, not this litany of prattle, but scaring him was not their intention. They preferred to covertly demonstrate that they were in control of him now. If they wanted to tease him, they could. In imagining increasingly ludicrous possibilities – 'The oxygen mask trick is effective, where the perp breathes pig manure vapor' – they were successful in their goal. Despite mocking their charade, Mick gradually succumbed to their authority. He was in their hands; by osmosis he ceded to their dominance over him.

'He's a city boy. Quick to puke when pure pig stink floats up his nostrils.'

'I'm sniffing pig right now,' Mick said.

Smart guy. They didn't mind that he fought back; part of the process to break him down. Mick was left with no false means of expression if and when they touched a nerve. He thought he was getting stronger, but his defenses were eroding. His lame threats provided the men with a baseline, so that he'd not be able to mask an honest reaction convincingly.

That moment arrived. Mick's panic was obvious when Cinq-Mars threatened to arrest his dad.

'You can't do that.'

'Says who?'

'He's got nothing to do with this.'

'You do?'

'I don't.'

'Sorry. Only if you're involved can you say that he's not involved,' Cinq-Mars pointed out.

The boy recognized that he'd snared himself in a knot. 'He's not involved, that's all.'

'Mick. That means you have something to do with it. Because – apparently – you know who's involved and who isn't. So tell us. What did you have to do with it all?'

He admitted to the flowers. He and his pals had been conscripted. To be paid later. They didn't know what happened to the flowers after they transferred them from one truck to another. They knew the job was not legit, that they were stealing.

'Are you aware that that makes you an accessory to murder?'

'What? No! Are you insane? It was flowers! Who the fuck cares about flowers?'

Cinq-Mars explained it to him. He was driving so couldn't look at him, whereas Casgrain was half-turned around in the front seat. 'The flower heist lured a couple of Mafioso to the farmers' market. They run a protection racket, somebody stole from their clients. A breach like that is not allowed. The two guys who arrived to check it out were gunned down. Ambushed, let's say. Could be that the whole point of stealing the flowers was to get the Mafia to show up. Are you aware of that?'

'Is that true? I had no part in that.'

'Well, you did. Maybe your father did, too. Maybe he's the ringleader. I'll bring him in.'

The news appeared to break the boy's heart.

At the station house, Cinq-Mars executed an order for Bogdan Ananyev to be brought in for questioning as a material witness. He instructed the uniforms to make their action public. Arrive under a siren. Keep the cherries flashing. Alert everybody on the block. Let the crowd that gathered see the janitor led away in handcuffs.

'We don't really have anything on him,' Casgrain noted quietly. He and Cinq-Mars took a few minutes alone. 'He went to the party. He doesn't know we know that. Be interesting, how he reacts when he finds out.'

Cinq-Mars agreed. 'Mick is weakest when we bring up his dad. His dad comes across as super-protective of Mick. Work them against each other. See what it delivers. For starters, why did he attend the Bondar party? Who did he know there? Did he conscript his son and his son's friends to steal flowers? He's going to tell me, or Mick will be introduced to, what did you say – pig manure vapor?'

'I should've said skunk serum.'

'No, I like the serendipity. If you call a cop a pig, you get to sniff pig manure. Seems fair. Time goes by, folks will start referring to us as sweet-smelling lilacs to spare themselves the fragrance-brutality method when arrested.'

Good to laugh. 'Should we pepper Mick some more?'

Cinq-Mars appeared distracted. Finally, he said, 'I'm waiting on Band-Aids. Let him stew. He made me run like I haven't run in a year. Still catching my breath and my head hurts. We can always nail him on resisting arrest, but I want him to feel my pain before we book him.'

Casgrain assumed he was kidding but was uncertain. 'Hope you don't mind me looping around while you did all that running. You're younger.'

Cinq-Mars scowled. 'So you know, *partner*, I expect you to do the running next time. After you went around you took a seat on the railway tracks, as if you were the tired one. Mind? Why would I mind I nearly burst my lungs out while you were working on your tan?'

Casgrain enjoyed a chuckle. 'Sorry your trousers tore.'

'Will the department pay?'

'Your department. My old one never would. Here's the Band-Aids. How's your head?'

A secretary brought in a first-aid kit and patched him up. She mentioned that the cuts should be stitched, certainly the deep one on his scalp, but he had no time for that.

'How's the head, Émile?' Casgrain asked again. His partner looked woozy.

'Damned concussion. I could use a nap.' He seemed to suddenly perk up. 'Hey. That gives me an idea.'

'Not sure I like the sound of that.'

'Come on. Follow me, Henri. Don't loop around this time.'

THIRTY-EIGHT

C oalface Willy parked on a side street. He tried to relax. He'd left himself a short walk to the strip club to feel the sun on his shoulders. At noon, two of his clan had been gunned down. He remained dazed by that. Less by the calamity than by the surprise, the possible repercussions. He was anxious to get a sense of how the news was reverberating through the community. Lately, Mafia henchmen were leaping into their graves. None volunteered. A virtual epidemic of bad guys snapped up by the fates.

He was supposed to be one of them.

Nothing to say he wouldn't be next.

Inside the club he took a seat at the bar and waited. Surprised
to be left alone, he tried to maintain a calm demeanor. His under-
arms began to sweat. Then Slew came out of the men's room,
drying his hands on his shirt, so that part made sense.

'Willy boy,' the manager greeted him.

'Slewfoot,' Willy said. He didn't know why he chose to state
the man's full nickname. It popped out. Legend told a story that
Slew fought a cop in a street brawl as a young man and brought
him down with a deft trip. He had the policeman on his back and
at his mercy where he could easily kill him. He had the opportunity, the weaponry, the motivation, the mindset and the rage to do it,
yet restrained himself. Later the cop nicknamed him Slewfoot, to
commemorate his tricky footwork in pinning him to the ground,
and to honor the man who spared his life. They became something
that approximated pals. Willy had not witnessed the fight but spoke
the nickname in full, to remind them of old times, perhaps, and
by extension to commemorate their long collaboration.

The old guy seemed to take it that way. He cocked an eyebrow
and smiled. 'Beer?'

'Ex. Thanks,' Willy said.

Slew went behind the bar and uncapped a Molson Export. He
poured tap water for himself, with ice.

Must be on the wagon, Willy noted, and said, 'Interesting times.'

'What do you know about it?'

'Any names released? Pasquale, my guess, and Le Gris.'

'Their mugs were on TV. Why do they have to use mugshots?
Le Gris looked unconscious. Fucking Pasquale looked stuffed.
Like a moose head on a wall.'

They clinked water glass to beer bottle and drank. A genial
toast to the dead.

'What's your take?' Slew wanted to know.

Willy preferred to ask questions, yet it made sense to do the
talking. He was connected to the source on high, whereas Slew
worked the ground. At least, that's how he billed himself.

'Battle's on,' Willy declared.

'Who and who?' Slew asked.

They were talking on opposite sides of the bar. That created a
considerable gap and Willy signaled the aging manager to lean in.
No one else was around. No dancer on stage. Not a single patron

seated. One guy still mopped the previous night's scuzz off the floor with a lassitude fitting the task. He was out of earshot. Still, beyond a need for confidentiality, Willy desired a heightened level of intimacy to connect them.

Slew, leaning forward, plucked a toothpick from a container and stuck it in his mouth to chew on.

'Battle's on,' Willy repeated. 'I'm here on a mission. We don't want a tip-off contact. Everything is dangerous as we speak. Follow me so far?'

'No. I don't.'

'Your job: take the message, one on one, where you live. The Hells need to know this.'

'Pick up the phone.'

'We'll meet. I don't mean me and you. The Hells and Ciampini. But we don't want the other side to see it coming.'

'What other side?'

'You told me. Didn't you? Sure you did. Where do you get your girls from now?'

'You're at war with The Rabbit?'

'Who do you think did Pasquale and The Gray?'

'Ciampini himself, my thought. Or something personal?'

'Add on Nic Jobin and The Dime. That's personal? The two guys in the countryside you told me about, personal? One screwed up whack-job to take so much so personal.'

Slew concurred that the death toll was adding up to something more than coincidence. He'd come to that conclusion long ago, even before Willy walked in the door.

'Why tell me? Like I said. Pick up the phone.'

'Ciampini's not confiding directly, OK? I can give you my honest opinion. I can be wrong.'

'Listening.'

'We don't know where the Hells are at. We need somebody to explain the opportunity under their heels. No more is it a secret they got their own ambitions.' Slew looked as though he wanted to raise an objection to the charge, that he took it as a charge, but Willy quickly mollified his concerns. 'We'll work with that. We get it. By "we", I mean Ciampini, of course. I'm the messenger. My idea, you're the trusted one, Slew, the messenger inside the Hells. You're long in the game, even if you're on the sidelines now, no offence.'

'Old age comes to us all, Willy-boy. More sooner than you think.'

'My point, Slew. You're neutral. No involvement. Long in the game. You have influence. I know you give directions. Like me, you're the perfect emissary.'

'Emissary, huh?'

'Go-between.'

'I know what the word means.'

'Then all right. This is what I want you to get across. The Rabbit does not act alone. He's not stupid. He's thrown in with new arrivals. Mostly Russians and Ukes. East Germans, too, so I hear. Not to be taken lightly. This is why we want you. Who can say this better than you? The Rabbit wants the sex trade. The Hells want the sex trade. Trust me, that's not the big secret you think it is. You and me, we know the Hells are looking at the drug action, too, asking why they're only down on the street. Why aren't they raking in the big dough on high? Slew, there's room for collaboration here. I'm saying that. You need to convince them. Ciampini is still the man with the contacts, in politics, with the police, with the internationals. What flows in, flows through Ciampini. He needs help, that's true. He's willing to face that fact. A collaboration can walk down the road. If you ask me, it's inevitable. Right now, it's the women. That's an action the Hells can take for themselves. The strip clubs, the hookers and primrose pimps, the Hells can take it on. But only if we kick The Rabbit's butt ass. Otherwise, Ciampini might go down but what rises up in his place won't be the Hells like they think, it'll be the East Europeans. Trust me, the Hells don't want to mess with those KGB mind-fucks.'

A helluva speech, with implications, ramifications – words that were part of Slew's vocabulary. He worked his toothpick around in his mouth, contemplating it all, naturally wary.

'You want me to say all that to the Hells?' Slew said.

'It's not a pick-up-the-phone type thing, is it? It's a discussion. More than that, a persuasion. It has to come from a wise voice. Not from an outsider. I know that you are more than who you say you are, more than what you show.' Willy raised a hand to prohibit any objection, although none seemed forthcoming. 'The Irish didn't give the Hells a leg up, without they didn't keep a piece. The Hells are French. The Irish and the French get along. Always have. It's history. The French don't like Italians being head of the pack on their turf. Not when they want the turf. Not saying this is the whole shebang. But it's a bigger jump than they can do otherwise, and it keeps out a bigger threat than old, dying-out Italians. We need the Hells to join the battle now against The Rabbit and who he's bringing in. Make this a war. Any war, there's spoils on the ground to pick up. Count on that. But any war is also survival. Your people need to understand that.'

'My people.'

'The Hells.'

Clearly, Slew was not going to concede an inch.

'Slew, I can say this to you because I know you understand,' Willy said. He took a long slug of his beer, partly to quench his thirst after so much talking, partly for dramatic effect.

Slew fell for it. 'Say what?' he asked, curious.

'Do all this – go to war even – it's got to be behind the sign.'

A winning argument. The phrase was an old one, unused in decades, but Slew was an older man who appreciated older times. The phrase referred to cartoons of cops in their patrol cars concealed behind billboards. They'd be up to mischief, drinking the moonshine they'd confiscated, munching donuts, undressing a damsel they arrested. Unsuspecting speeders were barreling down the highway, involved in follies of their own, similar to the policemen's. The phrase 'behind the sign' meant that you could mess around all you wanted, like the cop, except be ready to pounce from behind the sign, shock the guilty culprit on the highway when that made sense. Didn't matter that you were no better than him.

Afterward, return to the usual mischief behind the sign.

Slew made no commitment. He did not say no, either.

THIRTY-NINE

Spartan, windowless, harshly lit, the interrogation room offered metal chairs and a center table only recently secured to the floor. The walls reflected a yellowy institutional tint. With attitude, Émile Cinq-Mars strode into the room. Mick's nervousness redoubled. The boy adjusted his spine in reaction to the detective's angry step.

Entering second, Henri Casgrain presumed his partner's mood to be a ploy. He took a seat. Cinq-Mars had intimated that the wounds on his head plugged into a strategy; Casgrain was curious to learn how that took shape.

His boss opened on that point, unraveling a connection.

'The fight, Mick. The brawl in the lane. What was it about?'

'Told you already. Girls.'

'You did say that. Italian girls. What were you doing hanging around Italian girls?'

'Sorry? Have you seen them?' He came close to making an adolescent, lewd gesture with his palms to indicate breast size, but checked himself. 'Some kind of good-looking,' he said.

'Caught your eye?'

'These ones, oh yeah. For sure.'

The comment earned a grunt from Cinq-Mars. 'OK, so you're checking out Italian girls, and now you're stealing from Italian merchants. Is stealing supposed to impress the girls? Or were they part of it all along, Mick? Did they induce you to steal?'

'What? Come on. The girls? That's ridiculous.'

'You know you can go to prison for this, right?'

'For what? Flowers?'

'You think it makes a difference if you steal flowers? Theft is theft. Henri, isn't that true in the eyes of the law?'

Henri Casgrain confirmed it with a nod.

'The law has eyes, Mick.'

The boy's faint shrug suggested that he thought it would make a difference, that the theft of flowers was a lesser crime than, say, that of automobiles. Cinq-Mars didn't mention that any number of prosecutors and judges would agree.

'We're not talking Boys' Farm here. You're too old for the farm. We're talking Bordeaux Jail or St Vincent de Paul Penitentiary. The worst criminals wind up there, along with handsome boys like you. You've heard about those places.'

He had. Terrifying, the stories that filtered down.

Any lingering insouciance dissipated.

'Then who did?' Cinq-Mars had learned to ask questions a

suspect could not possibly follow. Rattle him that way. Then explain what he'd missed, making him feel a step behind.

'Who did what?' Mick asked.

'Keep up, will you?'

The boy turned both sullen and fearful.

'Who got you to steal if it wasn't the girls?'

Not a question he wanted to answer.

A carrot, along with the stick. In time, a suspect would lose track of which was which, or not have a clue what was coming next. 'I might believe you, Mick, if you told me the girls lured you in. Plus, that might help get your dad off the hook, wouldn't it?'

'My dad's got nothing to do with this.'

'What about the girls? Do they have something to do with this? Was that how you got involved with Italians? Your background is Russian, Mick. Your friends are Russian, Eastern European. Not a natural fit with Italian crime. Italians don't normally hire East Europeans to do their grunt work or steal their flowers. So . . .'

'So?'

'What was the fight in the lane about?'

'I told you.'

'You lied.'

'You're off it. You don't have anything right.'

'Only because you're lying. Either the brawl in the lane happened because Italians were hiring you and other Italians took exception to that fact, or you were getting chummy with Italian girls and other Italians took exception. In one case, you're working for an Italian gang when you stole the flowers. In the other case, you're working for an Eastern European-type gang. Possibly directed by your old man. See how this is important? Which was it?'

'Could be none of those. You're not thinking straight.'

'Am I not? That's possible, after what you did to my head. You might've knocked my brain loose. Did you think I'd let you get away with that? I'm bringing in your dad, Mick. What'll he do? Will he sell you down the river? Not likely. No, he'll take the blame on himself. He'll give me what I want as long as I promise to let you off the hook for assaulting an officer, beating my head in. You know that's true.'

'He didn't do nothing. Anyway, I didn't beat your head in.'

His lament sounded like a whine, a worried frustration, not something he believed. Mick was bright enough that he heard the lack of conviction in his own voice, which brought him closer to tears.

'He'll see my head, Mick. So tell me what the fight in the lane was about. You organized a V-shape, or was it a U-shape, to help even the odds. You knew what to do. Who taught you that, Mick? Your dad? Tell me, why did a gang of boys from the next neighborhood think it was OK to fight you on your own turf? What was at stake? Were you supposed to prove yourselves? Show the Italians what you were made of? Tell me that before your dad gets here. Depending on what you say, it might be the only hope he's got left.'

Mick squirmed, wrestled with whatever knowledge resided within him, knowledge he was unwilling to share. Spinning under the barrage of questions, he was not given time to answer any, which caused him to feel that answers were being created for him.

'Which was it anyway?'

Keep him confused. He'll feel concussed without any physical blow.

'I don't understand.'

'Pay attention. Your life is at stake here.'

'OK. I am! Which was what?'

A knock on the door.

'Was it a V-shape or a U-shape?'

Mick could scarcely believe the question and squirmed around. Casgrain rose from his chair and went to the door.

'U, I guess. What does it matter?'

'What matters is who trained you to do that, on the fly like that. Who, Mick?'

Sullen and silent.

'I can guess.'

'My dad had nothing to do with it, I told you.'

A whispering at the door. Casgrain closed it again and told Cinq-Mars that 'Bogdan Ananyev is here.'

Cinq-Mars saw the boy's face drain. He stood up then. 'He's not here to see you, Mick,' he let him know. 'He won't be talking to you. We'll be talking to him. That's how things go now. Everything in life has changed for you.'

'He didn't do nothing,' Mick repeated, a murmur, more a wish and a prayer than a statement of fact.

'You said that already. Too bad you don't believe it, eh, Mick? You might've made a difference for your dad if you believed in his innocence yourself.'

The detectives left the room. The door locked behind them.

'Hard,' Casgrain said.

'Necessary,' Cinq-Mars replied. 'He's breaking. Needs more time is all.'

'What line are you taking with the dad? Do you have one?'

Cinq-Mars thought about it, then decided, 'Crush him. I expect he's a tougher nut to twist than he's shown. But he's got a soft belly, that would be his son. We'll aim our punches there.'

'You're no priest,' Casgrain commented.

'Henri, how can you say that,' Cinq-Mars jibed, 'when I'm so willing to listen to this guy's confession?'

Bogdan Ananyev sat behind a table in a room similar to the one where his son was detained, except that the walls reflected a mauve tint. Under the stress of being picked up, handcuffed and brought in for questioning, he possessed a composure that might easily be mistaken for relaxation. Cinq-Mars interpreted his passivity as a form of aggression, well disguised.

'Mr Ananyev, we've introduced ourselves previously.' The man's wrists remained cuffed, his hands in front of him.

'Your names I remember, yes.'

That could be interpreted as a threat, although it could never be formally labeled as such.

'We have your son in another room.'

In a trice, his composure fell off the rails. 'Why? He all right? Why Mikhail here?'

'He resisted arrest, sir. Ran from the police. You'd agree, not an expression of innocence. You'll notice my bandages – the cuts on my forehead and scalp. Mikhail didn't put them there *directly*; still, I blame his actions. A serious crime, resisting arrest. My wounds won't look good for him in court. I'll preserve them in pictures. Sir, Mikhail has admitted to the flower heist at the farmers' market today.'

'Flower heist?' the building janitor inquired. 'What is flower heist?'

'Come on now,' Cinq-Mars said.

Ananyev looked from one detective to the other, confused.

'Your son,' Cinq-Mars explained, 'led a pack of young men to the farmers' market where they stole two truckloads of flowers. That might seem like a minor crime to you. It's not. The dollar amount makes it a felony. Mr Ananyev, your son has admitted to the crime. He faces prison time.'

The man looked socked. He crumpled inwardly. His body virtually slumped to a reduction in suit size. He no longer sat stiffly or defiantly.

'Why Mikhail do this?' His voice sounded faraway. 'That make no sense.'

'Mr Ananyev, you attended the get-out-of-jail party for Johnny Bondar. Why?'

The question puzzled rather than alarmed him. 'I know his mother. She ask me to go.'

Not a bad answer. 'We'll check that out, of course.'

'Why?'

'Johnny Bondar killed a policeman. You attended his party. A gang of thieves invaded your apartment building. One of your tenants has gone missing after a man was murdered in his bedroom closet. Another gang attacked your son's pack of boys in the lane. Your son stole flowers. In all of this, we have well-organized boys who must be receiving careful direction and training. You're on the periphery, always. Also, same country of origin as many participants.'

'Proof of nothing, my country.'

'Agreed. But we don't require more proof than what we already possess to send your son to prison. Adult prison, Mr Ananyev. Ours are not exemplary institutions. He will not want to be there. The truth is, I have a conscience. I don't really want to put him there. If you can help us with more serious crimes, perhaps the theft of flowers will be forgotten. If you give us information on critical matters, the charge of resisting arrest can go away. That one will be difficult for me, due to my head. You need to be very convincing with your information. The fact is, Mr Ananyev, you went to a party to celebrate the release of a man from prison who would soon murder a policeman, as well as another individual. You're not moving in the best circles. Understand?'

He nodded that he did, although his posture improved. His inner fortitude was returning.

'I tell you something. Then you release my boy, yes?'

'If we regard what you say as significant.'

'I can tell you who do the murder in Mr Willy's apartment. That is significant, yes?'

Indeed. Cinq-Mars stared him down. Casgrain leaned in, then asked, 'You know the killer's identity?'

'That's right.'

'You will tell us that it was Willy. That doesn't buy you much. Explain why you know that. How you know it.'

'Not Mr Willy.'

Although surprised, Casgrain remained intent on him. 'All right. Not Willy. You have an identity? Not somebody in the dark with a mask and a cloak?'

'I give you his name. You release my son.'

Ananyev shifted his stare from Casgrain over to Cinq-Mars. Their eyes met. Both sides waited for a resolution. Then Cinq-Mars agreed. 'Deal,' he said.

'Me,' the janitor said.

They waited. Cinq-Mars asked, 'What does that mean?'

'I kill the man in Mr Willy's closet.'

No, Cinq-Mars was thinking. *Too easy. It wasn't you.*

Another knot to unravel.

'Release my son,' Ananyev said.

'Let's talk this through first.'

'Release him now, or I say nothing. A lawyer I get.'

Cinq-Mars and Casgrain exchanged a look. Casgrain proposed a solution. 'Your boy is in a locked room. We'll let him out. He can sit at my desk, in my chair. We'll tell him to wait there until he can speak to you. After that, he either goes home, depending on what you tell us, or we arrest him. Your choice.'

Ananyev never said yes or no, but a slight bob of his chin indicated his acquiescence. Casgrain left the room to comply with his side of the arrangement. He then came back and resumed his seat. The whole time, Cinq-Mars stared at Ananyev, who never looked up from gazing at the tabletop.

'All right then,' Émile Cinq-Mars began. 'What can you tell me about the slash marks?'

'Slash . . .?'

'Chalk marks outside the back doors of the apartments in your building.'

'I saw yes. I don't know about.'

'You saw them. When did you see the marks? How many were there on each door?'

'After the robberies, I saw. Two marks. Some places. Other places, no. None.'

'Always two marks?'

'Yes. Two. You saw three, four? That was you. Not me.'

Cinq-Mars worked to keep the pace rapid, to deny the janitor time to edit his responses. With his accent, his slowness in English bought him time to think. Cinq-Mars wanted to take it away. His questions did not need to make sense. He needed Ananyev to start spilling words, thoughts, reactions, without coloring them first.

What was the purpose for the marks do you think?

Why mark the doors?

What do you know about the cameras?

Do you possess a master key to the apartments?

How do you think the marks were connected to the robberies?

Do you know about the rubber band in Willy's apartment?

The man fumbled his responses. He maintained innocence with respect to the robberies, admitting only to murder. 'What rubber band?' he asked.

'We'll get to that.'

'When?'

'When I'm ready.'

'When will that be? I murder somebody. An intruder. I not know about robberies.'

'Come on.'

'What do you mean *come on*? I am the killer. What rubber band?'

'You know nothing about the robberies?'

'Nothing I know.'

'How many apartments were robbed? Seventeen? You knew nothing?'

'They were quiet. I was sleep—'

He caught himself far too late.

'You see the problem, Mr Ananyev. You weren't sleeping. You were upstairs killing a man. So either you were not upstairs killing a man, and instead you were asleep and know nothing about the robberies, or you were committing a murder, in which case it follows that you were also aware of the robberies. A phrase in English: you can't have it both ways.'

Ananyev followed the line of his logic. 'I know about robberies,' he admitted, reversing his position.

'Maybe so. That answer lets you be the killer. Still, you have two strikes against your believability. Unless you want to tell me about the slash marks.'

For a change, Cinq-Mars gave him a moment to think about his response. Then Ananyev said, 'Me. I mark apartments.'

'Of course you did. How did you mark them?'

'You know.'

'Tell me, please, sir. For the record.'

'Two slashes. Yellow chalk.'

'Two. Never one, never three.'

A hesitation. Still, he said, 'Two.'

A knock on the door. Casgrain got up and answered, listened to a whisper, then indicated that he'd be gone a moment.

The janitor had a question of his own. 'You said two strikes. What is other strike, please?'

'Two strikes against your believability. The chalk marks are strike one. Originally there was one chalk mark per door. Later, two.'

Cinq-Mars saw another strike whizz past the man. He had reacted to the mention of one slash mark, surprised that Cinq-Mars knew that. At this stage, why had he hidden that benign detail? It struck the detective as odd.

'The other challenge to your believability, sir, is that you would so easily cop to a murder for which you were not a suspect. Maybe down the road, if you're guilty and your son is still in trouble, you might do that. But not so soon, so easily. It makes it hard to believe you. That is strike two with your story so far, Mr Ananyev.'

'It is my conscience. I confess. I kill this man.'

'Then let's talk about it. See if you can convince me. I warn you, I'm skeptical. I'll be extra hard on you and on your son if you lie to me.'

Cinq-Mars stopped when Casgrain returned. He waited for his partner to seat himself again, but he didn't. Casgrain put a hand on Cinq-Mars's shoulder and whispered in his ear, 'Touton on the phone. Your desk. Take it now.' He was beginning to know the man, so added, 'Don't argue for once.'

Cinq-Mars left.

Casgrain sat again and played with his watch. He took his time – as though the watch indicated how long – before he looked up at their suspect. 'The way it started out, I expected a routine day. It's been full of surprises. No matter what, I'm going home at the end of my shift. Doesn't matter what you say here.'

The janitor spread out his palms to the limit the handcuffs permitted, an indication that he had no clue what the man was talking about. Casgrain kept to himself that a sharp change to the course of their conversation was about to occur.

Cinq-Mars returned. He took his jacket off and slung it over the back of his chair. Sat down. He pushed his chair away from the table and let his posture slump into it, slouching his spine, spreading his legs out ahead of him to either side. He placed an elbow on the chair's armrest, a hand on his forehead. Thinking, yet in an attitude that portended that he could not think coherently anymore. As though he was bracing himself for what he'd already learned.

He finally looked at Casgrain and shook his head. Then sat up straight again, moved closer to the table and rested his forearms on it. He said, 'I talked to a friend of mine.'

The janitor waited.

'Fortunately for you, or unfortunately as the case may be, my friend has friends. As do you, Mr Ananyev. You have friends.'

The man was baffled.

'Would you like to tell us about your friends, Mr Ananyev?'

'Friends in gangs, you mean? You think I am a leader of gangs of boys. I am not. But I know such men. I not deny.'

'You'll not deny,' Cinq-Mars repeated. 'I didn't mean those friends. Perhaps you have friends who are worth having as friends.'

Both Casgrain and Ananyev waited for an explanation.

Cinq-Mars spoke again. 'It's your friends in the CIA that we should talk about, sir. They say you're one of theirs. They say you're one of the good guys and we should treat you as such. I wonder, sir, if we can now talk more plainly than before?'

Perhaps they could; perhaps not. Ananyev mulled over this reversal to the direction of their talk. He had been treated as an adversarial material witness. Abruptly, he was considered an ally. He was looking for a way back into their talk, or alternatively, for a way out.

After a spell, he said, 'This is a world we live in, Detective.'

The declaration was unexpected, one that invited a philosophical discussion, rather than a talk about their difficult straits. Cinq-Mars stood and leaned over the table. He took a key out of his pants pocket. He released Ananyev from the handcuffs, then sat back down again. The man rubbed his wrists.

'Do you know, Detective Cinq-Mars, story of young man in room built for coal? Maybe you know this story. Maybe not.'

'The world,' Cinq-Mars remarked, 'is the world we live in, Mr Ananyev.' Equally obtuse. Then he said, 'He had to cover his face with coal dust before a light was turned on. Then he faced the other man in the room.'

Bogdan Ananyev was nodding as a cow might chew its cud, deliberately, compulsively, and without conscious awareness. In whatever labyrinthine corridor his mind wandered, it eventually brought him back to their present room and immediate concerns. They could tell when he was ready to speak again, as the intensity of his nodding wound down.

'One slash mark I put.'

'Only one,' Cinq-Mars said.

'Mr Willy, he said make it two.'

'Why two? One was visible enough, to indicate the apartments with deadbolts.'

'A signal. Not to criminals. To investigators. Maybe, Mr Willy said, somebody might see. Trust the man who sees, he told me. If nobody sees, don't worry about it. But a man who sees will know about him. Trust that man, in case.'

'In case?' Casgrain butted in.

'In case Mr Willy is dead. He did not say that. He meant that.'

'Mr Ananyev,' Cinq-Mars inquired, 'why, initially, didn't you say that you made just one mark? Why say two?'

'Mr Willy told me to make two marks after I make one. How do I explain that without I mention Mr Willy?'

'Who killed the intruder?'

'Me. Mr Willy help. I did not want to say that to you. I warn him they were coming. He open closet door. I swing my knife.'

'Did you know the dead guy is ex-KGB?'

'He is?'

'He was.'

Ananyev grimaced. 'No "ex". If he was ex-KGB, he was KGB when I killed him. Still is KGB, even dead. They used to send smarter killers. We were a big surprise to him. He did not expect that. He did not know we know he was coming.'

'How did you know?'

'They found me. These kind of KGB Russians, the ones in the world now to make big bucks. I was gone from them a long time. I don't know how they find me. Boys in neighborhood maybe. Johnny Bondar, like him. They help bad people find who lives in the neighborhood. The Russians, the Ukrainians, the Poles. They check everybody. When somebody cannot be figured out, they look closer. Find out who really he is. Who he was in old country. They find out about me. Soviet engineer. I helped Americans. A reason for that. I say nothing more. I got out with my son. My wife had a way out, too. KGB, they caught her when she leaves. She is disappeared. They told to me, "We have your wife. In gulag. You do this for us, maybe she not die this week." I don't know if she is alive or dead. I had to protect my son. My wife and me, we agreed on that, firm, to get out with Mikhail, no matter what. I tell to Mr Willy my story and we plan.'

'Sounds as though they wanted you dead. Why did they want Willy dead?'

'They did not. I don't think so. Mr Willy is not sure. These Russians want to take Italian business. The drugs, the protection, the prostitution. Everything. Mr Willy is aware. Mr Willy knows how everything is working. Nobody wants him *dead*. We discuss. They want him *alive*. He is hard to kill but not why you think. They came here, I think – Mr Willy also believe it is possible, but he is not sure – they came not to kill him. To *take* him. Make it look like he is a criminal who steals from neighbors. Steals their toasters. Petty criminal. That way, everybody thinks he ran away. That he runs. Nobody thinks he is prisoner. As a prisoner he say to these KGB Russians everything he know about how Italians' Mafia work their business.'

'And he would tell them everything, why?'

The question seemed nonsensical to Mr Ananyev. 'They torture him, he talk. The Italians, Mr Willy said to me, train biker gangs. The Russians want to stop that. They need that knowledge for themselves, not for bikers. Mr Willy, he has that knowledge.'

Cinq-Mars thought it strange, as their talk went along, that he seemed to be conversing with an old companion, someone with whom he'd traveled through decades.

'What was the purpose in robbing toasters?'

'Also wallets. Don't forget that.'

'True. Wallets and purses. And radios.'

His wrists uncuffed, Ananyev sat with his hands folded together except to raise them, still clasped, to scratch an itchy eyebrow.

'They want people think Mr Willy is a bad man. Also, they recruit,' he answered. 'These Russians. They look for talent. Not everybody who steals is a thief. You know, in the heart. A black heart you can find. But a black heart who will do what he is told, loyal, smart, that is hard to find. I make sure my son, Mikhail, is not reliable to them. LSD he took. That night. Gangs don't like that. Neither I don't like it. But that night, he had permission. I don't want them to like him. They liked Johnny Bondar. Look at him now.'

'Do you know who Willy is to us, Mr Ananyev?'

'He told to me, yes.'

'He related the story of the coal bin. He must have trusted you to tell you that story.'

The Russian's smile was not a typical reaction, Cinq-Mars suspected, therefore genuine.

'At first, no. Long story. Short story is, at first, he was very suspicious of me. I suspicious of him, too. Like you do, we investigate each other. Find out the other one not our enemy. Both of us, our situation we live, very glad to have a friend to trust.'

'May I ask,' Cinq-Mars requested, disengaging from the cop–suspect aspect to their conversation, 'why you were at the Bondar party?'

'To see who show up.'

'Who showed up?'

'Two dirty cops. You want their names?'

'I know their names. Mr Ananyev. We want to bring Willy in.

Do you understand what I mean? To take him out of the battle he's in and return him to regular life. We also want his knowledge, as other people do. Do you know where he is?'

'This I do not know. It is possible Mr Willy does not know.'

'Do you know what he's doing? Surely, at this point, he's been compromised. People want him dead or held captive.'

'What he is doing I can tell you. There is one hope, he believes. He leaves you out, the police. The law, he leaves out.'

'He has his own solution?'

'The world we live in. I tell to you, these are his words.'

'I see. What's his plan, Mr Ananyev?'

'It is a fool's plan, Detective Cinq-Mars. He wants to talk to these Russians, the bikers, the Mafia, and he wants each gang to trust him. You ask me where he is. Dead by now, I think. I fear for him. Always how it was with us. I give my advice to him because he is more foolish than a man who knows better. I am afraid for him. But. That's him. That's Mr Willy.'

'And the plan is?'

'The plan is each gang goes to war against other gangs and nobody knows who is a friend, who is the enemy. Who wins, that gang will be weaker than before. And then, only then, the police go in, pick up pieces. Not my plan. His. Mr Willy's.'

'He wants the gangs to kill each other off? That's his solution after all these years?'

'He say no choice. No more does he believe in the law. Not Mr Willy.'

'What are his chances, do you think?'

'To survive for him? Very slim.'

'I meant, to start this gang war?'

Ananyev thought about it. Said, 'If he's alive, he might start it. Don't ask me who finish it. He believes the Mafia survive, do only unions and construction after that, import–export business, mostly drugs. The Russians he wants defeated. He is afraid of them the most. The bikers will grow stronger. That will not be good, but they will finish weaker. They are not ready to take control without they fail. He wants to slow them down. His plan, will it work? To answer, I must know, is he alive or dead?'

Cinq-Mars sat back. More to unravel, more to comprehend, more to weigh and evaluate. A man on the loose with the power to implement a monstrous, murderous idea was dangerous. All-out warfare among gangs might seem beneficial from a singular viewpoint, but chaos and wickedness set loose in the midst of a law-abiding population was never wise. The progress of any gang war was unforeseeable and predictions of its final result dubious.

'Why, Mr Ananyev,' he asked, 'did you admit to killing the KGB agent so quickly? I know you want to help Mick, but that seems drastic – very foolish – to me.'

Ananyev pinched his shoulders forward, then apart. 'To help Mikhail, yes? Also, I thought, I help Mr Willy. If people think he not the man who did the murder, but only me, a crazy janitor, maybe he be safer. In his world. A good lawyer gets me off later.'

For a moment, Cinq-Mars entertained a nutty thought out of nowhere, that pinning the tail on a donkey could sometimes be a tricky maneuver. Especially if the donkey turned out to be a different sort of animal. Try pinning the tail on a lynx in the wild.

'Was it true? Did you kill the foreign agent?'

'This time, my mouth I keep shut.'

That seemed wise. 'Why does he do it, do you think?' Cinq-Mars asked the janitor, the former engineer. 'We call him Coalface. How does a man darken his soul and go into the life knowing he's underground for decades? Who takes that on, and why? Why did you do whatever it is you did, Mr Ananyev?'

Briefly, they returned each other's sharp glance. Ananyev's response was unsuspected and cut through to the quick.

'Why do you?' he asked.

The remark made Henri Casgrain smile.

The room filled with silence for extended moments. Perhaps they were all asking the same question of themselves.

'My son,' Ananyev put to him.

The man had more than lived up to his end of the bargain. Cinq-Mars tacked on a stipulation anyway. 'I expect a full apology for my head wounds, and for running away as he did. I wasn't dressed for that chase. Please find out from him who was behind the flower heist. I want the merchants to realize that the Mafia could not protect them, but that the police helped. After, he walks. Of course, you both do.'

Bogdan Ananyev found the proposal equitable, and took on a stern, paternal expression as Casgrain stepped out of the room to fetch Mikhail. The boy stole flowers for one mob or another. He should never have done that. Time to own up to it and come clean.

FORTY

Willy took a chance that Joe Ciampini was on his farm. Probability favored the notion. The farm was a fortress with a guards' station installed at the top of the long drive. Guards passed the time in a black Caddy parked across the entrance. They emerged as Willy drove up. The man who greeted him had a pistol in his right hand tucked behind his thigh. His partner gazed out over the Caddy's rooftop, an Uzi at the ready.

Willy remembered selling the man that weapon.

He should have charged him more.

He was unarmed himself. No point doing otherwise.

The guards communicated with the farmhouse via walkie-talkie. Once identified and frisked, Willy was directed to park off the highway and enter on foot. A hike. Dusk beginning to settle. Birds sang their final riffs and a breeze kicked up as the sun descended. In the barnyard, a man with a rifle frisked him again, in case he'd gathered rocks as he strolled in or fashioned a slingshot out of willow branches. This guy was more intrusive than the guard up the road.

'Front door,' the man said.

'Thanks for nothing,' Willy said.

'My job.'

'You had to enjoy it so much?'

Willy got it. Either the Mafia was under attack, or they had killed their own people, in which case they wanted it to look as though they were under attack. In his mind, the fortress mentality was for show.

After the precautions outside, he was comforted to find the

interior of the country home devoid of such measures. Just him and Ciampini, and the boss wasn't nursing a Glock on his lap. The older man sat him in a comfortable armchair and crossed the room to pick up glasses. He offered bourbon and Willy accepted. Willy detected a weariness in the man's eyes. Rumor had it that he'd been interested in retirement years ago, a return to Sicily. He had family, friends, and a villa there; he might find solace in his waning years. Other rumors maintained that his retirement was put on hold after Ciampini's daughter went to prison for wounding a cop in her basement. She'd held a young woman hostage as a favor to her dad. Strings were pulled on her behalf. Still, the mob boss could do no better than secure a light sentence, and until she was paroled, he had to stick around. Who knows what would happen to her on the inside if he left the country? He was stuck in place.

Ciampini crossed the room yet again to return with a bottle of Knob Creek. 'Kentucky bourbon,' he stated, and poured. 'I'm thinking about getting into horses down there.'

'The horses, yeah?'

'Thoroughbreds. Buy a Kentucky farm. See how that goes.'

A pipe-dream. He'd never be admitted to the winner's circle. Willy assumed Ciampini knew it, too. Everybody nurtured unreachable dreams, if only to keep themselves alive.

'Didn't ask you to come here, Willy. Without no invite, you knock on my door. For what?'

'Boss, I'm lying so low that's not hair growing out of my nostrils. It's grass. I promised I'd be in touch when the time came.'

'What time has come?'

'The farmers' market. Doesn't happen every day. Thought the time was right to check in, like I said I would.'

'What you think, Willy? Those two, Le Gris, Pasquale, going down like that. A tragedy.'

'Yes, sir. A tragedy. Maybe they had it coming. Not for me to know.'

'What's that supposed to mean in my language?'

'Boss, those two guys wanted me dead. Maybe you know why. I don't. Maybe they weren't loyal to you, and when a man has enemies, you know it yourself, accidents happen. Maybe they had it coming.'

'Who can say?' Ciampini raised his glass.

'Who can say?' Willy asked him back, and raised his glass, also.

'To life!' Ciampini toasted, with sudden relish.

'To life.'

They clinked and drank, their homage to the dead.

Ciampini gave the liquid time to raise his spirits before speaking again. 'Somebody must die,' he said. 'How do things go on the street, Willy? Give me your report.'

Willy was sitting on the edge of his chair, knees apart. The coffee table between them provided a resting place for his Knob Creek. He made certain to use a coaster. He didn't know if Ciampini's family was at home, and didn't want the woman of the house to show up and berate him for not using a coaster. He'd had that happen.

'It's like I said,' he revealed. 'Worse, but I expected it. I expected the worst.'

'What have you learned, Willy? Do you have a strategy?'

Now or never. 'Like I said, it's the Hells, boss. They need to be brought into line. You can't go fighting them right now. You've lost too many of your own. Go to The Rabbit. I talked to him. He's willing. Give him the women across the city, the coming-into-town girls with the local trade he already has. He'll give back a fair piece. In exchange, teach the Hells a lesson. They want to take the women over themselves, and the drugs, too. With The Rabbit and his Russians, you keep the drugs, you lose the women, but you get a piece for your loss. With the Hells, you lose the women, you lose the drugs too, and you don't get a piece until they're afraid of you again. That might never happen. This is maybe a last chance, your only chance, to take them out. They don't know who's available to you, who's willing. Call The Rabbit, boss. Pop off a few Hells. They'll still work for you but under control after that. Take back the city.'

Ciampini listened quietly. He had probably drawn a similar conclusion. Willy knew that. The best advertising reinforced an existing preference.

'Enjoy your bourbon, Willy?'

'Delicious. I been too busy to have a drink lately. This goes down like pure medicine. Right to my toes.'

'Willy,' Ciampini said, 'there's you to be talked about, too. Not only the Hells. Not only The Rabbit and his new crew. Don't leave that part out.'

'I'm sorry to hear it, boss.'

'Don't be sorry. We clean up the situation.'

'That's good. Yeah. How?'

'I had an old foe. A cop. We're like a couple of old dog warriors. Both bitten, both chewed up, but we both still bite.'

'Old dogs. I like that. Old junkyard dogs.'

'I don't live in no junkyard, Willy.'

'Of course not. No. I misspoke.'

'Neither does Touton.'

'That old cop?'

'He's the one. We fought each other over the years, Willy. Good fight.'

'He's bothering you again?'

'If he is, I don't care. He's got a right. But some young guy's been brought in he told me about. I don't like him. I don't want him in my city. He sent my daughter up for shooting a cop. It was only a wound. Hard to believe he thinks there's no consequence for that.'

'Yeah. Heard of him. Strange name.'

'Strange name. Yeah. Cinq-Mars.'

'Right.'

'Put him in the river.'

'What?'

'I think you heard me, Willy. Or are you telling me that you gone deaf? Giving you a direct order here in case you didn't notice. Don't hesitate on me.'

'No, boss. No. It's just . . . That's not my usual ticket. You know that.'

'Willy, Willy, I'm losing guys left, right. Everybody has to step up. Do different jobs. Fill in. Especially guys who want to prove to me. If I wonder about a guy, I give him that opportunity to prove to me.'

'Are you wondering about me, boss?'

'On my mind, Willy. You. Lately. I got guys up from New York, couple guys in from Detroit. Good guys in a fight. Still, the local crew got to do its part. You know? This cop, this Cinq-Mars, he needs to buy his own Kentucky farm. Ride a horse in the sky. Play the fucking Kentucky banjo in the clouds. Your job, Willy. You don't have to do it yourself. Arrange if you want, except don't use our boys. Bikers like that kind of shit. What they don't know, they bump a cop, we start fighting them, right there we're on the right side of the law, they're not. See how this can work? The fight can go that way. See what you work out. Me, I believe if you want a job done, do it yourself. Up to you, Willy. Either way. Get it done. Just make sure it don't point back to me. That could get my daughter in trouble. Here's what I want.'

Willy waited while Ciampini wet his whistle with bourbon.

'Tomorrow,' the boss continued, 'big cop funeral. For that dick Poof-Poof the kid whacked. Cops coming from across the continent, marching downtown with their big-sack bellies. Swing their arms. Lift up their knees. Turns out, the dead guy is partner to Cinq-Mars. I would've liked it was him he shot, but didn't happen like that. OK, instead, tomorrow, before the funeral or in the middle or after, it's his funeral anyway. We bury Cinq-Mars. A message to cops. *Don't mess with us.* They been messing with us here, New York, Miami, fucking Chicago, Las Vegas. It stops here. Do it or arrange it, Willy. You want a war? You been *pushing* for a war? All I hear out of you. OK. But I want you in the fight yourself. Deep in. Not just putting it on me or on the Hells or on The Rabbit. You fight, too. You're a killer now, turns out. Show me, Willy. Take Cinq-Mars out for a swim. Seal your place. Great opportunity. Any problem?'

Willy held the man's gaze. 'No problem,' he said. 'You bet, Mr Ciampini. This Cinq-Mars, he's in the river.'

'Good.' Ciampini lounged back on his sofa, pulled one leg up and extended it across the seat. 'I didn't want you to think you can open a dam, let the water out, without you don't get wet yourself.'

'Understood. I'll dive in, boss. Deep as you want.'

'Good. Drink your bourbon, Willy. Then plan this. You got a brain. My advice? The voice of experience? Don't leave nothing to chance.'

Willy had arrived at the farm on a whim. Now he sensed that Ciampini had expected him to show up all along.

FORTY-ONE

Thirty hours to take out a policeman and implement a scheme of his own. A tight schedule. As Willy drove, ideas leaped across the glare of his headlights. This sudden change to his fortunes, if he handled it right, he was beginning to think could be for the best.

He found it ironic that he started his life's work as a peacekeeper in the Canadian Army. He was assigned to United Nations Command Military Armistice Commission, charged with supervising the end to the Korean War. Buddies died when their Jeep drove over an unexploded bomb. There and then he understood that a ceasefire did not mean peace. As a soldier, he patroled a zone between battling forces that desired to kill each other. He now walked a similar demarcation line, only not as a peacekeeper. He wholly intended to ignite a war.

In the army, he received letters from his mother, usually about his dad. Reports that grew increasingly dark. His dad had been a soldier, too, and like his son had a stubborn streak that was unassailable. A mobster wanted protection money from his dad's used-car dealership. A car was set ablaze. Then three more. *He won't pay!* his mother informed him, and it was difficult to know if she was infuriated with her husband or especially proud. Then the family home was firebombed. Out of control, raging, the man sought vengeance. Mobsters intercepted Willy's dad. Clubbed him into a coma. Willy was granted compassionate leave and might have engaged in a regrettable fury of his own were it not for his mother falling ill under the strain. He returned to duty while she remained hospitalized with congestive heart failure, soon to pass away two weeks after her husband.

He never learned who specifically was responsible for his father's death. His experiences in Korea taught him that it didn't matter. If executed, whoever had been responsible would be replaced. Criminal forces perpetuated themselves that way.

Out on the front lines, walking vacant roads between warring factions, a desire was born in him to roar back at the heart of the mob – in reality, any mob – eliminate it from the face of the earth. For his dad, for his mom, for all those who had been victimized.

He talked to random people about it, out on the front lines. He wasn't posturing. He was daydreaming.

Then a few very specific people talked to him.

They were Americans.

They worked something out after he left the army. More training. His commitment tested.

He passed with flying colors.

He remembered those days.

That fire within. It still burned.

Time took a toll. Revenge remained a core motivation, but he had changed, and his comprehension had altered. He had lived among the vile too long. Some guys intrigued him. He was swayed by their humanity, their humor, their fears and fearlessness. The ruthless, the jaded, the murderous were commonplace in his world now. He had become one with them. The things he'd done. Sold guns. Pitched good advice. Regulated the bookkeeping. Kept the prostitutes busy, the drug-runners safe. He had earmarked the innocent for extortion and cast his glance away when violence was ordained. Now he wanted mob justice to decide the course of events. He did not trust a fearful judiciary and despised a police department he knew to be corrupt. Apart from that, he understood that a job done properly meant that he should be taken down with the rogues' gallery himself. He deserved to be impaled on the spear of justice. He'd joined forces with his enemies and, like them, true for any mobster, yearned to keep his secrets concealed.

He did not want to speak of them.

Once he had been an idealist. No more.

Once he had been in fighting trim. He'd purposefully let himself grow soft. Touton had suggested it as part of his disguise. Though he never pulled his teeth out or indulged excessively in candy.

Ironic, also, as he stepped on the accelerator and merged into traffic, that Ciampini had mentioned Captain Touton. The man who met him in a coal bin. Touton warned that whatever reason he gave himself to embark on a life undercover would not hold up through the years. That proved true. His original impetus, for blatant revenge, which he hadn't admitted to anyone, lingered in his bloodstream like a dormant virus. Overruled now by an impetus more prevalent, more determined.

He needed to ignite a war, not for revenge, but for the sake of his own salvation.

To make his life whole, or worthwhile, to forgive his manifest transgressions, he needed the gangs to implode. Otherwise, his life underground had been futile.

Captain Touton, he believed, had seen it coming. He'd like to talk to him again. Perhaps, if the conversation swung that way, enter for the record a full confession, a tally of his sins.

A tally of his contributions, too. Few knew of them.

And yet. He had killed two men. Fingered two others for death. An end to a peacekeeper's life.

With it, an end to other lives ahead. Quickly, likely, an end to his own.

To be determined. Time to drop a dime. That was paramount now.

His end game was upon him.

Willy drove straight to The Rabbit's nightclub. As if his mind was on accelerant, he exceeded all speed limits. No hassles. He wasn't the first speeder to get away with his foot to the floor. He counted on cops prepping for the funeral procession the following afternoon. Whether they were or not, he made it into town in record time.

He had twenty-nine hours left to kill a cop and start a war.

The bartender punched The Rabbit's number into an intercom then passed Willy a Molson Ex. Word returned to take the stairs. Wow. Either he'd moved up in the world or his fate was sealed. The bartender shrugged, indicating he could neither ask that question nor answer it.

The Rabbit slouched in the swivel chair behind his desk. 'Willy, my Willy,' he greeted him.

'Hey, The Rabbit, how's it going?'

'One big favor, Wills. Cut off the balls of this world. A rusty hacksaw I got for that.'

'OK,' Willy said. He didn't know if the man was doped up or generally off his nut. He sat down opposite him.

'Give me best news you got. What goes on?'

'Cops from everywhere are in town for a funeral tomorrow.'

'Heard that. A cop funeral good news to me.'

'Joe Ciampini wants to make a statement. Expect fireworks. Maybe a late-night dance.'

'They should come to my place, these cops. I got whores don't mind jerking off a badge. One girl, strap on a Glock, bugger 'em the way they like it.'

His language in English might be stilted, but he could create an image.

'I'll leave those arrangements to you, The Rabbit.'

'I know. You like your pecker clean. Wash in turpentine. What else new in the fat?'

Willy was familiar with the old reference. Among those who pilfered and swindled, extorted and fought and bled for a living, *the fat* referred to the fat world where people held property and jobs, had families, pensions and vacations. The bitterness behind the phrase derived from a conviction that the criminal element lived off society's scraps, that they represented the lean, the hungry, the disadvantaged. A man such as The Rabbit might use the phrase to distance himself from the world of civility, despite being a fat cat among criminal felines. He devoured the fat of the land and the excesses of the city yet did not portray himself that way. In that sense, he admired his enemies, the bikers, who pocketed millions yet looked like human debris. To him, they had the right idea.

'Time to step up, The Rabbit,' Willy told him. 'The war's on.'

The man considered the statement in silence. Then decided, 'I make my own war.'

'Maybe you initiate your own,' Willy pointed out. 'If it comes at you, what will you do but fight?'

He had a point The Rabbit could not repudiate.

'What you know?' he asked Willy.

'Ciampini has guys in from New York and Detroit. Bolster the ranks. You know they don't show up unless it's serious. Won't be enough, I don't think. The Hells are making a move.'

'Farmers' market? That them?'

He had to be wise. For all he knew, The Rabbit had carried out that attack himself, with Ciampini's blessing or without. Ciampini could have hired him for the hit. The Rabbit's question, then, could trap him if he knew more than he let on.

'I'm not privy, The Rabbit. Let's say that Ciampini don't seem too upset. Except, he called in reinforcements. Ask yourself for what. He's vulnerable, that's true. Not weak. Don't misunderstand me. Understaffed in the short term is all. He's willing to semi-retire, peel off an enterprise, keep a piece of every action, otherwise let things go on as they are.'

'You talk to him. You have offer?'

'Depends on the war. The Hells are coming after you—'

'Wait minute, what?'

'I hope you're ready. They're coming after you because they want to take over the sex trade. That's their action. They figured out you're after it, too.'

'They don't know who is with me. You don't, neither.'

'That's to your advantage, no? They're coming anyway. I'm here to warn you to be prepared. Also to remind you that Joe Ciampini is on your side. Wants you to win.'

'You mean he hang me on a line like washing.'

'Not that way at all, The Rabbit. Still, if the Hells look like they're winning, then yeah, I'd say you should start shooting Mafia too. Take no chances that way. Then it's all-out war. A three-way. But understand, nobody wants that, except maybe the Hells. They think the Mafia is on their side. What a surprise when they find out different. They want the sex business, and the drugs, and Ciampini is willing to relinquish only the women. To you – if you pay back a slice, and if you win this fight.'

The Rabbit uttered an unintelligible noise that sounded like a scoff. 'You talk like tough guy, Willy. Who you are?'

'The messenger. Don't shoot me. But even me, I have to prove myself. Tomorrow, I shoot a cop. Boss's orders. Don't tell nobody, all right? Between me and you.'

The Rabbit remained quiet for a beat. The news serious, a surprise. 'Willy, you?'

'Me. Yeah. Everybody has to step up. Guys have gone down. So, yeah. Me too.'

'When this fight is start?'

'When you hear a knock on your door. Could be bullets. Could be a grenade, that knock, or a Molotov. Sooner. Not later. It's coming all right. Be ready. And then, fire back, The Rabbit.'

*   *   *

Sergeant-Detective Émile Cinq-Mars sat alone in his apartment at night. Lights off. A fan gently whirred on low. After midnight, quiet was an elusive prize. Alley cat tangles, dog barks, infant wails, a domestic shout, a distant siren; a car accelerates rapidly to show off the loud, deep subwoofer of its muffler; a truck brakes with a prolonged screech; a teenager's car passes, the radio turned to a level that will impair a driver's hearing by the age of twenty. Stillness – sudden, penetrating and disorienting that way – when it comes, feels triumphant.

The cacophony of the day has been quelled. Noise after dark is identifiable and precise, rather than a constant thrum of generic racket. Daytime roar is now a syncopated percussion. Cinq-Mars is aware of the aural interruptions to his meditations that keep him awake. He's risen from tossing and turning to get dressed with nowhere to go.

Wiggles his bare toes.

Content to be solitary, initially. After a notion strikes, he reaches for his phone. Armand Touton is home, he knows. He calls.

'What?' the other man barks.

'You with all the contacts.'

'Who do you want to meet? A president? The Queen? Anybody but the Pope. He's not taking my calls these days.'

'Someone to take a conversation into the core of the Hells Angels.'

Touton's gruff nocturnal breathing.

'Armand?'

'I can give you a name. He works days. Sleeps at night like the rest of us old farts.'

'I can wake him like I woke you.'

'Better I do. Me, he knows. You? He's chainsawed guys for less.'

'Call. I need to talk to him tonight.'

After The Rabbit, Willy rolled into Slewfoot's strip club while it was in full swing. Stepping from the quiet of the streets in its out-of-the-way, other-side-of-the-moon location into the high-bedlam-attack-volume inside created a polar shift. The dance music was raucous, the choruses of hooting drunks profane. Quieter men occupied tables in the rear. Some sat still with their drinks. Others conversed loudly. Still others invited women over for a private dance. The ladies put their high-heeled feet onto the dancing stools they carried with them and accepted fives and tens and twenties in the elastic of their thongs they'd slide to one side for a view. Willy saw that a contingent of out-of-town cops had found its way inside. Their haircuts, mustaches and interactions gave them away, as did their accents and demeanor. He bellied up to the bar.

'You here?' the bartender asked him.

'What, I'm a mirage? What the hell kind of question is that?'

'You're not usually here so late, Willy.'

'I need to talk to Slew.'

'He's not around. You know that. The sun's down.'

'You think I didn't notice? Talk to somebody who can talk to somebody who can call him. We need to meet up tonight.'

'It's important?'

'When did you buy a loaf of stupid?'

Kids today.

He declined a drink. It took about five minutes before a phone was put down on the bar in front of him. Willy picked up.

'Can you come in?' Willy asked. 'Or I can go to you. Critical.'

'Pen and paper, Willy. Give you an address.'

He had his own pen. A napkin served as a pad.

A north end bar. 'Give me twenty,' Willy said. 'In case of traffic.'

'If you're packing, leave it behind in your shitbox. Otherwise, no guarantees on your life expectancy.'

He headed north on Boulevard St Laurent, the Main, the official divider between east and west Montreal. To a degree, it marked the division between French Montreal to the east, and the conglomeration of everyone under the sun to the west, including both English and affluent French. Along the Main, nationalities commingled, and he drove into the garment district and parked down from the bar where he was meeting Slew. He didn't park right up close, not wanting to create the impression he had a quick getaway in mind. All he intended was a heart to heart with a wise old owl of a criminal to see if he could set him on a path to war, to tear down the house the Mafia built, and raise Slew's adopted gang – the Hells Angels – to a new threshold. That Willy meant to send the bikers into a lethal tailspin, he'd keep to himself.

The north end bar Slewfoot selected was dark, with a few regular citizens playing footsie under the tables or entwining fingers above them. He saw Slew in the rear of the narrow space but took no more than three steps inside before being accosted. He was covertly frisked by a massive hirsute man in a suit who was usually more comfortable in biker leather. Permitted entry, Willy joined Slew in the back.

Slid onto the booth's banquette.

'You're not armed,' Slew said, 'but I am. You woke me up. For that, I'll blow your balls off if you waste my time, Willy. Understand, this cannot be no habit.'

Willy ignored all that. 'Good to see you too, Slew. Interesting times, hey?'

'Drink?'

'Why not? I'll have an Ex.'

Slew didn't react. He said, 'What am I, your waiter? Raise your own arm.'

Willy did so. The waiter had been hesitant to come over without an invitation. He knew who he was dealing with.

The two men understood to wait until the beer arrived and the waiter had vanished again so that no word of their talk would be overheard. The beer tasted warm, but he wasn't going to complain.

'War's on, Slew. No stopping it now. Ciampini's bringing in boys from New York and Detroit. The Rabbit's loaded up a bunch of imports from overseas.'

'Overseas? What the hell does that mean?'

'Russians, Slew. Ukrainians. Poles and East Germans. A tide you better stem before it's a flood. They want to be the new Mafia. Get a foothold in North America that way. Maybe let you guys be their muscle, the same way Ciampini uses your French pals to keep them on the farm.'

'That's the plan, huh?'

'The Rabbit's put on a vest. He's not even the mover. He's just the door they're walking through. They need the door. Do you get me?'

'Close the door. Why doesn't Ciampini do it?'

'He needs to know first, who wins that fight? What goes to the victor, Slew?'

'Is that an offer?'

'The sex trade is on the table. Your boys were planning to fight the Mafia for it anyway. Fight The Rabbit instead. And look, everybody figures your boys want more. Not just the street drugs but the international trade. We get that. Ciampini gets that, but he's not giving up everything he's got, OK? He's ready to retire but not that fast. He wants stuff to pass on. You will get the sex trade. You even get a leg up the ladder with the drug trade, I can help with that, as long as you control the street action. Keep the prospectors out. After that, well, that's the future, isn't it? I'm not here to talk about the future. I'm here for today and tomorrow.'

Slew showed complete interest while indicating nothing. He shuffled around in his seat finally. Unlike Willy, he was drinking water, and took a long draught.

'You on the wagon?' Willy asked.

'Doc says I have to keep my kidneys wet. Stay hydrated.'

'Sorry to hear that.'

'I'll live. Keep that in mind.'

'I'm on your side here, Slew.'

'I bet. About you, Willy.'

'What about me?'

'I have my doubts.'

'I understand that.'

'Do you? How do we know you're not running your own game? Beginning to feel like it, though I can't figure out what's in it for you. Survival, maybe. Anything else?'

'What game? I'm talking to the boss is all. Letting you know how he sees it.'

'I talk to him too.'

'I know that.'

'So what's your skin, Willy?'

'Mine? Not much. All I got to do is shoot a cop tomorrow.'

That brought on a moment of silence.

'Any cop?' Slew asked.

'Specific. The one who sent his daughter up.'

'Makes sense,' Slew said.

'I'm allowed to hire it out. But I'll do it myself. Let it be a sign.'

'A sign.'

'To start the war. I kill a cop. After that, cops are less concerned if a few bikers shoot up The Rabbit's shop.'

'Is that what we're doing?'

'You can wait until he shoots up your place first, if you want. Not a pimple on my dick. Not good for business, though. Not to mention what you brought up to me before.'

'What's that?'

'Your life expectancy.'

Slew mulled the implications. 'Ciampini?'

'On your side. He expects a fallout. As long as you hold up your end, he'll have a trigger finger when it comes to Russians. Clean out a bunch, put the rest on the run, take over the sex trade top down. Your boys will be on the ladder to success and you don't go through an all-out war with the Maf.'

Slew soaked his kidneys again. Put his glass down.

'First things first, Willy. You get to start it off. We see you take down this cop, only then do we take out The Rabbit. Minimum five guys drop. That should make an impression on Russians, close the door. But you first, Willy. So we know this is how it will be, that you're selling me good dope.'

'You think I'd dare cross you? I thought everybody knew I was smart.'

'Counting on it, Willy.'

'That's why I'm here so late at night, Slew. I got opportunity tomorrow. Big cop parade. The funeral for my mark's partner. My mark will be there.'

Willy held the other man's gaze, then resorted to his beer.

'Tell me your plan.'

'Orders just landed. No complete plan yet.'

'I need your plan.'

Willy devised one on the spot. He'd been mulling it over on the trip in. 'Look, the parade is out of the question. I'm not going to kill a cop with two or three *hundred* international cops marching by, plus another two or three hundred local flics. It's not like I'm a sharpshooter in a bell tower. This has to be up close and real personal.'

'It does. Tell me.'

'The gravesite. Why not? The parade, the memorial service, lousy with cops. The gravesite? No more than a few. My mark will be there.'

'Why? How do you know? Maybe you're only hoping for the convenience.'

'He's the dead guy's partner. He has to stand with the family, no?'
Slewfoot nodded. 'Makes sense.'

'Pick my opportunity. If I'm lucky, it'll come after most of the cops disperse. Hostage my way out.'

'High risk.'

'Damn straight. The dead guy's daughter was on the TV news. See her? A babe in arms. *Babe in arms*, Slew. *Two* hostages for the price of one, and no one's taking a pot-shot at me standing beside a babe in arms. If things work out, I keep my skin. I'm also the manhunt focus. Except, nobody can find me. I've got that covered already, and anyway they don't know me. I got my disguise going. Meantime, you get to face-plant The Rabbit in a gutter. Let him bleed into a sewer. Show the Russians you won't be pushed out. Send them back to Moscow. When they're ready to return, let it be to New York or Miami or fucking Toronto. Anywhere but here. Your boys will be in charge by then.'

Slew wasn't listening to advice on how to conduct his own affairs. Still focused on Willy's plan.

'You need help?'

'Should be able. Don't want to complicate the situation.'

'We'll be watching.'

'Why? Well. OK. Up to you. Your concern. If you help with the get-out, if that's necessary, that's even better. Otherwise, let's keep it neat.'

'It won't be. Always count on that.'

'OK. Right.'

'Change of pace for you, eh, Wills?'

'Yeah,' Willy agreed.

'My advice? Extra pair of underwear, in case you lose your shit.'

'Yeah, all right.' He slid out of the booth and stood. 'How about you buy this round?'

'Kidding me? I'm drinking tap water. You can buy your own damn beer.'

Willy nodded and went over to the cash. His plan was in play. Ciampini had inserted one helluva wrench into the machinery, but his plan was definitely in play. Follow through, and the bad guys would be wrecking the hell out of each other for weeks. Who knew who survived once the smoke cleared?

Who knew if he would?

First, he had to follow through.

Put Cinq-Mars in the river.

The bad guys covered the angles. The cops, the prosecutors, the judges, the witnesses, the courts, and when things went wrong, they even controlled the prisons. Everything and everyone could be made to heel. He hated them for that. His way, Willy determined, was the only way. How far would he push it, that was the last remaining question. Maybe he wouldn't know until the moment of truth bore down upon his back.

FORTY-TWO

Inside the bar, Émile Cinq-Mars was stopped by a man with biceps splitting the seams of his suit jacket.

'You need a new tailor.'

'Spread,' the door monitor said. Bushy eyebrows. Facial hair that infringed on his nose and cheekbones. Hair to his shoulder blades.

Cinq-Mars declined to comply. 'I'm not armed.'

'I decide.'

'Touch me, I'll be back with the SWAT. You won't like the charge.'

'We got lawyers.'

'You won't like it.'

'I'm patting you down, copper.'

'What you do to little boys.'

'That's supposed to mean what?'

'Your lawyer won't like it, either. Nobody you know will like it. You'll get off – eventually – but who will believe you, really?'

An impasse.

'Back alley,' the man suggested.

'I've wrestled horses bigger than you.' Not a lie. He'd pinned more than one horse in an ornery mood to inject him or pry wire from a foreleg. 'Just so you know.'

Cinq-Mars had height on him, not weight.

'Serge,' a voice said. Both men sought it out. The bartender's. He cocked his head to indicate the back of the room. There, Slewfoot was waving Cinq-Mars past his own security guard. The big man with the hairy face stepped aside.

Cinq-Mars walked back and sat opposite the older fellow.

'You're Slew?' he asked.

'Cinq-Mars,' the other man greeted him. 'How's old Touton anyway?'

'Tough as shoe leather. Thanks for seeing me.'

'Me and him, we go back a distance.' The man altered his tone to a singsong voice, adding, 'Out of the mists of time. He calls, I give his man a listen.'

Not typical gangster locution.

'He got around,' Cinq-Mars stated, 'back in the day.'

'Truth is, I work a dayshift now. Started that to get out from under his damned Night Patrol. Since he retired, still my habit to work days. Plus, like him, I'm as old as a post.'

'He always boasted that under his watch he wouldn't allow biker gangs in the city.'

'I was West End Irish back then. We kept our heads down. Bikers were run out of town.'

'The Angels are French.' He was expressing a concern.

'They can fit in one or two old Irish if we make ourselves useful. Not to worry. I'll convey whatever story needs telling where it needs to be heard. Touton calls, says to see you. I see you. What's up?'

Touton had not been specific on the man's position within the Hells Angels. Lean, a short ponytail tied in a bob, the hint of a tattoo along his collar line. Cinq-Mars could imagine him looking the part on a Harley. He could also look like a regular citizen with a hint of the hip. He could move through different milieus. Even on a Harley he could come across as a benign geriatric biker if he preferred. Clearly, the man was smart, articulate; Cinq-Mars suspected he could alter his diction to suit the conversation. To a lesser degree, he possessed similar ability. Their take on being multilingual.

'I want a war called off,' Cinq-Mars told him.

Slew did not deny the possibility, which came across as respectful. 'You're current, Cinq-Mars. You know about a war nobody knows about because it hasn't started yet.'

'I see I'm talking to the right person.'

'I might be knowledgeable. How do you expect to stop what's not begun?'

'Voice of reason. Anyway, two men dead in the farmers' market is a start. If I may be blunt, the Hells have gained ground, but a war that nobody wins sets you back in time. It'll draw attention. Damage inflicted by Russians and Italians. The official retribution will also hurt. That's bound to come down later, if not sooner.'

'Not sure that Italians will damage us. I'm impressed you heard about Russians. Right up to speed. Maybe you should work for us.'

'I know the side I'm on. Not sure you do.'

'Don't get you there.'

'Don't count on Ciampini.' He followed up with an educated guess. 'Don't count on Willy, either. He might not be who he seems.'

The next pause was a lengthy one. By naming him, Cinq-Mars was protecting Willy, dashing any potential notion that he was connected to law enforcement. At the same time, he sought to undermine any plan he was cooking up, along the lines of what the janitor suggested.

Noticing that Slew was drinking water, with hand signals Cinq-Mars requested the same from the bartender, who hopped over with a glass.

'What do you think?' Cinq-Mars asked.

'Under advisement,' Slew said. He leaned in, lowered his voice. 'You have your own reasons not to want us dead. That puzzles me, but I'll put it aside for now. I'll treat this as a favor delivered. For that, and for old times' sake with Touton, I'm giving one back. Clear the debt that way.'

'No debt, but OK,' Cinq-Mars said, leaning in as well.

'You're a marked man.'

'Ah, this would be from your crew? Why?'

'Not mine. You warned me off Ciampini. Well, you sent Ciampini's daughter up the river. Did you forget? Ciampini didn't. Payback's on the way.'

Cinq-Mars settled back in his seat. 'Who's he got left to do it?'

'Think about it. Something might occur.'

Something did.

'When and where?'

'No time like the present. By that I don't mean this minute. As for where, stay alert if you hear any whistling.'

'Whistling.'

'Best I can do. I'm nobody's snitch. Favor to Touton, I'm giving you fair warning. You didn't give me much more. Debt paid.'

'OK. Thanks. Have I made any progress, Slew?'

'We'll see. Good to meet you, Cinq-Mars.'

'Likewise. Do you have a real name?'

'Slew is for short. If you ever book me, book me as Slewfoot. The last name's O'Grady.'

They exchanged a smile and a handshake.

Cinq-Mars neither smiled nor shook hands with the guard at the door, and departed.

FORTY-THREE

B y tradition, funeral services for slain Roman Catholic policemen were conducted at the city's downtown cathedral. A restoration underway there forced Detective Norville Geoffrion's service to be relocated to Notre-Dame, an historic church in Old Montreal that was frequently chosen for state and celebrity funerals. Underappreciated in life, Nord would be going out with a pomp and grandeur normally reserved for eminent figures.

Tower bells alerted the heavens above and citizens below to his passing.

Police from most American states, every Canadian province and numerous cities arrived to pay homage to a fallen brother. Invited to accompany Nord's daughter, with her baby in arms, Émile Cinq-Mars observed officers fill the pews in their dress blues, greens and reds. As the coffin passed down the broad aisle under the organ's fanfare, he whispered, 'Well done, Nord. Good on you.'

Nobody was calling him Poof-Poof today.

Estranged from her mother, and now her father was gone. Nord's daughter, Gina, was grateful for Cinq-Mars's company. She welcomed his assurance whenever she was overwhelmed by the somber pageantry. She extended an invitation to ride in the hearse that would wind through the streets of Montreal, cross the east side of Mount Royal, and ascend the mountain to the cemetery where the Police Brotherhood had provided a plot. In death, Nord was to be remembered, and according to the granite inscription donated by the department, revered forever.

The modest graveside internment service suffered a delay. Officials had been snarled in traffic in the old part of town. Another police embarrassment as they couldn't handle traffic control. Those who were first to arrive at the cemetery waited by the roadside, prepared to walk a distance in. Among them, Cinq-Mars nodded to the older priest. They'd met. A second priest helped organize an expanding line of dignitaries. Not the mayor but his second-in-command, not the police chief but his first assistant, plus the head of the Police Brotherhood and Captain Delacroix from his *poste*, were present. Ranking officers from visiting forces and higher-ups in the local bureaucracy mingled together, followed by an official honor guard of constables with long rifles. The older priest attempted to wave these men to the front and seemed annoyed by his junior's ineptitude.

Bugged by the chaos, Cinq-Mars let it go. He'd stand by Gina.

The next limo carried Captain Armand Touton and Detective Henry Casgrain. His partners past and present were seeing this through to the end, perhaps more for his sake than Nord's memory. Touton joined the assistants to the mayor and chief of police. Casgrain, a little lost, sidled up to Cinq-Mars.

He had a bone to pick with him. 'Touton said you called last night. You went out?'

'Took a meeting, yeah.'

'You shouldn't take them alone, Émile.'

'You had a ball game on. Anyway, no overtime. Did you win or lose?'

'The game was long over by the time you went out. What's going on?'

'I guess you lost. Sorry about that.'

'Émile—'

'Me and the Hells, Henri. We're pals now. Inseparable for life. Why'd you lose?'

'Couldn't hit with runners on. Your humor eludes me. Are the gangs at war?'

'To be determined. What about your pitching?'

'Not bad for once. Next time we'll get them.'

'Henri, do you know anything about whistling?'

'I can whistle. What's to know?'

'I'm told it's dangerous.' Cinq-Mars checked that Gina was beyond earshot. Thankfully, her husband and child were keeping her occupied. 'Word is, I'm a target. Ciampini wants revenge for sending his daughter up the Old Mill Stream.'

'The Hells told you this? Émile, don't take it lightly.'

'I'm not. Why I'm telling you now. So, whistling. Anything?'

'Nothing. I mean, we're in a graveyard, there's that.'

'There's what?'

'You know. A graveyard. Whistling.'

Cinq-Mars returned a blank expression.

'OK. It's an English expression. Why should you know it? Can't recall how I do.'

'What's the expression?'

'Whistling past a graveyard.'

'What does that mean?'

'Goes back in time. Used to mean bucking up your courage when you walk past graves. Helps to deflect the whistler's apprehension about dying. Or of ghosts. Since then, it means being cheerful in a crappy situation. Or, ignoring what's risky to get a job done, hoping for the best outcome by ignoring pitfalls, that sort of thing. What's this about?'

He blew out a gust of air. 'I'm supposed to watch my back if I hear whistling. So don't, I might get jumpy.'

'Émile. Take it seriously. Look where you are.'

He looked. He got it. 'Naw.'

'A French guy warned you? Maybe he didn't know the English phrase, either.'

'Irish, actually.'

'Émile. Irish? They recite a phrase with hidden meaning just to brush their teeth.'

Something to that, perhaps. He'd wanted Casgrain as his partner to have a mind close by capable of perceiving unique angles to any situation. He knew he should listen.

'Émile, you're out in the open. Ciampini knew you had to be here today. He's had time to prepare. The trees, the tombstones, he could hide a dozen shooters on the perimeter. High ground and clear escapes. I'd shoot you here. A walk in the park, so to speak, for a gunman.'

Cinq-Mars resisted the notion. 'Sharpshooters aren't a local MO.'

'This started with KGB in a closet. How is that local MO? The Rabbit has Russians flying in from Vladivostok. Yesterday, Mafioso stepped off a plane from New York. We weren't informed, of course, until they vanished from view.'

No further convincing necessary. 'OK,' Cinq-Mars determined. 'Eyes peeled. Ears wide. Let Touton know. Warn anybody you trust. Be wise with strangers. Probably pointless, but we'll take precautions.'

'Do I tell Delacroix?'

Cinq-Mars sighed. 'Sure. Ignore him if he barks orders.'

'You should leave.'

'Can't. I'm looking after Nord's daughter and granddaughter. Go.'

Casgrain briefed Touton on the possible threat. Both had a word with Captain Delacroix; from a distance Cinq-Mars observed their intensity unfold. Obvious that Delacroix proposed something the other two argued against. A second plan was proposed and modified before they nodded in agreement.

Those three moved through the mourners. Anyone not in uniform was asked to identify him- or herself as the pack started moving down the serpentine path to the gravesite. They cleared a knoll where their destination became clear. A hundred yards off, a mound of earth stood out as available backfill. There, the hearse took position on a crest against an azure sky.

Gina trembled, seeing it again, and gave her wee daughter a kiss.

One priest walked ahead of the honor guard, the other right behind, followed by Cinq-Mars and the Geoffrion family. Then came a mishmash of dignitaries. Delacroix fell into step, while Casgrain and Touton continued to wade through the gathering, checking ID.

They reached the gravesite.

Armand Touton flashed the OK sign. A long shot to think that an assassin strolled among a gathering of police, many armed. Whistling, then, did not pertain to the cemetery, although Casgrain's notion of a sharpshooter in the woods could prevail. Impossible to guard against that contingency now.

The mourners steeled themselves for the imminent emotional slurry. Pallbearers adjusted the casket on a mechanism to lower it tenderly into the earth. Gina broke up then, muffling her sobs on her husband's shoulder. A final commemoration was spoken, followed by prayer. The older priest made the sign of the cross. The younger hesitated, then did likewise. His vacillation was of no consequence, and might have gone unnoticed, had he not decided to redo his error. Cinq-Mars's antennae alerted him. He nudged Touton. The sign of the cross did not catch the retired detective's attention, the priest reversing his mistake did. In correcting himself, the cleric shot a glance at Touton. No stopwatch could calculate how briefly they locked eyes, a fraction of an instant. Breaking off that connection, it took another split-second for recognition to fully dawn on the older man. His attention riveted back to the young priest. Cinq-Mars and Touton both took a step simultaneous to the priest reaching under his cassock, which ill fit him. Too loose. Cinq-Mars and Touton bounded ahead. The younger of the two was quicker, the elder closer; they assailed the second priest as a conjoined unit.

The priest's right hand fumbled under his robe. The same right hand that had done the sign of the cross from right to left, not the Western custom of left shoulder to right. A faithful Roman Catholic priest from Quebec would not do it that way, the motion instinctive through prolonged habit. This one probably taught himself that morning and only well enough to notice his gaffe.

Long strides forward. Acting on instinct, not verifiable evidence, until the pistol came out, then Cinq-Mars and Touton charged. They were on him as the gun was upraised, Touton taking the body, Cinq-Mars frantic for the shooter's arm. He clutched the man's wrist and swung it upward, thrust the arm high and back, nearly dislocating his shoulder. The gun fired. Stunned mourners shouted now and cried out. Cops spun on their heels. The man went down under the two warring detectives. Casgrain next, then Delacroix joined the kerfuffle, pinning the squirming body to the ground, and two burly officers in plainclothes identified earlier as FBI kneeled on the priest's calves.

Constables in the honor guard stood stock still, their mouths agape.

Handcuffs appeared, more than enough, and the priest was formally restrained. He coughed under the weight of bodies, the wind knocked out of him. They stood him up while he tried to stay bent over, his lungs frantic for air.

Casgrain and Cinq-Mars pinioned the priest's arms between them.

The funeral abruptly on hold. Gina Malinger looking as though she was living through an earthquake. Nord's coffin, and in a way his life and death, held in suspension.

'I swear,' their captive protested, 'I wasn't going to shoot. You know that, right? Making it look good. We have to make it look good.'

Delacroix ordered a uniform to take care of the pistol, but Touton, on top of that, brushed the young man off and seized the weapon himself.

The now defrocked priest suddenly struggled and kicked.

'Calm down, Coalface. It's over for you,' Cinq-Mars said, and pulled his hair back hard.

'Coalface?'

'My nickname for you, Willy,' Touton told him.

'Cool. I like that.' He stayed half-bent at the waist.

'Glad you approve. What name do we book you under?'

'Book me?'

'Attempted murder.'

'OK, right, I get it. Make it look good. Book me. My fake name. We don't want the bad guys to think they've been had.'

'*Who's* been had?' Casgrain asked. Not a sincere question.

'You're not serious? You can't be. I wasn't going to shoot anybody. I was making it look good, believe me.'

'If you don't mind, I won't. We're overdue for a chat,' Cinq-Mars said.

'I'll enjoy that.'

'Less than me.'

'Of course. Of course. I get it. *No!* Don't pull me up!' He'd been hunched over, catching his breath. Cinq-Mars and Casgrain straightened him and turned him to face the way out. 'You don't get it! It looks friendly if I'm just walking along. Come on, it has to look good. Don't stand me up!'

He tried to stay bent at the waist. When that didn't work, he let his knees give out, slumping down.

'We can carry.' A suggestion from a burly FBI guy. He looked strong enough to tuck him under one arm and haul him away like that.

Cinq-Mars declined. 'I think we got this. Come on, Willy. First you walk. Then we talk.'

'Hit me. Make it look good. Better yet, let me make a run for it.'

Casgrain had had enough and put a knee in his gluteus. Willy didn't expect the blow.

'Good one!' he said. 'Now let me run. Shoot at me.'

'Damn,' Cinq-Mars murmured. 'These Americans will go home thinking we're into police brutality.'

'Aren't we?' Casgrain asked.

'I'd call it kid gloves,' the FBI guy chimed in.

They lugged Willy to his feet and started marching him down the winding path from the gravesite. Behind them, people were relaxing enough to commiserate with each other. Touton walked a stride behind carrying Willy's Glock, having emptied the chambers.

Willy kept squirming and being a pest.

'We need a cattle prod,' Cinq-Mars said.

'How'd you know it was him?' Casgrain asked, then grunted from the effort of holding on to their prisoner. 'Cut it out!' he warned Willy.

'Between him and me, I make the better priest.'

'I screwed up the sign of the cross, all right?' Willy barked. 'Fuck you! Sue me. I did it on purpose, you *idiots*, to tip you off.'

'Sure you did,' Cinq-Mars said. 'You counted on us noticing. That was clever.'

'Not my final move.'

'We'll never know that now.'

'Doesn't matter. The way you rushed me. Looked good. Arresting me, good move. Hauling me out like this, almost perfect. It'll work better if you let me loose. I make a break for it. You shoot me on the run.'

He made no sense to them. Cinq-Mars was thinking that Willy and Moira Ellibee were two peas in a pod.

'You can miss,' Willy let them know. 'I'll fall anyway.'

'How did *you* know, Captain Touton?' Casgrain asked over his shoulder. 'Same?'

Willy answered on his behalf. 'That one recognized my eyes. Fucking amazing. I knew he did. I saw it. Had to draw my weapon then. Before that I was going to wait. I wanted to catch Cinq-Mars alone. Fewer people, anyway. I had another scenario in mind. This works, too. But seriously, guys, let me make a break for it. Then shoot in my direction. You don't have to aim.'

Touton had his own version of events. 'I didn't recognize your eyes. Are you nuts? What I recognized was a man trapped in his own game. Seen that look before. It's called panic.'

'I didn't panic!'

'You're saying you planned to shoot me,' Cinq-Mars summarized, 'when I was alone.'

'Wait. How did you know I was here to shoot you?'

'Thanks for the admission of guilt. That's refreshing. We're making progress.'

'No. Listen. Making it look good is all. Keep myself from being shot for real, maybe.'

'Who by?'

'We have choices. The Hells. The Mafia. The Russians.'

'You're popular.'

'Very.'

'Why would you do that, Willy? Shoot me when you get me alone but warn me first that you're planning to shoot me, then only *pretend* to do it. Strange behavior. Not a story that gets you off.'

'You're not cooperating! We're being watched.'

'Excuse me?' They stopped walking.

'We're being watched. This has to look right, guys. Hit me again. Beat the shit out of me.'

'I can't tell you how tempting that is,' Casgrain said.

'Not going to happen. At least, not out here in the open,' Cinq-Mars told him.

'This'll work, this'll work. Let me make a break for it. I'll run. Then you shoot me. In the leg. Maybe you don't miss. If you miss, I still go down. *Then* haul me out of here.'

'How nuts are you, Willy?'

'We need a war! What's wrong with you? It's the only way. We need war. Let me escape. Come on. Trust me. Shoot me. Or shoot *at* me if you don't have the balls. I'll fall, then—'

Willy did not assume he was being watched through a sharp-shooter's scope until a bullet whizzed past them. It went above or between Émile Cinq-Mars and Coalface Willy and chipped a corner off a tombstone. They sensed its velocity in the air then heard the retort from the woods ahead.

'*Gunshot!*' Cinq-Mars bellowed, and others did, too. He and Casgrain gripped Coalface between them and for a moment pulled in opposite directions. Then went left, to seek shelter when a second shot fired. Willy was hit. He yelped and went down. Blood and flesh flitted into the air. Shouting and bedlam around them now. Cops and citizens scattered, hollering. Willy's wound looked bloody and painful, but it wouldn't kill him. The detectives jerked him to his feet, he yelped again, ducked low and ran. A third bullet struck the ground behind them, kicking up a divot. A fourth caused Coalface Willy to crumple onto his face when Cinq-Mars and Casgrain both stumbled to the ground. That was close. The detectives hoisted him up again and a burly FBI guy helped out by grabbing his feet. They trotted him across the grass then threw themselves behind low upright slabs of granite gravestones. The detectives gathered themselves and peered over the stones, as other officers across the cemetery were doing.

Civilians kept their heads down.

Nothing to see. Distant woods provided cover for any assassin.

Cops lacked a legitimate response. They stayed down. Delacroix suddenly shouted commands to the honor guard, and they scampered forward to take up secure positions amid the graves with their long rifles. On command they aimed at the woods from where the shots had been fired. At trees and boulders. Then at the sky when Delacroix commanded them to shoot high. No telling how many people were wandering around up there.

'Volley one!' Delacroix called. 'Aim high! Fire!'

A bullet from each weapon in the hands of eight young men.

Then the cemetery and the mountain turned perfectly still.

Silent, save for the receptive echo of gunfire.

No call for volley two. Little point.

One of the riflemen said, 'You know we only shoot blanks, right?'

Irritated, Delacroix swore that he knew that and told him to shut his yap.

Touton crawled over from one hiding spot to another. He pulled himself up against a grave marker and checked it out. 'I got Osmond Jenkins. What kind of name is that? Died in 1929. Wonder if he was a jumper. A market crash type.'

'I got Francine LeClair,' Casgrain chipped in. 'Died in 1941. At eighty-two. Long life.'

Cinq-Mars said, 'Avelino Maltais. Nineteen years old. 1951. Car crash, I bet.'

'Rest in peace, the bunch,' Touton summed up. 'You must be happy, Cinq-Mars.'

He knew the man had a quip on his tongue. Reluctantly, he asked, 'OK. Why am I happy?'

'For the last minute or so, you're not the only one saying a prayer. For sixty seconds, we all got religion. We're still down on our knees.'

Cinq-Mars cracked a smile. Casgrain enjoyed a chuckle. Then asked his partner, 'Was that meant for you, you think?'

'The bullets? Could be,' Cinq-Mars said. 'But they hit Coalface. Maybe no coincidence.'

'No coincidence,' the man replied. 'They want me dead.'

'Who?'

'Half the world. My one way out was to kill you, Cinq-Mars.'

'I now have motive. You're really helping yourself. How's the wound?'

He'd been hit under his left shoulder. The bullet had gone through flesh and there'd been blood loss. He was doing OK but required attention.

A tall, barrel-chested man in uniform with a marine-type haircut, pistol upraised, ran up, then sank alongside them. 'Special Agent Franklin,' he said. 'FBI. We just commandeered the hearse. Let's put the wounded man into the rear, then out to the parking lot.'

'Straight to a hospital,' Cinq-Mars said.

'You got it.'

The hearse maneuvered among the headstones. The driver didn't plan his turn well.

Lying on his side, Touton was ten feet away. 'FBI, huh?' he asked. 'ID?'

The question seemed totally unnecessary to Cinq-Mars and Casgrain. Touton didn't think so, and neither did the Special Agent. He showed his badge. Closest to him, Cinq-Mars accepted its validity. He looked over his shoulder at his old partner crossly.

'Was Coalface really a priest?' Touton asked, dismissing their unspoken criticism.

Point taken.

The black hearse peeled onto the twisting driveway and sped down toward them. The driver braked. Coalface Willy was hoisted up by the four men, each taking a corner, and they awkwardly shuffled him toward the vehicle. They were exposed in the open air again. But no shot was fired.

The driver, an FBI agent unaccustomed to the vehicle, had difficulty figuring out how to lift the tailgate, but did so finally. The injured man was slid into the space usually reserved for the dead. Two more FBI guys joined him.

'Let's go!' Special Agent Franklin leveraged himself into the front seat, the driver leapt in behind the wheel, and the hearse took flight like a winged chariot. Cinq-Mars, Casgrain and Touton stood on the path with the shock of the day's events hitting home.

'Cinq-Mars!' Delacroix cried out. 'Take cover! Casgrain! Touton! Take cover!'

They didn't.

No bullets were flying, despite the men being fully exposed, freestanding targets. That obliged Captain Delacroix, reluctantly, to get to his feet as well, although he enjoined others to stay down.

'The Hells, you think?' Casgrain asked.

'Not their style,' Touton opined. 'Their two weapons of choice are bombs on timers and chainsaws. They prefer the drama. They've never had a sharpshooter.'

'Ciampini?' Cinq-Mars wondered.

'Up close to the back of the head,' Casgrain noted.

'Yeah,' Cinq-Mars agreed. 'And The Rabbit prefers beating his victims to a pulp. If they don't die easily, he pulls out a shiv. His friends? These KGB or ex-KGB, whatever they are? They might have brought a sharpshooter in. Not that he was all that sharp.'

'Willy got hit. Or was he aiming at you?' Casgrain probed that one possibility again.

Cinq-Mars pursed his lips. 'This is Russian, possibly under the

Mafia's direction, with The Rabbit as the go-between and the
Hells' approval. Could be I was the target. Could be Willy. They
miss me, they shoot him. Not impossible. Until we track the
shooter, we won't know.'

Assuming he was on the run, with a mile head start, they weren't
tracking the shooter immediately. With a forest to conceal himself,
he had undoubtedly fled the mountain and probably not on foot.

'Heard you're in trouble,' Touton commented, scarcely above
a whisper. 'Henri said.'

'The Hells let me know,' Cinq-Mars admitted. 'Ciampini's
chewing his cud.'

'I'll take care of Ciampini.'

'Don't shoot him, Armand. I'll have to arrest you.'

'Your bleeding heart. I'll let him know that anything happens
to you, his daughter's safety in prison cannot be guaranteed. You
tell him that, he'll laugh his ass off, a priest like you. I tell him,
he'll get the message.'

They looked over the shambles of the funeral gathering. Most
people remained down. A few were dusting themselves off and
coming to their knees. Fewer still were standing. Cinq-Mars spotted
Gina Malinger cooing to her child. She was on her knees, her
husband providing coverage between her and the woods. Other
policemen in the vicinity were doing their best to offer a word of
comfort.

Cinq-Mars looked back to where the hearse raced off with
Coalface Willy. It had already left the parking lot. The vehicle tore
down the road leading off the mountain. Hospital-bound, but that
was not the only possibility. A penny dropped.

'What just happened here?' he asked. He looked at Touton to
answer.

Touton shrugged, smiled. 'I told you. He was not my man.
Coalface has finally come in. Not to us. Now it can be said. He
was an FBI plant from the get-go.'

Cinq-Mars did a complete 360-degree spin and looked set to
paste him. 'What are you telling me? He was FBI? How? Why
didn't you say so?'

'Not for you to know, Émile. I wasn't allowed to say.'

Cinq-Mars folded his arms over his chest, trying to contain
himself. He and Touton were glued on each other now, wholly in

each other's orbit; a kind of kinesis, where each motion by one caused the other to feint, or hunch, or react with a reciprocal physical reflex. Like a pair of heavyweights preparing to spar.

Henri Casgrain noticed and held his peace. Waiting.

'What was this about then?' Cinq-Mars asked.

'What? This? Or—'

'This! This! If he wanted to come in out of the rain to the FBI, why come here to do it? Dressed as a priest? With a gun in his hand? He could just go home with them.'

Touton nodded. He understood the quagmire, the mud they were stepping in. 'Two choices,' he acknowledged. 'One, he wants to come in, but also wants his gang war. He lived among them too long. My guess? He built up personal grievance, his own animosity. He wanted to take them down and figured out a way. He might have shot you, Cinq-Mars, to accomplish that. In the head or in the hip – to make it look good, like he claimed – I can't say. His second choice was *not* to shoot you. I don't know how he could work that one. His secrets have a longer shelf-life if the gangs don't realize they've been compromised, and don't know by who or for how long. My guess is no better than anybody's.'

Casgrain shuffled, his head and neck slightly more stooped than usual. Then lifted his gaze. 'How did this come about, sir?' he inquired.

Touton brought his shoulders up, then let them drop. A weight released. 'Back in the day, my old boss, Pax Plante – you heard of him, famous man – he signed on for it. The FBI knew Pax as an Eliot Ness-type. They trusted him. He had a reformer captain – that would be me. The Americans found Pax easy to convince. Me, not so much. In the end, I had no choice, and swore to keep the mission quiet. Their plan was to embed an informant in the local Mafia to keep tabs on how they supported their American cousins. Willy gave them steady dope – good dope, I hear. Us? A few crumbs from the table. We provided limited cover. If he got arrested, he might contact me to clear the decks, that sort of thing. He did his job. He disappeared down a dark rathole and stayed there. The locals didn't know they had a spy in-house because he was tipping off G-men on stuff south of the border, letting the locals get away with murder, literally. My guess, we won't see him again. Nobody will.'

They stood amid the gravestones, aware that their quarry had been snatched from their hands at the last moment, as if lifted into thin air, into flight.

Cinq-Mars tried to manage being both furious and stunned. He tried to revert to being philosophical, if only to ease his upset. 'I'll never know why he did it. I wanted to ask him that. Why go under? For what?'

Touton did not favor the question. He asked, 'Why do you?'

'I'm not under.'

'Aren't you? In your own way you are.'

He deflected the subject. 'I also wanted to find out what he knows.'

'Some folks are against that. I could name a slew of people.' He extended the word *slew* as he spoke it. 'I have my connections, Émile. If anything comes back from Coalface that we can use, they should contact you. That connection becomes yours.'

Delacroix was walking up behind them.

'I suggest we proceed, gentlemen,' he said. 'Lower Norville Geoffrion to his rest. Toss in a little dirt. Complete that formality. Then let's get the family members out of here. We'll deal with this sorry mess later.'

As if he still had authority, Touton concurred. 'Yeah,' he said. 'Let's do that.'

Cinq-Mars gazed across the field of grass and tombs and caught a glance from Gina Malinger. Her child was now in her husband's arms. Nord had enjoyed his pomp and ceremony, and also a fight on his last day above ground. Disregarded in life, he was going to be remembered in death by everyone present.

'Yeah,' Cinq-Mars agreed. 'Let's bury him properly. Our best behavior, gentlemen. Send him on his way with dignity. I insist.'

Not necessary. No one had any inclination to say or do otherwise.

FORTY-FOUR

Detective Henri Casgrain asked to come along. The day would be his last on what he called 'The Sunshine Shift'. Cinq-Mars appreciated that Henri preferred to be the senior officer in a pair. He saw the value in having a trusted colleague who worked the streets at night. The converse was true for Casgrain.

Émile offered his partner an early exit to his shift. What he had in mind for the rest of his own day was 'Definitely not sunny.'

Casgrain declined to skip out. The mission would close out their time together in a way that was fitting, as it highlighted another side to Émile's nature, one possibly in opposition to the other. Priest or cop was no longer an issue. Cop and part-priest remained.

Cinq-Mars accepted that being a detective was his true calling, yet the decision did not dovetail with the whole of his nature. The fact that he was undertaking this particular task, one he was not obliged to do, underscored that inner schism. He was perpetually conflicted.

He almost climbed into his Volkswagen Beetle when he noticed his partner looking at him. Of course. He'd been thinking he'd drive the Bug, allowing him to continue straight home after work. With Henri along, that would leave him a distance away from his own car. He locked up the Bug, looking sheepish, and took the squad car.

'Finish early,' Cinq-Mars suggested, 'then a farewell-for-now beer?'

'I'll even have a whiskey. What are the chances of finishing early?'

Good point.

'We'll see.'

Miraculously, to Émile Cinq-Mars's ecclesiastically-inclined mind, the parking spot always available to him when he visited the Reverend Alex Montour was open again. He parked. 'O ye of little faith.'

'What are you on about now?'

'You probably believe this parking spot is an accident. A fluke.'

'You don't?'

'Like I said. O ye of little faith.'

'Nut bar.'

'Infidel.'

They knew the humor was not meant to merely pass the time. They needed to comfort their worried minds for the sadness ahead.

'Speaking of infidels,' Casgrain chided him as they walked

toward the United Church, 'what are you doing hanging out with Protestants?'

'Lesbian Protestants.'

'Makes my case.'

'Seems like I've discovered I have more in common with lesbian Protestants than I do with lapsed Catholics.'

'I'm a never-was, except by birth.'

'You're baptized, boy. Grin and bear it.'

'You'll fall, sunshine. I'll welcome you back to logic. Anoint your head with Balmoral.'

'Never been to logic. What's it like there? Hellish?'

'Some days. You're in heaven, I suppose.'

'Not lately. Not often, truth be told.'

They were admitted by the deaf Portuguese custodian and warmly welcomed by the minister. They accepted tea. She pointed out that they were early. 'They have enough on their plate. Don't want to surprise them popping in before they're ready. How are you two doing?'

Like most men, they had little to say on first reflection, not until Casgrain took the opening that presented itself. 'I'm fine, Reverend, but our friend here is in a spiritual crisis.'

The minister was nobody's foil. She knew his comment was meant to tease.

'Our friend,' Montour agreed, 'is in a never-ending spiritual crisis. Then again, a spiritual life that is not in perpetual crisis is probably no spiritual life at all.'

The heads of both policemen turned to her in sync, for she'd suddenly won their attention and, to a greater degree, their admiration. Cinq-Mars smiled, as though he had finally put his finger on the nature of his own existence.

Casgrain noticed his friend's reaction. 'Careful, Émile. She'll turn you into a Protestant.'

'You're in more danger, Henri. She'll turn you into a believer.'

He laughed, but seemed a touch embarrassed to have that known in front of clergy.

'Not to worry, Henri,' she said. 'I knew from the moment you stepped foot inside.'

'Did you? How?'

'God told me.'

A moment's dismay, before the three of them broke into laughter. Kooks abounded whenever the issue of God came up, which allowed legs to be pulled by anyone who could play the part. Cinq-Mars was reminded of Moira Ellibee, whom he'd come to enjoy. How much had she pulled his leg, he wondered? But no, as much as he might want that to be the case, he had to accept that the poor woman suffered a pathology. Spiritual and sexual, both. Or they were one and the same.

Ice broken, they enjoyed their tea and discussed recent events. Reverend Montour had a question. 'About the toasters,' she asked. 'How in God's name, or anybody else's name, did they land on your old captain's doorstep?'

'We have no idea,' Casgrain stated, only to have Cinq-Mars raise a contradictory hand.

'I woke up this morning with an idea.' He winked at the minister to share his joke. 'Maybe God whispered in my sleep.'

'We know you're a nut bar. What did God whisper?' Casgrain asked.

'I think the only people who might care enough to pull some silly trick on Captain Touton would only do so if they knew he was my former mentor and sought his council. Otherwise, the toasters would never mean a thing to anybody. They'd not think well of him to subject him to their humor. They'd have to have a connection to the young crooks, or to any gang of thieves aiding and abetting the kids, contributing to their juvenile delinquency. That's borne out because the culprit was obviously in possession of the toasters.'

'I'll bite, Émile. What does God say?'

'He's confused, also,' Cinq-Mars allowed, which pitched the other two forward in laughter. Then he added, 'He's willing to suggest that it might have been Detective Alfred Morin and Sergeant-Detective Jerôme LaFôret. Or one and not the other. Both had motive, maybe, and opportunity, maybe, and we will never know, maybe or maybe not, that they did it. Anyway, I'm inclined to go along with God's suggestion until the Devil comes up with a better one.'

'Or logic,' Casgrain quipped.

'That too. I have an open mind. There's another part of it, though. I'm putting one of those two guys, if not both, behind the fake call supposedly from Moira Ellibee to get me out at night. Who else would know that a visit to Moira's in the middle of the night would be a cruel joke?'

The three of them knew what they were doing: procrastinating, delaying the inevitable. When Reverend Montour finally lifted her hands, they understood. Time to go.

Outside on a lovely day, the minister agreed to travel with them in the squad car. 'If you get into a high-speed chase, don't slow down on my account.'

'Let's hope for bank robbers,' Casgrain said. 'I'm in the mood for a high-speed shootout.'

'You two,' Montour said.

'This is our last day married.'

'What? Why is that?'

'We're getting divorced,' Cinq-Mars said, playing along.

'Couples therapy, it's my specialty.' Montour could play their game as well.

A momentary quiet. Casgrain decided not to let it go. 'So, you counsel men and women on how to stay married?'

'Sure. Unless the woman is really cute. Then I recommend divorce.'

'You should have been a cop,' Cinq-Mars concluded.

'I can dig it. Ride around in a car all day, cracking jokes and eating donuts.'

'Whereas your life,' Cinq-Mars noted as he pulled over, holding his thought until after he parked, 'is not so easy.'

A pall descended upon the occupants of the car.

'Come on. Let's go.' They all thought it. Reverend Montour said it.

They clambered out.

The three climbed the stairs to the apartment of the family whose daughter was missing. The young woman's body had been located sixty miles downstream. Beyond recognition. The dental records conclusive. The official record would be recorded as a 'probable suicide'.

A wretched afternoon. As a father, Henri Casgrain experienced physical as well as emotional pain throughout the encounter, feeling the couple's torment but also fearing it, for the same could happen to him or to someone he knew or to anyone anywhere at any time.

The couple's grief came home, their unwarranted guilt, the calamity of their lives overwhelming them. Cinq-Mars and Montour walked them through their sorrow, reminded them of sweeter memories, eliciting a revival of their daughter's life, the blessing of her, of whom she'd been for the time she'd been here. This was not the time to heal, a long way off, and they would never forget, but they held out hope for a time of restoration, and the comfort of each other and their children going forward.

Cinq-Mars told them that he had not taken the time to visit their daughter's wall murals yet, but on his first day off, he would do so. Reverend Montour thought that was a grand idea, invited herself along, and suggested that the parents join them.

A date was set.

On the landing outside, departing, Casgrain wiped a few tears that welled up. Cinq-Mars touched his elbow, knowing how his reflections provoked his love for his own children. Casgrain wanted to say something but, pent up, couldn't get the words out immediately. They went down to the car in silence and got in. The detective with poor posture rested a hand on his partner's shoulder, as if upon a crux, to restrain him from starting back just yet. Then said, quietly, 'Cop and priest both.' He nodded. 'Both of you. More one than the other. One is more cop, one is more priest. You figure out who's who. Cop and priest, both, each of you. Nothing wrong with that.'

They let the exchange and the afternoon's talk settle on them, then the Reverend Alex Montour spoke up from the backseat. 'If I'm the one who's supposed to be more part-cop, then how about we go for donuts?'

The two men turned around.

Casgrain broke it to her. 'We don't actually eat donuts.'

'We had planned on a beer after work,' Cinq-Mars said.

'Or a whiskey,' Casgrain said.

'Whiskey! Now you're talking. If you don't mind, I'll take my collar off before I step into the bar. It tends to give patrons the willies.'

'No problem. Hey,' Casgrain teased, 'how about we go to a strip club?'

'We're not going to a strip club,' Cinq-Mars intervened.

'Why not?' Montour asked, sounding disappointed.

'It's against my religion.'

'He's a fanatic,' Casgrain explained.

'He's the fanatic,' Cinq-Mars struck back. 'A married man.'

'Damn,' Montour said. 'Too bad. Good idea otherwise, Henri.'

'Yeah,' Casgrain conceded. 'Too bad, though. He's right. Bastard's right half the time. It's uncanny.'

'Don't you just hate that?'

'Most of the time, Reverend. Most. Of. The. Time.'

'Not me,' Cinq-Mars said, and started the squad car.

The reverend wanted the last word on the subject. 'You guys,' she admonished them. 'You really ought to develop a greater appreciation for donuts.'

They had a laugh. They needed it.

Cinq-Mars turned the police band radio up loud for the reverend's benefit, in case bank robbers became active, and the three headed off to a local watering hole.